NOVELS BY **MERCEDES LACKEY**
available from DAW Books:

AERIE

AERIE

MERCEDES LACKEY

DAW BOOKS, INC.
DONALD A. WOLLHEIM, FOUNDER
375 Hudson Street, New York, NY 10014

ELIZABETH R. WOLLHEIM
SHEILA E. GILBERT
PUBLISHERS
http://www.dawbooks.com

First Paperback Printing, October 2007

1 2 3 4 5 6 7 8 9

DAW TRADEMARK REGISTERED
U.S. PAT. OFF. AND FOREIGN COUNTRIES
—MARCA REGISTRADA
HECHO EN U.S.A.

PRINTED IN THE U.S.A.

Dedicated to the RPCongress for keeping me sane.
You know who you are.

(www.rpcongress.com)

 # ONE

KIRON, Wingleader of First Wing of the Jousters of Sanctuary, woke from a dream that his lover Aket-ten was nuzzling his ear to find that his ear was being nuzzled, but not by Aket-ten.

He sat up with a yell, startling the half-grown kitten that had been trying to nurse on his earlobe into instant flight. He felt its sharp claws dig momentarily into his shoulder as it leaped away into the darkness, and though he had certainly felt worse pain in his life, he bit back a curse.

With a growl, he turned over on his pallet and tried to get back to sleep. Below him, channeled up through the stair cut into the living stone of his dwelling, he heard Avatre snoring gently, or at least, as gentle in snoring as a dragon ever got. He couldn't actually see anything, because it was pitch-dark in this room. He wondered how the cat could see.

Avatre was below him, not just beyond the door of the little room he'd been calling "home" for the last several months, because ready or not, the Jousters had been forced to make the move to the desert city they had initially dubbed "Dragon Court" and now called Aerie. The city they called Sanctuary, the place they had all thought would serve for years, was filling up with people, and fast. Priests, acolytes, the army of servants and slaves required to tend to them—those had come from Alta and Tia alike. The press of priests and their followers alone had shoved the Jousters out of quarters they had only just gotten used to. And that didn't even begin to deal with the visitors . . . all eager to see the first Voice of the Gods of both Alta and Tia ever. And the first Voice of the Gods, period, in a very, very long time.

The presence of Kaleth, the Voice, gave legitimacy to Sanctuary; turned Kaleth's plans to make it into a city of priests, for the training of priests, into something more than someone's odd ambition.

Kiron stared into the absolute darkness of his new home. It was still a bit unnerving to wake up in the middle of the night here and see that. Or rather, not see that. Even on moonless nights during the rains back in Alta there had been *some* light, but here there was nothing, because he was, for all intents and purposes, inside a man-carved cave. There was a window hewn through the rock to the outside, but the shutters he had gotten made and refitted to the places where original shutters had clearly been were closed to keep the bats out. Not because he didn't like bats; he actually liked them quite a bit. Because the cat persisted in thinking of them as mice with wings and chasing them. It never caught one, but it never stopped trying either. This meant a night full of the sound of running and jumping, and occasionally of having his body used as a launching platform. But having the shutters on made it literally as dark as a cave in here at night. For someone who had spent the best part of his life sleeping unsheltered under the moon and stars, such darkness took some getting used to.

As for why he and the rest of the Jousters found themselves being all but ordered to leave, well, the reasons were complicated. And because those reasons fed right into Kaleth's actual plans for Sanctuary, that made it exceedingly difficult to say "no," and, frankly, Kiron hadn't had the heart to do so.

To begin with, Sanctuary was living up to its

name. The priests of both Alta and Tia had had
a bellyful of finding themselves victims. In both
lands, the manipulative Magi, working through
the rulers, had been able to decimate the priestly
population of those who had even a hint of
magic about them. The Altans had managed to
save the greater part of their Winged Ones,
thanks to warning by Aket-ten and a rescue by
the Jousters, but the priests of Tia would be several years, perhaps even a generation, in recovering. In a city of their own, where priests ruled,
this would be—not impossible, perhaps, but far
less likely.

And most of the priests of both lands agreed,
in principle at least, that if the peoples of Alta
and Tia were to become one, it was time for the
temples to merge. This was going to take some
very creative work. And probably a few divine
revelations. Some of the gods of Alta bore a suspicious resemblance to the evil gods of Tia, and
vice versa. It was probably a good idea for this
reconciliation to take place far away from the ordinary run of worshippers.

And so they had come, the teachers, the High
Priests, the scholars and scribes, from temples
large and small. This was not a stripping of the
temples bare by any means; though Sanctuary
was indeed becoming a city, it was by no means
big enough to hold more than a fraction of those
who served the gods of both nations. Neverthe-

less, there were more than enough takers for every available scrap of living space. The *kamiseen* winds, which had been so generous in uncovering portions of the buried city as they were needed, were scouring bare desert plain now. There was nothing more to be uncovered.

That influx of people had been more than enough to push the Jousters out.

And, truth to tell, a city full of the priestly castes was not a comfortable place to live, not for Kiron at least, and mutterings from the other Jousters made him think that they felt the same. The latest batch of youngsters, chief of which were Coresan's hatch, were already at Aerie, and though repairs were far from complete, there seemed every good reason why the move should be speeded up. When they had first come to Sanctuary, they had taken over a temple complex that seemed to have been dedicated to Haras, or some god very like him. That had been all well and good when there were only a handful of priests, but the devotees of Haras had descended in droves, and had made it quite clear that while having dragons and their Jousters dwelling in the workshops of the god was not precisely blasphemy, it was certainly being looked at with a somewhat stern eye.

Having the Priests of Haras looking over one's shoulder with a certain amount of impatience was more than enough incentive to find some other quarters for the dragons.

Well, now the priests had taken possession of the god's temple. They were happy. Presumably the god was happy. The Jousters were far from the eyes of the priest, and so it was to be hoped that they were at last happy. And, truth to tell, when it was finished, and even now in some ways, Aerie was far more suited to the dragons than Sanctuary was.

Here they had good shelter from the *kamiseen* winds and sands, as good or better than he'd enjoyed in the dragons' own compound in Mefis. There were cliff tops for dragons to bask on, and a hot spring for the humans to bathe in. Here, pens were set up as the bottom floor of these rock-carved "houses," so there was no need, ever, to shelter them from the rains. They were central to all the good hunting grounds, and there was enough browse here for them to keep their own herds to supplement that hunting. Eventually, when Kaleth's scheme to farm incense and rare plants here came to pass, they would even be self-sufficient. And here dragons could prowl or romp in the canyon bottoms that served as streets, unlike in Sanctuary, where they could scarcely fit in the narrow avenues between buildings and where an increasingly large number of people regarded a free-roaming dragon with apprehension.

There was a lot to appreciate here, even if the place had been abandoned for centuries. So had Sanctuary, and Kaleth, the original band of refugees from Alta, and the Blue People had made it livable *while* living in it. If they had done so to Sanctuary, the Jousters could do so for Aerie, and if the Jousters were not particularly suited to the task, well, neither were those who had initially followed Kaleth out here.

And he ought to be personally grateful for this much; as someone who had been camping out here for some little while—first when he was keeping an eye on the half-wild dragon Coresan's nest, and later, after the destruction of Alta's fabulous city and port in order to get some desperately needed privacy, he'd been able to lay claim to a spot before anyone else. He'd gotten one of the dwellings cut into the sides of the canyons of this place that had required the least amount of repair: two rooms with very high ceilings, one above the other, and the lower room had been hewn out to be lower than the street level, which seemed to be the case with roughly half of the dwellings. He had to wonder again if dragons had once been quartered here. The dwellings seemed designed for them, for sand wallows on the lower floors. There had been no need to do much to the place other than have the shutters made. A little subtle magic worked by one of the priests during a *kamiseen* and enough sand to make a tolerable pit for Avatre had been deposited literally at his door; the canyon street had been knee-deep in it. He (and everyone else who had moved to this section) only had to shovel it inside.

Shovel it inside! It was a good thing he had spent most of his life as a serf and was used to hard labor! Even with Avatre's help—and she had been, surprisingly, a lot of help. Digging and shoving alongside him, once she understood that the sand was going to be her new wallow—it had taken a lot of backbreaking labor. At the moment, there were very few spare hands to be had in the canyons of Aerie, and the Jousters were all getting their hands dirtier than they ever dreamed possible. For most of them, it was more physical work than they had ever done in all their lives put together. There had been a lot of complaining about sore muscles, and a great many people soaking their aches in the hot spring before they went to bed.

Furniture had been problematic; it was whatever anyone could bring across the desert or could spare, and there wasn't much of either, though more was coming in all the time. Most of it was Tian, since the priests were bringing caravan loads of things with them.

Kiron was of two minds about that. Tian furniture was more practical out here, made for a desert climate, but seeing it gave him twinges from a lifetime as a captive. At least he had an Altan-style mattress and blankets to sleep on. He could not imagine how the Tians managed with their benchlike beds and neck rests instead of pillows. It didn't look comfortable. In fact, it looked rather like the sleeper had been laid out for the embalmers.

He had collected bits of furnishings through begging, trading, and actually fetching a few items himself when he had to take Avatre across the desert to tend to more serious matters. So far, he had collected a chair, his bed, a clothes chest, a desk, a brazier, and some lamps. Avatre had her wallow, properly heated now by magic. It looked bare, in the big, empty room, but then, he didn't actually spend a lot of time here. There was just too much work to be done.

He punched his pillow a few times and settled back onto his side. But something in him kept listening for that pesky cat.

He was not sure how he had acquired the little beast. It seemed to have decided that he was the one privileged to play host to it. Which wouldn't have been bad, since it definitely kept down the vermin, except for the way it kept trying to suck his earlobe when he slept and use him as a ramp to get itself into the air.

Some priests had followed the Jousters out here to Aerie, prompting a couple of snickering remarks about priests looking for captive worshippers. But it was not to be denied that there were temples here, too, and no real need for any Jousters to claim them. The priests of the cat goddess Pashet had found what seemed to be an ancient temple to their deity and had claimed it, bringing with them a veritable horde of four-legged avatars. Cats being cats, the *mau*-cats brought to Sanctuary had thrived and bred . . . cats being cats, the ones brought here did the same. Not that they weren't useful, because the half-ruined city swarmed with all manner of things that the cats simply gobbled up, but cats did have minds of their own, and some of them were minded to find places to live other than the temple. This despite the fact that they were literally worshipped and adored at the temple, and had their pick of the daintiest portions of the kills and sacrifices that went to feed the dragons.

So they were likely to be found not only in the temple, but outside of it. Some of them didn't seem to realize they were supposed to be in the temple at all—One of them being the *mau*-cat that kept trying to derive nourishment from Kiron's earlobes.

He sighed, now wide awake despite the fact that it was so pitch-dark he wouldn't be able to see the cat, or know where it was until it—

He refrained from leaping to his feet and screaming when it dashed across the length of his body and used his shoulder for a launch point into a tremendous jump.

He heard it land, heard a brief scuffle and a squeak, and then heard the wet sound of a cat dining on a fat desert rat.

Neither Avatre nor any of the other dragons bothered the cats, or bothered about them either, much to Kiron's relief. He wasn't sure how he would explain to the priests that one of their avatars had gone down the gullet of a dragon. Fortunately, dragons were too slippery for cats to want to sleep on, and most of them preferred warm human and blankets to warm sand of the wallows.

The wet sounds in the darkness ceased. And a moment later, the nameless cat strolled up Kiron's legs to his hip, and stood there, attempting to knead it into a soft bed. Its claws were very sharp and long, and he gritted his teeth as they stung him even through the thick wool of his blanket, reminding himself over and over that one must *not* strike the avatar of the Goddess Pashet. . . .

He knew better than to roll over to try to dislodge it. Doing that in the past had resulted in the cat sinking its claws into his hip in an effort to keep its balance.

Finally, the cat gave up hip kneading as a lost cause and strolled down his legs again. Presumably, now that it was full, and he had, once

again, proved to be a less-than-satisfactory
sleeping partner, it would pad down the stairs to
Avatre's magic-warmed sands and curl up on a
ledge at a respectful distance from the dragon.
After all, she might not intentionally harm it, but
dragons did occasionally heave themselves up
out of their sands and roll over. They also were
known to lash their tails in their sleep, or flail
their wings. Kiron, on the other hand, was not a
satisfactory place to sleep. He was too bony, and
he moved too much, and he would not allow the
cat the two thirds of his pallet that it wanted.
Clearly, he was being ungenerous to the avatar
of the goddess.

Maybe that was why he couldn't get Aket-ten
to stay here. Pashet was the goddess of love as
well as cats, cats being well known for their
amorous nature. Maybe he had offended Pashet
herself.

That . . . could be bad. He made a mental note
to find something to make the cat a warm bed
with down on that ledge. And find another way
to keep it from sucking his earlobe. And make
an appropriate sacrifice at Pashet's Temple in
the morning.

Aket-ten was one of a handful of Jousters who
were staying in Sanctuary to run courier to the
new city the Great King and Queen were building on Great Mother River between Tia and Alta.
He could hardly blame her for wanting to stay

there instead of here. Her family was there, or at least, her mother and father were; most of her brothers had gone back to Alta to take care of the family estates and help resettle the refugees of the city. The only one of her brothers who had stayed was Orest, who was one of the first of Kiron's wing in Alta. He was here in Aerie, though.

Maybe she's living in Sanctuary to get away from Orest, he thought with amusement. The two had something of the usual sibling quarrels, exacerbated by Orest having decided quite on his own that, since all of his brothers were off and their father was immensely busy helping Great King Ari reconcile Altans and Tians, it was his duty to "keep an eye on" Aket-ten.

Maybe he ought to give Orest more to do.

Maybe I ought to give all of us more to do.

Maybe. But there was already too much work. That was the problem, really. It was all work they weren't particularly good at. There were just not enough hands to make Aerie livable, to free up the Jousters to do—

To do what? Yet another problem. What was it that the Jousters should be doing? Not fighting each other. Not fighting each others' nations. What could a man and a dragon do that half a dozen fighters couldn't?

Honest answer: not much.

Still turning this question over and over in his mind, he finally fell asleep.

*   *   *

Avatre greeted him as he came down the stone stairs with a croon of pleasure. He couldn't help but smile. Since she wasn't bothered by the cat, he never put the shutters over her window unless there was going to be a *kamiseen* storm, so the light of midmorning reflected off the sands of the canyon and into the room.

It was a bit more rough-hewn than the one above it, leading him to wonder once again what the original purpose for it had been. There was no sign that dragons—domesticated ones, anyway—had ever lived here. And yet— There were the sunken, rough-cut lower rooms. What would you put in such a room if not a dragon?

Could they have been stables? Pens for livestock? Not stables; no, probably not. The first time Tians or Altans had ever seen horses, they had been in the hands of the Nameless Ones.

But pens for livestock. Goats. Maybe camels. Donkeys. That made sense. And it explained the huge doorways even a dragon could pass through. You had to have a doorway that wide or you'd have a devil of a time getting livestock to pass through it.

Now that there were no patrols to be flown, the dragons could awaken at their own time and pace. Now that they were each flying out to hunt alone, it didn't matter that the wing never

flew together anymore except during rare prac-
tices. Avatre, given the choice, was a late riser.

"Ready to hunt?" he asked her. He was never
entirely sure how much she understood, but she
certainly knew what that meant. She snorted eagerly, and positioned herself to best advantage
for getting harnessed up.

He paused for a moment to reach his arms up
toward her. She bent her head down on her long,
long neck and rested it over his back while he
embraced her neck. In so many ways she was his
first love, and for so long she had been the best
thing in his life. Truth to tell, she and Aket-ten
were tied for first position now. If he lost either
of them—well, he just didn't want to think about
that.

She was beautiful, and not just in his eyes.
Her colors of scarlet shading to gold and topaz
on the extremities only grew deeper and more
intense as she grew older. When she was in the
air, those colors shimmered against the hot
turquoise bowl of the sky. She might not have
been the *most* beautiful of the dragons, but
everyone who saw her was struck by her combination of color and regal bearing.

He scratched the soft skin under her jaw for a
bit, then patted her neck. "Come, my Sunrise.
Let's get you fed."

He intended to go a great deal farther afield
today, to give the regular hunting grounds the

opportunity to replenish. And while he was at it, he was going to look for more dragon nesting sites. Though he was going to make it a condition of egg ownership that the potential Jouster have his own dwelling and pen with hot sands ready and waiting before any egg was bestowed.

And what was he going to do about the girls?

He strapped on Avatre's saddle and flying harness, adding the flat bulk of the game bags to the rear over her haunches, just in case. He threw open the huge double doors to the outside, and she crouched, extended her neck, and eased herself out the doors. It never failed to amaze him how the dragons could stretch themselves out and make themselves thin to fit through places one would never dream of seeing them go. She didn't even scrape her harness on the door, though in time he would probably have to saddle her outside to prevent that from happening. No one really knew how long a dragon could live, nor when they stopped growing. The best guesses were "about as long as a man" and "until they die."

Ari's Kashet, for instance, was still larger than any of the Altan-born dragons, and fitting him into one of the new pens here would have been a challenge. Fortunately, that was not an issue. For now, Kashet and Ari were dividing their time between Mefis, where the old quarters for the Jousters were, and the new city that did not yet have a name, with side trips to Sanctuary. Quarters for Kashet, and for The-on, Great Queen Nofret's dragon, had been the first things finished on the new palace. The Great King and Queen were still sleeping in tents when Kashet and The-on were luxuriating in their wallows.

Those pens were built to the old plan, open to the sky, sheltered from the rains by canvas awnings that could be pulled across the top, with huge doorways. The pens were big enough that Kashet and The-on could triple in size—which wasn't likely—without running out of room.

Kiron didn't even need to command Avatre to let him mount now; she crouched down and extended a leg as a stepping place as soon as she was out in the open. She kept glancing up with one eye at the sky overhead; clearly she wanted to be gone and hunting.

Well, so did he. Morning and evening hunts were about the most amount of time he got to spend with her now, and it displeased him not at all that the hunts for the next several days or even weeks were going to be longer. And it actually would not have been all that bad if what he was doing was merely physical labor. No, he was spending most of his time acting as de facto leader for all the Jousters . . . except that, of course, there were those who were objecting to

that on the grounds of his youth. Which he
wouldn't have minded in the least, if only they
had put forward some reasonable person to take
over in his place.

But Baken didn't want the position, and neither did Haraket. The only people who did
weren't Jousters, and Kiron had had a bellyful of
being ruled over by people who knew nothing
about dragons, Jousters, or the unique bond the
human-raised dragons shared with their
Jousters.

Well, for right now, he wasn't going to think
about it. He was going to hunt with Avatre, and
that was absolutely all he was going to concentrate on.

He felt her muscles tense under him, but she
was on her best behavior, waiting until he
checked the quiver at his knee for broad-headed
hunting arrows, made sure of the tension on his
bow, and that the straps holding him into the
saddle were sound and cinched down tight. In
the old days his dragon boy would have done
all that. He didn't particularly want a dragon
boy actually. Where would he put one? In his
own home? He liked having the privacy. He
liked being able to be with Aket-ten, knowing
that no one would bother them.

Satisfied that everything was in order, he
gave Avatre the wordless order with hands
and legs, and she launched herself up with a

leap and a tremendous downbeat of her wings.

He was so used to the bounding surge of her flight that he didn't even think about it now, he just automatically shifted his weight with her movement. But he never lost the thrill of flight, of watching the earth below, of soaring among the falcons and vultures. He loved feeling Ava-tre shifting the planes of her wings as she spi-raled up a thermal, then glided down to the next. He loved the heady rush of speed when she folded her wings and dove into an attack.

Ah, but he also missed the thrill of combat....

He would never admit that to Aket-ten, but it was true. He had enjoyed every aspect of com-bat. He knew, however, that she didn't, and that she was relieved that the only "combat" taking place now was competition to catch streamers from one another.

Well, there was still the hunt.

He took Avatre far out past her normal hunt-ing grounds and well into scrub-covered hills. This was good territory for her to hunt in, too; the trees were twisted things with tiny leaves, and hid nothing beneath their contorted limbs. There were no canyons for game to run into and hide. There was more browse here, which should mean more game—

Just as he thought that, he saw a cloud of dust on the horizon. A cloud like that was only kicked up by the hooves of many herd animals, and sure enough, as Avatre drew nearer, he saw it was a herd of antelopes, a bit smaller than the oryx he was used to hunting. But that was fine; a herd of wild oxen this size would have been too dangerous for Avatre to tackle by herself.

He pulled an arrow from the quiver at his knee, nocked it on the bowstring, and gave Avatre the signal to make a fast pass over the heads of the beasts.

He was hoping to spook them into dividing, and it worked. He signaled Avatre to chase the smaller of the two groups, sighted carefully along his arrow, and fired.

The beast he had chosen took the arrow in the ribs, stumbled, and tumbled headfirst into the ground in a cloud of dust and tiny clods, and a moment later, Avatre's front claws connected with her chosen victim. He braced himself for the impact as she used the momentum of her strike to spin herself around with the beast in her foreclaws as the pivot point. The rest of the herd thundered off into the distance. He dismounted and made sure the one he had struck was dead.

He let her feast, bundled the remains up in the game bags and fastened them to her harness, then glanced up at the sun and sighed. He'd be back by midmorning. Plenty of time to be cornered by half a dozen people with agendas of their own.

Oh, well. Putting it off was not going to make it go away. He sent Avatre into the air again, and prayed that today, at least, he was not going to find himself enmired in someone's private quarrel.

As he approached Aerie, he could see younger dragons and riders practicing in the thermals now rising above the canyons. None of them had colors yet, though each of the original eight had his own wing now. Besides the population explosion of Sanctuary, there had been a population explosion of Jousters and dragons after the final battle between Alta and Tia that had ended the war with victory for no one. Many of the dragons that had gone wild when their controlling *tala* became useless had mated and laid clutches, then abandoned the eggs. And surviving Jousters and aspiring Jousters alike had gone out and kept watch over dragon nest sites, just in case that very thing happened. Eggs kept warm and tenderly cradled in carts full of sand were brought back to Sanctuary, then Aerie. And now there were eight wings of eight dragons each, with this year's hatch only now taking to the sky.

Only Aket-ten had no wing of her own. . . .

Not that she didn't want one. It was only that she wanted one composed only of young female Jousters.

And while he sympathized with her desire, he also knew what a hornet's nest he would stir up if he gave eggs to young women when there were so many males—dragon boys, former Jousters, and warriors—who wanted to join the ranks of the new Jousters. This, despite the serious load of hard work it took to become one now that the dragons had to be human-raised.

Maybe that was why she would not move in with him. She was still angry at his last refusal.

She had a great many logical arguments. Women were smaller and lighter than men. Women tended to be more nurturing, which was what a young dragon needed. Women had good senses of balance and were good with bow and arrow and sling. And since there was not, and (the gods be willing) never would again be aerial combat between Jousters, other than ribbon chasing, there was no need for great strength.

She was right about all of that. He couldn't argue with her on those points. But the plain fact remained that until he had satisfied every single male who wanted a dragon, he did not dare distribute a single egg to a young woman. The resulting outcry would be more than he cared to think about.

Aket-ten could only see that there were plenty of young ladies like Nofret who felt the same longing for the companionship and freedom of flight and, yes, *love* that the bond of human and dragon brought to the human. She couldn't see that people still thought of the Jousters as warriors. That he was still training the Jousters to be warriors. She thought warfare was over. And so it was—between Alta and Tia.

But what about the lands to the south? And what about those to the east? That was where the Nameless Ones had come from and might come again.

And besides all of that, there were the desert raiders who plagued the Blue People and made the old caravan trails dangerous to use.

When those eight wings were wings of warriors again, well—

It wouldn't be just incense trees and rare plants that supported them all.

But first he had to get through this.

 **TWO**

THESE people were Jousters, at least. They
let him get Avatre unharnessed and turned
loose, to go and socialize with other dragons if
she wished (which she did but very rarely) or fly
alone, or go back to her hot sands and sleep off
her breakfast (which was what she usually did).
And they let a Jouster whose dragon had not
been as good or lucky a hunter as Avatre come
and claim the extra meat from him.

But then they descended on him with their
problems.

The first to reach him was a trio of the newest
Jousters, one older former rider of a swamp
dragon from Alta, the other two dragon boys
who had gotten themselves fertile eggs. All

three of them wanted use of the few workmen they had here. Kiron listened patiently to their arguments before he made a decision.

"Resket-teren gets priority," he said finally, and held up a hand. "I understand. All three of you have housing problems. But Resket-teren's can be fixed the fastest. When people have all got about the same level of urgency, that's how I'm deciding who gets priority."

The other two grumbled a bit at that but reluctantly admitted that was fair. "You two might help each other," he suggested to the "losers" in this situation. "You aren't trained workmen, but there's a lot that can be done with four hands rather than two."

They exchanged a wry look, because this had become one of his favorite answers these days. No one could deny the wisdom of what he was saying, even when they didn't much like it.

With that disposed of, he went the rounds to see how each of the eight wings was faring. Not, of course, that he didn't already *know* how they were faring. The names changed within each wing, but each of them had the same triumphs and the same problems. In each wing there were two people who simply did not get along, mostly because of personalities. In each wing there was at least one show-off who would have to take a fall and learn his lesson. In each, there was one dragon slower to learn than the others.

There were some riders who were better at co-
operating than others—the recalcitrant ones did
tend to be the older riders—and these would
just have to get over their attitudes, or eventually form a wing of their own, which was certainly a viable proposition, and one he was
considering already.

In fact, the more he thought about it today, the
better the idea seemed. In the last day or so there
had been two incidents of older riders flaring up
at their wingleaders, objecting to serving second
or third to "some jumped-up dog boy." The
older riders were, by and large, all aristocrats,
and the differences in social standing were beginning to rub some of them raw. Finally, after
listening to Huras sigh over his particular problem rider, he came to a decision, and as soon as
practice was over for the day, he collected the
wingleaders in a group while the rest of their
Jousters took themselves off to work on their
housing.

By now the sun was fully overhead, and it
was like a furnace down in the canyons. Kiron
squinted against the white-hot glare on the
white sand covering the bottom of the canyon,
feeling the heat reflecting from the surface as
well as hammering down from the sun-disk.
Small wonder that the Tians regarded the Solar
Disk as a destroyer, rather than the life giver that
the Altans called it. It was even hotter up on the

cliffs, which was exactly the way the dragons liked it. There were jewel-bright dragons sprawled over every available ledge, wings spread out to absorb the sun, turning the cliff tops of Aerie into an abstract mosaic of color.

Avatre had forsaken the dark and her hot sands to soak up sun just like the others, a sprawl of gilt-edged ruby glistening in the sun. She had her favorite perch atop Kiron's dwelling, and, on hearing his familiar step, she raised her head a little to look down at him with her great, golden eyes. She made a little crooning sound on spotting him, and put her head back down again. He smiled up at her, and then simply gazed around the canyon for a moment, taking in the peacefully napping dragons. Every one of them was within snapping distance of at least one other. A couple of them were even lolling side-by-side. This was normal behavior for wild dragons; unheard of in the Jousting dragons that had never been raised by humans.

Oh, yes. This was a far cry from the hissing, complaining dragons of the Jousters' Compound in Tia . . . hissing, complaining, and at times, dangerous. The wild-caught dragons, even when drugged with *tala*, needed to be chained and regarded other dragons as potential rivals needing to be trounced. Though they had never hunted on their own, wild dragons classed human among the "prey animals," and

there was no telling which of the young drag-
onets brought in by hunters might have feasted
at one point or another on a two-legged meal.
Nor how many of them might remember doing
just that thing, and try another two-legged
morsel.

So far as these dragons were concerned, humans were fellow dragons, nestmates and parents, and the very little naughtiness they got
into could readily be dealt with by a fist to the
top of the nose. Not that they did very much;
most misbehavior occurred before fledging,
when they were still small enough to discipline
easily, and when they learned that a fist to the
top of the nose meant they had been bad.

And never had a human-raised dragon even
snapped at a human, not even when most irritated. They were safe around adult humans; that
was a surety.

Maybe not children. No one had volunteered
to test the theory so far as a young child went.
Though there was no reason why they shouldn't
be just as safe; with Aket-ten there to "explain"
to the dragons that a child was a nestling. . . .

With that safeguard in place, so far as Kiron
was concerned, it could be done. It definitely
should be done before very much longer. Sooner
or later there were going to be small children
running about here. Once there were more workmen, more folk raising those incense trees, and

yes, servants—those would attract bakers and brewers and tradesfolk—there would be families and children. They had better have the problem fixed before it became a problem.

When he looked back down at the faces of his friends, he saw that they, too, were gazing at the lazy dragons with a combination of pride and affection in their eyes. Well, all the new sort of Jousters, even the most argumentative of the "old" Jousters who had gone through the difficulty of hand-raising their new dragons, shared that pride and affection. So that much bound them all together; you couldn't raise your dragon from a wet-winged hatchling to a flying adult without loving it, and surely that shared experience would help to sort things out, if the irritations could be brought down to a reasonable level.

They filed in the front door, crossed the little distance to the stair cut into the wall, and went up it one after the other. The upper room was full of reflected light, betraying his attempts to paint Avatre on one blank wall of his home, plastered over for the purpose. The painting looked out of proportion. The neck and legs were too long, the head too big, the wings too stretched out and too thin. Well, he was no artist and had never pretended to be. At least nobody laughed at it.

It might be furnace-hot in the canyons, but in

the back of Kiron's second room, it was cool and comfortable. Kiron half closed the shutters to cut down on reflected glare from outside. With a sigh of relief, the nine friends sprawled out in various positions of comfort, some of them taking advantage of the cool stone floor to let the heat leach out of their bodies.

Kiron didn't exactly have a kitchen area— perhaps that was another reason why Aket-ten wouldn't move in with him—but he did have some heavy storage jars with even heavier pottery lids that kept the vermin out. From them he took out strips of dried and cured meat and flatbread, and dipped out beer into pottery cups that he handed round. Hardly fancy fare, but none of them were complaining. Perhaps later today, though, he should stop by what passed for a marketplace and get some onions. About the only time he got cooked food anymore was when he visited Sanctuary.

"So, what is it that is buzzing in your head, Kiron?" asked Orest lazily. "Not that I mind all of us getting together for a change. We don't do that nearly enough." Aket-ten's brother, like all the Altans, was of a paler skin tone than the dark Tians, though the people of both kingdoms shared the same straight black hair and dark eyes. He had matured immeasurably over the last several moons. Then again, they all had. He used to be forgetful, and could be terribly lazy when he had to do something that didn't particularly interest him. Not anymore. Though he still had not broken himself of the habit of speaking first and thinking after.

Kiron nodded at that last with a pang. For people who had been such close friends, and had gone through so much together, it troubled him that they saw so little of each other these days. And yet, there just was not enough time in a day for them to do everything they needed to. If only they could get some workers out here, or youngsters willing to serve as dragon boys for the chance at an egg themselves one day! Or both—actually, preferably both. Then, ah then, they might have some time to themselves . . . some time to get together when there wasn't something that needed to be talked about.

Soon, if the gods were only pleased to grant it. Well, at least Ari was not ungenerous about supplying them with funds. They could certainly hire people, if only they could find them.

He sighed.

"It's the older Jousters," he said carefully. Orest snorted.

"They're spoiled," Aket-ten's brother said without preamble. "All they do is complain and talk about how much better it used to be. They had everything done for them in the old days, and they want that back."

"And you don't?" Kiron raised an eyebrow, and Orest had the grace to blush.

Old days, Kiron couldn't help but be amused. The "old days" were mere moons ago.

"Well—" Orest began.

Huras, son of bakers who had lost everything when Alta's capital and port were destroyed by the Magi-caused earthshakes, sighed. "We all do," he admitted without a sign of embarrassment. "And maybe we'll get all that back one of these days. I hope. And I don't blame the older Jousters for wanting it either. My two— Well, I think they are doing pretty well, considering all they're having to do and learn just to be Jousters again. Having to cope with the way things are now is hard on them. But—I'll admit to you, I am getting tired of the complaints myself. It's not as if we have extra workmen and dragon boys hidden away somewhere and are keeping them to ourselves, after all."

There Huras, practical and level-headed as always, had struck the main point. They were all having to cope with a distinct lack of comfort. There were only one or two who had come from positions in life so low that the cave-houses were actually an improvement.

"Well," Gan said, for once looking quite sober and serious, "I've thought about this a bit, and I've been keeping a bit of an eye on the old Jousters. No, they aren't comfortable. No, they

don't fit in. Most of them are of much higher
rank than the rest of us. All their lives they've
had servants, and not just as Jousters. Our cave-
houses really aren't much better than holes dug
in the cliffs." Interesting to hear Gan saying this,
ranking the situation into "we" and "them" and
classing himself in the "we." Interesting, because Gan was noble-born himself. And before
he'd become a Jouster, he'd had a bit of a reputation for putting on airs. "They're *trying*, they
really are, but I wonder—I wonder if it wouldn't
be easier for them if they didn't have to adjust to
everything at once, and do it in the company of
a lot of—ah—"

Here, he clearly ran out of words for a polite
description of the motley collection of former
slaves, former serfs, common-born, and noble
youngsters that comprised the bulk of the new
Jousters.

"A mixed lot, and most of us are quite young
compared to them, and not well-born," Kiron
finished for him. "We are the sort of people who
would have been their servants, and not their
brothers-in-arms."

Gan nodded.

"I've been thinking the same," Kiron said
frankly. "And it seems to me maybe they would
be more comfortable in their own wing. Granted,
that would mean a wing that's pretty much
comprised of former enemies, but—"

"Yes, but isn't that what Ari and Nofret want? For Altans and Tians to start working together?" Gan replied with a shrug. "Anyway, they're thrown together with former enemies as it is. Not much change for them there. It might be they'll find more in common with each other than anyone thinks right now."

Pe-atep, who had been yet another servant— the keeper of great hunting cats for a noble master—laughed. "At the very least, they will all of them have the same complaints about the 'young upstarts.' That ought to be a common bond."

Kiron had to chuckle wryly. "Of course, I could be letting myself in for a lot of trouble," he pointed out. "When you think about it, I'm putting all the people who would rather I wasn't acting as leader of the Jousters in one wing."

"Yes, but you'll have all of them in one place then," Orest pointed out. "With them scattered out across all the wings, there's always a chance their grousing will have an effect on some of the new ones who look up to them. Tucked into their own wing, they can't influence anyone but each other."

"I also don't want them to think I'm trying to exile them—"

Oset-re nodded, a knowing look on his handsome face. He was another well-born Jouster, and another who had matured in unexpected ways. He had been vain, and Kiron had not been sure he would last out the training at first. Now he was as steady as Huras. "They're more likely to take advice from another noble. I can talk to them individually, find out if they would *rather* have their own wing, then let them finally come around to delegating me to ask you to transfer them into a wing together. And I'll take them, if you like. I already have two of them, and they at least listen to me with respect because of my birth." He sighed dramatically and stared with melancholy at his rather dull meal. "The gods know rank doesn't get me anything else anymore."

Orest snickered. Gan pouted with mock sympathy. "Oh, the tribulations we of noble blood must endure!"

Menet-ka, once so shy, flung a pillow at his head. He caught it adroitly. "Why, thank you, brother. This is exactly what I needed," he said with a mocking bow as he tucked it under his rump. "How kind of you!"

Menet-ka made a rude gesture, and they all laughed. "Seriously, though, that is a good idea," Kiron said, rubbing the back of his neck with one hand.

"Of course, it's a good idea. It's mine, isn't it?" said Oset-re. "If you start shuffling them about, Kiron, they'll resent it. If they think it's their own idea, they'll decide that 'the whelp' is finally learning to show some respect to his betters. Politics and people; it's all politics and people. I'm not the expert Lord Ya-tiren is, but those are the circles I grew up in, and I do know something of what to expect from folk in those circles."

Kiron spread his hands. "In that case, as you volunteered, I accept." He sighed. "I didn't really want this position anyway."

"You're the only one that isn't a worse choice," Huras said thoughtfully, in his deep voice. "I don't mean to say that the others are not competent, or at least most of them are, but—"

"But we have a problem with some of them being truly unacceptable to the older Jousters," Gan pointed out. "Haraket, for instance. You would think, seeing as he was the Overseer for the Dragon Courts, that they would think of him as one of them. But it doesn't work that way. Overseers are people you hire so that you need not dirty your hands with trivial details. And Baken—he was a slave. Doubly unacceptable. The very few nobles that are *not* unacceptable to us because they don't know a dragon from a doorpost are already integral members of Ari's advisers and far too busy for anything else."

"What a comfort, knowing that I am the least objectionable rather than the best qualified," Kiron said dryly, and the others laughed. "I suppose that will have to do in lieu of approval. Though I would rather have Lord Ya-tiren or Haraket in charge here."

And that was when another thing occurred to him. These were his friends. They were Aket-ten's friends . . . who better to ask for advice about his quandary. Not the personal one, but the one that affected the Jousters.

"I have another problem," he said, a bit forlornly, which made them all prick up their ears. "And it's one that I can't think of any kind of solution for. Aket-ten wants me to give eggs to— girls."

"Why?" Orest asked, looking just a touch contemptuous. "A girl wouldn't last ten days. Well, my sister and Nofret notwithstanding, I don't think a girl could take all the hard work involved in raising a dragon from the egg—"

Gan and Huras rolled their eyes. Pe-atep snickered. Orest looked bewildered. "What?" he asked. *"What?"*

"If you ever in your life wish to have pleasurable company from a young lady, never voice that sort of opinion aloud again," Huras said gravely.

Orest's stunned expression made them all snicker. "I don't understand—"

"Girls," Huras said carefully, "become women. Women often become mothers, raising children, who are far more trouble and take much longer to mature than a hatchling dragon. You belittle that work at your peril, for all females are very well aware of this role from quite early in life."

Orest still looked bewildered, and Huras just shrugged. Kiron sighed. His friend was unbelievably dense sometimes. Just because Orest's mother had possessed a horde of servants to do all the unpleasant parts of child rearing for her, it simply did not occur to Orest—and this despite the fact that he himself was now having to do without servants— that other women did not enjoy similar privilege.

Or if it did, he probably thought that older children in the family would take the jobs that servants did for the well-off. And to an extent, that was true, but that only meant that common-born girls became accustomed to the burdens of child rearing at a much younger age than their well-born counterparts.

Oset-re pursed his lips. "I can see the problem. There are, well, a *lot* of young men and boys, most of whom have already had at least something to do with dragons, if they weren't already Jousters, waiting for eggs. And after them, more who were warriors. Giving even one egg to a girl— That is truly asking for trouble from those who have been waiting for a very long time."

Kiron nodded. "But she is very unhappy that I have not at least considered it."

Gan's eyes widened. "*That* kind of 'unhappy'? I wouldn't have thought that of her."

"Not—exactly. But she has been making it—obvious—that she thinks I am being unfair." He sighed heavily. "She brings it up every time I see her, and she does have some good arguments. And all I can say is that it's impossible right now. Which doesn't please her, needless to say."

"Too bad you didn't win a girl who only wanted jewels," Oset-re said with sympathy.

"Have any of you any ideas?" he asked, looking from one to another of them hopefully. "I thought about telling her we would train any girl that managed to find her own egg or nestling, but—"

Pe-atep shuddered. "A very, very bad idea," he said. "It's bad enough that some of the ones on the waiting list are going out with the old fledgling hunters trying to find a way to steal hatchlings. People will shrug and think it is sad if it's a fellow who gets hurt or even killed doing that. 'He knew the risks,' they'll say. If if a girl got hurt or killed doing that, the blame would be on you. And maybe the ghost, too."

"I wonder . . ." Menet-ka gazed off into the distance. "Now, here is a thought. Obviously, we're trying to accommodate former Jousters and dragon boys first. They have the experience and something like the expertise, and even Aket-ten at her most stubborn would have to admit that. But when we finally get to people who want eggs but know nothing about dragons . . . I have a notion." His eyes returned to Kiron's and he smiled slyly. "And it will solve a problem as well. Make it known that from now on, anyone who wants to be a Jouster that doesn't have the experience must serve an—apprenticeship, call it—as a dragon boy. Or girl. For at least a year. Six moons serving an adult dragon, and six helping with a hatchling up to fledging."

"Oh—oho!" said Gan appreciatively. "By the gods, that is a plan!"

Kiron nodded slowly and felt himself beginning to smile as well. "Anyone who does this will find out precisely how much work an adult dragon is, and will see how much *more* work a hatchling and a fledgling is."

Pe-atep pursed his lips dubiously. "We could have a very high loss of dragon boys. Some will quit within the first moon, I suspect."

Kiron had to shrug at that. "And this would leave whoever had lost an apprentice at precisely the same point he was before he had an apprentice at all. I think all of us are used to the work now. Besides, it's better they quit as apprentices than take on a fledgling and abandon it."

They were all silent on that point. No one had—yet. The closest that anyone had come was when Toreth had been murdered, leaving his dragon bereft. Aket-ten had saved it, comforting it mind-to-mind so that it rebonded with her. But what would happen if a hatchling was abandoned? There were no other Aket-tens about to comfort it. No, this would be much, much better, solving a potential problem and Kiron's own dilemma at a single blow.

Huras nodded. "Personally, any help at all will be welcome. If it is only for a short time, it will still be welcome." Kiron smiled at him. That is exactly the sort of thing he would have expected of the easygoing Huras.

"Then that is exactly what I will do," he said, with a nod. "And if a young woman does not feel easy being an apprentice to one of the existing Jousters, she will just have to wait her turn being apprentice to Nofret or Aket-ten. That seems fair to me."

And hopefully it would appease Aket-ten at last.

Kiron looked up at the sky where the young dragons were soaring in the thermals of late afternoon, then back at the lists Haraket was presenting for his perusal, and sighed.

"You know," he said unhappily, "no matter what I decide on this, someone is going to object."

"I know," the former Overseer said, running a

hand over his shaved head. "I know it only too well."

"Of course you do," Kiron sighed. There were two lists. The first was of items of construction and furnishings that had just come in from the arduous crossing of the desert. The second, and much longer, was the list of who had requested what items. There were at least two and often a dozen claimants for a single object.

"So what do I do?" he asked forlornly.

"If it were me? Take a walk. Look over what people already have. Some of them have already paid for things out of their own pocket, or brought them in on their own dragons. See what they have, cross things off their list that they've gotten for themselves. Then start with the people that haven't hardly got a stick. Give them each one thing, and work your way down the list. Don't give anyone more than one thing. That's what I'd do."

Kiron nodded thoughtfully. This was the first "official" caravan of goods coming directly from Mefis and the vizier of the Great King and Queen. There would be more; Ari had finally gotten them scheduled. But every new arrival would mean the same clamor for what was on those camels.

He sighed. "Which means another list. Who's gotten what from the caravan. So it all gets parceled out equally until everyone has what they need."

"That is what I would do," Haraket said. "It seems the fairest and wisest course of action." Again, he ran his hand over his hairless head. "I am glad it is you who is responsible for the decisions," the former Overseer said ruefully. "I got a belly full of the results when I was in charge of the Dragon Courts, and that was in our days of plenty."

Kiron rubbed his hands over the heated skin of his biceps. "I appreciate the aid, Haraket," he said, with a grimace, "But I still would rather it was you."

"You're getting all bound up in this nonsense, boy," Haraket said, then grinned. "Excuse me. Captain of Dragons. Go take Avatre out. Hunt if you want to, but get in some practice, too. Combat practice, even if your targets are nothing but thorn trees. There's an itching in my bones that says that dragons and Jousters will be fighting again, maybe sooner than we think."

Kiron looked up alertly at those words. Haraket shook his head. "No, I've never been god-touched, but I do get feelings, and they're more often right than wrong. Get some practice in. If nothing else, you'll feel better for it."

Since the alternative was an afternoon listening to people complain about things he could do nothing about, he took Haraket's advice, left the lists in his quarters, and called Avatre down from her sunning post. She did not look at all loath to quit it, and kept her head up, gazing about alertly as he saddled her and added the combat weapons. He'd always had the feeling that she had enjoyed combat, too, and her reactions seemed to confirm that.

So did the fact that she leaped into the air as soon as he was firmly settled in her saddle.

He gave her no directions, however; since the other dragons of Aerie were not out hunting, it would not matter if she entered someone else's hunting ground. It was by general agreement that no two dragons, with the exception of Avatre and Re-eth-ke, shared the same hunting ground. They were generally as good and as reliable as the best-trained hunting dogs, but—

But another thing that no one had tested, and no one wanted to risk, was having two dragons come down on the same kill. Dragons in the wild fought over kills. Would the human-raised ones? No one knew. Avatre and Re-eth-ke cooperated because Aket-ten was there to tell them to, speaking in thoughts and images in their minds. Without Aket-ten there—

They might simply posture and circle, like a pair of cats that had not yet made up their minds to fight. But if they fought, if the riders didn't get off and out of the way quickly enough, death or severe injury was inevitable. And although Kiron had never seen a dragon fight go on to serious hurt in wild dragons, all that meant was *he hadn't seen it.* That didn't mean it didn't happen. There was a lot that wild dragons did that he hadn't seen, nor had anyone else. No one had known, for instance, that a dragon mother would leave her youngsters in the care of another, if she felt that other was trustworthy enough. That was how Great Queen Nofret had gotten *her* dragon,

It made sense, though, and it explained something that had been reported—one or more of the previous hatching's females hanging about the nests and not being driven away. It occurred to Kiron, as Avatre spiraled up a thermal, that this was very like what common-born women did, appointing an older child as a tender for the toddlers and infant. The young female got to practice her baby tending under the careful eye of her mother, then just before fledging, which was the moment when the babies really were sturdiest, the mother could fly off, leaving her older daughter in sole command of the nest. In the next few years, this lesson might be repeated, so that when the young female matured enough to mate, she was not relying on instinct alone to guide her in rearing her first hatch—

Such philosophical thoughts were rudely interrupted by the sound of shouting and screaming below him.

Startled, his involuntary movement made

Avatre go into a sideslip, and he looked down over her shoulder.

Below him, men on horseback, attacking a laden caravan. With a start, he realized he and Avatre had gone farther afield than he had planned. And that this caravan was taking the more dangerous short route between Sanctuary and Ten-hen-tes, the so-called City of Caravans.

Dangerous, not just because of the lions that roamed this area, but because of the bandits, sadly on the increase. Renegades and lawless men, and some merely desperate, but all deserters from the armies of both Tia and Alta, seeking to make their fortunes by taking the fortunes of others.

The fighter in him instinctively responded, and Avatre in her turn responded instantly to the little signals his muscles gave by going into a steep dive.

His mind was startled, but his body was already reacting, shifting and leaning forward, while his hands reached for his sling and stone bullets. As the defenders of the caravan milled in confusion, and one bandit darted in to cut lead reins of the rearmost camel and lead it off, no one looked up, until the dragon and her rider were literally on top of them.

Kiron slung a stone, but they were already past his target, what he took to be the leader, at the point where bandits and defenders alike suddenly became aware that something incredibly large, bright ruby in color, and possessed of more teeth and claws than anyone sane really wanted to confront, was rushing at them at a high rate of speed just above the ground.

The bandits scattered; so did the defenders. The camels knew this was a predator that could—and would—eat them and tried to bolt. Only the fact that their lead ropes were each tied to the pack saddle of the camel in front of them, and the fact that they all tried to flee in different directions at once, kept them from succeeding in vanishing over the horizon. The men of the caravan all went facedown in the sand, freezing in place like rabbits in hopes the dragon would overlook them.

Not so the bandits.

Some of them tried to rein in their horses to stand and fight, but the horses were having none of that. They also knew what was plunging down out of the sky at them, and were not at all willing to become dinner. Unlike the camels, they were not bound together; they could, and did, bolt in whatever direction seemed the most unobstructed. Not even the strongest bit, not the strongest rider, was going to hold back a horse in a state of panic.

Avatre pulled up, shooting straight up into the sky, as Kiron clung to her saddle and looked for the missing camel. He spotted it just under them. The rider that had tried to steal it was now on the ground, with no sign of his horse—

Unless his horse was the one currently heading north, riderless, at a high rate of speed.

Kiron sent Avatre in a wingover to make a second pass, scattering the riders further. By this point the horses were in full gallop and not likely to stop for miles.

At this point, there really was nothing more he could do to help—and in fact, landing Avatre would be rather counterproductive, given the reaction of the camels, so after that second pass he left the caravan workers to take care of the few remaining bandits themselves. He turned Avatre's head homeward; she seemed content now to go.

But if he had needed it—there it was. The proof that there still was useful work for the Jousters.

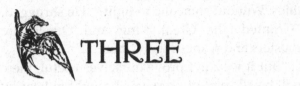 THREE

"So," Kiron announced with glee to his swingleaders. "There's still useful work for us."

"Not just useful, I'd say it's important," replied Huras after a moment. "Uh—I hadn't wanted to bring this up before, but . . . without an enemy army to fight, Jousters aren't exactly a necessary sort of thing to have about."

Orest snorted. "Neither are pet baboons, but no one complains about them."

But some of the others looked thoughtful. It was Oset-re who spoke up for all of them. "The thing is," he said reluctantly, "The pet baboons aren't eating enough meat every day to feed an entire village. For a moon. It was one thing

when we were protecting people from their ene-
mies. Without someone to fight?" He shrugged.
"Granted, the Great King and Queen are
Jousters and want dragons, but . . ."

"But if we can't prove ourselves useful, there
will be all sorts of pressures brought to bear by
nobles and common leaders and maybe even
some of the priests," Gan said bluntly. "We are
quite visible, and quite costly and the things that
go to support us could go to someplace else at a
time when both Tia and Alta are trying to recover from terrible losses." He pursed his lips
thoughtfully. "Granted, it is true that with the
weather no longer in the control of the Magi,
this year should be a normal one for crops. But
there are fewer farmers in the fields as well, at
least in what's left of Alta. I don't suppose
Kaleth has had any revelations from the gods
about how the harvest will be, has he?"

Orest raised an eyebrow. "I don't think that's
the sort of thing that Kaleth hears about."

"Well, a fellow can ask, can't he?" Gan was
not in the least abashed. "I doubt the gods
would be offended by so simple a question."

"I want to hear about what sort of tactics we
should be using," said Kalen firmly. "Driving off
bandits is not the same as fighting trained soldiers. And what do we do with any that we
might capture? We won't have an army underneath us to act as our support in the field. We

need to think of these things before we have problems, not after."

"Should we be getting permission to do this?" Menet-ka worried aloud. "This is nothing we've been told to do."

"But we also haven't been told not to do it," Kiron told them all. "And my thought is that if we wait for permission, we might be waiting for moons, but if we just go and *do* it, by the time anyone thinks to order us to stop, the merchants will be so used to the protection that the howls of protest will sound like a pack of wild hounds with prey in sight."

Gan grinned. "You're learning," he said smugly. "You are learning."

Kiron just shrugged. In so many ways, the old order of things had been uprooted and they were all having to learn new paths. He looked around at them all, his friends, the young fellows he had fought beside and helped to train, and suddenly it was as if he was seeing them for the first time.

"We've—all changed," he said aloud, feeling just a little stunned.

Because they really had changed, all of them, some out of all recognition. When he had first seen them, lining up before him to be told what being a raiser of dragons would be like, they had been an oddly assorted crew. There had been the commoners: quiet Huras, the baker's son; tall

Pe-atep of the booming voice, who had tended the great hunting cats for a noble; small, wiry Kalen, who had done the same with falcons. There they had stood, in their soft commoners' kilts, no jewels, no eye paint, their hair, like Kiron's, tied back in a tail. Common as street curs, all of them. Kiron could not boast any great bloodline, for before he had been a serf in the power of the Tians, he had been nothing more than an ordinary farmer's son.

And the others. Orest, son of the great and wealthy Lord Ya-Tiren; Kiron's friend, yes but under normal circumstances, they would never have met, much less become friends. So Kiron had met them because he had rescued Orest's sister Aket-ten from a river horse—so they had become friends because Kiron had done so by flying in on the back of the first tame dragon that the Altans had ever seen. A simple farmer's son would never have been a Jouster in Altan society; the notion was as outlandish as the reality—that a serf bound to the Tian Jousters had stolen a fertile dragon egg, hatched it, raised the hatchling to adulthood, and escaped with her. Impossible.

Yet there he was, and there they were. And he had been set the task of teaching a new lot of Altan Jousters how to have truly tame dragons, that obeyed out of training and love, instead of drugs and training.

Then there were the others, that he had not until that moment met. Ganek-at-kal-te-ronet, known to his friends as simply Gan, the oldest of the lot, handsome to a fault, with a languid air of laziness and a passion for women, with the highest bloodline of all of them but one. Menet-ka, also nobly born, though of a minor house, shy, but like the others, wearing garments and jewels, eye paint and hairstyle that proclaimed him to be far above the common touch. Oset-re, almost as nobly born as Gan, almost as hand-some, with a superficial vanity that had swiftly fallen before his desire to partner a tame dragon.

Kiron preferred not to think about the one who was no longer with them. Prince Toreth, who had stood between the Magi and the power of the Altan throne, and thus, had died at their hands. . . .

Now, though . . . now, there was no telling which of them was common-born and which noble. They all looked alike. There was no eye paint, no one wore his hair in the elaborate braids of nobles. All were clad alike in the wrapped Jouster's kilt; all were equally tanned and hardened by work. All had the hands of warriors, and some scars, too. Except for some superficial differences of face shape and size, they could have been brothers. Paler than Tians, but like Tians, black of hair and brown of eye, what marked them most was the look they all

wore, what Heklatis called "the look of eagles."
Even Aket-ten had that look about her, now that
he came to think about it.

They were no longer what they had been.
Now they were men.

And one woman . . . no, two. Because Kaleth had
crossed the threshold into adulthood before any
of them, and with him, Marit, his lady, and her
twin sister Nofret.

It was Menet-ka who understood at once what
Kiron meant. He nodded. "We have," he said
gravely. "Now I think it is time we truly showed
that."

Orest made a face. "Alas! We must be *responsible?*" he said in mock mourning. "And here I
had hoped that when the wars were over, I
could live my life as an idle ne'er-do-well! Ah,
well. Fate has other plans for me, I suppose."

The others laughed. With the Altan capital in
ruins, even had Orest been dragonless, he would
scarcely have been permitted to be an idler. For
that matter, it was vanishingly unlikely that his
father would have permitted him to enjoy such a
path even if Kiron had never come to Alta. And
he, and everyone else, very well knew it.

"So!" Orest continued, with relish. "Tactics!
How will a Jouster, or a wing of Jousters, best
deal with bandits?"

Kiron smoothed out a patch of sand and laid
pebbles in a line on it. "Caravans always travel

in single file; this makes them vulnerable to attack from one or both sides. What this means for the bandits is that they must find a place where they can wait concealed." He heaped up sand on either side of the line of rocks, and placed more rocks behind them. "Since there are only so many places along the caravan routes where they can do this, we need not spread ourselves overly thin, nor play watchdog for the caravans as they traverse their entire routes."

The others nodded, but it was Huras who said slowly, "For now."

"For now," agreed Oset-re. "Without a doubt, once the bandits realize what we are doing, they will change their tactics. But I think we can adapt. Let us concentrate on 'for now,' and worry about the change when they make it."

"Against a small group, the old fighting style against ground fighters worked very well," Kiron continued. "The horses were frightened into bolting, and none of them had the presence of mind to shoot at me. Of course, this, too, will not hold for long. So what I think we must do is this. We will begin by running patrols in pairs. For now, having two targets will keep the bandits confused enough. We will determine where the places of cover are along the caravan routes and keep them under watch."

"We will be limited to flying no more than half a day from Aerie," Kalen pointed out.

Again, Kiron nodded.

"For now," he repeated. "This will change. Perhaps the merchants will suggest ways in which we can feed our dragons along the routes besides hunting. Perhaps the Great King will establish outposts of Aerie. But, for now, this will do. We will be giving the caravans some protection. And those who are now questioning the need for us will shortly be the ones insisting on such things. So. We have much territory to cover, and not so many of us. I would hear your words, wingleaders. Who shall we set to what patrolling, and still remain able to feed our dragons with hunting?"

Two days later, much as Kiron had expected, Aket-ten swooped down out of the sky on Re-eth-ke, just as he was harnessing Avatre to go out to hunt. Re-eth-ke backwinged smartly, throwing up an enormous cloud of sand, a piece of rudeness on Aket-ten's part that Kiron found less than appealing. She flung her leg over the saddle and slid down Re-eth-ke's blue-black flank as he dusted himself off, her face a study in anger and admiration mingled.

"Great King Ari and Great Queen Nofret send their greetings to Kiron, and compliment him on the successes against the bandits that have been raiding caravans," she said, with an attempt, not very successful, at icy formality. "They command you to continue in these ventures, while their advisers study the results. And I would like to know—" she continued, her eyes flashing, "—why no one told *me* that there was going to be fighting!"

"Because you were with the Great King and Queen," Kiron replied mildly. "I only just launched the first strike by accident two days ago. We are still working out what pairings are best, and what we will do when two dragons are no longer enough. And do not think to add yourself to the roster. Not until the Great King and Queen release you from messenger duty, at any rate. I cannot countermand their orders, and you will flout them at your peril."

Aket-ten looked quite ready to bite something. "Any dragon past fledging could run messages!" she protested.

"But not just any Jouster has the full trust of the Great King and Queen," he pointed out with inexorable logic.

He didn't expect that to mollify her, and he was right. She actually growled.

But at least this had put all complaints about the lack of female Jousters right out of her head for now.

Aket-ten surveyed her handiwork and smiled.

So Kiron thought he was going to be clever about her plan for more female Jousters, did he?

"Allow" it as long as they got their own dragons? He had clearly forgotten who he was dealing with. She loved Kiron, no doubt, but sometimes he drove her mad. He should have known by now that when Aket-ten made up her mind about something, she found a way to get it done.

It didn't hurt in the least that she was serving duty as a courier between Mefis, Sanctuary, and Aerie. And there in Mefis were all those dragon pens, lying empty. . . .

And in the hills beyond the Great Mother River, all those former Jousting dragons, some of whom, at least, retained some good memories of their service to humans, none of whom were the least bit experienced in hatching eggs and raising youngsters.

It had all been a matter of patience, really. Patience, and having Great Queen Nofret's ear. Nofret would immediately see the value of having female Jousters as well as male; for one thing, dragon courier service was proving extremely valuable to the Great King and Queen, and they certainly could use more than just Aket-ten to serve as messengers. For another, just because Jousters were very good at fighting, that didn't mean that fighting was all they could do. Men were so single-minded! Kiron *assumed* that because she'd fought alongside the rest of them, that was what she wanted to do, too! She had never liked the fighting. Never. The acrobatics, the training, all of that, yes, but never the fighting. But girls could scout the borders of the Two Kingdoms without ever engaging an enemy, making the regular patrols that Tian and Altan Jousters always had, and that could free the fighting dragons to be ready to spring into action if a threat did appear! Girls could give Great King Ari regular reports about conditions within the Two Kingdoms, too, if that ever become necessary. In flood season, they could fly rescues as Kiron's own wing had when the capital of Alta fell. They could ferry a single passenger, say a Healing-Priest, to places where he was needed—much, much faster than the fastest chariot could bring him. From the air, they could learn how to recognize blight in crops and map out the exact area that would have to be burned in order to save the rest of the crops.

And that was only what she could think of without working too hard. She was certain she could think of more things, and all of them would be tasks the men would—face it—scorn to perform. Or, well, at least the hotheaded young men, and the hidebound old ones. Probably Kiron and most of his wing would see the need. But they'd be glad to have girls around to do the jobs, so they wouldn't have to.

Once she had girl Jousters, anyway. At the moment, she only had one . . . or rather, she had one girl and one egg, shortly to hatch. Still! it was a start!

The Palace still needed its food rooms cooled; that hadn't changed, and the heat removed had to go somewhere. Sending it to the dragon pens as it had always been sent was the logical choice, even if there were only two dragons here to benefit from it. Or three, if Aket-ten was at the Court. But now there was another occupant here besides Kashet, The-on, and Re-eth-ke.

Secretly, Aket-ten had been very pleased when the only girl to present herself as a candidate for the lone egg she had retrieved had been a fellow Altan and a former serf, as Kiron had been. That had seemed a very good omen. Getting an egg hadn't been trivial, but it hadn't been impossible either. The problem had been that so many of the first-time mothers among the former Jousting dragons had laid infertile eggs and had abandoned them for that reason. It had taken a lot of patience and incubation to find one that was fertile and hadn't sat so long that the egg had died. She must have had drovers haul in over three dozen that she'd had to discard. Only when she was sure she had a fertile one had she felt prepared to look for the right girl to play mother to the incipient dragonette.

But Peri-en-westet was definitely the right girl, someone after Aket-ten's own heart. Gentle and patient, she nevertheless had a mind of her own and a stubborn streak that had kept captivity from breaking her.

Her history was rather interesting. She had attached herself to a woman with a feeble-minded daughter when the three of them had been acquired by the same master here in Mefis. She was by nature an affectionate person, and since her own family was gone, she had naturally gravitated into helping to care for the daughter until Ari had freed all the serfs and given them paid employment or restored them to their lands again. In this case, the woman Peri had adopted was quite skilled, thanks to her own cleverness in getting into the master's kitchens. Her talent at baking had blossomed, and now she was one of the bakers for the stoneworkers quarrying limestone across the river. Her daughter was not so impaired that she couldn't be set to grind flour and pat the loaves into shape. That had freed Peri from having to look after her.

Unfortunately, it had also left her without a job. She had no lands to restore, and no real skill other than child tending, something almost any slave could do. Then she had heard of Aket-ten's search for someone to take on a dragonet, and she had answered it.

There was a complication, of course. There always was. The woman herself was pretty well determined that Peri would be married to her son, when and if she found him. But Aket-ten was confident that the young man was probably dead, and even if he wasn't, he'd probably found some other young woman to marry. Peri herself seemed attached to the idea only insofar as it made her putative mother-in-law happy to plan for it. In the meantime, though, she was keeping the nature of her new "job" a secret from her friend, because evidently this woman was one of those who had set ideas about one's place in the world—and a peasant girl had no place in the world of the Jousters, to her way of thinking.

Peri had moved into the pen where Aket-ten had installed the egg, living as any young Jouster did, but enjoying much better living conditions than the Jousters at Aerie. Granted, she had no servants, but as a farm girl she was used to that, and tending to her egg and learning about dragons from Aket-ten was scarcely an onerous job. Re-eth-ke had no objections to taking up a strange rider if Aket-ten asked it of her, and Peri's riding lessons had been going very well.

There had been tapping and movement in the egg over the last couple of days, and Re-eth-ke was showing mild interest in it. If Aket-ten was any judge of things, today would be the day that the egg hatched. Aket-ten perched on the wall of

Peri's pen, looking down at girl and egg with Re-eth-ke craning her neck and head up beside her—though Re-eth-ke was far more interested in Aket-ten's idle brow and chin scratches than in what was happening down on the sand. The egg was moving visibly.

It would not be long now, and Aket-ten waited to see if the girl was going to live up to her hopes.

Peri-en-westet waited beside her egg—*her egg!*—with a hammer in one hand, watching and listening as Aket-ten had taught her. Though she looked calm, inside she was anything but. As she listened to the tapping and waited for the baby dragon inside to pick the one spot it would try to break through, it seemed to her as if her entire life had been working toward this moment.

Not that such a thing had ever entered her mind before she embarked on this venture. Far from it. She had always thought that she would follow the path every woman in her family had ever followed, that of a simple farmer's wife. Or, well, "always" as well as any small child understood the word. She had never really considered any other life, and truly, even now she would have been content with that path. But the war, which had changed so much for so many people, had destroyed any hope of pursuing the same life as her forebears.

In fact, it had destroyed her family altogether. But not in the usual manner . . .

No, unlike Letis-hanet, soldiers had not over-run Peri's village. Her family had not been slaughtered, nor taken away as serfs for some trumped-up charge. In fact, in a way, the in-vaders had been a blessing, for they had, at least, fed her and cared for her when they found her.

No, Peri's family had fallen to the floods that had followed those terrible Magi-wrought rains. Upstream of their village, the waters of Great Mother River had risen, and kept rising, and kept rising, all in a single night while the vil-lagers slept unaware until, just before dawn, dis-aster struck.

The wall of water that engulfed the village had melted the mud houses as if they had been children's dirt forts. The unlucky had perished there, smothered by their own walls. And had Peri not been sleeping on the roof of the family home to escape the bickering of her siblings, who insisted on ending every day with a quar-rel, she would have been one of them.

As it was, she woke in a panic, fighting her way out of sleep and up to the surface at the same time, by sheer good fortune catching hold of what had been someone's roof timber. She clutched at that piece of wood with all her strength as she was whirled away under storm-racked skies, until she was fished out, nearly insensible, along with five or six others from her village. The fact that it was soldiers of Tia, the enemy, that fished her out made no real impression on her, not even when they turned her over to the Royal Slave-master to begin her life as a serf.

And even then, that life was nothing near so onerous as that of others. She had been numb and sunk in grieving for some time, so she hadn't really paid much attention to her surroundings, but her master had not been unkind. In fact, her master was scarcely seen at all, and his cook, to whom she had been assigned, was taciturn but fair.

Perhaps all that had been due to the fact that there were no lands attached to her. She was too young to tell those who had picked her up where her family farm was, and there was no use hunting for records after the flood had swept through the place. The only other records would have been in the Altan capital, and Tians would hardly be welcome there. So there was no reason for anyone to try to be rid of her to free the property of encumbrances, and every reason to keep her alive and healthy to continue to serve. As others had noted before this, there were laws in place regarding the treatment of slaves, but serfs were war captives, and subject to much less oversight. As a consequence, for the same amount of work that could be got from them, they were much cheaper to keep.

It was in the kitchen that she had encountered Letis-hanet and her daughter Iris, and if ever there was a story of the woe of an Altan family in the hands of the Tians, it was theirs. Though Letis' husband had never fought against the Altans, he had the misfortune of possessing fine property. A Tian wanted it. And so, spurious accusations were made, soldiers sent—

Letis was understandably less than coherent about what had happened then. All Peri really gathered was that her husband was killed on the spot, Iris was hurt, and the family broken apart, their son going with the house and the rest attached to the farmlands. Then as those lands in turn were parceled out, the remaining members of the family were further separated, leaving only Letis and her feeble-minded daughter together.

Their masters had ranged from careless to cruel until they and the remaining parcel of land they were tied to was bought by Peri's master. "Absent" was better than "cruel," at least. The trouble was, what to do with Iris while Letis was at work in the master's bakery?

That was quickly solved when Iris proved moderately useful in the kitchen and the kitchen garden. Ordered to keep the girl in her charge, Peri had been perfectly happy to do just that, seeing to it that no one teased or tormented her, making sure that when she was given a task she completed it. Letis had been overwhelmingly grateful, and as time went on, the two became friends, then nearly as close as mother and daughter.

That was when Letis had started talking about her son. How he was Peri's age. How Peri was exactly the sort of person Letis had envisioned as her son's wife. And from that, it had drifted until the unspoken became the accepted, at least on the part of Letis—that when her son was found and the family reunited, Peri would marry him.

It seemed a harmless enough daydream. Letis had few such dreams to sustain her, and Peri was disinclined to shatter this one.

But then, without warning, at the moment in which victory was confidently expected by their captors—the war ended. The Great King was dead. His advisers were dead. Most of the Tian army was dead. And suddenly, there was a new Great King and a Great Queen, too—and she was Altan. And he ordered the serfs freed, and their lives to be sorted out, with recompense given to them.

Of course, there were thousands upon thousands of them. And it was taking a very long time to sort through records and claims and counterclaims. So while she was waiting for *her* claim to come up through the magistrates, Letis had been given a job that paid well, a place to live, and help for Iris. And Peri had—

—this!

She heard the tapping suddenly take on a new urgency, and she heard, felt, exactly the place where the dragon was trying to break through. Now she moved, the hammer in her hand tapping firmly, but carefully, against the shell. Hairline cracks started from her point of impact.

Soon, but not soon enough for her rising panic that she wasn't doing this right, a piece of shell popped off, and a fist-sized golden snout with two flaring nostrils poked out of the hole.

She sat down hard in the sand with a sigh of relief. Now, according to Aket-ten, the baby would just breathe for a while, resting, before going back to hammering its way out of the shell. If she were a mother dragon, she would be licking the shell to weaken it. She couldn't do that, so she had to weaken it with the hammer.

And before too long, that was what she was doing. Periodically, the baby would stop to rest, and so would she. The baby had begun her attempts—Peri was sure it was a "she"—to emerge in midmorning. It wasn't until midafternoon that a big piece of shell finally fell away and the gold-green bundle of wet skin tumbled out of the larger half of the egg to land at her feet.

The baby raised her—it lacked the horns, so it *was* a female—head on a neck that seemed too fragile to support it and looked up at Peri with confused golden eyes. She opened her mouth to emit a muted squeak. And Peri fell entirely in love.

Aket-ten watched her protégée do everything exactly right, watched the moment when Peri fell into entirely besotted adoration, and smiled.

Everything was going according to plan.

Once other young women saw Peri—who was *not* a Great Queen, not even a noble—was a Jouster, Aket-ten was certain more would step forward, eager to join her fledgling flying corps.

In fact . . . she just might proceed with this plan *without* telling Kiron. Just deliver it as a *fait accompli.* That would show him, him and everyone else, that she knew what she was doing.

But she ought to get Nofret's permission, formally, for a girl group. It was one thing to experiment with one girl and one dragon; quite another to invent a whole new kind of Jouster.

"You'll need food for her shortly," she called down to the young woman, who had the baby's head cradled in her lap, with the wings spread out over the hot sand to dry. Peri looked up, startled, at the sound of her voice, as if she had forgotten that Aket-ten was there.

She probably had, actually,

"I'll make sure someone brings you the sort of thing she'll need for her first meal," Aket-ten continued, jumping down off the wall. Re-eth-ke lost interest in the proceedings as soon as Aket-ten stopped scratching her, and stretched out to bask on her own sands.

Aket-ten hurried off, feeling uncommonly cheerful.

 # FOUR

THE trade routes for half a day's flight in all directions from Aerie had been carefully surveyed. Places where ambushes were likely had been found. In fact, in the very act of making those surveys, two separate groups of bandits had been flushed and defeated, a fact which both elated and dismayed Kiron.

This meant that his plan was a good one. It also meant that the help he and the other Jousters were about to supply was more desperately needed than he had thought.

On the other hand, this development electrified even the older Jousters; he hadn't quite realized how badly they had missed having duties to fulfill. But now that they knew there really was a need, they were on fire to begin patrolling, and had begun practicing on their own, adapting the tactics of war to a different sort of combat.

Right now, the tactics were simple: dive out of the sky and spook the animals. The riders would either be carried off with the panicking mounts, or dismount—or be thrown. Once on the ground, they were easier prey. And that was where the first difficulty came in.

No one had any compunctions about killing these brigands. The question was what to do with them if they surrendered.

If there was a caravan about, the law was clear, and Great King Ari had repeated it. Bandits were war captives, and as such, became serfs. The caravans could take them and sell them to the highest bidder, or use them as labor. With all of the Altan serfs freed, there was a bit of a shortage of that sort of labor now. More strong captives would be welcome.

The problem came if there were no caravans about. What to do then? There was no good way to transport them back to the nearest settlement. They certainly couldn't be brought back by the Jousters; there was no way to do so safely. They couldn't be released. That was utterly out of the question. So what to do with them? Killing them out of hand was utterly repugnant to Kiron. So was leaving them trussed up in the sunlight to die.

He still hadn't solved that problem on the day that the first official patrols began.

But it was still a relief to lift into the sky on Avatre's back, in charge of a flight of the "greenies," Jousters who had never actually seen combat. He wasn't worried about them; they were merely flying support for Orest's wing, which was composed of very experienced Altan Jousters, survivors of those terrible days when the Magi had sent them into combat with the ruthless intention of getting rid of them through battlefield attrition. Anyone who had come through that was not going to find a few bandits at all intimidating.

Kiron's greenies, all sporting ribbons of his signature color of scarlet, striped in colors picked randomly, were acting as scouts. They ranged ahead and to either side of the trade road in pairs, taking it in turn to fly back to Kiron and the fighting wing to report. He really, truly, did not expect any fighting this day, something he had even warned the others about. It wouldn't do for them to become disappointed and disillusioned the very first day.

For the first half of the morning, the most exciting thing that happened was that one of the green youngsters spooked up a lone camel and decided it looked tasty. Green dragon, green rider, and a prey much bigger and tougher than even some experienced hunters would try; it was a good thing that they *were* flying support, for they were in trouble in moments, and it hadn't taken the sight of the youngster's partner flying back in a panic to let most of both wings know something was amiss.

There was a sudden cloud of dust on the ground where no dust should be rising, and most of the dragons in both wings suddenly turned their heads in that direction, as if they sensed something wrong.

Avatre did a wingover and headed in that direction on her own, but by the time they arrived, the situation was already well in hand. The camel was down, with Orest's blue atop it, tearing at the prey, while the youngsters stood off, the dragon's posture one of chagrin and envy. It wanted the meat. It also knew it was only going to get what Wastet left behind.

A pointed lesson for both dragon and rider.

But Wastet had eaten, and eaten well, before he flew. And Orest had no real difficulty pulling him off after he'd had the choicest bits. Not that—in Kiron's opinion, at least—there was anything particularly choice about a camel.

This meant a delay as the rider of the offending dragon was dealt with. Finally Kiron decided that the best possible punishment would be to leave him behind.

The dragon, oblivious and greedy, gorged

himself, while the rider stood unhappily by and nodded at Kiron's orders. "Clearly, either you are not gauging how much to feed him, shirking your hunting duties, or not paying enough attention to his behavior," Kiron said severely. "You are the human, and you have to think for two. He is a dragon and only knows what he wants to do in the next few moments. So when he is finished eating, you will butcher up what is left and fly back to Aerie. Tell Kalen that I am assigning you to his wing for more training in understanding your dragon."

The older riders in Orest's wing looked pleased at this. Even in the old days, when the dragons were drugged, it had been of prime importance to understand their moods and behavior. And working in the hot sun, butchering a smelly camel, was good punishment for the young man. This was a form of discipline that they strongly approved of.

For his part, that made Kiron feel a little more like a proper leader. *Maybe I can make this work,* he thought, as he mounted Avatre and sent her up, the rest of his greenie wing (but one) straggling after him.

There was a cloud of dust on the far horizon; from here, like a tiny smudge against the blue bowl of the sky, as if the "glaze" on the rim was not quite perfect. He signaled to one of his greenies and sent him on ahead to find out what it was, but since it *was* on the road, it was a good bet that it was a caravan of some sort.

A caravan . . .

There was a particular spot on this trade route that they'd already chased off one group of ambushers a day or so ago. Could it be that this had been no accident? Were the bandits actually expecting this caravan?

He signaled to Orest, who flew Wastet to within shouting distance. "I have a hunch!" he called, and gestured at the dust smudge. "We might just get some action—"

Orest grinned, teeth gleaming whitely in his dusty face. "We're ready for it!" he shouted back. "Lead us in, Captain!"

As Orest returned to his wing, Kiron signaled the rest of the greenies, and got them in rough formation behind him. Their riders were lighter, the dragons themselves a little smaller, and hence, just a little faster than the older ones, at least in straight flight. There was always a trade-off of weight, power, and speed. Lighter meant faster in racing flight, but not in a dive. A small dragon could never be a powerful one. But a powerful one might not be able to catch him.

A powerful one might not be able to dodge an arrow.

Kiron had memorized this stretch of the road, and now led the group straight to the ambush point. For now, he doubted very much whether bandits were looking *up* for trouble. They had no real reason to. And even if they did, seeing the dragons in the sky would probably make them scatter, which was the point anyway—

The others might not see it that way, he realized after a moment. *They might be spoiling for a fight.* He made a mental note to remind them that they weren't soldiers anymore, they were police, and preventing something from happening was just as good, if not better, than flying to the rescue.

He'd just have to convince them of that.

But not, it seemed, today. For ahead of them, in the ambush point, there were little dots that he didn't recall being there. And Avatre began to strain forward, which told him that her superior eyesight had made out those specks to be animals or people or both. He took a chance, based on the fact that the dots weren't moving, and waved his hand over his head in the signal for "Enemy sighted."

And none too soon either, for the greenie he'd sent out was racing back toward him signaling "Caravan," and he could see the dark streak against the desert floor beneath that dust cloud that told him the same.

He sent the greenies up higher, moved Avatre into a middle-height position, and signaled to Orest to bring the seasoned wing in to the forefront of the formation.

By that point, the dots had resolved themselves into riders, waiting to swoop down over the crest of the hill as soon as the caravan came within reach.

They were not looking up.

Although, a moment later, as Orest's wing came diving down out of the sky, and their camels began to bolt, they were.

By the standards of the war it was a short, and very much one-sided, battle. Kiron even allowed his greenies to dive down and herd riderless mounts off into the desert as far as they could be chased, while the seasoned fighters concentrated on the bandits themselves. This was plenty of excitement for them.

The bandits, however, were enough of a menace that the seasoned fighters, individually, had their hands full. Some of them must have dealt with Jousters before this, for a handful of them went back-to-back in a circle, roughly half with spears, and half with bows.

The bowmen were good shots.

A deep maroon dragon bellowed in outrage as an arrow pierced his wing web, and as his rider cursed and ducked, an arrow bouncing off his helm, Kiron was glad he'd ordered the experienced Jousters into their scavenged armor today.

But rather than making them back down, the successful attack on their fellow Jouster infuriated the rest. The angry cry from their injured wingmate ignited the ire of the dragons, and as if they had been given orders from Aket-ten, Kiron watched in astonishment as they did something he had never seen Jousting dragons do before.

They ignored the commands of their riders and landed, clustering all on one side of the knot of bandits. Then, as one, they half-reared and began furiously fanning the air with their wings.

A landing dragon had always kicked up a miniature *kamiseen*. This was eight dragons all blowing up sand and dust and purposefully aiming it at the humans, who were not expecting it.

Blinded, uttering cries of pain of their own as they dropped weapons and tried to shield their eyes, or clapped their hands over eyes full of sand, they stumbled backward, turning away from their attackers.

Only to be felled by arrows, javelins, and slung stones and lead bullets. Accustomed now to hitting running game at long range, the cluster of incapacitated bandits at short range was no challenge. They were armored—armor that, it appeared, had been salvaged from Tian and Altan officers—but nothing covered their throats, the backs of their legs, or their eyes.

The Jousters were ruthless. When they were finished, there were none of that group left standing. It left Kiron feeling a bit sick, but—

This was war, another sort of war, and this time he had not a lot of sympathy for the enemy. They preyed on the people who were only trying to make an honest copper, who already had to contend with wind and sandstorm and all the other hazards of trade. They stole and killed without provocation. He clenched his jaw and said nothing. The bandits could have surrendered, and the gods only knew what they were guilty of precisely, but they were—at the least— guilty of trying to rob people who had never harmed them.

It was a short, hot fight, but in the end, it was one-sided.

It took longer to round up the survivors. Some lay where they had fallen, wounded, or having thrown themselves to the ground, but others—

"We have runners, Captain," said Kelet-mat, rider of a bronze-and-yellow beast of placid nature, when a half-dozen brigands waited, trussed hand and foot, in the sun. "What should we do about them?"

Kiron pondered that for a moment. "Do you think they'll get anywhere?"

Kelet-mat grimaced, and raked his black hair out of his eyes with one hand. "I would have said 'no,' since there's nothing but sand and scrub as far as the eye can see—but these rats aren't soldiers. They have the luck of Seft himself, and it would be just *our* luck that one of

them would go telling what had happened in
some scummy tavern and the next lot we have
to deal with will be ready for us."

"Eventually someone will tell—" Kiron
pointed out reluctantly. "But it would be good if
we could keep the advantage of surprise for a
while longer." He scratched his head and looked
out over the horizon. "All right. You senior riders track them down and round them up. And
don't take unnecessary chances."

It wasn't until the caravan itself arrived that
they finished, and as the astonished merchants
halted their beasts to stare, Kiron was pondering
the second problem; what to do with twenty-
some bound captives.

It was an interesting tableau, actually. On the
road, the line of laden camels, blowing and looking nervously at the dragons. The dragons, ignoring them, all lounging happily, basking in
the sun. The merchants, torn between apprehension and curiosity, The Jousters in their armor,
some of which had already been removed because it was so cursed hot. And the captives.

Finally, curiosity won, and one of the merchants swung his leg over his saddle, slid down
the side of his camel, and headed straight for
Kiron.

The merchant was nothing if not bold. "So,
Captain," he said as soon as he came within
earshot. "I can see you're Jousters, but for which

side? And why've you trussed up these men like chicken going to market?"

Kiron smiled. "We're Jousters for Great King Ari and Great Queen Nofret, which makes us royal police of a sort. You could say we're on your side, come to that. As for why these fellows are trussed up—if we hadn't been patrolling when we were, they'd have ambushed you on this very spot."

The merchant nodded. "Then you surely have our thanks. But this isn't the sort of thing that Jousters do—"

"It is now," Orest interrupted, with pride written in his very posture. "The Great Royals have given us our orders. We serve the people. We'll watch the borders, and we'll guard the roads."

The merchant's eyes started to light up; it was clear he saw all of the implications of this. "Are you police, or army?" he asked carefully.

Kiron thought that over. And felt a sharp pain in his ankle. Orest had just kicked him.

His startled glance won him a grimace from his friend, and the silently mouthed word "nomarchs."

What—he thought, and then it struck him. The army answered only to its Captains, and the captains only to the generals and the generals only to the Great King himself. But the police, Royal servants though they were, answered to the nomarchs, the governors of provinces, and their line of command ended at the Royal Vizier, not the King. Their services could be commanded at any point by almost anyone in authority down to the headman of a small village.

So the Jousters, few as they were now, could find themselves spread thin over too much territory, and dependent for the keep and the care of their dragons on people who would think that the three-day-old stinking leavings from the butcher were "good enough" food for something like a dragon.

"The army," he said quickly, earning a nod and a flash of grin from Orest.

"Ah," the merchant looked a bit disappointed, but then his eye fell again on the bandits, and he brightened. "Then that makes these men war captives, true?"

Kiron nodded. The merchant grinned toothily. "Well, Captain, in that case, I am authorized to take them off your hands." He fished inside the neck of his tunic and brought out a medallion on a cord. "I am an authorized dealer in war captives."

"Tian, I presume?" Kiron asked, peering at the circle of stamped faience. He couldn't make heads nor tails of it—

But Kelet-mat was Tian, and Kiron waved him over. He glanced at the medallion and grinned. "Looks like our problem of how to transport this scum is solved, Captain," he said. The faces of the captives fell.

Kiron decided that some scare tactics might be in order.

"Well, it's a good thing this fellow came along," he said gruffly, loud enough for the captives to hear. "The Great King gave me field authority. I was going to try and execute them right here." He paused. "I don't know, I still might. The dragons are hungry."

For one moment the merchant looked horrified, but as Kiron gave him a broad wink that the captives couldn't see, his eyes narrowed and a ghost of a smile appeared.

"That's a waste of good workers, Captain," the merchant protested. "You can easily hunt down their camels to feed your dragons—"

"He's right," Orest chimed in. "Besides, there's more meat on a camel."

"All right, then," Kiron said, sounding as if he had been persuaded, but was still a bit reluctant. "What's the procedure here?"

The procedure proved to be fully as bureaucratic as he had suspected it would. Two copies of the list of captives with names and general condition had to be written up on the spot, with Kiron taking one to turn over to whatever Royal Scribe was in charge of such things. From there, he had no idea what would become of list or captives—

But, presumably, the lists would be checked against each other and against the actual captives before they went into the market. Kiron had heard that Ari had made a few changes to that procedure, to make sure that serfs weren't treated as Kiron—then called Vetch—had been treated. These men had no notion just how much better their lives were going to be than his own had been.

Pity they didn't deserve it.

 FIVE

"A FEMALE Jouster group?" Great Queen Nofret asked, astonished.

Mind she didn't look like a Great Queen at the moment; she was in the same sort of linen tunic that Aket-ten was wearing, with her hair held only by a simple headband. She wore no jewelry at all, much less a crown, and she groomed and saddled her dragon, the magnificent purple-and-scarlet The-on, as well as a dragon boy.

But this was the one time of the day when she was able to relax and not be Great Queen Nofret, when she could become something she had never actually been before: something *other* than royal. Merely herself. In many ways, Aket-ten did not envy her at all. As she helped to wipe

The-on down with oiled cloths, Aket-ten stole glances at Nofret's serene profile and considered the Queen who was also her friend.

All her life she had been groomed to be on a throne. First, she had been one half of the female pair of Royal twins that would share the thrones of Alta with the male pair of Royals; that was the way of things in Alta, as the Great Kings and Queens of Alta were always two sets of Royal twins. As the only female pair in the bloodline of reasonable age, she and Marit had always been in the Court, schooled and trained as the probable heirs, and very well aware that their choice of mate and life had been taken out of their hands by the gods.

But Nofret and Marit had accepted it; well, it wasn't as if they had any other course of action before them. And they had liked Kaleth and Toreth quite well—

Now here, Aket-ten wiped down the purple flank of Nofret's dragon with a feeling of uncertainty. Marit had quite been in love with her destined mate. But Nofret?

Nofret was hard to read and always had been. Much more phlegmatic than her twin, much more practical, Nofret had clearly enjoyed Prince Toreth's company and had not shown any sign of discontent with her prospective life. But . . . when Toreth was murdered by the Magi of Alta in the next stage of their bid to take over

governance of the entire Kingdom, Nofret's dis-
tress had not been . . . as intense as Aket-ten
would have thought it would be, had Nofret
loved him as anything other than a friend.

Now, coercion into a marriage with a pair of
faux-Royal twins the Magi had cobbled up in
order to take those thrones—that had gotten an
intense reaction.

And still Nofret had been Royal, and not able
to escape the ever-increasing restrictions. Until
she and Marit had escaped Alta into the desert,
and the lost city they called Sanctuary. And
there, for a brief moment of escape, she had been
something other than Nofret, heir to the throne,
Royal twin.

After all, they were all too busy scraping out
life in Sanctuary to think about relative triviali-
ties like royal birth.

But with only that brief time, things returned to
what was "normal" for Nofret; she was a Royal
again, this time selected to marry the only other
Royal—if illegitimate Royal—left of the Tian
bloodline. And that had been Ari-en-anethet,
who had until that moment been perfectly content to live his life as plain Jouster Ari. It was just
a good thing for both of them that they were very
fond of each other, very fond indeed, and fond
quite quickly became loving. But it still meant
that Nofret had had only brief moments of being
herself, and not a title and responsibilities.

Aket-ten sighed in sympathy; Nofret had gotten a short taste of freedom, and without a doubt she treasured the few moments of freedom she still was able to garner.

No one troubled her when she was with her dragon, even though, aside from exercise, the only flying she ever got to do anymore was when she and Ari made a Royal Appearance on dragonback.

Perhaps that was why she looked askance at Aket-ten, and repeated, "A *female* Jouster group? What would they do? We have not got work for the wings we have—"

"Yet," Aket-ten replied, and tried not to smirk. "Kiron is testing his idea of sending out every dragon he has to guard the trails soon, if he has not already begun. Every wing in Aerie will be flying guard on a trade road. I suspect that it will not be long before the traders and the merchants who depend on them for goods will be petitioning Your Highnesses to find more Jousters for the same duty."

"Knee," Nofret said absently, and her dragon obediently lifted a purple-to-scarlet leg for her to use as a stepping place to mount up to the saddle over her shoulders. Once securely in the saddle, Nofret looked down at Aket-ten. "But why a group of female Jousters? Not that I object," the Great Queen added quickly, "but what can they do that the Jousters we have cannot?"

Aket-ten opened her mouth to answer hotly, shut it without saying anything, then opened it again. Frustrated, she finally answered, "Nothing."

Nofret sighed, and looked down at her. "And you will incur much displeasure," she pointed out. "Not that women should not be Jousters, though there will be some grumbling of that nature, but there will be many more complaints that you are taking dragons that should have gone to those waiting for them. And adding more hungry draconic mouths to fill."

Aket-ten set her jaw mulishly and squinted up at her, purple and scarlet and glorious against the hot blue bowl of the sky. "I know all this. And we will *not* be taking dragons that should have gone to those waiting for them. We will find our own eggs, our own baby dragons. We will not be pretty priestesses flying about for no good reason except to be ornamental. We will work. We will *find* work."

Nofret shook her head, then laughed. "I am the Great Queen. If I want a wing of dragons, rather than, say, a temple, I may have it," she said at last. "All right, Aket-ten. Find your eggs and your girls. Find your work. Make me a wing of female Jousters. If nothing else, I can claim I need you to escort me on temple duties, or," she made a face, "to escort me when I am flying at any time. You may have to play the part of pretty priestess flying about to be ornamental, at least for a while, but if you can find real work for your wing, then . . . I will release you to do it."

Since Aket-ten had been steeling herself for more reasons why this was a bad idea, she beamed with happiness. But the next thing that Nofret said was sobering.

"I shall require you to give up courier duty, of course," she said. "Not even the most accommodating of the old Jousters will be willing to act as the leader and administrator of this group. I can give you the full use of the old Dragon Courts, and I can lend you an overseer, but only you have the knowledge of what the dragons will need and how to train them. I doubt very much that any of the current trainers will help you. You will have to do this all yourself. And the only place besides Aerie that has the right resources for dragons is here. Mefis. You will have to remain here for the foreseeable future."

Give up courier duty— That would mean giving up seeing Kiron. . . .

Remain in Mefis. That would mean little chance to get away. Especially with baby dragons to tend, and new Jousters and dragons to train . . . all on her own. If Kiron wanted to see her, he would have to come to her. Would his own duties allow that? Nofret eyed her with speculation as she searched within herself. What was she willing to sacrifice for this? Did she have good reasons? Enough of them?

Merely believing that it was the right thing to do was not going to be enough.

But Kiron did all this, all by himself.

Well, that was one reason. She wanted to prove to herself, and to him, that she was as capable as he was, that she could do what he had done, on her own. And maybe she wanted to prove it to other people as well; she had a sense that to her mother and father she was still the little priestess, with minor powers, who really ought to make a good marriage and settle down and raise a big family. . . .

The mere thought of that made her grit her teeth. Not that she didn't want a family, but . . .

I'm more than that.

And before she did any settling with anyone, especially Kiron, she wanted him to know that, too.

But as the wind stirred her hair and cooled her forehead, and she looked up at Nofret and her increasingly restless dragon, she knew that this couldn't only be done because *she* wanted it, nor only for *her* reasons. The-on lifted wings of deep purple shading to scarlet at the tips, and folded them again, and looked down at her. And her instincts told her there were good reasons for other girls and young women to do this—even if she didn't know what they were yet.

But maybe those reasons will be as different as every girl who raises a dragon.

She felt it then, the certainty. "I'll need that overseer," she said then. "And the priests to make sure the sands are kept hot. And some of the old dragon hunters to help me. And a cold room and some butchers and a few servants to tend the rooms, and—"

Nofret laughed. "And, and, and!" she said. "The records for dragon keeping are extensive and exact, I believe my vizier can puzzle out what you will need. For how many?"

"Nine, including me and Peri," she replied. Her mind was already racing. It was not too late in the season to find eggs yet to hatch, and not too late to find nests of young dragons whose parents did not know how to tend them. She would, in fact, look for those first. Nofret had shown the way there with The-on and her siblings; accustom a baby to a human as its parent young enough and it had no trouble in accepting that human, indeed, all humans.

"And I will request to Kiron that he send me one of his young and inexperienced Jousters to be our courier . . . hmm . . ." Nofret's eyes grew distant for a moment. "If we are to have more than just four dragons here, it would be no bad thing to have more than one courier. Two, at least. No, four. Two for between here and Aerie and two for between here and Sanctuary, one at each end. If Kiron is going to start guarding the trade routes, we will need to speak with him very much more often."

"That is something we can do!" Aket-ten said instantly, glad of the opening for one of her ideas. "We females can fly courier, and since we are lighter than the men, we can probably fly faster."

Nofret looked down at her, and at that moment, Aket-ten saw the Great Queen, and not her friend. "That will be for the future, then. Keep thinking, Aket-ten," the Great Queen said. "The more reasons you can make, the easier it will be for me to defend your existence. Now, my dragon is getting restless, and so am I. Go and consult with my vizier and make your lists. And think of how you are going to tell Kiron that if he wishes to see you, it will be he who must come to you from now on. Because no matter how you tell him . . . he is not going to like being told."

Aket-ten sighed, and shielded her eyes as The-on took to the skies. Nofret was right.

That was going to be one of the hardest things she was going to have to do.

The easiest thing turned out to be finding the dragons themselves.

Two seasons on, and the freed dragons of Tia often still could not manage to grasp how to properly tend a nest full of babies. This was not so bad for the young ones when one of the parents was a fully wild dragon, but when both were former Jousting dragons . . .

Over the course of the next few days, Aket-ten went back to all those places where she had found dragon nests and marked them, hoping to find eggs that had been abandoned.

Now she looked for baby dragons that were not prospering.

It turned out that it was not at all difficult to find them. Baby dragons that were not being fed were hungry, and hungry baby dragons cried.

Now, occasionally a dragon who had laid infertile eggs would adopt the younglings; not wishing to find herself and her crew of carters staring into the face of an angry mother, Aket-ten spent time at each nest, waiting to see if the mother returned with adequate prey, or if she would fail to return at all. Once, where there had been two nests relatively close together, the gold dragon that Aket-ten remembered at the second abandoned the eggs that were clearly not going to hatch and took over the babies in the first nest. But all too often it appeared that not all of the baby dragons were going to survive being raised by indifferent or inexperienced mothers.

This was not unlike the experience that falconers had, when stealing young hawks. A good falconer would find a nest where one or two of the chicks was not thriving and take the strongest, leaving the other one or two that were left to enjoy the good feeding that the largest and greediest had been getting all for himself.

However, given the size and strength of even the smallest of young dragons, Aket-ten took the opposite approach. She and her wild-animal hunters took the weakest.

They waited until the mother and father flew off for the first of the morning hunts, then moved in. And the first thing that they did was to stuff all the babies in the nest with meat that they had brought with them. The babies were still too young to recognize a human as anything other than another moving object in their world, and when that moving object slid meat down their throats . . .

When the babies were full, they stopped whining and went almost immediately to sleep. That made extracting one from the nest trivially easy. Two strong men could carry one in a sling, and the rocking motion seemed to be soothing for them. Putting the sling between two camels for the trip back to Mefis proved to be just as soothing. Unlike captured fledglings, these babies were perfectly content to sleep in their swinging cradle and be fed when they woke and whined. Within seven days, Aket-ten had as many young dragons, and she took care to point out to her animal hunters how she had located these babies. There had to be other nests out there, with ill-tended babies. Kiron had complained that he had more would-be Jousters waiting than he had eggs or babies to give them. The Great Queen had observed that Aket-ten would incur resentment for "taking" dragons that "should" have gone to men.

Well, no one would now be able to say she had not done her best to help her "rivals."

Besides . . . she couldn't bear the thought of those beautiful little creatures slowly starving to death. . . .

When Nofret had approved the notion of the "Queen's Jousters," Aket-ten had hoped that young women would be as eager to volunteer for such a thing as the young men were. There never seemed to be any shortage of young women wishing to be priestesses, for instance, and that was equally demanding work. . . .

Not that she was going to take just anyone, but—

"I don't understand this," she said forlornly, as Peri helped her to feed the babies, which she had housed all together in one pen for ease in care. "Why aren't there more people who want to train as Jousters?"

"More girls, you mean," Peri said shrewdly. "Well that's easy enough. How is a girl going to find a good husband if she's riding around on a dragon?"

Aket-ten stared at her, dumbfounded. "You jest, yes?"

But Peri shook her head. "You have not spent enough time around ordinary people, Aket-ten," she said frankly. "Ordinary girls anyway. It seems . . . even among us when we were serfs, that was what we talked about. It was what our mothers and grandmothers talked about. It was all anyone ever talked about—"

"Not among the Winged Ones!" Aket-ten protested.

"Then perhaps you are looking in the wrong place," the girl said shrewdly. "Perhaps if you looked among the priestesses—"

Aket-ten blinked. That simply had not occurred to her. But—

But among the priestesses, her power was considered minor, uninteresting, and . . . to be honest . . . not at all useful. To be able to speak into the mind of an animal? To what purpose? Far more useful and cherished were those who could speak to another priestess at a distance, to see at a distance or the future or the past. To speak with spirits—that was another sought-for power. Most of all, to be a Mouth of the Gods . . .

All these things could serve the people. What would you learn if you spoke into the mind of an animal? Not a great deal that was useful.

Unless, of course, that animal was a dragon.

Aket-ten had been able to calm even the Jousting dragons that had gone to the wild. She could coordinate an entire wing. She could soothe fears and tell what was hurting.

What if every wing had someone like her?

"Peri," she said breathlessly, "you are a genius."

"I am a genius covered in bits of meat," Peri said ruefully, looking at her bloody, sticky hands. "Let us finish feeding these little ones so we can bathe before we become covered in biting flies."

Aket-ten laughed.

She hurried through her bath, though, a daily luxury she usually lingered over, especially in the hot days like this one. Not that she didn't take care with it; she certainly did that. After all, when one is going to visit a temple, one does well to look one's best.

But she also did not want to look as if she was one of those silly women who dressed to impress a man with how important and wealthy she was. Baket-ke-aput, the High Priest of Haras in Mefis, was not the sort to be impressed by what was on the surface of things.

She did pause at the Palace long enough to ask Nofret's vizier for a note of introduction to the priest, and waited while a servant went to take her request to the overseer. The Palace was pleasantly cool, the effect of the same magic that kept the sands of the dragon pens warm. Heat was removed from the Palace, where it certainly was not wanted, and sent to the pens, where it certainly was, something that at the moment, the dwellers in Sanctuary and Aerie would probably be very glad of. Aket-ten amused herself by examining the murals here, which were many-times-life-sized paintings of one of the Kings of Tia out hunting in the marshes for ducks.

Which was certainly a subject preferable to one of the many Kings of Tia out hunting for Altans in his war chariot . . . .

A note of introduction was going to be necessary to get past all the underpriests and scribes and functionaries of the temple, who were there in no small part to keep the High Priest from being bothered. The High Priest of Haras was not the sort of person one simply walked up to—well, not unless one was the Great King—

"Aket-ten!"

She looked up, startled, to see Ari himself striding toward her, hands outstretched, his bodyguards looking very unhappy to be forced to trot to keep up with him.

"Nofret's vizier knew that I am to have an audience with Baket-ke-aput shortly, or rather," Ari grinned, "he is to have an audience with me. I see no reason why your business with him, whatever it is, cannot be broached at the same time."

Aket-ten felt almost faint with gratitude. She had been anticipating, despite a note, having to spend most of the rest of the day, and possibly tomorrow, being sent from one underling and scribe to another.

This would cut all of that short.

Belatedly she remembered that this was not just Ari. This was the Great King—

And she quickly got to her feet and flung herself down on her face again.

"Oh—" she heard him say in exasperation. "Don't do that. Or at least, don't do it when we are private together. It isn't necessary."

Slowly she got back up to her feet and smoothed out her linen sheath with both hands. "If that is your will, Great K—"

"Not when we are private together," Ari said firmly. "And, to you, in private, I am nothing more than Ari. Now come to the Lesser Audience Chamber with me. Baket-ke-aput is a good man. If what you need is simple enough, he may be able to help you this very day."

Aket-ten had not really had very much to do with Ari back when they were all just the refugee Jousters trying to survive at Sanctuary. She was Altan, he was Tian, he was *so* much older than the rest of the young wing of Jousters created by Kiron, and at any rate, it had not been long before the plan of making him Great King and Nofret Great Queen had resulted in both of them being so embroiled in plans and strategies and negotiations that she had seldom seen him *or* Nofret. He had been Kiron's great friend and mentor, not hers. She hadn't really thought he had paid all that much attention to her, but—

"So I suspect this is about this plan of yours, the Queen's Wing?" he asked, glancing at her with a hint of a smile. She started a bit, and his smile broadened. "Nofret and I *do* talk, you know. I was intrigued. I'm not at all clear why you want to do this, but I am intrigued."

"I'm not sure it is a very good idea now," she confessed, subdued. "I am having difficulty finding girls who want to be Jousters."

"You're having difficulty finding girls like yourself." Ari nodded. "Not very surprising, really. People in Tia, not just girls, are accustomed to a rigid structure all about them. People expect to do what their fathers, and their grandfathers, and their many-times-great grandfathers did. If you are a farmer, your son will be a farmer, and your father was a farmer. You *might* go into the army, or, if you were very clever and very fortunate, you might go to the priesthood or apprentice as a scribe. But you wouldn't expect to leave your home village unless you went into the army. I expect it is even more rigid for girls, since girls don't go to the army or become scribes."

"No, they don't." Aket-ten frowned. "But in Alta . . . you might become a skilled craftswoman . . . or . . . or something." But she couldn't really think *what* else a woman might become. She had never been forced to look at things that way. She had always had such freedom as a Nestling, then a Fledgling—one of the special the chosen, the Winged Ones. And before that, well, as the cherished daughter of a great noble.

"Well, I really don't know what it's like in Alta. I do know that I was probably the only scribe ever to become a Jouster. And if I had been forced to learn to handle a wild-caught, *tala*-drugged dragon rather than a hand-tamed one to do so, you would probably find me sharpening my pens in the marketplace at this very moment." He laughed at her expression.

"I cannot imagine you ever being content to be a scribe," she finally said.

"Oh, I did not say I would have been *content*," he replied. "But here we are."

They had passed through a number of large, open rooms, most of which had been sparsely populated by people doing things at desks. Light came from ventilation slits up near the ceiling. Now they entered another large room, but this one was empty of everything but a very low dais with two thrones on it, and some stools against the wall.

"Go stand there, if you please," Ari said, gesturing to the left side of the dais. Aket-ten quickly obeyed. As a former Winged One and the daughter of a noble, she was accustomed to standing about for long periods of time doing nothing.

She adopted the relaxed posture she had learned was best for such situations, while Ari mounted the dais, put on the Lesser Crown that was waiting on the seat of one of the two thrones, and took an equally relaxed pose.

As if that had been some sort of summons, a tall, thin, ascetic man with a faintly harried expression came out of the next room, went to his knees and bowed, then rose again. "Great King, the High Priest Baket-ke-aput craves audience with you."

Ari looked very much as if he wanted to say, "I know that; he made an appointment." Instead he inclined his head gracefully and answered, "Then let the High Priest Baket-ke-aput approach."

The man who entered the room was tall and vigorous—certainly well past middle-age, but vigorous and strong for all of that. He did not abase himself—and why should he; the High Priest of any god was the equal of the Great King, and in fact, the Great King was also a High Priest as his wife would be a High Priestess. But the two greeted each other as friends, and Ari immediately ordered a stool for him.

Baket-ke-aput glanced at her curiously a time or two, but the matters of which they spoke were hardly secret. It seemed that Ari had a plan—

"—build or rebuild temples, with places for the gods of both Tia *and* Alta, was what I thought," he was saying. "Two moons of every year for six years, or one year in full to belong to the King to work on these temples. Men from both Tia and Alta would be working side-by-side, sharing the same rations, living in the same barracks, putting up with the same overseers. By the end of two months . . . well, they would go home knowing that the man from the other land is no monster. You cannot share bread and beer with someone for two months and still think of him as unholy."

Baket-ke-aput pursed his lips. "That fits in neatly with what I had come to ask you for," the old man replied with a nod. "Some way to enlarge our temples so that the corresponding god of Alta can be set side-by-side with his Tian counterpart. But enlarging the temples would take costly labor, and costlier stone. By your scheme, however . . ."

"You like it, then?" Ari asked eagerly, leaning forward on his throne.

"I think it is a stroke of genius. Let the Great King supply the labor, the temples themselves will supply the raw materials. And now—" the High Priest nodded his head at Aket-ten. "Perhaps you can tell me why this charming young person has been standing here all this time. It is surely not because she is merely a restful place to gaze upon."

Aket-ten blushed, as Ari gestured her forward. "Jouster Aket-ten, this is the High Priest of Haras whom you asked to see, Lord Baket-keaput. Let me make you known to each other."

"Jouster Aket-ten?" Baket-ke-aput's brows rose. "Interesting. And what can the Great Queen's courier wish of me?"

Hurriedly, Aket-ten explained her difficulty in finding young women to join what she, in imitation of Ari, called the "Queen's Wing." Baket-keaput listened to her with interest until she ran out of things to say.

"And how do you suppose that I may help you in this endeavor?" he said, with a half smile. "I know nothing about dragons, and not a great deal about young women. That is the sign of my wisdom, by the way, Aket-ten. In my age, I have come to understand how little I know of women."

She flushed. "Well," she said hesitantly. "I thought . . . I thought maybe . . ." she fumbled, "If there were other girls with my . . . ah . . . the Gift of understanding the minds of animals is not a very useful one . . . and even if they didn't have that, I thought maybe . . . priestesses would . . ."

Baket-ke-aput laughed gently. "Yes, it is true, the young women who become priestess are very often much more strong-minded and -willed than their sisters. So yes, Aket-ten, I will have the word spread, not only among the young Priestesses of Haras, but of other gods as well. This is serving the gods no less than offering incense and sacrifice and—" He smiled. "The kind of young lady who finds the notion of flinging herself into the sky on the back of a fearsome dragon to be fun is probably *not* suited to a life of prayer and contemplation!"

 SIX

WITHIN two days, there was a rider from the merchant caravan that Kiron had saved, arriving in Aerie with a request for another overflight, and with him, two more traders who had come there themselves. Success in that first trial had caught the attention of King and Queen and merchants alike, more than he had guessed, as it turned out.

Success piled onto success, with every patrol that the wings made that ended in saving a merchant caravan or a traveler. Sometimes the successes were small ones, setting right a traveler who had lost the road, or dropping a waterskin to someone who had run out. Sometimes they were large, like that first rescue.

The Jousters responded to it as well, with growing cheer and a sense that they were, once again, worth something. Perhaps more so now than when they had been fighters. Then they had been taking lives. Now they were saving them.

And as the Tian and Altan Jousters worked more and more closely together, a grudging respect, and then in some cases, real friendship began to grow.

And so it went, with more and more traders arriving all the time, asking for the same. *Send out more dragons, more riders. We need them. We need the help.* The merchants and traders were making sure that people knew what the Jousters were doing. It was hard to tell what those who had been complaining about how costly it was to keep dragons were saying now, without being in Mefis or one of the other cities where the complaints had been the loudest—but the merchants who came to ask for escort for their caravans specifically did not turn up empty-handed. Some brought small flocks with them. Some brought more of the goods that were so difficult to bring across the desert, most notably camels laden down with disassembled furniture. Over the next moon or so, Aerie rapidly became a much more livable place.

Then the craftspeople started arriving.

Considering how difficult it had been to get

them there initially, Kiron was shocked when the first stonecutters arrived. What was happening all became clear very quickly, though, when a single spice grower turned up with a caravan of carefully nurtured young trees and bags of seed. Aerie was that rare place in the desert, a spot where delicate plants could be protected from *kamiseen*, where there were no floods and storms, and yet where there was abundant water. Aerie was positioned well to be added to several trade routes, and it had the protection of the Jousters. It could not be a better place to raise incense trees and spices.

He had met with all of them. To all of them he had given the same answer. "We will do our best with the numbers we have."

But most surprising of all had been the representative from the Bedu, also known as the Blue People, the nomads of the desert.

He was busy, but not so busy that he did not miss Aket-ten. She did not come nearly enough, and he wished he could take the time to go wherever she was but—where was she? She could be anywhere—Mefis, Sanctuary, any of the towns up and down Great Mother River. She was being used as a courier more and more often now, and while he was pleased for her, perhaps it was a good thing that he was so busy, because it was lonely without her.

The request from the Bedu, however, had

some urgency. In many, many ways he and his owed them their very lives. This was a chance to pay some of that back.

He sent out all the wings today, including all but four of the youngsters that the Great King had asked specifically to be sent for courier duty. Four young hotheads that had trouble controlling their dragons . . . making boring, routine courier flights should soon steady them down. And perhaps—perhaps this would release Aketten to come here to Aerie. Oh, she would probably have to give them some training, but when she was done—surely she would come here.

He sighed, feeling impatience as he waited to go off with his wing until those four were ready to go. He really couldn't understand why she was so stubborn about this. It wasn't as if he didn't want her here after all. . . .

"You know the way," he reminded them, getting his mind back on the task at hand. They gazed solemnly back at him, so identical they could have been brothers; their height was nearly the same, all of them were of the same stocky build. All Tians, which meant they were darker-skinned than the Altans. All four were former dragon boys. It occurred to him that they might actually like their new assignments; they were going home, after all. They would get the use of the Dragon Courts, the quarters of the former Jousters; there would be no more need to hunt. By the standards of Aerie, those quarters were very luxurious. He found himself envying them. "You four must stay together. If one of your dragons decides to hunt, you all hunt. You must arrive together; this is part of wing discipline."

He looked the dragons over as well, to make sure that all was right with them, as they lifted their heads curiously to sniff the morning wind off the desert. Oddly enough, they were all four of the same color family, variations on blue shading to green. They would look very smart with bronze trappings on their harnesses.

"Hem-serit," he said, nodding to the most responsible of the lot. "You are temporary wing-leader. Any other disposition will have to be confirmed by—" he looked at the dispatch, "—Vizier Nef-kham-het. You will be reporting to him directly when you arrive. Land at the Dragon Court, and there will be a servant waiting for you. After that, what happens and who you report to will be determined by the vizier. If he is displeased with your performance, he will send you back here."

Hem-serit gave him the fist-to-shoulder salute of the Tians; he nodded. They mounted up—not together, and their dragons seemed inclined toward mischief, since they tossed their heads and pretended not to understand the "Knee" command until *he* barked it out. Yes, they had a ways to go before they were ready for any sort of responsibility on trail guarding.

He sent them off with a wave and they took off raggedly, diving down into the canyon to pick up speed, then pulling up and out of it and pumping hard for height; for as long as he could see them, they flew in tolerable formation, though blue dragons against a blue sky were a bit difficult to track after a while.

Then, finally, he was able to signal to his wing to mount up. *They* did much better, although they did not all mount at once with military precision. All their dragons promptly gave a place to climb up on the "Knee" command, and if there was still a little awkwardness getting settled into the saddle, that would pass soon enough. This time the signal to fly was when he sent Avatre diving into the canyon himself; he never got over the thrill, the feel of falling, hurtling toward the ground, bracing himself in the saddle. Then the sudden, hard *snap* of Avatre's wings opening, the fall turning abruptly into a climb as he was pushed down into the saddle on her shoulders, the ground being replaced in front of him by sky. His skin tingled, and a laugh of delight rose in his throat.

His wing was not going to be patrolling the trade routes, however. He had another assignment for them all.

The Blue People were being raided, probably

by the same lawless deserters and former soldiers that were making up the majority of the bandits. And it was not that the Bedu could not defend themselves; they most certainly could. The problem was that the raids were taking place at night, and animals were being stolen one and two at a time. Clearly the bandits were treating the nomads' flocks as their private larder.

So Kiron and his wing were doing a different sort of hunting today. They were going to look for the bandits' camp. It had to be within distance of the latest tribe to be raided, and since the nomads always occupied an oasis, the bandits might be filling their waterskins before helping themselves to a goat or a sheep. Or perhaps not. In the part of the desert where the Bedu tended their flock, water was not as difficult to come by as one might think.

The camp was almost certainly concealed from ground level. It might not be from the air.

After the debacle just before their first successful foray into bandit hunting, all the members of the wing were determined to carry this out with no "incidents." The dragons were all fed, enough to be full, not so much as to be ready to laze about. Every inch of saddle and harness had been checked and checked again. Their weapons of choice were where they should be.

Kiron nodded with satisfaction, then gave Avatre the signal to fly off into the north.

Well, there they were, all right.

I was right. Hidden from the ground, but not from the air.

This part of the desert was not barren; the Blue People would not have been able to live there if it had been. There was some water here, enough to allow the occasional oasis to dot the landscape, and enough that there was vegetation outside an oasis to allow grazing. There were acacia trees and scrubby brush, which the nomads used thriftily, to start fires, but never for the fire itself.

In short, this made a good place for the bandits as well as the nomads.

Kiron kept Avatre circling in the air above the place, studying it, while the rest of his wing made wide circles around them. The encampment, clearly not one of the nomads' nor of honest traders, was concealed in a narrow, twisting wadi below them, hardly more than a crack in the earth, and just wide enough to pitch a tent. A dangerous place to camp, because if there was an unexpected storm anywhere "upstream," there would be a flash flood with no warning at all, one that would probably kill most of them and would certainly wash away their gear and drown their animals.

On the other hand, they could dig down below the surface and probably find water there, making a "seep well" for themselves that would ooze a cup or two of water over a reasonable period of time. Several seep wells spaced out over the wadi would produce enough water for men and mounts with patience. That would mean they wouldn't have to raid the nomads' oasis for water as well as food. It was a calculated risk, made all the more clever by the fact that no one who knew anything about the desert would expect someone to camp in a wadi.

Now, the question was, what to do about them? The walls were high, the canyon very narrow. In no way would dragons be able to get down there, and so far, all of Kiron's tactics had relied on spooking the bandits' mounts as the first attack. The bandits were entrenched there; if they had enough bows, they could do some serious harm to the dragons and the Jousters.

He waved his wing off, and pointed into the distance. They needed to get out of sight of the camp before they landed to confer. He hoped he would have some ideas by then.

He led them off to an eroded, wind-sculpted hill with a flat top. It would make taking off easier for the dragons. He didn't dismount immediately. Instead, he fixed his gaze on the horizon in the direction of the camp, frowning, trying to think of something clever to force the bandits out. Short of finding one of the Magi to brew up a storm, he couldn't think of anything.

But somewhat to his surprise it was one of the older Jousters, one of the Altans, who slid down off the back of his young dragon. "Captain," he said with a formal salute. "Do you think we actually have to attack this lot now? Could it wait until tomorrow?"

Kiron pondered that a moment. "I take it you have an idea? As long as they don't move, no, there is really no need to try and hit them when we are ill-prepared."

The grizzled fellow nodded. "Then if you'll dismiss me, Captain, I'll go to Sanctuary first and talk to that Akkadian Healer, Heklatis. You see, sir, if he knows how to make it, there's something called—"

But Kiron already knew where he was going with this. His mind leaped back to the attack he and his original wing had made on Alta, to rescue Aket-ten. "By the gods, Thesis, you're right! No need for just you, we'll *all* go by way of Sanctuary! Because, yes, Heklatis does know all about it. He's already made Akkadian Fire—and my old Wing knows how to use it!"

Two wings of Jousters headed at dawn for the bandit nest. Yesterday, Kiron had taken the precaution of leaving one Jouster—the old veteran, Thesis—behind to keep an eye on the encampment to ensure that the bandits didn't move it before sunset. They hadn't, which was probably not surprising, since they were doing their raids on the nomad herds by night. Evidently, *they* had no fears of hungry ghosts in the night. Either that, or they reckoned that hungry ghosts were not as troublesome as empty bellies.

In any case, they probably wouldn't move the camp in the morning either. A night raid meant that they would likely be sleeping long past sunrise.

Each of the Jousters carried two pots of Heklatis' nasty Akkadian Fire concoction. Nasty—well, "vicious" was more descriptive of the stuff. Not something anyone he knew liked using.

But the bandits were just as vicious in their way. The Blue People lived on the edge at all times, often no more than a few goats away from starvation. By stealing from their herds, it was possible that these raiders were condemning this tribe to a slow death. . . .

Kiron hoped not, but the possibility was there.

He led the way, the dragons laboring through the cool air of dawn. This was not a time of day he would have chosen to fly them into combat, had he intended them to attempt the sort of combat that they had been undertaking.

But if this went well, this would not be the usual sort of fight at all.

As the two wings approached the wadi, they split, one going "upstream," the other, "downstream." Although they were not flying particularly high, there was no sign that they had been spotted. And in fact, a very thin, threadlike stream of smoke arose from where Kiron reckoned the center of the camp was. The desert air held few scents of its own at this season other than dust. The scent of roast goat was faint, but clear. There was no sign of any lookout, and no indication that the dragons had been sighted. The bandits must be very confident that no one would find them here, so confident that they didn't even trouble to leave a lookout.

Kiron and Huras lined up their wings on the wadi and sent their dragons down to fly a little above the ground, above the rim. He felt Avatre's relief as he gave her the command, and she went into a long, shallow dive. Flying this close to the ground took less effort than wing flapping at height. With no thermals to climb, she was already a little tired; she was strong, yes, and powerful, but she had just flown a long way, and done it on flapping rather than soaring. He leaned down over her shoulder, and peered along her neck; the wadi stretched out before them like a crooked snake.

He looked back over his shoulder, making sure the rest of the Wing was lined up behind him. They had practiced this last night with

bags of sand, with his original Wing showing
the Jousters of his wing and Huras' how to handle the jars of Akkadian Fire, how to drop them,
and how to time the drops. The trailing dragons
looked good; they were spaced properly without too much or too little distance between
them. With the wind of their passage in his face,
and as Avatre swiftly approached the wisp of
smoke that marked the camp center, he loosened
the first pot of Akkadian Fire in its bindings.

The empty wadi ripped by beneath him,
flashes of thin green from a patch of tough grass
or the leaves of a tree. He sighted his way down
ahead of him, watching for the regular shape of
a tent, a bit of color from clothing, anything that
shouldn't belong. As narrow as this wadi was,
the camp could be strung out along it for quite
some distance. The jar was heavy in his hand,
and he held it tightly by the "handle" of tough
cord wound around its neck. Then—there it
was, the shape of a tent! As soon as he saw
that—he threw the jar as hard and straight as he
could, and signaled Avatre to climb.

He heard the crash beneath him as she banked
to avoid Huras' purple-blue Tathulan, passing
the other dragon belly-to-belly as they often did
in mock combat when ribbon chasing. He didn't
actually see the effects of his strike until he was
high above the wadi; by then four more of his
Jousters had sent their pots crashing into the

camp, as had five of Huras' wing, and the camp was ablaze.

The screaming of men and animals mingled with the black smoke, as the rest of both wings dropped their first jars. Kiron felt a jolting, and a sick feeling in his gut. This wasn't clean. Suddenly, what had seemed like a good idea wasn't so appealing now. This wasn't even remotely clean.

The smell of burning hair, burning hide, and a sickly sweet smell of burning flesh wafted toward him as Avatre banked and climbed higher. His skin began to crawl. He reminded himself that these men were preying on people who had done them no harm; preying on those who had not, in fact, done anyone any harm.

But it didn't help. Yes, he had to be rid of these men . . . but . . . by any and all means? Did they deserve this?

By then, both wingleaders were lining up for their second pass. This one was to ensure that no one escaped, at least not up or down the wadi; they all dropped their jars far earlier this time. Kiron forced himself to drop his second jar. And this time, at least, the blossoming fires were not punctuated by screams of anguish.

As Kiron sent Avatre up again, the fires seemed to be going out; the plumes of smoke were thinning, flames no longer visible above the rim of the wadi. And there was no more screaming. Maybe the men hit with the stuff had managed to smother it; water didn't extinguish it, but sand would.

There wasn't much to burn down there, perhaps a few cloth tents and shelters. It wasn't going to become the kind of raging inferno a wooden house, a village of papyrus huts, or a ship would be. But anyone that stuff splashed onto—and from the screams, it had splashed onto a great many men—was going to have terrible burns.

Without a healer, they would probably die of those burns.

The only healers nearby were the Blue People.

Kiron did not think that the bandits would find much of a welcome in the Bedu camp.

Both Wings landed at the oasis to rest their dragons until there were good thermals, and tell the Mouth of the People, the individuals who spoke for each tribe with outsiders, what they had done.

The Mouth seemed somewhat taken aback. Swathed in veils it was hard to tell what he was thinking, but he was silent for a long time.

"This Fire—" he said at last, as the rest of the encampment went on about its business, with curious glances at the dragons. "It is a cruel thing."

Kiron bit his lip. He'd had second and third

thoughts about this as he had led the Wings away from the burning wadi. "It is," he admitted. "And it was not an—honorable sort of attack."

The Mouth considered his words. "Neither was theirs," he replied finally. "They did not kill any of us directly—but there are children going short of milk, because they stole milch goats. And we will need to call upon favors from other tribes to make up for our losses. We will not starve . . . but we will not prosper either, for some time to come."

That was an extraordinary admission from a Mouth of the Bedu, who were so notoriously secretive that they generally had only one person in each tribe—the Mouth—to speak to outsiders.

"Starvation is a cruel death," the Mouth said, meditatively. "It is why we left the tents of stone."

And then he walked off, leaving Kiron puzzled at his meaning.

Kiron sent his Jousters off one at a time to hunt. He also didn't want the temptation of the nearby flocks to overcome the dragons' training. Once they were all fully fed, they lazed about in the sun while their Jousters napped. It had been an early morning for them, with their flight beginning in false dawn rather than when the sun was well up and the flying was good, and it was catching up to them. The Bedu went about their business as soon as they were certain that the dragons weren't going to do anything or anyone a mischief. Huras gazed at them with curiosity, but at Kiron's silent headshake elected not to approach any of them.

By midmorning the thermals were strong enough for the dragons to take to the air again, spiraling up them lazily, looking for all the world like bits of debris caught in a dust-demon, only moving much slower than that. On a whim, Kiron decided to lead the wings a little off the direct route back to Aerie, to cover part of the route between there and the eastern border. Not that there was an actual road; there was not enough traffic for that. There might once have been a trade route, but that had ended when Aerie had been abandoned. Now anyone who wanted to cross that expanse of wasteland did so navigating by the stars and the sun, or went farther south or north to an established route. Even the garrisons of the army there went farther south, though straight across would have been far faster.

He was glad that he had when they were roughly halfway home.

The dot of color on the bleached earth caught his eye first; curious, he veered Avatre toward it. But as soon as he was able to make out what it was, he urged her to greater speed.

Because the blot below that lay without moving was the combined bodies of a man and a camel, the man slumped over the camel's neck, the camel collapsed sideways. And as soon as Kiron landed, slid down Avatre's shoulder and ran to them, he knew that both were dead. But the most critical thing about the bodies, aside from the terrible arrow wounds, was that the man wore the simple kilt, headcloth, and armband of a Tian border guard. And the last of the trail in the sand made it clear that he had come from the eastern border.

The rest landed, and stared with him at the poor victim, most showing at least as much alarm as he felt, if not more.

"Who—who did this?" someone ventured at last.

Kiron shook his head. The bodies were hit with several arrows, wounds that the victim had tried to bind up without much success. Kiron's heart was thudding with alarm. There had been no stirrings of trouble from the eastern border in centuries. The position of border guard was, as a consequence, not sought for. The guards were far from most of the amenities of civilized life, and spent most of their time walking exceedingly boring patrols, and occasionally sorting out the altercations in tiny villages dotted along their jurisdiction.

But now—

This—this was a very bad sign. This did not look like the result of a private quarrel. If it had

been—the man would have been tended to by
his own garrison healer. If he had done murder,
he would not have been trying to get back to civ-
ilization. Could it be the work of bandits?

Well it could, but if they had gotten fierce
enough to take down the border guards . . . it
would need the army to take them.

"Whoever did it, this fellow tried to get word
back—" Huras ventured.

They all looked at Kiron.

"Huras," he said finally, "you go to Sanctuary
and get a priest to look at this body, or at least
someone to fetch it back there. The rest of you go
on back to Aerie. I'll take word to Mefis."

No one argued. Kiron remounted Avatre and
sent her up, his mouth dry, his heart pounding.

It wasn't that the man was dead. Kiron had
seen dead men in plenty, far more than he liked
to think about. He'd killed before today; not
gladly, and certainly not easily, but he had done
so. No, his fear was due to the fact that this was
a sign, a sign that something was very wrong on
the eastern border. If this man was the lone sur-
vivor of a massacre—

Well, that was high on the list of what could
have happened. He must have been the only one
left, or the only one still mobile, otherwise there
would have been someone else with him. Something had gone badly wrong out there, and it
must have come with no warning.

He stopped only long enough to claim a meal for Avatre at a temple; he was in such a hurry that he didn't even notice which god the temple enshrined. Once she had eaten, he pushed her ruthlessly into the sky. She was in good condition; though tired, she was far from winded, and she obeyed his commands without a protest. She did keep glancing over her shoulder at him as she flew, as if she was picking up some of his anxiety. His mouth felt dry, no matter how many times he pulled at his waterskin, and he tried to reckon how long it would have taken that border guard to get to where he had been found. It didn't look to Kiron as if he had been lying there for more than a day—and he would have thought, with all of the dragons in the sky, someone would have spotted him if he had been lying there for much longer.

I wish someone had spotted him before he died, Kiron thought, and then, with a flash of anger at himself, he realized that someone might have. But lone riders crossed that stretch of desert all the time, and none of his Jousters had ever been instructed to examine or even make a close pass to try to identify them. If they had . . . they would have seen the dried streaks of blood on the camel, the man . . . they would have known both were dying, and might have been able to get the man to a Healing-Priest in Sanctuary in time to save him.

Now all they had was a mystery.

Just as the sun-disk touched the horizon, the first of the buildings of Mefis came into view, and recognizing that rest and food were close in reach, Avatre found a little more energy and pushed herself to a little more speed.

He welcomed her effort and urged her on, leaning down over her shoulder to help her. She recognized her old pen and backwinged straight down into it, landing lightly.

The two pens on either side of hers showed recent occupation, and those on the right both held blue-and-green dragons, two of the four he had sent here as couriers. Their Jousters were, as he had trained them, giving their charges the final grooming of the day—more for affection and bonding than for any practical purpose. They both ran into the pen as Avatre landed, clearly recognizing him.

"Find me someone who knows who is in charge of the border guards," he said without preamble, sliding down out of the saddle.

"That would be the vizier—" said the first, Wesh-ta-he, doubtfully. "Nef-kham-het. But he is surely at his meal—"

"Kiron would not have flown here if it had not been urgent, you goose!" exclaimed Aket-ten from the doorway. "Come on, Kiron, I'll take you to him."

"Take care of Avatre!" Kiron ordered. "She has flown long since her last meal."

Aket-ten turned and trotted down the long, high-walled corridor between the mostly empty pens. Even though the complex was empty, someone had still stocked all the torch holders along the walls with torches, and as they turned a corner, they passed a servant lighting them. The passages had a haunting familiarity to them; the beautiful, larger-than-life-sized paintings of gods and goddesses and dragons, the flickering torches, the smell of hot sand . . .

He wanted to ask Aket-ten what she was doing here, but she didn't slow down long enough for him to get in a word. As soon as they left the Dragon Courts, she broke into a run, pelting down the broad avenue leading to the Palace as if she were a runner-courier herself.

She headed not for the Palace itself but for the row of Great Houses near it, where important officials lived. Kiron almost balked at that; this might not be a matter for an overseer as important as that—

But then again, it might. And it was not his call to judge.

There were a few people out on the avenue in the dusk, one or two servants trotting along, and some of those important folks in their litters, borne aloft by slaves and lit by servants with torches. None of them even glanced at the two Jousters. Those servants had errands on their minds, and the important folk were likely thinking about what they were going to say and do at whatever banquet or meeting they were going to.

Aket-ten slowed down and stopped at the gate of one of those houses, speaking briefly to the servant on guard there. By the time Kiron arrived, the servant had stepped aside, and Aket-ten waved him on to follow her.

Another servant escorted them into the house, Kiron acutely aware of his disheveled and filthy state. He hoped that the servant was not going to take them to the dining chamber—he was in no fit condition to be seen in such a place.

But as they passed through the antechamber, lined with benches for those who would be waiting on the Vizier's attention, and painted with murals of the Vizier supervising the Queen's household, receiving the Gold of Honor, and dictating to a small army of scribes, another servant appeared at a door, followed by the Vizier himself.

He was not someone that Kiron knew, but evidently Aket-ten did, for the man greeted her warmly.

"I know you would not have summoned me from my meal if this had not been urgent," he said, with a wry smile. "You are not given to hysterics."

"Actually, my lord, I don't know what the situation is," Aket-ten admitted. "But I do know that Kiron would not have flown all the way from Aerie himself if it was not a serious problem—"

Now she glanced at him, and there was something else in that glance that made him uneasy. Something personal.

Still nothing to be done about that. He saluted the Vizier. "My lord . . . while returning from an action against bandits, my wings discovered a body."

He went on to describe everything that he could remember about the body and its disposition while the vizier listened carefully, arms folded over his chest. Torchlight flickering over the murals gave them a strange semblance of life, making it doubly odd to be talking to one Vizier while four more went about their business.

When he finished, the vizier nodded, face expressionless. Kiron's heart sank. He had disturbed a very important man for nothing—

"This could be of no consequence," the vizier said, and Kiron's heart sank further. "But—we cannot take that chance. The gods may have placed a warning in our laps, and we ignore it at our peril. You acted properly in bringing this to me."

Kiron felt a weight lifting from his shoulders.

"Then I will leave it in the wise hands of Vizier Nef-kham-het," he said. And he left it at that, bowing himself out, Aket-ten coming with him. He wanted to be sure Avatre had been properly tended, and he wanted a meal and a bath in that order.

However, he knew he wasn't going to get any of those things soon when Aket-ten turned to him just outside the vizier's gate and said somberly, "We need to talk. . . ."

 SEVEN

"**N**OW?" he asked, wishing he dared walk on, but knowing—unless he wanted a quarrel—he had better stop where he was.

Ah, but he had forgotten one thing. Aket-ten was a Jouster as well as a young woman. She pursed her lips and shook her head.

"Not this moment. Go see to Avatre." But she wasn't about to let him off that easily. "Once you're bathed, I'll have one of the servants bring food to your room in the Dragon Courts. We can talk then."

So he had a little respite anyway. He nodded, stifled a sigh, and tried to look something other than apprehensive. Then something struck him about what she had just said. And something that had been nagging him about the Dragon Courts occurred to him as well.

She had said she was going to have a servant bring food to his room. Now he usually stayed in one of the old Jousters' quarters in the Dragon Court on the rare occasions when he turned up here, but . . .

But there had never been servants here. Why should there be? There was no one here. And he didn't think that four self-sufficient young men here could justify installing servants again.

Could it?

Or was there something more going on?

Or was he just tired and overreacting to something that had no meaning?

He talked to her about little nothings as they walked together back to the dragon pens. How progress had just speeded up apace since the merchants had taken to being grateful . . . how he was even going to have a kitchen in his own dwelling before long . . . how some enterprising soul was planning to create some bathing and swimming pools . . . all of this to try and make her see just how much more livable Aerie was becoming, to tempt her back.

For her part, she responded with a neutral interest that would have been frustrating if he hadn't been too tired to be frustrated by anything. Flying was hard work; not as hard as it was for the dragon, of course, but there were constant adjustments of weight, shifting balance, and accounting for wind resistance going on to make things easier for the dragon. A Jouster didn't just sit there like a sack of sand. At least, a good Jouster didn't just sit there like a sack of sand.

It was dark in the pens, but Hem-serit was waiting for him. "We gave her a quick sand scrub, fed her as much as she would eat, and she flopped down and went straight to sleep," the courier said, anxious to assure Kiron that everything possible had been done to make Avatre happy.

"I'll just check on her," he replied, easing into the pen.

Had Avatre been hungry, anxious, or even just a little restless, her head would have been up the moment she heard his voice and footstep. Instead, all he heard was her steady, deep breathing. She was sleeping like a stone.

He dropped down into the hot sand and stroked her head anyway. She didn't awaken. She had been well-tended and now she slept the sleep of the exhausted.

But then he raised his head, because he distinctly heard the mutterings and meepings of— baby dragons?

Aket-ten heard them, too, and suddenly her demeanor changed—he sensed it in the shift of her posture. Guilt?

Was this what her odd behavior had been all about?

"Why are there baby dragons here?" he asked, treading carefully. If she felt guilty about something, she would be angry, too. Whatever she was up to—

Then it struck him, what she must have done. It was the only reason he could think of that she might be feeling guilty. And why she had not so much as brought a single couriered message in too long. And why Ari would have asked for four Jousters to serve as couriers. *Oh, blessed gods. She's started her own—*

"I have permission and the patronage of Great Queen Nofret," Aket-ten said, head raised, her voice taking on an edge. She was already starting an argument that he had no intention of getting involved in; whatever was done was done, and there was no point in fighting over it.

"I never said—"

Well, he might not want an argument, but she clearly was determined to have one with or without his participation. "I got my own babies." Now there was defiance in her voice, and challenge.

"I never said—"

Apparently, it did not matter what he did or did not say. She had the argument in her mouth, and she was going to get it all out. All that was required was his mere presence, it seemed. "And all but one of the new lady Jousters are priest-esses with the gift of communing with animals!"

He gave up. She had marshaled her forces and was going to charge the battlefield. If there was no opposing force there, her chariots were going to run down warriors of air.

She went on at great length about how she was not depriving anyone of anything, not even a scrap of meat. How her little priestess-riders were so completely in communion with their charges and devoted to them that it made *his* young Jousters look as if they were neglecting their dragons. How Queen Nofret thought this was an *excellent* idea and that eventually all the Jousters flying courier duty could be replaced with the "Queen's Wing." These were, of course, all good points. They would do nothing to silence the mouths of those who would not approve of female Jousters; they would do nothing to still the anger of those who had been waiting to become Jousters and would see any dragon gotten by the women as one that "should" have gone to them. There might be some who would be quieted when the women began flying courier duty, but there would still be plenty who would say that the dragons were a costlier alternative to runners and chariot drivers doing the same duty. And there were probably other things she had not even considered and he had not thought of.

And none of them mattered. She had wanted this badly enough that she had found a way to make it happen and arguments for and against it were useless. The thing had happened; there were lady Jousters. Now they must deal with the complications and consequences.

But she was still staring fixedly in her mind at her arguments.

The more she talked, the quieter he became; the quieter he became, the more she talked, until finally she had repeated every one of her arguments at least three times. It almost seemed as if she needed to fill the silence, as if the very silence was an argument against her.

It made no sense, of course. No sense at all. He found himself getting angry with her for being angry that he had not argued against her. It was stupid.

But so was his anger, and anyway he was too tired to sustain it.

At last she seemed to realize that the complaint had gone on more than long enough. She finally stopped, hands on hips. He couldn't see her face in the darkness, but he could see her silhouette. She was still angry, angry over nothing, essentially.

"Well?" she said belligerently, daring him to raise one of his counterarguments.

Not a chance he would do that.

Oh, no.

It might be time to try to placate her. Strange, that all the practice he'd been getting in handling his Jousters seemed to be giving him some ability to deal with her. . . .

At least, he hoped it was.

The soft breeze that always soughed through the Dragon Courts brushed against his skin, and he took advantage of the darkness and clamped and unclamped his jaw to ease some of the tension.

"You seem to have everything well in hand," he said, in as neutral a tone as possible. He really could not agree with her wholeheartedly. Not even halfheartedly. He saw far too many ways in which her brilliant plan was going to make everything worse, not better. She didn't want to hear anything of that nature; she would see his counters, not as things to be taken into account and to find answers for, but as reasons why she had been wrong. And if he agreed falsely with her, he had the feeling she would know he was being false. So the best he could manage was neutrality.

Evidently that wasn't good enough.

"*Fine*," she said waspishly, then turned on her heel and left, stalking off into the lit walkway between the pens, anger evident in every movement.

He sighed. Well, there it was. She'd had her argument. She had, in a sense, won it. But she hadn't won it in the way she had wanted to, and now she was angrier still. He had the sinking feeling that no matter what he said or did now, unless he came to her on his knees, saying that she had been absolutely right, that he had been absolutely wrong, and that he begged her forgiveness, *nothing* he said or did was going to ease her anger.

And he didn't even know why she was so angry with him, not really.

All he could think of was, *I am glad I am not depending on her for a dinner, or I would be eating Avatre's scraps.*

Which was about the most sensible thing that could be said at this point.

He petted Avatre a little while longer to calm his nerves. The cooling breeze off the desert was very soothing, and the sounds of the baby dragons somewhere nearby made him smile. However she had gotten these little ones, it was a fair bet that they would have died had she not fetched them out of the desert, so that was good. In fact, he found himself curious about that, then curious about these new lady Jousters. No matter what, Aket-ten would not have taken featherheaded lack-wits for her Jousters, nor would she have risked precious babies with girls who would not care for them as deeply as she did. He waited while the night sounds of a Dragon Court soothed him, let the breeze cool his own frustration, let the smooth feel of Avatre's slick-scaled head under his hands bring him back to an even temper, then took himself to the old Jousters' quarters, curious to see what the changes were.

Strange to be back here, where the place was so familiar and yet so unfamiliar. The pens, the passageways between them, were all roofless, but the walls were tall and thick enough that no dragon could reach over them to savage another. It gave the same impression, actually, as the city of tombs. The pens all had canvas covers that could be pulled over them to protect the hot sands of the dragon wallows from becoming hot sand soup during the season of rains. And each section, where the corridors intersected, was denoted by enormous paintings of gods and sacred animals that seemed to stir a little with life in the flickering light from the torches that had been placed in sconces at intervals along the walls.

The silence was what struck him. Except for the section where his Avatre, Aket-ten's Re-eth-ke, Ari's Kashet, Nofret's The-on, the four courier dragons and the babies were, the place was echoingly empty. As he moved toward the Jousters' Courts, the rooms arranged around simple but attractive courtyards that had once held all the Jousters of Tia, he wondered what it would be like to hear the Dragon Courts full again.

It was somewhat unnerving to hear the chatter and giggle of feminine voices coming from the Jousters' Courts. The first court, lit only by one torch, and by the dim light of a lamp shining in five of the eight sets of rooms was the one where his usual quarters were. By the presence of the lamps, that was where the four couriers from Aerie had been housed. He had intended to ask his fellows where he might get some food, but instead, he followed his ears to the spill of light marking the door to the second court when he realized that there were a few male voices among the females.

He smiled as he did so. He should have known, of course. These were young men for whom there were, as yet, very few young women in Aerie. The closest place to find female companions was Sanctuary, which was a good half-day's flight away. They would have gravitated to Aket-ten's girls like bees to flowers.

He stepped into the doorway and paused, letting his eyes adjust to the light. He found his four couriers and eight young ladies, all of them in the standard linen tunics his own Jousters wore at this time of year. They were sitting to one side of the ornamental *latas* pool, with dishes and cups and beer jars scattered among them. Their chatter fell silent as they saw him in the doorway, and his four couriers jumped to their feet and saluted him.

As the young women looked uncertain, as if they were not sure if they should do the same, he waved at his couriers to sit back down. "Jousters, be easy," he said. "I am not here to inspect you. There was some important news that I needed to deliver in person, and now I am merely a weary and hungry fellow like yourselves."

The young ladies relaxed as his Jousters sat down. He walked over to them and took a place on the pavement of the court among them.

"I trust you left something for me?" he said, with a smile. The young ladies giggled or tossed their heads, and began to pass plates and an unopened jar of beer to him. It looked exactly like the meals he used to get when he was a dragon boy here, tending to Kashet and Ari. Strips of cooked meat, flatbreads, onions, greens, thick, soured milk to use as a sauce, beer and honey cakes. It smelled wonderful, and his mouth watered as they passed the plates to him.

He made a tolerable meal, although the meat was cold. Still, it wasn't dried, which was a distinct improvement over what he got at Aerie. Fresh bread was always very welcome, and as for the honey cakes . . . he quite forgot Aket-ten's tantrum in his enjoyment of them.

When his hunger was finally sated, he looked around at the company. The torches around the courtyard itself and the little lamps placed on the rim of the *latas* pool cast a pleasing, warm light. He found himself approving of the girls as he examined them. Despite the giggles, none of them acted silly or too girlishly. All had done something equally sensible; they had cut their hair very short, right at chin level. All appeared to be Tian, with the darker skin tone than Altans had. That was a curious choice—but then again, there were not many Altans here in Mefis, so perhaps Aketten had no choice. . . .

None were wearing any jewelry fancier than a faience amulet on a leather thong or a string of faience beads. A glance at their hands told him they were no strangers to hard work. This was all very encouraging.

Finally, one of them got up, waved cheerfully to all of them, and left. At his curious glance, one of the other young women offered, "We have all the babies together in one pen, and we take it in turns to sleep with them through the night. That way everyone gets to sleep in a bed seven out of eight nights."

He blinked. Why hadn't *he* thought of that? It was the one complaint his young Jousters had about baby tending. Not everyone was as slavishly devoted to the welfare of a sleeping infant dragon that would not wake and would scarcely even stir all night long as he had been. . . .

Then again, they were with their babies all day long. He'd not had that luxury. He'd only had stolen moments with Avatre among all his other chores, and every moment he had been able to spend with her had been precious to him. So it rightly wouldn't seem as urgent to any of them to be with their babies at night as long as *someone* was with the babies.

"It's a good idea," one of the boys said defensively. They all looked at him as if they expected him to object.

He sighed. When did everyone get the idea that he was a crocodile? "I never said it wasn't," he replied wearily. "In fact, I think it is a very good idea. Just because *I* spent my sleeping hours with Avatre when she was a baby, it doesn't follow that it's a sensible idea. Well, it was sensible for me, but only because I was afraid she might be discovered if I left her alone. That's hardly anything any of you will ever need to worry about."

Several of the girls exchanged speaking glances, and one of them said, with a lopsided grin, "I told you he couldn't be the soul devourer that Aket-ten said he'd be."

Oh. So this reputation was Aket-ten's doing. . . .

"I devour neither souls nor babies," he said firmly. "A good honey cake, though, stands no chance with me." And to prove it, he boldly reached for the last and ate it in three bites.

Whatever motive Aket-ten had in darkening

his reputation, now he was feeling rather annoyed with her. He then set about firmly countering the image by simply being pleasant. He supposed she must have warned them all that he was going to object to their presence, their mere existence, and probably be aggressive about it.

On the surface, there was very little to object to. The Queen's Wing had the blessing and patronage of Nofret, and if the Great Queen preferred to have a wing of dragon couriers rather than a temple in her name, no one was going to dare say her nay. Aket-ten had found a way on her own to get baby dragons without depriving any of the men waiting for one—

Come to think of it, he was very curious about that, though, wondering just where and how she had gotten them.

—and the Great Queen's patronage ensured that the wing got support without taking anything from the existing Jousters. Aket-ten had found sensible young women who were not only capable of taking care of their dragons, but were actually better suited to the task than the young men, by virtue of their ability to understand animals and make themselves understood by them.

I must find young men who can do that. . . . Surely that particular ability was not confined to females.

As to whether or not they would actually

work out as couriers, there was no saying. They probably wouldn't have difficulty with the hard work, but the flying itself—not everyone took to it.

It looked as if she was finding them something they could do, that would actually free the male Jousters to counter the bandit threat. That could only be good for Aerie and the Jouster Wings there.

So really, there was overtly nothing to object to, and he wasn't about to bring up.

Other than that . . . he was not stupid. It was fairly clear that the duties of training both dragons and girls were going to keep Aket-ten here. Which meant that the chances of his getting her to move back to Aerie were nonexistent. Maybe part of the reason she was angry was because she knew that.

Curses.

"Where and how did Aket-ten get nine dragons?" he asked into a lull in the conversation, going to great pains to sound interested and approving rather than accusatory.

"She scouted the nests," said one, who had been very quiet until now, and had sat a little apart from the others. "When eggs were abandoned, she had them brought back here to hatch. That was where my dragon came from. And as for the rest, she continued to watch the nests, and had some of the old dragon-hunters come and take babies that had been abandoned, or the weakest of the nestlings when it was clear that one or more was not getting enough food to thrive."

Clever, and he hadn't thought of *that*. He had just taken it for granted that out of a hatch it was likely that there would be failures and let it go at that. This made sense. Especially if he could find young men among his Jouster candidates who shared Aket-ten's power . . . he could do the same.

He continued to ask the girls questions, not just about their dragons and how they were taking to life as young Jousters, but about their former lives as priestesses. He didn't have to feign interest; he *was* interested, and he got the impression that his four young couriers were no little annoyed with him for taking all of the girls' attention.

Well, let them be annoyed. He would be gone tomorrow, and they would have the young women all to themselves again. In fact, it was rather amusing to see which one of them got annoyed over which young lady. And which young lady cast a glance at which young man when he spoke to her. It wasn't long before he had who was interested in whom fairly well sorted out.

This was going to make for some complicated times, especially as rivalries were definitely a potential. He was just as glad that *he* wasn't going to be the one to have to deal with them.

Oh, yes. Hurt feelings, jealousy, broken hearts . . . let Aket-ten deal with that particular aspect of having female Jousters. True, he had not anticipated those problems either, but she was the one that had wanted females in the first place. He made a mental note that if Ari asked for any more couriers, to find a reason why he should not send them.

Not that he wanted his Jousters to do without female company! By no means!

But life was complicated enough with the possibility of quarrels over young women when those young women were not Jousters. The dreadful ramifications of having to sort out female Jousters fighting over males, and vice versa—add to that the sensitivity of the dragons themselves to the emotions of their riders—it made his head spin. He was beginning to understand why the old-style Jousters had been discouraged from anything but the most trivial of affairs and trysts with "flute girls."

Let it all be on Aket-ten's head.

Petty revenge, maybe, but she had made him out to be a monster of sorts, and then she had gone tearing off in a temper when he hadn't said a word against her new Jousters.

But . . . he should have a word with his fellows, before he left. Something. Warn them about letting women get in the way of their duty or—

He'd think of something.

Actually, after a moment of listening and staring at the little flame of a lamp, he realized that he wasn't thinking of anything. Well, a bath perhaps.

Should he tell them about the dead border guard?

Perhaps—no, not yet. It might be nothing. It still could turn out to be nothing. It might have been the tragic result of a private quarrel. There was simply no way to tell.

He realized after a moment that he had fallen silent while the others kept chattering on. All but one, that one girl that sat apart from the others.

Now that he had food in him, he wasn't as tired as he had thought. And a bath was beginning to feel like a good idea. He excused himself and walked into the shadows, into the next courtyard, aiming for the rooms he generally used as his own when he overnighted here. There were no torches burning in this court, and only a single lamp in each of the rooms assigned to him, but he really didn't need much light. As he had hoped, the bath jars were all full, everything he needed in readiness, a clean kilt and loinwrap laid out on the bed. Whatever Aket-ten thought of him, the servants knew their jobs, and were not letting him go unattended.

He felt much more human after a good bath, and not quite ready to go to sleep. But he also didn't feel much like going back to the group he had just left. He stood in his own doorway for a moment, looking in the direction of the pens, wondering if he ought to go look in on Avatre, when a movement in the deep shadows beside the pool in this court made him start and bite back an exclamation.

And that in turn startled the person in the shadows who jumped and squeaked.

"It's all right!" he said hastily. "Don't be alarmed—"

As he said that, it occurred to him how much things had changed since the Magi were gone. A few moons ago, he would have gone into a defensive crouch, perhaps even called for help, certain that whoever was there was a spy set by the Magi, or one of the Magi themselves.

A breathless laugh answered him. "It is I who should be begging your pardon, Lord of the Jousters," said the quiet young woman who had sat a little apart from the rest, apologetically. She got up and walked toward him, into the faint, warm glow of the lamp behind him. "I often come here when the chatter of the others goes on a little too long," she added. "They are kind, and quite friendly, but they all come from the same circle, and they—" Now she hesitated. "I know that we are to think of ourselves as one Kingdom now, but I cannot help saying—they are Tian."

Now that she had said more than a few words, he knew her accent. "And we are Altan," he agreed. Even after all these many moons of working with the Tian Jousters . . . there was still that sense of "us" and "them." He suspected it would take years, perhaps even tens of years, for that to leave them.

It was a very good thing that Ari was a patient man.

"And I am the daughter of a farmer, and they were priestesses," she sighed. "I know that rank does not matter among Jousters, but . . . they speak of things of which I have no knowledge, of rituals and ceremonial things, of powers, and the people who have them. I only know how to bake bread and make beer."

"And without someone to bake bread and make beer, those who serve the gods would quickly starve," he pointed out, sitting down on the rim of the pool. "Besides, as you say, rank and origin have no meaning among Jousters. I am a farmer's son myself. To tend the earth is an honorable profession. Please, sit and talk to me. I had as soon hear someone do other than flirt."

"It is good to hear the accent of my home, even if I have no home to go to," she said, then took a seat of her own. "It wasn't the war, it was a flood. I think I may have been the only one left alive out of my village."

He sighed. "If it was a flood, it was the war," he said sadly. "The Magi of our own homeland caused those, sending terrible storms against the Tians to destroy their crops, to terrify the people, to keep the dragons grounded. The only problem was that the water all had to go somewhere, and it flooded Altan lands once it had done with the Tians.

"But—" she protested. "Did the Magi not realize this would happen?"

"The Magi did not care, so long as it served their purposes," Kiron said wearily. "They aimed to rule both Alta and Tia, even if to do so meant leaving no more than half the people in either land alive. And I beg of you, ask someone else of this. Ask the other ladies; they are priestesses and no doubt know a great deal more than I. I only know that this was a war that could have ended long ago, which the Magi of Alta fostered, and they battened on it as a hyena feeds on corpses. Let us speak of other things. Let us speak of—your dragon."

Kiron learned quite a bit about this new female Jouster as both spoke until they were tired enough to go to bed. He learned that her name was Peri-en-westet, that her young female dragon was the only one hatched here and that Peri had helped the egg to hatch just as he had helped Avatre. Peri described her gold-and-green beauty to him in such loving detail that he had to smile, hearing in her voice the same adoration he heard in every Jouster that ever raised an infant. She told him that she had named her dragon Sutema, which meant "reed," because she was so slender and graceful. He very much doubted that any baby dragon could be described as graceful, but he was not going to tell her that,

He also learned something of her history, which proved to him that at least not all Tians were as vile to their serfs as his masters had been. In fact, they seemed to have been even moderately kind. Certainly Peri had not been made to starve as Kiron had, had had decent housing, and had even made some friends.

He also learned something she had probably never told any of the priestesses; that her friends had no idea what she was doing nor that she was going to become a Jouster. They all thought that she had some position at the Dragon Courts—cook or cook's helper. A servant such as she was would be required to live where she worked. And as the lowly ex-serf, she would seldom be allowed time of her own.

"But why?" he finally asked. "Wouldn't your friends be proud of you?"

She shook her head. "My friend is always talking about how important it is to know your place and keep to it. She is scornful even of those who send sons to the temples to learn to be scribes or priests. She would think I was being presumptuous."

He shook his head in disbelief at how anyone could be so rigid in their thinking. "Well, she'll have to learn someday," he pointed out. "Once the Queen's Wing starts flying, there will be no way of hiding who the riders are."

"I'll find a way," she replied; he heard the stubbornness in her voice and had to smile.

"I expect you will," he said then. "I expect you will always find a way to do something you truly want, Peri." He stood up and stretched. "And with that, it is time for me to sleep. Avatre and I have a long flight ahead of us tomorrow. I hope that the wind will be at our backs for it."

"I hope so, too," she replied softly as he returned to his rooms.

 EIGHT

THE *body told us nothing, and the ghost had fled. We will have words with you soon.*

That was the ominous message from the priests at Sanctuary, a cryptic statement that was waiting for Kiron when he and Avatre landed at Aerie.

Avatre landed in the golden light of early sunset, with the wind at her back, a fortuitous bit of weather that meant she was a great deal less tired than she had been after the flight to Mefis. Haraket was waiting there for them and handed him the note as soon as he slid down from Avatre's saddle. It took less than a glance to know that all it meant was that the priests did not like the look of this either.

He looked to Haraket who had delivered the information, unspoken questions in his eyes as they both unsaddled Avatre, then fed her with the meat Haraket had brought. The older man rubbed his shaved head, and shrugged. "Do not ask me what it means," he said. "Other than the obvious. They can't tell what happened, they don't like it either, and I think you can expect a summons to Sanctuary within the next few days."

Well, that drove all thoughts of Aket-ten and his irritation with her out of his mind entirely. The flight had been long, and he'd had plenty of time to brood over her unreasonable behavior during the course of it. What had happened to the good-tempered, sensible girl he'd known in Alta and Sanctuary? Had she become jealous that he was the leader of the Jousters now? If that was her problem, he would have been happy to let her have this so-called "honor." It was one he could well do without.

Well, that was what he told himself in frustration, but there were layers and layers of truth there. Part of the truth was that none of the Jousters, not even his original wing, would have accepted her as Lord of the Jousters, when they only grudgingly accepted him. Part of it was that he thought he just might be doing a reasonable job with this—although he dreaded to think what it could be like when and if there were more Jousters than just the few they had. And part of it was that he did like it that people were no longer treating him as a nonentity, nor as a boy who couldn't possibly cope with the responsibility.

The idea that she begrudged him this made him angry.

He'd managed to stew himself up into such a state of irritation that when he'd found a kill for Avatre on the way back, she attacked it with the savagery of a dragon that was starving. In helping her make the kill, he'd managed to work off most of his anger, and got rid of the rest in butchering the remains for Avatre to eat at her second pause on the way back.

Now, though, it was clear he was going to have other concerns.

"I wish they would be less cryptic," he groaned.

"They're priests. I think it is an unwritten law that they must be cryptic at all times," Haraket replied with a half grin. "Let me help you get your girl fed and bedded down," he added, with a glance at the setting sun. "Then we'll get you fed. I envy you those meals in Mefis—"

And that reminded him of Aket-ten and her half-thought-out scheme, and he groaned again. "Oh," he said bitterly. "You would not envy me if you knew what I found when I got there."

He unburdened himself freely to Haraket

who, he reckoned, would be the best person to advise him on whatever troubles love affairs might bring his Jousters.

"In the name of Re-Haket!" Haraket swore, when he heard what Aket-ten had been up to. "Now I know why I never took a wife. Women! If it is not one thing, it is another with them. They are more trouble than a cage full of apes, and not nearly as entertaining."

He looked so disgusted that Kiron smothered an involuntary laugh, and he glared at Kiron

"It is not amusing," he growled. "*You* have not yet needed to separate two men gone so wool-headed over a stupid wench that they went at each other with knives. And that was a mere flute girl, some doe-eyed bit that would have found herself a richer patron within the moon. These—this *Queen's Wing*—" he made of the name a curse, "—will be full of creatures that cannot be turned out when the sun disk rises. Bah!"

"The Queen's Wing is in the old Jousters' Courts in Mefis," he pointed out mildly. "And we are here."

"And we will stay here," Haraket snorted. "I will not complain again about the lack of bathing rooms, or the food, or the heat, if these things all keep those confounded women out of Aerie!"

He found himself wishing that Aket-ten could

be here to hear all this herself. It would do her a world of good. He had no doubt that Haraket had a hundred tales of the horror that conflict over a woman could bring into the lives of the Jousters, and he found himself nursing a feeling of grim satisfaction that Aket-ten had failed to investigate this side of her plan.

The cat woke him before dawn. It had been sleeping on his stomach when he went to sleep himself, but it must have left for a while because suddenly he woke all at once as his shoulder was hit from behind. He snapped out of dreams, flailing for a moment, before the sound of clawed feet scampering off made him curse and sit up.

And just as well, too. Mere moments after the cat had made him a landing platform, some youngster he didn't recognize came stumbling up the stairs, oil lamp in hand, to wake him. Warm light splashed across the stone wall before him, while behind him, his shadow danced, elongated and distorted. "Jouster Kiron!" the boy called, peering into the darkness toward Kiron's sleeping place. "Jouster Kiron! There is a Priest of Haras here to see you! The Blue People brought him!"

That was more than enough to bring him fully awake. "I am coming!" he called, fumbling for his clothing. "Go back and tell him I will be with him in a moment."

"He is at the Temple of Haras," the boy said, and now Kiron thought he recognized the youngster as one of the acolytes of that god. "I will tell him you are on the way." He turned and fumbled his way down the stairs, taking the light with him and leaving Kiron kneeling on his bed, putting on his loinwrap by touch.

It was by no means the first time that Kiron had dressed or left his home in the dark, and for once the cat did not try to trip him on his way out. Feeling his way to the stairs and down them, he kept one hand on the wall as a guide as he passed through Avatre's pen. Avatre hadn't even been disturbed by the intruder; she was still soundly asleep in her warm sands and did not stir as he passed by.

As he stepped out into the canyon that was the "street" here in Aerie, he glanced about at the other dwellings carved into the cliff faces. None showed any light, and a cold wind off the desert made him shiver. Hard to believe in just half a day it would be so hot that anyone sensible would be inside, where the rock walls kept the heat at bay. Evidently what the priest had to say was for his ears alone, at least for now.

Overhead, there was not yet a hint of dawn light, the stars all burned down, brilliant beads of electrum, from where they ornamented the Robe of the goddess Nofet, for whom Great Queen Nofret-te-en had been named. The moon was down already, leaving only Nofet's Robe to give light.

But farther down the avenue, where the several "buildings" stood that had been taken as temples by those priests who had elected to leave the comforts of Mefis and what was left of Alta to establish a home for the gods, there was the warmth of lamp and torchlight reflecting off the carved rock. The temples tended to be illuminated all night long anyway. The work of the temples began early and ended late. For all that Kiron sometimes lamented the hard work of being a Jouster, the work of a priest was harder still.

He trod softly down the sand of the canyon floor, wondering yet again who it could have been that had carved this city out of living stone. The place was still something of a mystery, though they all knew now why it had been abandoned. In digging it out, they had decided that the wreckage had been wrought, not by the hand of time, but by one or several earthshakes very close together. They had found the places where several springs had been buried.

The water sources had been closed up so thoroughly that they must have been completely inaccessible right after the shakes. Although water was now available, it looked as if it had only lately been working its way to the surface.

Those, they had cleared enough that the water seeped up again, into holding pools created from cementing stones together and lining the inside with ceramic tiles, not as the old pools had been, carved out of the rock. In a place like Aerie or Sanctuary, in the heart of the desert, every drop of water was precious. One of the very first things anyone had done here, in fact, was to start securing all the possible sources of water. All the cisterns and cache basins at the tops of the cliffs had been repaired and made ready for any rain. Provisions had been made to keep and use every drop of water; if it was not suitable for drinking, it was saved and went for irrigation.

And, last of all, they had found something they had not yet cleared: what they thought was an entrance to a great underground cavern, like that in Sanctuary, a place where one of the daughters of Great Mother River snaked her way through the cool shadows beneath the rock and sand. That was a discovery without price. If it did prove to be a water cavern, it would mean a very great difference in people's lives.

The springs they had found were sufficient for the population they had now—but not for one with the herds and flocks and carefully irrigated plots of garden that a city like this *must* have to sustain all the people that had once lived here. Only access to a water source like that in Sanctuary could have permitted that many people to live and thrive.

When that source had been cut off, in less than a moon the city must have begun to die. Certainly in less than a year it had been abandoned by all but the most stubborn. And, probably within ten years, even they had given up. Certainly not much had been left behind, not even things that would survive such as stone tools or metal objects.

The discoveries had been a stark warning to all of them, he thought as he passed one of the dwellings that had still not been cleaned out, restored, and taken over. They had the example before them; this could happen again. What they would do if it happened, he did not know. So far, all anyone had done was to make sure that no place that people had claimed to live in had any fractures running through the rock. Perhaps that was all anyone could do. Or perhaps someone might have ideas of how things could be reinforced, how they could find ways to make sure the water sources were never cut off again.

A torch burned on either side of the door of the structure that had been claimed by the priests of Haras, and there was light shining through the doorway, though there was no one outside. The two enigmatic carvings on either side of the door stared out and up at the stars. Kiron mounted the three steps between them and entered.

He paused a moment for his eyes to adjust to the light, but was almost immediately approached by the boy who had come to wake him. There was a lot of light in here; torches and lamps burned everywhere, with the scent of incense and perfumed lamp oil that would have told a blind man he was in a temple of some god.

"Priest Them-noh-thet is waiting for you, Jouster Kiron," the boy said, bobbing his head diffidently. "Please—" he gestured toward an inner room.

The places that had been chosen as temples were not much like the ones that Kiron and the others had taken as their own. Here, the ceiling was higher, to accommodate the enormous, stylized statue in the first of the rooms, identical to the ones on either side of the door, a statue that looked enough like a hawk-headed man to satisfy the Priests of Haras. As Kiron knew, the structure was carved three to four times farther back into the rock than the ordinary dwellings, and dividing walls had been built inside to separate the sanctuary from the rest of the temple.

The boy took him to one of those rooms, hardly more than a cubicle, that contained a single lamp, two stools, and a table. One of the stools was already occupied.

Kiron did not recognize the priest, but he was young and looked fit; he'd have had to be fit to

make the rigorous crossing of the ground between Aerie and Sanctuary in the short time
since the body had been discovered, reported,
and investigated at Sanctuary. Only someone on
one of the racing camels belonging to the Bedu
could have made the trip so quickly, and then
only under the careful guidance of one of the
Blue People themselves. The racing camels were
not noted for a comfortable ride.

"Jouster," said the priest, nodding at the other
chair. "I have come on behalf of Sanctuary to beg
a favor of you."

That was not what he had expected to hear.
He sat down quickly. "Just me, or the Jousters as
a whole?" he asked. "Though, of course, we are
all at the service of the temples."

"The Jousters as a whole, at least a few of
them, but you specifically," said the priest, both
hands clasped together on the table in front of
him. "You see, what we discovered when we at-
tempted to trace the path of that unfortunate
guard, was . . . nothing."

Kiron blinked; that didn't make a lot of sense.
He was vaguely aware of a chant beginning out
in the main room. The first rituals of morning
must have just begun. This must be grave indeed for the priest to be here, and not out there,
among his fellows. "Nothing? I am not sure that
I grasp what you are saying."

"We found no trace of his passage, nor of any

links to any border stations. It is as if he had never existed. When we made the assumption that he had come from the nearest border out-post and we had the Far-Sighted examine the place, we also found—nothing." The priest paused significantly. "It is empty. There are no guards, no animals, no one and nothing in the settlement that supports it. There is no trace that anyone ever lived there, not so much as a single sacred cat."

Kiron's mouth went dry. How was this possible?

"Now, we are not entirely certain that the Far-Sighted are Seeing this correctly," the Priest went on. "It could be that someone with magic is interfering with them. The Mouth of the Gods has no guidance on the subject, and is as baffled as the rest of us. We would like you to take however many Jousters you think necessary and fly there to investigate."

He nodded quickly; it seemed the only possible plan. Whatever was going on, this death could not be the result of a simple quarrel. "We can do that. We cannot get there in a single day, however—"

Them-noh-thet waved away Kiron's caution-ary words. "No one expects you to. But by dragon you can go there much faster than any-one else. And you and your senior riders have had some experience with Magi. I am to come with you if you have any dragons that can carry two. I am—" Kiron saw his jaw tense "—highly conversant with dark magics. I can protect you from them, and if there has been any such thing employed there, I may be able to detect the traces."

"We'll find a way to take you," Kiron told him immediately. There was no question in his mind about that. "It will take a little time to organize matters so that things run smoothly here in our absence. We will leave as soon as possible."

Them-noh-thet nodded. "Then I will hold myself in readiness."

This did not seem the time for an exchange of pleasantries. "I will start now," Kiron replied, standing up. "I will be seeing you very shortly, I think."

The priest gave him the little bow of equals, and Kiron took himself out.

He felt his own jaw tensing as he made his way out of the sanctuary, pausing only long enough for the deep bow of respect to the image of the god. This was not good, not good at all. What could have happened to make an entire settlement vanish?

Wait—not an entire settlement, he reminded himself. One had escaped.

Now, more than ever before, he berated himself for not having had the foresight to send out riders on a regular basis to scan the desert for lone riders. It would have been an excellent exercise for the younger Jousters. If he had—

Never mind. Now they must try and make up for that neglect. And the sooner he got his riders in the air, the better.

Breakfast was . . . very interesting that morning in the Dragon Courts of Mefis. Peri-en-westet said nothing about Lord Kiron to Wingleader Aket-ten. She didn't have to. The other young ladies were saying quite enough as it was, rather too much in fact, and Aket-ten was clearly getting very irritated about it. The more nice things they had to say about Lord Kiron, the deeper a frown line grew between Aket-ten's brows. They seemed oblivious to the effect they were having.

Or perhaps they were enjoying it. Some of them had rather mischievous natures.

For Peri's part there was something more going on, something she was afraid to tell anyone just yet.

She had spoken for quite some time to Lord Kiron last night. And until that conversation it would never have occurred to her that Lord Kiron, the leader of all of the new Jousters of the Two Lands, the friend of the Great King and Queen, could possibly be the same person as the missing son Kiron of her friend Letis-hanet.

Even now the speculation seemed unlikely.

A logical person would say that there was not the least little chance in the world that something so impossible could be.

But—

Lord Kiron was a farmer's son, from the borderlands between Tia and Alta, from lands taken by Tian troops.

The missing Kiron was from those same lands, and was about the same age as Lord Kiron.

Lord Kiron had been separated from his family as the lands were divided. Letis had lost her son almost immediately in one such division.

Lord Kiron had had at least one sister but was the only son. Letis, of course, still had one of her daughters with her, had lost others, and had had only one son.

Now, Kiron was a common Altan name. Kiron, son of Kiron, was not at all uncommon. Every village had at least one Kiron. But . . .

The more she looked at it, the more it seemed that there were too many points of similarity between the two. Kiron even looked rather like Letis; there was a great similarity in the eyes.

The complication was this: Letis had made it very, very clear that once her son was found, she was going to do everything in her power to make a match between her boy and Peri. And up until last night, Peri had always considered that idea to be the wildest of fantasies, somewhere between laughable and suitable only for the sort of thing one would amuse a child with.

Now . . .

If this was Letis' son—

She left the rest of them teasing Aket-ten and went back to her baby dragon. No reason why she couldn't continue to consider all this while she took care of the little one. Her hands could work undirected while she thought things through.

As she tended Sutema, tenderly oiling the baby's delicate wing webs, feeding the little one until her stomach was round and full, then leading her to flop down on the hot sands in the sun to doze contentedly with the rest of the wing's babies, she thought about Lord Kiron, and what it would mean, could mean, if he was her friend's lost son.

He was a Jouster. He was Lord of the Jousters. And what better mate could there be for a Jouster than another Jouster?

Letis would heap scorn on her for having airs and presuming above her station for being part of this creation of Aket-ten's under any other circumstances but this. If her own son was not only a Jouster, but Lord of all the Jousters of the Two Lands—to scorn that would be to scorn her own long-lost, longed-for son. She could say nothing to Peri, who would be the fittest bride there ever could be for such a man.

As for Kiron the man—

He was handsome, fit, young, but most of all, he was kind. If someone had come to Peri and said, "What are all of the things you could desire in a mate? Only say, and the gods will create such a man for you," then Lord Kiron would have come very close to that ideal. She'd had moments, and many of them, when she had thought it likely she would never marry. And back when she was a serf, she had wondered if a mate would be forced on her, an old man, or someone cruel. Lord Kiron . . . Lord Kiron was like something out of the sort of story that a market storyteller would recite to charm the coins from pretty unmarried girls.

Well, it was worth thinking about this as at least a decent possibility. Why not? Even if Lord Kiron was *not* Letis' son . . . now that Peri was herself a Jouster, was there any reason why she should not look on Lord Kiron as someone she might attract?

Not really. He was not of aristocratic blood. He was, in fact, as common as herself.

The only other possible rival—

Aket-ten.

As for the other young ladies—Peri thought she was on fairly safe ground there. Judging by the way that Kiron had spoken of the Tians in general last night, she thought he would never consider anything but another Altan. So her fellows of the new Queen's Wing were easily dismissed. And they were priestesses, people with whom he had very little in common. It was one thing to pursue a pretty priestess or noble for light love, but Letis was right about one thing. When a man chose a woman for something permanent, he liked to have someone about who wouldn't make him feel inferior, nor make him feel as if she was doing him a great favor by being with him.

Now, Aket-ten was, of course, the very first female Jouster. She and Kiron must have shared many adventures together, and Peri thought she might have heard some vague tale of how Kiron had rescued her from the earthshake that destroyed the capital city. Or maybe the story was that he had rescued her from the Magi. She, too, was Altan, and what with all that previous acquaintance, she was ahead of the game. But Peri had two advantages that Aket-ten did not have. *She* was of the same background, and the same rank, as Kiron. Aket-ten was nobly born, with all the unconscious arrogance of someone who never needed to think about whether or not her orders would be obeyed. This didn't matter to someone who was already an underling, but at some point, that had to grate on a man.

And there was a third advantage, if Kiron really *was* who Peri thought he was. Peri already had Letis' approval. Approval? Letis had essentially handpicked her as the mate for her son.

Aket-ten could never get that, try as she might. Letis did not at all approve of looking above one's self for a mate; she did not at all approve of what she called the "presumption" of the "jumped up." She had many things to say, none of them complimentary, about such liaisons. She would say them to her son's face if he went, as she would put it, "chasing the hem of the skirts of a noble." When Letis chose to use the weapon, she had a very, very sharp tongue. Mind, with the excitement of being reunited, it was likely that Kiron would be willing to agree to just about anything his mother asked of him, and Letis would never have to use that particular weapon.

But from the way that Aket-ten herself was acting, well . . . it did not look as if there was any interest there at all. Look at how she had portrayed Kiron to the others! And when he had been among them, she had given him very short shrift indeed. It was more as if Aket-ten considered Kiron a rival, and not a potential mate.

Perhaps that was precisely the case. She had been a priestess herself, after all. Priestesses were accustomed to power, and being merely one Jouster among an increasingly large number, with *no* chance that she would ever be given any leadership role, must have grated on her.

But now she had the chance to make, not only a single wing of lady Jousters, but perhaps a force to equal or rival the males, if enough work could be found for them. But Kiron's Jousters were essentially competition for her; at any point they could demand to be brought back here to the Dragon Courts, and there was no reason not to accede to that demand. Once they were here, what could the Queen's Wing do that the male Jousters could not do as well or better? That, at least, would be what the naysayers would claim.

Surely that was the only explanation for the way that Aket-ten had made Lord Kiron out to be the worst possible sort of authoritarian and some sort of monster to boot, why she had insisted that he would immediately disapprove of each of them individually and the Queen's Wing as a whole. Peri had expected someone large, rude, and angry, someone determined to put "the women" in their place, someone who would see nothing good and much evil in the very existence of the Queen's Wing. And possibly someone old enough to be her grandsire.

She had certainly not expected the young, polite, affable and self-effacing young man who turned up at dinner. He had been good company, he had gone out of his way to make them all comfortable in his presence, and—above all—he had not made any of them feel as if he disapproved of them or what they were doing. Possibly that was all a deception, but if it was, he was a better fraud than Peri was able to detect.

But if Aket-ten saw him as a rival, as competition, it would certainly go a very long way toward explaining her attitude.

The one possible complication was this: in Peri's admittedly limited experience, young men did not, as a rule, appreciate discovering that their mothers had picked out wives for them with no regard for what *they* wanted. Yes, in the first flush of the joy of finding each other, Kiron probably would do just about anything his mother asked. But once that wore out, he might very well decide he could pick his own wife, thank you.

If, however, Peri could manage to become friends with Lord Kiron . . . if she could even gain more interest from him than that, then when Letis discovered the identity of her lost son and presented him with a putative bride . . .

. . . a bride who was already someone he liked . . . and who was a Jouster herself . . .

Peri smiled to herself. That would be very good indeed.

So, now, all she needed to do was to find a way to get herself and Sutema moved to Aerie.

 **NINE**

FOUR Jousters—Huras, Oset-re, Pe-atep, and Kiron himself—set off from Aerie at the best possible time for flying, when the sun was at zenith and the thermals were at their strongest. Huras' big female, Tathulan, who had begun from the moment of hatching by being the largest of the lot of hand-raised Altan dragons, and had remained in that position, carried the priest Them-noh-thet as well as Huras. The priest had clearly been impressed by her when he had seen her, and rightly so. Not only was she the largest, she was the most striking, with her coloring being an indigo blue shading into purple, which in turn shaded into red at all of her extremities. She was a quiet and dignified dragon, and even as a baby had not been given to much in the way of absurd antics. Steady and unflappable, she was the best possible choice to carry a second rider, although they would all take it in turns to carry the priest once Tathulan started to show signs of fatigue.

The dragons were fully fed and would be carrying their midday meal. They would hunt this evening, before they stopped for the night. It was very likely that nothing would trouble them in the night—it would take a foolish predator to attempt to kill a single adult dragon, much less four—but even if something did attack them, these dragons, who had trained to fly at night, would hardly be daunted by darkness. They should be able to make short work of attackers.

Them-noh-thet said that he could find water. Kiron hoped that was true. That was the one concern he had for this journey. He knew that if they found an oasis or a well, it would probably be in the hands of the Bedu, and that was all right. He had tokens of friendship and right-of-passage and water-right with him; any of the Bedu would honor those, particularly after the way that he and his Jousters had cleaned out that lot of bandits for them.

The real question was if they would be able to find the water in the first place. This was a part of the desert that Kiron knew nothing about, nor did the Bedu with which he normally dealt. They knew that there were tribes here, yes, but not exactly where their water sources were, nor if they would be on the line of flight. The dragons could probably get by on one day without water, but not two.

The desert grew harsher the farther east they flew, until at last they were passing above stark sand dunes with no sign whatsoever of plant life or, indeed, any life whatsoever. The heat blasted up at them from this inhospitable zone, as the sun blazed down on them from above. Only the dragons seemed to thrive here, actually flying better than Kiron had ever seen them before. The Jousters all bent their heads beneath the scant shelter of their headcloths, and did their best to endure the uncomfortable journey.

It was a good thing that they were carrying the dragons' midday meal, because there was nothing larger than a beetle down there to hunt.

It wasn't a large meal; they didn't want the dragons to be ready to drowse. It was furnace-hot down there on the sand, and while that might be perfect for the dragons, the humans would bake like flatbreads in a hot oven.

Even up in the relatively cooler air, with the effective wind on them from the dragons' flight, it was difficult. The sun felt like a hot pressing iron on them, flattening them against their saddles, and every place where flesh touched anything else, sweat oozed.

This was the part of the desert called the Anvil of the Sun, and well-named it was, too.

The Bedu crossed it, but few others. Most, if they had any sense at all, went north or south, to places of easier passage. But this was the shortest possible way . . . the fastest, if you could fly.

If you could endure the furnace heat.

Kiron tried not to think about it. He concentrated on the air moving over his skin, on shifting himself so that parts of him remained in shadow, on watching Avatre's behavior. He had never yet heard of a dragon being overcome with heat . . . they reveled in it, soaked it up . . . but he'd never yet heard of anyone flying a Jousting dragon over the Anvil of the Sun. There'd been no reason, really. Jousting dragons had always gone North, to the border with Alta. Not East.

There was, after all, no reason to go East; the East was quiet. There had been no trouble on that front for ages.

From time to time, in the distance, tall pillars the color of smoke slowly drifted across the landscape. Sand demons, some called them, whirlwinds that were easily avoided, but which could strip the skin from anything that was unfortunate enough to be caught in their path. Those weren't bad; it was the Midnight *kamiseen*, the huge sandstorms that could go on for a day and swallowed up the landscape. Those storms buried entire cities and—as in the case of Sanctuary—unburied them.

Kiron *thought* that the dragons could probably fly above such a storm, but he didn't really want to put that idea to the test. What would he do, if they saw such a storm on the horizon?

Turn back, maybe. Hope that they could outrun it to shelter. Or try and see where the edge was and get there.

So he watched Avatre for signs that she sensed anything of the sort, and watched the horizon for that thin, dark line, the sky above it for the hazing of flying sand in the distance.

Slowly, the sun-disk traveled to the horizon so that it was at their backs. Slowly, the fierce heat eased a little.

On the horizon, Kiron spotted a haze of color that was not sand, did not have dust in the sky above it, and was hard and unmoving. He looked over at Tathulan, and waved his hand until he got the attention of the priest, then pointed.

The priest peered at the eastern horizon for a long time, then finally looked back over at Kiron. *Water,* he signed, using the signals they had all agreed on. *Hunting.*

Kiron sighed with relief and bent over Avatre's shoulder. They had crossed the Anvil of the Sun without incident. The worst of the journey was behind them now.

He hoped.

At least, it was the worst he could plan for.

The dragons approached the area of the eastern border of the Two Lands in the last light of the fourth day of their journey. It would have taken a rider on a fast camel nearly a moon to make the same trip. The trek across the Anvil of the Sun, if it could be made at all, usually took days all by itself; traveling by day and night, knowing that getting across that hideous stretch of desert was more important than rest.

This was still desert land, but it was the sort with which they were all familiar. There *was* water here, there was wildlife, plenty for the dragons to hunt. The eastern border could even be termed "grazing land" as there was enough there for goats and camels at least.

But as they neared the outpost where they reckoned the dead man had come from, and the one that the priests most definitely wanted investigated, it rapidly became evident that there was something very wrong.

There were goats, donkeys, and camels everywhere.

"Everywhere," being relative, of course; what he was actually seeing was the occasional little herd of goats drifting in the distance, a lone camel or so, a couple of donkeys. But there should not *be* goats roaming loose in little herds of three to a dozen so near a settled place. If they were wild, someone would have made a point of catching them and adding them to his herd. And if they were not wild . . . then what were they doing roaming loose, away from the watchful eye of their shepherd?

As for the camels and donkeys, they were even more expensive, and therefore a hundred times more likely to have been caught and penned. The price of a good camel could easily feed a man and his family for several moons.

The animals were fairly evenly spaced out as if they had been roaming loose for days. Herd animals did that, especially in sparse grazing areas.

This was delightful for the dragons, of course. It was easy hunting, and they were quite happy with it. But Kiron had a queasy feeling in his stomach, and he knew he was not the only one wondering with dread what they would find.

Behind them, the sun-disk drew near enough to the horizon that the light began to change, growing more golden, less white. Their own shadows stretched long on the ground beneath and ahead of them, as did the shadows of the scrubby trees and the occasional animal. Heat now radiated up at them from the ground, rather than burning down on them from above. And those passing shadows the dragons cast— they made the animals below them startle and flee, suggesting that other dragons had been coming here of late for the easy hunting.

There was a bump, a group of irregularities on the horizon, the wrong shape for a natural formation.

The town. Kiron gave the others the signal to drop down closer to the ground. He needed to be able to see what—if anything—was moving down there. The shapes disappeared for a while into the general landscape, then sharpened out again, now close enough to make out that they were buildings. And there was just nothing there besides those buildings. No sign of humans. No one on the road. There should have been people on the road, people coming into town from gathering deadfall, herdsmen bringing in the herds—

There should have been smoke from cooking fires.

Nothing.

As they approached their goal, more than just the absence of people going toward it struck Kiron.

It was silent.

A border town should be a noisy place. After all, it had sprung up purely to serve a garrison of men far from home. "Two taverns for every temple," was the saying about such places. At this time of day there should be men carousing in the beer shops. There should be people calling in families for dinner. Flute girls and storytellers should be setting up near the beer shops. Children should be crying, goats bawling, donkeys braying.

But the only sounds were the barking and growling of dogs in the street.

Cautiously, they circled the dragons overhead, but the only things moving anywhere were animals, all running wild, mostly dogs and cats, with a donkey drowsing at the side of one of the town wells, and a goat incongruously on a rooftop.

And a pack of jackals slinking down the street, that dropped their ears and ran at the sight of the dragons overhead.

As they circled, Kiron glanced over at the priest, who was frowning in concentration as he gripped the straps that held him in the double saddle. But the priest finally shook his head and gave the hand sign for "land."

Kiron had to hope that the man hadn't sensed anything hostile.

He picked what seemed to be a logical spot, just at the outskirts of town and near one of the taverns, open and with plenty of room for the dragons to take off again if they had to. He was glad now they had all come armed. Five men and four dragons—that was formidable if they were up against humans. But if they weren't—

He'd never seen a demon, nor any other supernatural creature, and he really didn't want to. He couldn't doubt their existence, given that he had seen the Magi at work, and had heard Kaleth speaking as the Mouth of the Gods, but that was all. He didn't know anyone who had, much less anyone who had fought one. There were legends, of course; the trouble was, unlike Ari, he was no scribe to remember them all.

The dragons landed one at a time, Avatre first, as he gave her the signal to be wary. Armed with spears, bows and slings—and in the case of the priest, presumably magic—they moved cautiously into the town.

The streets were as deserted from ground level as they had appeared from above. They approached the first building cautiously. It was a tavern, with two small tables and six overturned stools outside, and a bundle of barley painted crudely on the wall next to the door. Huras motioned to them to stop, moved forward a few paces, and sniffed.

"Don't smell anything rotting," he said.

"Jackals—" Pe-atep pointed out reluctantly. "Wild dogs—"

Kiron shivered. That wasn't anything he wanted to think about. If everyone was dead, that was almost unthinkable. But jackals . . . if jackals had gotten to the bodies here, this entire town would be haunted by hungry, unburied ghosts. And they would be very angry.

"I don't think we should stay here after dark," Oset-re said, nervously.

Huras squared his shoulders, and eyed the open door. The canvas door flap was down, so they couldn't see inside. "I'm going into the tavern."

"We're all going into the tavern," Kiron said firmly. "And for right now, we're all sticking together. No one is going wandering off by himself, no matter what. I don't care what we see or hear, we all stay in a group. Let's go."

They advanced on the building with no idea of what they were going to find when they pushed aside the door flap. Kiron felt sweat prickling all along his spine, and he gripped his spear tightly with both hands. The four dragons stirred and flipped the tips of their wings nervously, their eyes fixed on their riders.

Kiron reached for the canvas flap, and shoved it over on its rod, letting the last of the light from the setting sun come streaming into the main room. And what they found was . . .

Nothing.

No bodies, no blood, no sign of an armed struggle. The room was in a shambles, of course, but it looked random. Not the sort of thing that would happen because of a fight. *Plague* had been Kiron's first thought, that the people here had been sick. That didn't explain the soldier they had found, but maybe his fate was unrelated. People could have just crawled inside to die, leaving the streets deserted.

This had been a beer shop, as opposed to the sort of tavern that also sold food. They found overturned stools, opened jars of beer spilled on the two tables, and strangest of all, money on the counter, exactly as if someone had paid for beer and no one had collected his money. If there had been a fight, if some overwhelming force had come and taken the town, that money would not be there.

And if it was plague—people in a plague town don't keep going to beer shops.

It looked almost as if something had gotten the attention of everyone here, something so startling they had all gone out into the street to look at it. But there was no sign of what had then happened to them. The back of the shop had been set up as living quarters, and there were no signs of anyone there either. The only thing that they *did* find that was an absolute indicator that something had happened very abruptly—the family oven had been full of bread, which was now burned to a cinder. So whatever had happened here, it had happened some time between when the shop opened and when the bread would have been taken out of the oven. Late morning or early afternoon.

It was clear that scavengers had been in the kitchen, but also in the beer shop. Any foodstuffs had long since been run off with. Some enterprising creature had determined that he could break the beer jars by shoving them off the shelves; presumably he and his friends had lapped up what they could before it ran away, dried up, or sank into the dirt floor. The floor under the shelves was littered with broken pots.

But that must have happened after the people had gone . . . and where did they go?

Kiron's stomach turned over. Surely the entire town wasn't like this? All right, finding bodies would have been horrid, but this, in a way, was even worse.

They made their way—with less and less caution—up the street, checking every building, and finding—nothing. No people. Shops and houses in disarray. It looked for all the world as if suddenly, in the middle of the day, everyone in this town had put down what they were doing and walked out.

From the barracks—where they found neatly-made pallets, weapons stowed, and where the kitchen had been torn to pieces by animals hungrily devouring every scrap of bread and meat they could find—to the huts of the shepherds, it all looked the same. Everyone in the town was gone. They found piles of soft swaddling where infants had been picked up out of their corners. They found withered flowers and sticks and little clay dolls where toddlers had been taken away from their play in the dirt. The half dozen student scribes in one of the temples had put down their pens and their potsherds and walked out, along with their teacher.

Everyone in this town had vanished without a trace.

Well—

Everyone but one; the lone soldier who had almost made it to safety. And not even his body had been able to tell them anything.

Aket-ten was more than irritated with Kiron now; she was just about ready to remove his skin and salt him. Bad enough that he had only turned up when he had some bad news to deliver to an official, worse that he just vanished in the morning as soon as he could get Avatre in the air without even *trying* to see her. For that alone she had every right to feel slighted. But then to have gone out of his way to be charming to every Jouster here *except* her . . .

The girls, in particular, were very annoying the next few days after he had left. They had been rather disgustingly impressed with his charm. And yes, he could be charming when he felt like it. It was rather too bad that he felt sure enough of her feelings that he didn't bother to be charming to her anymore. But the girls certainly could have done without being so . . .

. . . ugh.

It was "Lord Kiron said this" and "Lord Kiron thinks that" until she was ready to scream, throw something, or both. The only one that was sensible was Peri, who, as usual, was quiet and spoke only about her dragon, and didn't go on about "Lord Kiron" as if he was the God Haras come down to earth.

Let them have to deal with him when he's being excessively dense some time and see how they feel about him then.

Maybe it was that the other girls had all been priestesses. Aket-ten remembered what it was like back when she had been a Nestling and a Fledgling. The other girls never seemed to tire of talking about young men. Young priestesses all seemed to have more time on their hands than they should, though why that should be, she couldn't imagine. *She* had always managed to find plenty of things to do with herself—studying for one. There were always new things to learn. Just because you didn't *have* to learn them, that hardly meant you shouldn't.

She was pondering just that when she passed by the pens and saw all of the babies in the middle one, piled in a drowsy heap with Peri and two of the others watching them, and she wondered where the other five girls were. And even as she wondered that, shrieks of laughter made her compress her lips and follow her ears.

She found them quickly enough. With three of

the four couriers, who were taking them in turns on short little rides dragonback . . . they weren't even wearing proper two-person saddles. The young men had the girls up in front of them, and were holding them in place with arms around their middles.

She reined in her temper with an effort, and stood very visibly in the door, arms crossed over her chest until someone finally noticed her.

It was one of the girls who wasn't getting a ride who turned, saw her, and yelped.

That got the attention of everyone except one of the couriers and his passenger, who rather quickly reacted when one of those on the ground blurted, "Wingleader Aket-ten! What are you doing here?"

The three dragons dropped to the ground, and three girls slid down off of them wearing three very different expressions. One was defiant, one highly amused, and one simply looked bored. Of the other two, only one looked properly apprehensive, the other, the one that had yelped—

Was she actually looking down her nose at Aket-ten, like one of those lazy, good-for-nothing girls that did nothing but lounge around a Court all day, looking decorative? Who did she think she was anyway? Every one of these girls had been *minor* priestesses with the very minor Gift of understanding the thoughts of animals. In the ordinary way of things, they would all, every one of them, have been sent off to some minor temple—or else, if nobly born, been relegated to wafting incense about or holding an ostrich-feather fan for the rest of their lives.

"I should be the one asking you all that question," she said sharply. "I am where I should be. And that is no way to address your superior. So what, exactly, is going on here when you should be watching your babies?"

The one looking down her nose smirked. "Lord Kiron thought it was a good idea for us to learn how to fly so we would be ready when the babies were."

Kiron again! Aket-ten opened her mouth to lash out at the girl, when suddenly something occurred to her, and instead, she smiled.

Nastily.

Apparently that smile got through to them. The identical expression of apprehension crept over all five faces.

She narrowed her eyes. "Lord Kiron suggested that, did he? Well, although I rather well doubt *this* was what he had in mind for *his* couriers to be doing, he just might have been right." She turned her attention to the three boys. "I'm sure, couriers, that you have far more important things to do with your time, and your dragons, than give pleasure hops. Training, after all, never really stops, does it?"

They took the hint. One of them even saluted her as all three flew off.

She turned to her girls and crooked a finger. "Come along," she said, in silken tones. "I want to introduce you to some new equipment. Since you all want to learn to fly so quickly, you are going to truly enjoy this. It is widely considered to be the highlight of training."

She had, with an eye to the training, been looking for the same sorts of apparatus that she and the rest of the original Altan wing had used to learn how to stay in the saddle when combat flying. It had taken her some time to track down where it had all been stored. Now, she had no intention of having the Queen's Wing in combat; much though she disagreed with Kiron's strenuous objections to the idea, she also knew that he was scarcely alone in his objections. There were things she would be able to do without offending the sensibilities of people in a position to stop her. Putting the young ladies in combat was not one of them.

But she was not going to tell these girls that. Actually, she had no intention of telling them that what she was about to put them through was combat training. After all, if they had to fly through sudden turbulent weather, they'd need this sort of practice.

And a few bruises, wrenched shoulders, or occasional black eye would do them good. It

would remind them that they were here to serve
the Two Lands, not as some sort of decorative
accessory. She had been very clear on that when
she had brought them in, after all; the Queen's
Wing, regardless of what other people were
being led to believe, was not merely here to provide a dramatic and beautiful backdrop for the
Queen's Royal Appearances.

If they wanted to be decorative accessories,
they could always go back to their temples. Sys-
trums and ostrich-feather fans were in plentiful
supply.

"Here we are!" she said cheerfully, ushering
them into the empty pen with unheated sands in
it, and the selection of six bits of apparatus waiting for them. They stopped just inside and eyed
the things with misgiving. "You wait right here,
while I get some servants. Since you're all so
eager, there is no time like the present, right?"

It didn't take her long; all that was required
was one stop in the kitchen to send someone for
six of the husky slaves who used to perform this
very duty for the training Jousters. By the time
she herself got back to the pen, the slaves were
already there. But then, she had taken her time,
wanting the girls to think about what they
might be faced with. The slaves had surely run;
she had sauntered.

The six men stationed themselves at each of
the sets of apparatus. She walked over to the

first of them. "I'm going to show you what real flying training is all about," she told them, getting into the saddle at the end of the long pole poised on a fulcrum, and fastening the straps tightly before she stood up. She made very sure they were good and secure, too. "This will make sure that you're really ready when your baby dragons are. After all, this is not that different from being a charioteer, and no charioteer trainer would ever put a green driver and green horses together."

She nodded at the slave, who levered her up into the air, then let her carefully down again. Up, down, up—this was like the gentle flap-glide-flap of a relaxed dragon in perfect flying conditions. The girls relaxed a little.

"This is what your flying will be like under ideal circumstances," she said. Then she raised an eyebrow. "But I am sure we all know just how often ideal circumstances come about. So most of your training will be so that you can stick with and guide your dragon under the worst conditions possible."

She nodded again at the slave, who proceeded to throw her end of the pole in every direction possible for the admittedly limited equipment, as hard as he possibly could. She gripped the padded end of the pole and the saddle strapped to it with legs and arms, shifting her balance as the dynamics of the seat shifted, grinning a little as the slave grinned at her, grinning still more at the look of alarm on the faces of the girls. Oh, they had no idea. This was the *easiest* of the flying training.

Finally she signaled to the slave to stop. He let her down onto the sand, and she unbuckled the straps, then stood up, motioning to the others.

"Come on, then," she said. "I thought you wanted to learn how to fly."

By the time the babies were ready for their next feeding, the five who had found themselves "volunteered" for flight training were indeed sore, bruised, and even a little sick. "You'll be here every day, twice a day, from now on," Aket-ten told them. "You'll take it in turns. Four of you will watch the babies and play with them, and start teaching them what *they* will need to know, while the other four of you train. I'll send the first four back to get the other four when I think you've had enough."

And then—we will graduate to the second stage.

Two of the girls suppressed groans, but Aket-ten wasn't done with them yet. "It's also more than time you started learning about dragon harness. As you just felt for yourself, properly fitted harness can save your life, while improperly fitted harness will kill you. You should never depend on a dragon boy to be certain your harness is right. You'll be spending part of every morning learning how to care for, fit, and even repair your harness."

"But—" the supercilious one began faintly.

Aket-ten cut her off with a look. "You are going to be couriers. You will spend at least half of your time somewhere where there will be *no* dragon boys, no harness makers, no one who knows how to help you. So you might as well start getting used to taking care of yourself, your dragon, and everything about both."

They looked at each other, then back at her.

Finally, the supercilious one straightened and squared her shoulders. "Yes, Wingleader," she said formally, saluting. "Now, by your leave, should we be getting back to the babies? By the sun, it should be feeding time."

Aket-ten gave her an approving nod. *Kenemaat,* she thought. *I have to start remembering their names properly.* "Indeed you should, Kenemaat," she replied evenly. "I will see you all at evening meal."

That one just might make a good Wingleader herself, Aket-ten thought as she headed for Reeth-ke's pen.

This thought, however, did not ease her anger with Kiron.

He had put this notion into their heads. Furthermore, he had undermined her authority in doing so. If he thought they were ready for flight training, he should have told her, not them.

In fact, there were a great many things he should have been telling her. Such as where to find those saddle trainers. There were the other sorts of advanced trainers, too, the barrels strung on the ropes—one of the slaves had told her about those. She'd have to find someone who knew where *they* were stored.

And on top of all of that, why had he simply left without even telling her good-bye?

She felt her temper flaring again and stopped right where she was in the corridor to force herself to calm down.

Then she used one of the meditative techniques she had learned as a priestess to clear her mind. Because there were surely things she could do to make all this work better if only—

Ari was a Jouster. He knows where all of those things are. And he can probably outline the training for me.

She almost hit herself because that had been so obvious. It wouldn't take him but a moment. He'd probably enjoy taking a little bit of leisure out to describe what he thought would be a good training regimen for her couriers. And *he* wasn't set on undermining her.

She relaxed a little further and—

I can ask that Nofret be made captain of all the couriers here in Mefis.

That would take care of the little matter of Kiron's couriers playing lazy games with her lady Jousters. She smiled. She could *certainly* think of things for them to do. Things that would keep them within the bounds of Mefis. There were plenty of errands to be run for the temples that would be done faster and more efficiently with a dragon courier. And as for them being ready at all times—she could have someone put up a pole and fly a pennon from it if the absent courier was needed.

She began to smile again. Yes indeed. That would keep them out of mischief.

And as for the girls . . . the day she couldn't think of ways to keep *them* out of mischief, she might just as well find another rider for Re-ethke and retire to a secluded temple somewhere because she most certainly would have lost touch with reality altogether.

 TEN

THE sun had just touched the horizon. The eastern sky had grown dark. And Kiron noticed now that even the smell of this town was wrong. The air was almost like that of the empty desert, with just a touch of musky goat to it. It should have smelled of unwashed bodies coming home from a day of hard work, of incense from the temples, of cooking food, of beer, of the cheap perfumed cones that flute girls used and the expensive ones that the well-to-do sported.

Everything conspired to make his skin crawl. This was different from Sanctuary and Aerie. There, the towns had been abandoned for so long that they had ceased to be places where you could imagine that in the next moment,

someone would come around a corner. Here . . .
this was like being in a nightmare. You just
knew that at any moment you would wake up
and the streets would be full again. Except that
didn't happen.

Avatre whined unhappily behind him. The
dragons had been trailing them all through the
town as if they, too, were uneasy about this
place. Now Avatre came up behind him and
bumped his shoulder with her nose, wanting
comfort. Absently, he cupped her snout against
his face.

"People just don't vanish into thin air," Pe-
atep said suddenly, looking up, and raking his
sweat-soaked hair out of his eyes with one hand.
"They leave a trail. Assuming they *all* went to
the same place, that would be a pretty wide
track. I'm going to find where they went before
it gets too dark to see their traces."

With that, he stalked off, leaving the rest of
them to scramble to catch up. Kiron was the first
to move, motioning to the others to follow, and
the dragons straggled along behind. Once, they
startled a little herd of goats, which tried to run
toward the desert; as if they were coordinating
their attack, each of the dragons pounced on a
different victim. All that hunting practice made it
absurdly easy for them; they caught and gulped
down their prey in nothing flat, and were shortly
following close on the Jousters' heels again.

They'd made a circuit of about a third of the ragged periphery of the town in the gray twilight when they discovered that Pe-atep was right in all of his assumptions. The people that were gone had gone *somewhere*, with some appearance of purpose. They had all gone in the same direction, it looked as if they had all gone at the same time, and they had left a trail.

Under normal circumstances the hard-baked desert ground would never have retained enough impression of feet for any of them to read; they were not, after all, skilled hunters or trackers. Pe-atep was the closest in that regard; he had trained the great hunting cats for the nobles of Alta, and thus had some minimal hunting skills himself. But the rest of them— Kiron had been a farmer's son and then a serf for most of his life, big Huras was the child of bakers, and Oset-re the protected child of nobles. What they knew of tracking could have been written on a fingernail with room left over.

But this was not a "few" people. Clearly, the entire town had passed this way, funneling through the streets and between the houses until they were channeled here to this spot. The scuffs and kicked-up dirt of an entire town's worth of people, all condensing into a kind of army, and all heading in the same direction left a path as wide as an avenue in Mefis and as easy to see. The only reason they hadn't spotted it before, from the air, was because they had approached low, and from the opposite side of the town. By the time they were near enough to see it, they had been concentrating on the empty streets, and thinking more of possible ambush or horrors to come than of what might lie on the eastern outskirts of town.

For this trail was headed east, without a shadow of a doubt. Men, women, children, children too small to walk on their own—all had come this way and gone off with no known reason. Across the border into lands the Altans knew nothing about.

"East?" Kiron said out loud. "What's east?"

Could there have been plague, or at least sickness? Was there some famous healer in that direction that everyone had decided to go to? Had there been a prophecy, some utterance from one of the gods ordering everyone out? Kaleth wasn't the only Mouth of the Gods in the world. . . .

And there were also plenty of people who would claim that title without having any right to it, too. Could someone like that be entrancing enough that people would do whatever he told them to do?

All four of the young men looked to Themnoh-thet, who was stroking his unshaven chin and frowning at a sky growing rapidly black. "This . . . is odd," he said slowly. "Very odd.

There's nothing for them to go to. There is supposed to be nothing to the east of Tia, nothing at all, save a few wandering tribes of herders. No tradesmen, no merchants have ever bothered to go there. Not even the Bedu go there; it is wilderness . . . but . . ."

His voice trailed off.

"But?" Kiron prompted sharply. There was something about the priest's expression that he did not like. "If we are to solve this, we must know even your speculations."

"But this is where the Nameless Ones came from," the priest said slowly and reluctantly. "They came marching across the border at a place very near here, according to the old records. That is why there was a border garrison here in the first place, to watch for them should they come again." He rubbed his eyes with one hand. "There is no reason for anyone to go marching off in that direction, much less all of the people in the town. Something is very wrong here."

Kiron snorted. That much was blindingly obvious.

The priest glanced aside at him. "I mean, something more than the obvious is wrong. I was sure I would find traces of magic here, that whatever had happened would be obvious to the trained Sight and the kinds of things I have with me. But—no. There is nothing other than the absence of the people and this track. None of my talismans are telling me of the presence of the kind of dark powers that the Altan Magi used," the priest continued, peering uneasily down at the ground as the darkness of full night quickly descended. "In fact, I sense . . . nothing even of what I can see with my eyes. No more than did the Sighted among us from Sanctuary. I can see the buildings. I can see the signs of ordinary life everywhere. But what I see does not correspond to what I See. It is as if there never was a town here, that nothing has ever lived here but wild things. People leave echoes of themselves anywhere they have lived, and those echoes take years, not days, to fade. Yet those echoes are not here."

Silence answered his words, and Kiron shivered. He knew nothing of magic except that it did follow rules—and the priest was talking as if all those rules had been completely violated. *He sounds like I would, if Avatre suddenly turned on me with no warning.*

"I am going to hunt while there is still a little light left," Pe-atep said abruptly into that silence. "The dragons have fed, but we have not. We were counting on people to be here, on the garrison to take care of our needs when we got here."

Kiron nodded slowly. "Yes, we were. But who could have thought—"

"No one," Pe-atep said immediately. "This is not something you could have anticipated, Kiron, but it isn't going to stop our hunger from making us weak if we don't take care of ourselves. I will kill one of those wandering goats. That will be meat enough for us all, if nothing else."

"I will see if there are stores of flour or the like," Huras said slowly. "The scavengers can't have gotten into everything. There plainly is nothing in this town to fear, not even ghosts—" He faltered to a halt. Kiron could empathize. When a place was this deserted, even a ghost would have been welcome, in a way.

And at least this was something constructive they could all do. Kiron took command of the situation. "Pe-atep, that is a good plan. We must sleep, and we must eat. Going to bed with our stomachs aching will not let us sleep. We cannot do much, even to return to Sanctuary, without food and rest. So let us divide ourselves—but carefully."

He pondered for a moment. "Pe-atep and I will take the dragons to the courtyard of the Temple of Haras, then hunt. Them-noh-thet, go you to the Temple of Haras with us, and light the fires and the torches and see what you may find there. We will make that place our refuge; the wings of the God will surely shelter us."

A pious statement that the priest nodded at,

but which Kiron himself was not entirely sure he believed. After all, the priests were all gone, too . . . the wings of the God hadn't done them much good.

But right now he preferred they didn't think about that. They all needed some place that would at least feel a little safe. "Huras and Oset-re, see what you can find of foodstuffs that animals haven't pillaged, get us water, and we will all meet back at the temple."

The priest nodded; it was clear he was not loath to take himself back to familiar confines. Kiron couldn't blame him, a temple must feel to him as a fortress felt to a soldier.

And perhaps, since he was Sighted and Gifted, he might be able to turn the temple into a truly protected spot. A border garrison town was hardly going to attract priests of any kind of power. In fact, it would have been surprising if even the Healer here could do more than pray and offer herbs and the knife.

"I think that the homes of the wealthier here might yet yield something we can eat," Huras said. "Once we find torches, I will make a fire and kindle them, and then we will be on better footing." The big man led Oset-re confidently off back into the town. They looked almost like a father and child, Huras towered so much over Oset-re.

"Let us seek the temple then, while we can

still unharness the dragons without stumbling over straps," Kiron said, catching up the reins of Wastet and Tathulan before they could follow their masters. There was a moment of resistance, a little tugging, and then the two yielded to Kiron's insistence. They had been well trained, but more than that, they accepted Kiron and the other riders of Kiron's wing as substitutes for their true masters.

"And while I can find the stores of torches and lamp oil," the priest said and sighed. "At least I need not concern myself with being frugal. Clearly, no one is going to object if I burn a sennight's worth in a single night."

"Hardly," Kiron said dryly. "Rather we are more apt to ask you to make more lights, not fewer."

Treading carefully, the priest walking alongside them, Kiron and Pe-atep took all four of the dragons, which were beginning to make anxious sounds again, off to that courtyard. As were many temples, this one was set up to play host to dragons if need be. It would catch and hold the sun all day, and at night, the stone would radiate back that stored heat. There were stone basins that could be filled with fuelbricks made of straw and dung to provide more warmth if the dragons got too cold. There was ample room for the four, and they all stopped whining and began to relax as they realized they were soon going to be allowed to sleep. Pe-atep and Kiron set about getting them out of their gear and stowing it off to the side, each set going to a different corner and stacked neatly. The priest greatly aided their efforts by bringing four torches as soon as he could find them and get them lit. The moment that saddles and harness were off, the four curled up together to share warmth and immediately went to sleep.

By this time it was fully dark, but the moon was already rising, and this turned out to be all to the good. It was a full moon and as Kiron and Pe-atep knew from experience, a full moon provided almost as much light to dark-accustomed eyes as any number of torches.

Leaving the temple to the priest, they stepped out into the street, and waited for their eyes to adjust. Kiron wished Aket-ten was with them. She would have known where the goats were . . . she could probably have lured one right into their hands.

On second thought, that was probably a bad idea. Maybe if they were actually starving to death, it would be different. But luring a goat with your thoughts just so you could kill it . . . no, there was something profoundly wrong with that idea. He made a mental resolution at that moment never even to suggest such a thing to her.

Better just to use what scant intelligence he had. How to think like a goat . . . ?

"If I were a goat, where would I go to escape jackals and lions for the night?" Kiron mused aloud.

Pe-atep chuckled, the first pleasant sound he'd made since they arrived here. "Have you forgotten already that goat we saw on a roof? He was not stupid, Kiron, he was quite clever. Lions and jackals can't manage steep staircases very well, they wouldn't be able to actually see goats on the roof, and it's possible that they might even be so confused about where the scent was coming from, they'd never think to go up. If I was a goat, I would head for the rooftops, too, and I think I remember where he was."

Pe-atep led the way quietly and carefully up the street. Carefully, with weapons in hand, because they had seen jackals, and there was the very real possibility of lions. With all the easier prey about, a lion or even a pack would probably not trouble themselves with humans, but why take the chance?

But they encountered nothing worse than dogs going feral, and Pe-atep's memory was quite correct.

As they approached the house in question, they could actually hear the sound of hooves clicking a little on the stone of the roof, and heard a bleat of complaint. It sounded as if the first goat had been joined by several more. Well . . . on the one hand, goats did like to herd up. And if a lion *did* figure out it had to go up to find them, having several more goats up there would mean that the lion would have more than one target.

But on the other hand . . . having more goats up there meant more noise and more chance that a lion *would* figure out it had to go up.

I think, if I were that goat, I would go find my own roof.

"Hmm," Pe-atep whispered, and scratched his head. "I had rather not go up there, try to take one, and frighten them. Being in the middle of a herd of frightened, kicking goats in the dark—"

Ugh, Pe-atep was right about that. Goats could do a great deal of damage with those sharp little hooves. Not to mention the horns.

"The first thing to do is see what things look like up there," Kiron replied, after a moment. "It's not as if they're going to charge us or anything. The worst that will happen if they see us is that they'll startle and try to run."

"Huh. That might not be bad. If they jump off the roof—"

There was a thought. Surely there would be one out of the lot that would land wrong. "Keep that in mind. It's not the worst plan I've ever heard."

The two of them circled the building until they found the narrow, precarious stair that led up the outside to the roof. Feeling his way along the wall and taking great care not to trip, Kiron climbed up first and cautiously poked his head up over the low wall that rimmed the top.

There were about six goats there, most of them standing packed closely together with their heads hanging. Their even breathing told Kiron that five of the six felt secure enough here to doze. But one of them, a piebald, pricked its ears up at Kiron and craned its head forward, sniffing. It didn't seem alarmed. In fact, after a moment, it took a step toward him, and then another.

Feeling a little like a traitor for getting it to trust him, Kiron made a *tsk*ing noise at it, as Pe-atep moved up beside him and went into a crouch. Switching its tail, the goat ambled over, looking as if it expected a treat.

It must have been somebody's pet. Kiron tried not to think of the child that had probably made it into a pet . . . a child that without a doubt must have other things to worry about now than its pet goat. Assuming it was even in a condition to worry about anything.

Still, this was rather like—like Aket-ten using her Gift to lure a goat to doom. It made him a bit queasy.

He tried to remind himself that the poor goat

was just as doomed. If not at their hands, a wild beast would surely get it before long. A goat that was a pet did not have many survival skills.

Kiron moved down the steps backward, still making little calling sounds. When the goat was about halfway down the steps, Pe-atep pounced, long knife in hand. And suddenly, this was a lot like helping Avatre make her first kills. He moved in to help.

It was over very quickly, without much in the way of noise or struggle to alarm the other goats of the herd.

"Should we try to frighten them?" he whispered. "See if we can get a second one?"

Pe-atep cleaned his knife and sheathed it, then paused to consider. "No," he said finally. "We have enough to eat with this one, and without a cold room . . . no, I don't think that's a good idea. Besides, tomorrow we can start finding everything there is to eat left in this place, and we can make sure the dragons hunt for all of us. We won't starve."

Kiron nodded. With Pe-atep taking the front legs and Kiron the hind, they carried their prize back in the direction of the temple.

As soon as they rounded the corner, it was very clear that the priest had been very hard at work in their absence. The customary two torches burned on either side of the door, and light streamed out onto the street from that door.

It was a welcome sight, and mitigated, a little, the undeniably disturbing effect of the otherwise silent and empty town. It was a sign of light and life.

Them-noh-thet himself greeted them by hurrying out from the back of the temple when their footsteps sounded on the stone. "Ah, good," he said with relief. "I admit to you, this place is disturbing me."

"It's just too empty," Pe-atep replied fervently. "I am glad you were able to get this temple looking more lived in."

The priest shrugged. "As much as a temple can. The rear part is better, the part where the priests and acolytes live. I have a fire going in the kitchen, and I have cleaned it up somewhat so we can work. I also found foodstuffs in storage jars, and herbs. We will not be eating half-raw, half-burned goat like barbarians; I have pickled onions and dates, and honey, and some other things, things the vermin and animals didn't scent. Come, follow me."

The temple kitchen was, as such things went, rather spacious. Open to the air, of course, though sheltered by a roof in case of rain. There were many storage jars in a room off to one side, a wide counter to prepare food on, a mortar for grinding grain into flour, troughs for kneading dough, two ovens for bread, flat stones one could build a fire on to heat for cooking, and three fire pits where things could be stewed in pots. And it looked as if they weren't going to be starving any time soon. One waist-high storage jar alone held enough lentils to feed them all for a week, and there were several dozen such in that storeroom. Kiron was not unaccustomed to kitchen chores, but he had to admit to relief when Huras and Oset-re returned bearing the fruits of their own rummaging. He gladly stepped aside to let the son of a baker take over directing the rest of them. Huras was a big man, with correspondingly large hands, which performed startlingly deft work with the knives and other implements that Them-noh-thet had found. Once they had water from the well, the question of what they would eat in the morning was easily solved; lentil stew, which would use the scraps of goat that were left when they finished eating tonight.

The result was a surprisingly good meal, which they elected to eat right there in the kitchen area. It was, however, eaten in grim silence and with many glances over the shoulder toward the small open court behind the kitchen. The silence was intimidating, though at least here, they could pretend they were in the kitchen of a country house and not in the middle of a town.

At last Them-noh-thet cleared his throat awkwardly. "I intend to try to reach my fellow priests in Sanctuary tomorrow," he said, "as well as attempt more magics that might tell us what has happened here. I think that we cannot return until we investigate this situation more—"

He looked at Kiron as if he expected Kiron to object, but the Jouster only nodded.

"As long as we have hunting for the dragons and food and water for ourselves, I don't see any other course," he agreed. "An entire *town* just walked off into the wilderness; we don't know where they are, why they left, or who did this to them. We have to find out whatever we can, here."

The other three nodded in agreement, and the priest looked relieved. "I don't think we should sleep without a watch being set, though," Kiron continued, "And I think we really ought to sleep with the dragons. It offers that much more safety." He thought for a moment. "In fact, I—all right, this may sound strange, but I think we ought to sleep tethered to a dragon's leg. That way, if something comes along and makes us want to go wandering in the desert, hopefully our dragons will wake us out of it."

Huras scratched his head, looking relieved. "That's a good idea. And I don't think it sounds strange at all. Tathulan is very good about telling when there's something wrong with me."

"I think they're all good at that," Kiron agreed.

The priest looked from one to another of them, and finally asked, very quietly, "Would you mind if I joined you?"

It was not a restful night. But then, no one really expected it to be. Only the dragons slept soundly, and didn't really seem to notice when their riders took heavy cords and tied themselves to a front foot. Then again, they'd had a hard several days getting here, and they were probably exhausted.

The Jousters should have been exhausted, too, but Kiron could tell that the others were sleeping fitfully if at all. Even Huras, who normally slept through everything, was tossing and turning. He took his turn at night watch, then settled down with Avatre again, and finally some time before dawn, did drop into an uneasy slumber.

It was a relief to do something normal and take the dragons out to hunt. They let all four of them kill and eat as much as they could; it would be no bad thing for them to doze most of the day and recover their strength.

They left the priest stripped down to his kilt, busily laying out all manner of things in the sanctuary of the temple. He looked up as Kiron passed. "It is a very good thing," he said in measured tones, "both that all Temples of Haras are required to keep everything needed for the greater magical rituals, and that no one, so far as I can tell, has ever used these things here. I have pristine tools and materials."

"Will you be needing anything from us?" Kiron asked, hoping that the answer would be "no."

The priest shook his head. "I could do with a trained acolyte, but in matters this complicated, an untrained helper is worse than none at all."

Kiron nodded. "In that case, during the morning we intend to consolidate everything useful here, and in the afternoon, we are going to follow the trail of the missing townsfolk for as long as we can."

The priest's mouth thinned. "I do not know what to hope for. It could be that 'nothing' is the best thing you can find."

Kiron tried very hard not to think about that as he went out with Huras to scour the northern half of the town, including the garrison, for foodstuffs and water jars. After two trips with the latter, which were heavy, awkward, and bulky, he was feeling distinctly out of sorts. He really didn't want to contemplate what it was going to be like to have to fill all the jars that Huras had lined up along the wall of the kitchen. The temple did have its own well, but it was still going to mean a lot of water carrying.

I thought I had done with toting water when I was no longer a serf.

Eventually, Huras deemed that they had enough jars, and he was able to go on to carrying—

Equally heavy things. Irksome. Exhausting. By midmorning he was sick of it. Fortunately, so was Huras. "Enough," the young man said finally. "I am like to turn into a donkey at this rate. We have looted the best houses in this town; anything we find elsewhere will be inferior. We will look for gardens, I think."

Kiron groaned but agreed.

But the gardens had long since been eaten up by the goats, which understandably preferred tender, well-nurtured plants to what they could find in the desert. The best that Huras could manage was to dig up some half-grown onions whose green parts had been eaten down to the ground.

Pe-atep and Oset-re fared no better, and the rest of the morning was spent filling water jars until their arms ached. Huras rewarded them, though, with a decent meal, and Kiron mentally congratulated himself that the big man was along, even though Huras had been picked for the size and strength of his dragon and not his culinary skills.

The priest came in as they were finishing their meal looking so bleak that Kiron put down, untasted, the honey-smeared flatbread he had been about to bite into. "What?" he asked apprehensively. "Your face is as long as Great Mother River—"

"I cannot speak with Sanctuary," the priest replied. "Even though my powers find *nothing* in the way of dark magic here, or even any magic at all, I cannot sense them, nor, I suppose, can they sense me."

All the dire things that Kiron could think of were quickly dismissed. The priest was an expert in his magic; he would surely have thought of everything Kiron could think of as the reason why he could not reach his fellows. Still. If magic was like water, could it be drained away? "No magic?" he said instead. "None? Isn't there always some magic about? Amulets, charms, even if only half of those are genuine, shouldn't you be able to sense them?"

Them-noh-thet gave him a sharp look. "What are you thinking?"

Kiron had to shrug. "I don't really know. Is there something that drinks magic?"

The priest stroked his chin, which was now shaven again. "Huh. It is possible. I have never heard of such a thing—" He stared past Kiron for a moment, then abruptly turned and stalked back into the sanctuary.

Kiron and the others shared a look. "Priests," Oset-re said dismissively. "Aket-ten is like that."

"So she is," Kiron replied, feeling both a touch of irritation and a touch of smugness, both overlaid by a profound wish that she was here. When she wasn't being irritating, she had the ability to cut through to the heart of things, and to see them quite sensibly.

But—now. Bad enough that they were here themselves. That he was here. He didn't want her in this place, this unhaunted place, where not even ghosts were lingering.

"Let's get the dragons up," he said, rather than saying anything more about Aket-ten. "We'll follow where the people went for as far as we can."

The track was easy to follow. And unnaturally straight. It looked for all the world as if the people had simply trudged over everything in their path, not stopping to go around obstacles and climbing down wadis and up the other side. There was no actual mark on where the border of Tia ended, of course; this was wilderness, who would care? The garrison had just been placed in a spot that seemed good for keeping an eye out to the east. But Kiron was fairly certain that they were well past that nebulous "border" by midafternoon. And the track showed no signs that the people who had made it were getting tired and needed to rest.

But then the dragons glided over the top of a rise—and the track abruptly ended in a muddle of footprints as if whatever had drawn those people out into the desert had stopped calling them, leaving them confused.

And on the other side of that muddle, another track began.

The four of them swooped in to land.

"Camel droppings," said Pe-atep at once, pointing to the pile of dung. "And camel tracks." He slid off his dragon's back and began walking about, bent over, frowning. "Whoever was here, they weren't here by accident. They camped here two, maybe three days—there's a fire." Now he pointed at a blackened smudge half covered with loose earth. "And look how the brush is browsed up. Whoever was here, came here expecting to intercept these people. They *knew* the townsfolk were coming."

"They weren't here to invite them to a feast either," said Oset-re suddenly. He rose up from behind a bit of scrub with something in his hands, his face grim.

They all clustered around him. What he held in his hand was a bit of leather with a ring on it; it had broken where the ring was riveted to the leather, rendering it useless.

It was a slave's neck collar, and the ring was meant to run a rope through, so that the slaves could be strung along like a string of pack animals.

Well. Now they knew why no one had come back.

"The dead guard," Oset-re said, slowly. "He was probably riding patrol along the border, and whatever happened back there, he didn't get caught in it. Then, when he got back to town, he followed this track, just as we did."

Kiron nodded grimly. "Now we know who killed him. But where did these slave traders take our people?"

Pe-atep was already walking the site in ever-widening circles, and suddenly stopped. He looked at the other three and spread his hands in frustration. "I was thinking—a town full of people—that's a lot of slaves. And there were a lot of slave traders here. A *lot* of slave traders."

Kiron went to join him, and saw what Pe-atep meant. Camel and human tracks radiated out from the spot where Pe-atep stood. This must have been—like a feast for these traders. Because there were no signs of any struggle. Whatever held the townsfolk in thrall continued to keep them docile.

And as for where the townsfolk were—they were scattered to the four winds.

The four Jousters looked at each other in dismay. By now there was no telling where those people were. There were only four of them, and a dozen slave traders or more, and that was assuming that the traders had moved so slowly that the dragons could catch up with them—with more than a sennight of head start.

The townsfolk were gone, beyond recall.

With heavy hearts, they mounted back up, and turned back to the deserted city.

There was still a mystery to solve. Who did this? Why?

And how could it be avenged?

 **ELEVEN**

DESERT wind flowed through the ventilation openings just under the temple's roof, carrying away most of the thick incense smoke. Which was just as well, since the Priest of Haras had been undertaking so many rituals that it would otherwise have been impossible to breathe here. "I can find nothing," Them-noh-thet said with frustration. He looked worn to a rag. He had not slept except when he had to, and Huras had been bringing him meals because otherwise he would not have troubled to eat. "Except that, yes, something is drinking the magic. I cannot tell where it is, because it drinks the magic as fast as I bring it up."

Kiron rubbed his head. They had been here

three days now and were no closer to solving the mystery. Nor were they in any position to do anything about bringing the stolen people back, and the longer they remained here without being able to speak to Sanctuary, the longer it would take for anyone else to know what had happened. Finally, he shook his head. "We must go back. We can do nothing more here."

The others looked as if they were about to protest, then thought better of it. With a resigned look, the priest shrugged and knelt down to begin packing up his magical and ritual instruments. Kiron nodded with sympathy. "I understand. We have accomplished nothing other than to find a deserted town and to discover that the people and garrison are almost certainly now slaves. If any of you can think of *anything* we have not yet tried, I should like to hear it."

Nothing. No one had any clever answers. They were all too tired to even try to think of some. As he had known was the case, since he wasn't in any better condition than the rest.

He wanted a real meal, and he wanted a bath. But he would do without both if only they were getting answers here. Since they weren't—it was piling misery atop futility to stay here.

"Very well, then. We fly back. Perhaps the priests at Sanctuary will have better ideas." He glanced at Them-noh-thet, who shrugged wearily. The priest looked as if he had come to the last of his ability to think, and that was not a good state to be in. They were relying on him for defense against magic, but if he could not think clearly, that was a potential disaster.

He could tell them not to feel guilty, but it would be useless. He rubbed the back of his hand across his cheek and felt the grit under it. Enough. The wise commander knew when to order a retreat. The sun was going down; there was a beam of light pouring in through the ventilation slit in the western wall, to fall three fourths of the way up the eastern wall. That only happened as the sun-disk approached the horizon and was a good cue to tell them all that nothing more could be done this day. "Get a good night's sleep," he advised. "If you cannot do it any other way, broach that last jar of date wine. We'll hunt before we leave and take as much as the dragons can carry."

At least now he knew the locations of the watering places on the way back. The locations were engraved, not in his memory, but in the far better memory of the dragons. That would make things much easier for everyone; the dragons would make a straight flight from one to another, without the need to hunt for it this time. A dragon never forgot a place where there was something it needed, as he had discovered with Avatre, who would return, time after time, without prompting, to the same little wadi where she had cornered a gazelle, presumably hoping that another one would find the place to its liking. And more often than not, she did find some sort of prey there, though once it had been a very disappointing fennec fox that had slipped right between two of her talons and scampered away.

They all resorted to the date wine, even the priest. Huras put together a truly excellent if very limited dinner for all of them, but it seemed rather like a funeral feast. In a way, perhaps it was; the people they could not help might just as well be dead now. It was more than enough to make one think very hard about taking refuge in the wine. No one indulged too much, however; no one wanted to awake in the morning feeling as if his head had been put in the olive press and his gut was a colony of scorpions. And when the jar had been split five ways, Kiron noted as he went to bed that at least half of each portion had been poured out frequently for the god. He hoped that Haras got good use of it.

In the morning, it did not take long at all to hunt enough to take care of everything the dragons would need for a day. The goats that had taken shelter in the town made easy prey. The dragons ate well, and they all lumbered into the air burdened not only with their midday meal, but their evening as well.

Kiron pressed them all hard, and no one objected, not even the dragons. But once they were a day out of the border town, the priest *had* been able to tell his fellows what had been discovered—sketchy details, at least. Once they were down for the night, he had performed a very simple ritual that allowed him to scribe characters on a specially prepared piece of papyrus paper which somehow would end up on another like it in Sanctuary. And he, in his turn, could read characters that appeared on his piece of paper.

Return to Sanctuary quickly, was all that he got, which was what they were doing anyway, after all. The return trip was the mirror image of the trek out, with one exception, and that was when they split their party on the last day.

Kiron took up the priest behind him and veered off to Sanctuary, where Avatre drifted down to her old pen in the very last glimmer of twilight and sank down onto the heated sands with a sigh. At their midday stop, the priest had sent Sanctuary another message, telling them to expect him and a Jouster around sunset. So there were servants waiting with food for Avatre and another to help Kiron unsaddle her.

"There is a bath waiting for you, Lord Jouster," said one of them. "And clean clothing. There is drink waiting at the bath, and I will bring a hot meal when you are finished."

"That sounds . . . very good," he replied, trying to maintain at least a semblance of dignity.

He followed the servant to the bathing room that had been set up in the Temple of Haras, to which the dragon pens were attached, and with a sigh of gratitude for water he did not have to personally haul, upended the first bath jar over himself.

The priest, of course, had immediately hustled off with two acolytes that had been waiting for him.

And when he returned from his bath, the waiting servant told him that Avatre had roused herself long enough to eat, then flopped down and spread out her wings and was asleep in moments.

As for Kiron, fed and clean and finally in clean kilt and loinwrap for the first time in days, he thought he would surely be called on to contribute. The pens they had built here in Sanctuary were of the type that he himself had pioneered, with the Jousters' spartan quarters in the pen itself, and this was where another servant bought him food, drink, and a small lamp to see by. But as he ate the meal that was brought to him, no summons came. When he found himself nodding off over the empty bowl, he gave up and stretched out on the pallet.

Dawn broke, and still no summons. After getting himself some food from the kitchens of the Temple of Haras, and waiting until Avatre herself woke and began to look restlessly about for food, he finally shrugged, found someone to pass the message to Them-noh-thet and Kaleth that he was leaving, and saddled Avatre up.

He was just about ready to mount up, when a boy came running up, and with him servants carrying meat that Avatre eyed with great hunger. Sanctuary still operated leanly, despite all the priests and temples here. Last night's meal for Avatre had been a necessity, because they had arrived too late to hunt. The couriers were expected to hunt their dragons to feed them.

For Sanctuary to feed Avatre twice told him that the orders he was about to get were not to go back to Aerie.

"Jouster Kiron," the lad said, breathless from the run. "You are asked by Kaleth, and through the priests of Haras by Great King Ari, to say nothing of what you found. Not even to your best friends."

The servants spread out the meat for Avatre; it had already been cut up so that she could simply gulp chunks down rather than tearing at larger pieces, and she did so while he blinked at the boy's words. This took him rather aback, but he could certainly see why this edict would be issued. Given that no one knew how the people had been lured from that town, nor who had done it, there might be panic if people thought even for a moment such a thing could happen again.

Might be panic? There most certainly *would* be. And rightly. It could happen again, and at the moment, they had no means of preventing it.

There were no answers to why it had happened, only more questions.

He nodded. There was great wisdom in this edict, but there was certainly more to come.

"You are further asked to go, not to Aerie but to Mefis, where the Great King wishes to speak with you at length," the boy continued. "A courier will be sent to Aerie with your instructions for the Jousters."

He thought carefully. A courier . . . there wasn't a great deal that he needed to actually give in the way of instructions. Perhaps if the others were all untrained—but in fact, there were people at Aerie who were far better schooled in the management of dragons and their Jousters than he was. "You can send something from temple to temple, yes? Very nearly as swift as thought?"

The boy nodded.

"Then tell them that they are to continue as I left them." His wing of wingleaders was more than competent enough to continue as they had been. Until the bandits changed their strategy, which was not likely for some time, there was no real need for him to be there, and even then—

well, there were men with the Jousters now who all had more combat experience than he, the "old" Jousters, who surely, surely would be able to deal with such problems. All the administrative nonsense could be handed by Haraket. . . .

He felt a distant relief and a little guilt. Haraket had not wanted it.

But Haraket was good at it. As the Overseer for the Dragon Courts of Tia, he had handled all these things before: disputes over quarters, getting supplies, finding ways and means of doing just about everything. The circumstances had changed, but . . .

Well, perhaps Ari could come up with a way to sweeten the circumstances. And he was certainly now in a position to make such a request. *Lord Haraket, with his own villa and land . . . not a bad thought.*

Meanwhile it seemed he *was* needed elsewhere, and he had better put all possible speed into it.

Avatre finished the last chunk of meat and raised her neck to look at the sky, spreading her wings slightly. She was impatient to be gone, and she turned her head gracefully, to look at him as if prompting him.

"You are to make all speed, Lord Kiron," the boy said, echoing his thoughts.

"We will," he replied, and before he had finished the second word, Avatre, responding to his shift in weight, gave a tremendous leap and upward thrust of her wings and sent them both aloft.

They landed to the kind of reception that Kiron remembered from the old days of the Dragon Courts here; servants, rather than dragon boys, but otherwise it was a taste of the old days, except he had never been on the receiving end of the attention back then. It was a little disorienting, actually, to see the swarm and have the reaction that he should be down among them. He had scarcely unbuckled his straps and slid out of his saddle when there was a servant there unbuckling the harness, another with a barrow of meat for Avatre, a third filling her water trough. She looked surprised for a moment, then hunger overcame surprise and she dove into her meal.

Kiron, for his part, was taken away by yet a fourth servant, moving at a run toward the Palace. And if he had not felt the urgency of his situation so strongly, he would have been stunned at the mere sight of the huge building that crowned the avenue that the servant led him onto.

For all that his duties sometimes brought him here, this was the first time he had been in the Palace, and it simply did not compare to anything he had yet seen. The Dragon Courts and the temple attached to them were large, yes, and indeed the temple was fully large enough for a dragon, even several dragons, to walk about in comfortably. But he had gotten used to the low ceilings, the long, dark rooms of Aerie, the squat, sturdy buildings of Sanctuary. That was what his mind measured things by.

He had forgotten—if indeed he had ever truly realized—that the Great King's Palace in Mefis was intended to impress to the point of intimidation.

He found himself approaching a building that was at least as tall as the cliff walls of Aerie were—except that the dwellings of Aerie were carved from something natural, and this was entirely built by man. Fat, carved and painted pillars made to look like palm trees rose up three tall stories to support the roof, and the front of the Palace was so wide that forty chariots could have lined up in front of it. The front door, of beaten plates of bronze, would have admitted Avatre or even Kashet without requiring them to bend their necks or tuck in their wings.

Inside, the first room looked like the sanctuary of a temple, with more rows of carved and painted columns upholding the ceiling, which was so far above Kiron's head that Avatre could probably have flown in here, had the columns permitted it. And there must have been fifty torches illuminating the place.

From the dais and the two thrones at the far

end, this must be the audience chamber. But the thrones were empty and the servant was hurrying on.

They passed through another chamber like the first, but smaller; presumably this one was for smaller gatherings of more important people. There were larger-than-life-sized murals here, of tribute being offered and captive enemies, and on the wall behind the thrones, there was an almost-life-sized dragon, wings spread protectively above the thrones themselves. Just as many torches burned here as in the previous room.

The servant hurried on, leading him into a chamber of about the same size, but clearly one made for a very different purpose.

This was a room full of scribes' desks with rolls of papyrus paper in baskets beside them, ink and reed pens on them, and on one or two, works still being written and held down with scroll weights. Four doors led into this room, and, through them, he glimpsed servants coming around to light torches and lamps. There were a few, a very few lamps lit here, but not many. Work here was done for the day, unless the Great King or Queen would call for a scribe.

The servant led him through the right-hand door, taking him now toward the south, for the palace itself faced east. The next two chambers seemed to be places for officials to do business;

the decorations here were paintings of the god Teth, who oversaw such things, and the furnishings were desks, chairs, and baskets of scrolls.

A wafting scent of roast duck tickled Kiron's nose as they moved through the second of these rooms, and made his stomach growl. He hadn't had duck or fish or goose, or anything that lived on or in the water, since leaving Alta. Well, fish. But they were dried. Nothing like the glorious roast fish he used to enjoy as an Altan Jouster. He turned his thoughts resolutely from food. He needed to concentrate on what, if anything, Ari might be asking him.

They passed into and out of a huge courtyard with a *latas*-pool fully big enough for swimming, rimmed with palm trees. There were piles of cushions, palm-leaf fans in baskets, and other things that gave him the impression that this was a spot used for lounging. But by whom? He did not know enough about court life to even venture a guess. From there, they passed into another part of the Palace where the ceilings were still high, but only a bit above "normal" height.

So far, every area they'd been through had been graced with stunning wall paintings appropriate to the room. In the scribes' and officials' chambers, it had been paintings of the god of writing and of diligent workers. Here, where he supposed these rooms were for entertaining,

the murals were of dancers and flute girls, or of
hunting scenes, or of the gods giving gifts of life
and health to the Great King. The pillars were all
painted to look like *latas* flowers, with the pillar
being the green stem and close-furled leaves, the
capital the blue-petaled flower spreading out to
press against the ceiling. Here were low
couches, more piles of cushions, and small tables holding objects it was too dim to make out.
The effect was opulent beyond his dreams.

He hurried on, with the servant leading
through more rooms seen only dimly as torches
here had not been lit. They passed through another court with a pool, this one somewhat
smaller and set like a blue jewel in a green garden. And from the far side of this court he could
see what was presumably their goal, another set
of rooms, where light and sound were spilling
through an open doorway.

Glad to see an end to this journey, he followed
the servant in and found himself in a room
about the size of one of those that the officials
had used. There were Ari and Nofret, bent over
a table with something spread out over it. There
were no torches here; instead, lamps provided
much clearer, steadier light, including a lamp-
stand at each of the four corners of the table.
They were looking at a map, he saw, as he drew
nearer. But it was the biggest map he had ever
seen in his life.

A table to one side, pushed up against the wall, was laden with food: grapes, pomegranates, figs, flatbread and loaf bread both, honey cakes, butter and cheese, lettuce, green peas— and not that roast duck Kiron had scented but a glorious roast goose. It was missing one leg. The leg was in Ari's hand, and the Great King looked very like the old Ari as he took bites as someone—from the war helmet, Kiron thought it might be Ari's Captain of Thousands— pointed to something on the map.

"Kiron," said Ari without turning around. "Get food and come over here and tell us exactly what you found. Kamas-hotet, where's that map of Bukatan?"

A fellow with the sidelock hairstyle of a scribe went to a basket of scrolls and pulled one out without even looking at it, spreading it out on the table on top of the big map and weighing down the edges with little faience scroll weights in the shape of beetles so it wouldn't roll up again.

Kiron didn't have to be told what to do twice; his stomach felt as if it was pressed against his backbone. He heaped a platter with slices of goose, a slice of loaf bread spread with soft cheese, and grapes. "Kiron, come tell us everything you saw, from the beginning," Ari said. "Here's the map of the town you were in."

Between bites, Kiron related everything that

they had seen, from the moment they approached the place from the west, to the time the trail of the (presumably) now-captive townsfolk and soldiers ended and the trails of the slave traders began.

When he had finished, Ari and Nofret looked to the man in the war helmet.

"This was planned," he said flatly. "It was planned for some time, and carefully executed. Let us leave aside how the townsfolk were bewitched; that is a matter for the priests to worry over. But look at this—"

He drew a line on the map with his finger, from the outskirts of the town to the place where Kiron guessed that the slavers had been, now marked with a red pebble. "I have planned many, many evacuations, Great Ones. I have had to evacuate towns and villages in time of war and in time of flood both. That distance is nearly exactly how long a group of people carrying children and infants can go before some begin to fall back because of exhaustion. I am speaking, of course, not of a measured and calm march, but of a forced one. In the ordinary sort of evacuation, people drop back all the time. In a forced march, fear bites at their heels, and only when the weakest are too tired to go on will you lose some. Whoever planned this knew all about such things. And whoever planned this did not want to leave so much as an infant behind."

Ari nodded somberly. Nofret, however, looked sick and troubled. "Forgive me, but—as a Royal twin of Alta, where we bought and used many slaves, I know something of slave traders. It is not often they wish to be burdened with children; young children tire easily and cannot keep up with adults. They then must be carried or conveyed some other way. And infants—" She shook her head. "Infants on such a march? I never heard of such being taken. So why would they want *all* of the people in the town? It cannot be because they did not want to leave abandoned children to die—"

"You ask that—" came a low voice from a shadowed corner behind Kiron, so that he jumped in startled surprise "—whose land played host to those abominable Magi?"

There was a crisp tap on the floor of that corner as they all turned around to face the speaker. Nofret inclined her head. "It is something I would rather not contemplate, my Lord Priest," she replied. "That some of the Magi could have survived . . ."

The shadowy figure seated there in the corner shook his head. "Bah. They learned their tricks from somewhere. It need not be the Magi of Alta behind this—though I would by no means be surprised to learn that some had indeed survived. It could be others of the same sort. It could be these are the source of their evil. It could be that this is evil of the same kind but a different source."

Kiron made out more of the seated figure in the corner as his eyes adjusted to the shadows. It was a man in the simplest possible robes of a Tian Priest, with none of the ornaments that most boasted. With one difference. A clean bandage covered his eyes. He was blind.

"And don't call me 'my lord priest.' I am no one's lord. I am simple Rakaten-te. The name I was born with will do nicely."

The bandaged, sightless eyes turned in Kiron's direction. "So this is the young one you've put in charge of your new Jousters." Kiron felt a kind of coolness pass over him, and had the sense of being weighed and measured, but for what, he could not have said. "He'll do."

Although the priest had a face that was un-lined, and like all priests, his head was shaved so there was no telling if his hair was white or black, Kiron had the sense that he was long past middle age.

But there was that about the priest—not the least of which that he was seated in the presence of the Great King and Queen—that commanded a special respect. "Thank you, Rakaten-te," Kiron replied, with the Altan salute.

"Oh, you would not thank me if you knew what I am, boy," the priest said with a low chuckle. "I am the Chosen of Seft."

Kiron blanched. He had only heard of the Chosen of Seft in the hushed whispers reserved for tales of angry ghosts and terrible revenge. Seft was worshipped, it was true—or rather, it was more true to say that that dark god, brother to Siris, was propitiated rather than worshipped.

Now all the gods had their dark side. The benevolent Haras was known to go quite mad at times and forget even who his friends and allies were. Nofet was the gentle goddess of night and women with child, but she also ruled over plague. And of course, there was the sun-disk of Re-Haket, which brought life but also death, both in the most fundamental of ways—light after darkness, but also the hammer on the Anvil of the Sun. Warmth that called seedlings out of the earth, and the fire that burned them where they grew.

Still! Seft! He of the underworld, through which the sun-disk must pass each night, he who murdered his own brother that he might have Iris to wife, the Father of Curses, the Brother of Lies . . .

"When you wish to catch a thief, young Captain of Jousters," said the priest, a little smile playing over his mouth, "do you set a virtuous man to find him? Of course not. The youngest child will lisp the old saying, 'set a thief to catch a thief.' There is no one in all of Tia, aye, nor of Alta, that knows more about the dark magics than I. If you wish to hunt for the makers of the darkest of magics, you need someone who works such things himself. I am that person; I hold the Rod and Whip of Seft. It is why I was blinded when I was Chosen. The god himself marked me as his and made sure I could be nothing else."

Kiron gulped. *Blinded? They blind their priest? But—but—*

The priest chuckled. "I was Chosen at birth, boy. I have known nothing else. Do not feel sorry for me, I can know more things with my four senses than you can with five. And take my advice. Never wrestle with a blind man. You will always lose."

He turned his head back in Nofret's direction. "The dark magics are one thing. Blood magic is another. The more potential life is cut short, the more power is generated. I have no doubt that whoever lured those people away demanded the infants and children as compensation. You might find a grave full of them, but more likely, the scavengers have dragged them all away. A wise precaution and one any blood mage would take to keep them from haunting their killers."

Kiron felt a shudder convulse him, Nofret choked on a sob, and Ari's face went blank. Even the Captain of Thousands muttered a curse. The old man looked at them all with pity.

"The truths that no one wants to hear are the

ones most needful to be said," the priest told them all. "That is the way of things. My lord Seft is the god of all hard things. Hear this: the ignorant say that Seft slew Siris to take his wife. That is the fool and the common man who think this, for they would have done so, had their brothers taken to wife the Star of the Universe." He snorted with veiled contempt. "Here is the great mystery that we are taught in Seft's halls—Siris had to die to become Lord of the Dead. The Dead required a Lord and King on the other side of the Star Bridge, and Siris knew he must be that King. Yet a god cannot slay himself, and he laid it upon his brother, who is the Finder of the Way, to find the way to slay him. So Seft did, that Siris could cross the Bridge and take up the Crook and Flail among the Dead."

"But what of his taking the Lady Iris?" asked Nofret sharply.

"Oh, that," the old man said with a sly smile. "She was alone and a widow and the fairest of all the goddesses, with breasts as firm and round as young melons, and lips as sweet as pomegranates, so say the scrolls. Who could blame Seft for taking her into his house? Even a god is sometimes a man."

Nofret flushed, though whether from annoyance or embarrassment, Kiron could not have said.

"But you did not ask me here to hear of the

loves of the gods," Rakaten-te continued. "You asked me to tell you whether or not this was dark magic, and I tell you it is, of the darkest. That those children are gone tells me that. I cannot tell you who or why, but I will uncover the mystery." He turned to Kiron. "This will take time. You, Jouster, will wait here in the Dragon Courts while I do my work. I may yet require a dragon and his rider."

There was only one reason why the old man would want him to wait. . . .

He started to open his mouth to say that there was not a chance under heaven that he would take an old blind man out to the deserted city. Started. Then he thought better of it.

What, after all, did he know of magic? Not much. And of the terrible magics the Magi used? Nothing at all.

It might be that the only way to unravel the mystery would be to take this man to where the mystery was.

"If I can send a younger man, I will," Rakaten-te said, with a wry twist of the lips. "I have no more desire to undergo the rigors of such a journey than you want to take me on it. But it may be that I will need to go. Save the Great King, you are the most experienced Jouster riding these tamed dragons that there is."

Kiron nodded reluctant agreement.

"You also have faced the Magi personally,

Kiron," Nofret pointed out. "You know something of what to expect."

He nodded, though reluctantly, and the urgent discussion moved on to other aspects of the
situation. And try though he might to stay
awake, he found himself yawning when he no
longer needed to answer questions.

At last Ari took pity on him and dismissed
him. But only after calling in a servant to guide
him back out again. A good thing, too, or he
would have gotten lost.

He checked on Avatre; she could have been a
stone for all that she moved. He thought about
stumbling as far as his usual quarters—

But the sand was soft and comfortable and
he thought he would just curl up with her for
a little.

And that was the last thing he knew until dawn
brought a chorus of birdcalls and the stirring of
all things in the Dragon Courts to wake him.

# TWELVE

IT had all started like a perfectly unremarkable day. Sutema woke, ate, begged for caresses, and slept again. Peri then got her bath and fresh clothing, as always, reveling in the scent of the clean linen and marveling anew that she had the luxury of clean clothing every single day. Then she went in search of food for herself before the day's lessons, both for Jousters and little dragons, began. There had been some fuss over the last few days about comings and goings from the Palace, but really, though those who had been priestesses might find such things worth chattering endlessly about, for Peri, it was not anything that would make any difference in *her* life, so she ignored it.

And that was where "ordinary" ended. Peri stopped in surprise at the doorway to the courtyard where all of the Jousters and Jousters in training ate, and stared, hardly able to believe her eyes. It was Lord Kiron. What was *he* doing here? No one had said anything about him appearing. It wasn't as if he was a courier, to come and go unannounced.

He looked very tired, and he was plainly wearing a borrowed kilt, as it was a little too long on him and extended down over his knees. He must have arrived last night.

Perhaps all that business that the other girls had been so excited about had brought him; with so many comings and goings between all of the temples and the Palace, perhaps this was something that would make a difference to the Jousters.

Then something else occurred to her, that last night, it was rumored, the Chosen of Seft himself had made a visit to the Palace.

The Chosen of Seft! The Altan equivalent was Sheften, and in one of the rare cases of total accord between the Two Kingdoms, in both the Altan and Tian pantheons, the god had betrayed and murdered his brother, and tried to force his brother's goddess-wife into marriage. Seft was the lord of dark doings, of rumors and shadows and hidden knowledge. His Chosen almost never left the Temple of Seft.

For indeed, Seft was worshipped, as was Sheften, and openly; both gods had temples, but that was largely on the basis of the idea that it was better to coax the god into leaving you alone than it was to leave *him* alone and take the chance that he would turn his attention on you.

Among the ordinary people, the serfs and the slaves, the tales of what went on in those temples ranged from the prurient to the profane. In general, anyone wishing to propitiate the god into indifference simply delivered his or her sacrifice at the door, to be collected by the silent and faintly menacing acolytes, then hurried off. Seft's Temple was not a place where you wanted to linger—oh, no.

And yet—it was said among the Jouster-priestesses that, other than being a place where shadows instead of light ruled, and the most sacred sanctuary was all in darkness, the temple of Seft was, if anything, more ascetic, more spare, than any other in Mefis. That there were mysteries there too deep for common folk even to begin to understand. That Seft's priests never offered their aid with dark magics and cursing, even when one came to them precisely for that purpose, and that no matter what occurred there, it had a profoundly important purpose.

Frankly, Peri didn't believe them. First of all, they were all priests together, and priests protected each other, even when there was some-

thing bad going on. She remembered a scandal
from her own home village and one of the temples there, and not that of Seft either, but of
Ghed, who was a jolly god, and one of the few
for whom there really were no darker or more
violent aspects. People reasonably assumed that
any house of Ghed was a safe one for children.
The priest had been taking advantage of the little girls, inviting them to come and decorate the
altar with flowers, then filling them full of palm
wine, and when they were too dizzy to think,
filling them with something else entirely. And
what had happened to him when he was found
out? Nothing. Other than that he was whisked
away and another priest put in his place. He suffered no punishment at all so far as Peri knew.
The other priests of other gods would not say
nor hear a word against him, in turn saying only
that "The matter is dealt with."

Ah, no. Priests stuck together, and she would
trust nothing from former priestesses without
confirmation. Nor from priests either, but from
common ordinary people who had seen things
with their own eyes.

But there was no reason to doubt that the Chosen of Seft had made a long visit to the Palace
last night, and that was a curious thing indeed.
The very servants were talking about it as they
brought the meat for the baby dragons this
morning, and she had heard murmurs of aston-

ishment coming from over the kitchen wall before she had left last night.

Reclusive did not even begin to describe the
Chosen of Seft. He had not emerged from his
temple even when the Royal Family itself was in
the thrall of the Magi. So why should he come
out for the sake of one who was (to be totally
honest) a bastard offshoot of the Royal Bloodline? Was it only because Ari was all that was
left of that line?

That was what had the lady Jousters all a-
twitter last night. Temple talk, palace talk, again,
and once again, nothing she could really share.
She'd listened to it without speaking while she
ate, then took her leave. She had gone back to
Sutema and then, since this was a rare night
when she was not watching over all the babies,
she paid a visit to Letis, with the intention of extracting every bit of information about her missing son Kiron as ever she could. The more she
knew about the boy, the more likely it was she
could match him with the man. Or not. But that,
after all, was the point.

Letis, for her part, was never reticent about
talking about her long-missing son. She filled
Peri's ears with tales of the boy, which included
the sorts of things that Peri was really hoping to
hear, since they were stories that it was unlikely
some other boy would match. These were the
sorts of things that most mothers liked to tell

about their children, unique and often funny. One such was an incident where he and his eldest sister had gotten into a quarrel, and she, furious and helpless because her mother had supported Kiron despite his being in the wrong, had waited until he got too near to her, then dusted his hair with the flour she had just finished grinding. And that, in turn, had made *him* so incoherently angry that Letis had feared he would take the pestle and beat his sister with it, and had separated them both for the rest of the day.

Letis found that incident utterly hilarious; she thought it funny that the eldest girl, the one she seemed to think not much of, would be so angry at being put "in her place." And she saw nothing wrong with supporting her adored son even when he was wrong, because he was the only boy. Peri for her part could only reflect that it was, in a way, a very good thing that Kiron had been separated from the family at so young an age, or he would have been spoiled beyond all correcting as a child, and that alone probably would have led to an early death among slaves and serfs. But perhaps Kiron's father had taken a firm hand with his son and kept the boy from becoming too full of himself.

She had not had the slightest notion when she came back late from her visit, and fell onto her pallet, that her quest for ways of identifying Letis' son would be put to the test so soon. She stared at the apparition with blank astonishment that would have been embarrassing and obvious if Lord Kiron had glanced in her direction.

Lord Kiron, however, was not alone. Two of the other female Jousters in training were sitting at the same table as he was, and two of the four couriers as well, and presiding over all of them was Lady Aket-ten. All five of them were throwing questions at him without regard for the fact that the poor fellow was trying to eat.

She took a deep breath, and walked in with as normal a demeanor as she could manage, both excited, and apprehensive. What if he found her questions impertinent? What if he thought she was rude and intrusive? What if he turned out not to be Letis' lost son? She felt her throat tighten and her hands grow damp with nerves. The others, however, paid not the least attention to her. They were all too busy quizzing the poor young man on why he was here and why he had spent so much time at the Palace last night.

That was a piece of information she hadn't had until that moment. So he *had* come in last night! Probably he had arrived about sundown, after she had gone off to visit Letis. When she had returned, she had gone straight to her bed, so of course no one would have told her anything. She held her peace and simply watched and listened.

He ate slowly and deliberately, and did not allow them to rush him, nor make him try and talk through a mouth full of food. It shortly became painfully clear that he was not going to tell them why he was here, except that he was on "the Great King's business."

"And what of the Great Queen?" Aket-ten asked testily, brows furrowing as if she considered the omission some sort of slight.

"Hers, too," came the laconic reply. "They are one in this matter, as in most other things. Surpassingly in concord, are our rulers. Others could do well to follow their example."

Peri winced. Aket-ten did not seem to notice the veiled allusion to her own behavior. *It would be a lot better if Aket-ten didn't pick at him in front of the others. That can't be good for discipline.* "And what *is* this matter?" she persisted. "We are the Great Queen's Wing! Should we not be told?"

"There is nothing to tell," Kiron replied, and took a bite of bread and honey. "I have not leave to discuss any of it."

Let it rest, Aket-ten, Peri thought, wishing that her wingleader was as good at reading human thought as she was at reading animal.

"How long will you stay?" Aket-ten then said, taking a different approach.

"I do not know." Another bite of bread and

honey; Kiron chewed and swallowed meditatively.

Aket-ten bristled, as if he had somehow in-
sulted her with the simple answer. "I am the
Overseer of the Dragon Courts now," she responded, drumming her fingers on the table
with impatience. "I am responsible for provi-
sioning everyone here. There is another dragon,
another Jouster to feed, to care for. How am I to
plan for both of you if I do not know how long
you are to stay? What if my allotted provisions
run short?"

"As I am on the Great King's business, you
may apply to the Great King's vizier," Kiron
replied, and this time under all his seriousness
Peri was sure she saw a twinkle of amusement
in his eye. He was getting a certain amount of
pleasure from thwarting her, even tormenting
her with his secretiveness. "I am sure he will
leap to assist you in any way possible."

She heard laughter in his voice, then. So he
was teasing Aket-ten! She wondered if Aket-ten
realized this.

"You were at the Palace for simply ages," said
Min-kalet, she of the slender ankle and slightly
nasal voice: the former, which she displayed
whenever she could, and the latter, which she
seemed unaware of. She leaned over the table,
ignoring her own breakfast in her eagerness.
"Lord Kiron, were you with the Great King and

Queen? Was there a feast? What did you do there?"

"The Great King and Queen were my friends before they ascended the thrones of the Two Lands," Kiron replied looking as if he was choosing his words with great care. "It is rather surprising, really, that I have not been there before. They had need of me, so they summoned me here; it was a thing of duty, not of pleasure, though it is always a pleasure to see them. There was no feast, but we had roast goose."

"Glazed with honey and stuffed with dates?" exclaimed slender West-keri, who had an unbridled passion for food of all sorts. "Or basted with butter and stuffed with bread and raisins? Or stuffed with a duck that was stuffed with a chicken that was stuffed with a quail that was stuffed with an egg?"

It was a daily wonder to Peri that West-keri remained so thin. She and her young dragon were a good match; both always seemed to be hungry.

"Just plain roast goose," Kiron smiled. "Though that was more than good enough. At Aerie, we do not get such things; we are too far from any water for goose or duck, too far into the desert for much that is fresh of anything." He raised an eyebrow at the girl. "I do not think you would like it there. It is more like living in a camp in the desert than living in a city. One day, perhaps, it will be a place like any other city, but that is for the future." Then he shrugged. "At any rate, this was nothing more than sharing an evening meal. It was not a feast, as I told you."

"It should have been." One of the couriers chimed in, and Peri smothered a smile when she saw the hero-worshipping look on his face. "They should have summoned you to reward you. You should have been given the Gold of Favor and the Gold of Honor, Lord Kiron."

Kiron laughed aloud. "To what purpose? When I was his dragon boy, Ari had a chest full of the gold, and never even looked at it. I am no courtier to wear that nonsense about; there are no festivals, no feasts at Aerie, we are working far too hard for such things. Serving well is enough of an honor."

Aket-ten rolled her eyes, when Kiron was looking the other way. Then he glanced back and caught her at it and his eyes glinted. "I am going to get no satisfaction from you, am I?" she demanded.

"You said yourself, you serve the Great Queen and answer only to her," Kiron replied, a little smile playing over his lips, but sounding as innocent as a child. "Go and ask her yourself."

The exasperated look that Aket-ten gave him made Peri hide another smile. Peri's only real rival here was doing herself no service with her attitude. Not that Aket-ten seemed to care.

Finally, she found an opening in the conversation to ask about Kiron's childhood, a moment when he reminded them all that he was from a very simple background and was more at home in the rough surroundings of Aerie than the Palace—"Unlike you, Aket-ten." That was when Peri metaphorically pounced. He seemed very grateful for the change in subject, and as a consequence readily answered questions that under other circumstances would have been considered impertinent, not to mention prying.

And the more she asked . . . the more points of identity she had. He had the right number of siblings and the right ages. And although Letishanet was a very common name for an Altan woman—it meant "flower of the goddess"— still, there was that point of identity as well. Unfortunately all he remembered of his sisters were the pet names he had for them, which didn't match what Letis had called them. But other than that, she soon had almost all the evidence she needed. Until she pulled out the final jackal for her game board . . .

"Surely your sisters cannot always have been inclined to spoil you at every opportunity!" she laughed. "Surely there must have been times when you were at each others' throats! I have never in all my life heard of siblings who did not fight, especially eldest with youngest!"

He smiled a little. "Well," he began, slowly. "There was *one* time—"

And as he recited the story, with much laughter all around, she knew that she had what she needed and wanted. It was the same incident. Him winning the argument only because his mother said he should. His sister going red in the face with anger. The handful of flour thrown into his hair. *Him* going red in the face with anger as the "insult" sent him into a senseless fury. His mother finally intervening, separating them for the rest of the day, only to bring them back together again at sunset and force them to apologize to each other.

"Oh, now I can admit that I was completely in the wrong," he laughed. "And I know now that the reason I became so angry was precisely because I was in the wrong and would never have admitted it then. But I was an arrogant little toad then, and as sure that I was the ruler of all about me as any Great King."

"Aren't all boys?" she teased.

"And all girls are the Princesses of the Household, and just as arrogant in their way!" he challenged her. "There was many a time when my sister won an argument only because my grandmother supported *her* with no more reason but that she was a girl and must therefore know all things!" He chuckled. "That was the great ri-

valry in that house; my father's mother supporting the girls because my mother supported and
spoiled me. And yet, let a neighbor so much as
deign to hint that any of us were less than perfect, and lo! The ranks were closed, the armies
assembled, and they faced the enemy as one!"

Peri laughed, able to see it all so clearly, for exactly the same situation was true in most of the
village families she had grown up around.

By then, bored with it all, the rest had drifted
away, even Aket-ten, who looked rather determined to, in fact, go to the Great Queen and
demand to be told what this "business" was all
about.

Well that was her outlook. Peri was only interested now in one thing. This *was* Letis' son; this
was the young man that her friend was determined she wed. And she liked him—oh, how
very much she liked him, indeed!

And he was smiling at her as he had not
smiled at any of the others.

Her heart lifted, and an unexpected thrill
went through her.

She felt her breath catch, she flushed—and she
quickly turned the conversation back to his past.
Because now she wanted to hear it. All of it.

Because it was his, and no other's, and she
wanted to know everything, everything that
had made him what he was.

* * *

When the little female Altan Jouster in training took herself off to her duties, Kiron rose and stretched and immediately forgot all about her. Her simple questions, her conversation, had been a much-needed distraction, but now he needed to return to the Palace. Not to hare off after Aket-ten—though he was going to have to apologize to her at some point for teasing her in front of her wing—but because it would be better if no one had to send a servant to go looking for him if he was needed. And because if he was going to have to take the Chosen of Seft back to the border, he might need some special arrangements and the best person to arrange those was probably Ari's own vizier.

As he had partly anticipated, he was expected at the Palace, and arrangements were already in place for him to bypass most of the protocol that others had to thread. He did have to present himself to the Keeper of the Door as any other petitioner, but once his name was known, the man nearly turned himself inside out to get Kiron straight to the rulers. Within moments, he was put into the guidance of one of Nofret's personal servants and taken straight to Ari and Nofret's private quarters, just as he had been last night. This time, however, the rooms that had been empty were thronged with people, many of whom looked at him with curiosity, envy, or both as he passed.

It was to a different set of rooms that he was taken this time, in the womens' wing, and by the opulence, the wall paintings of Queens being greeted as equals by various goddesses, it was Nofret's own suite of rooms. Which was—and he would have expected this, if he had just thought about it—where he found Aket-ten, alone in one of the rooms set aside for those who were especially favored of the queen. Servants there offered them both drinks and little dainties; he declined, but Aket-ten took a delicate goblet of pomegranate juice absently, staring at him with a rueful expression on her face.

"Aket-ten, I really need to apologize—" he began.

Just as she blurted, "Kiron, I have been a pig-headed goose—"

They looked at each other, and laughed nervously.

"You have, and I have," he said. "And we were both wrong, and that is of little importance right now. Now . . . did they tell you what is toward?"

"A very little. Enough to frighten me half to death. *Could* some of the Magi have escaped?" she asked, and she truly did look frightened. "Do you think they really have set themselves up in the east?"

She shuddered. Well, he couldn't blame her. She, not he, had been the one they had held captive. She, and not he, had been the one that had seen the evils of the Magi in a very personal way; they had, not once, but twice tried to drain her of her power and spirit, and she had felt their dreadful power at first hand.

They had cut her down out of the sky and taken her captive, and the last thing she had seen as they dragged her away had been Re-eth-ke lying in a crumpled heap on the ground. She, not he, had been the one to think she had lost her dragon forever.

To contemplate the idea that some of those same Magi could still be alive must be the stuff of her worst nightmares.

He had to shrug. "There is no telling. That is what the Chosen of Seft hopes to learn, I suppose. But as he rightly said last night, the Magi are not the only ones of their sort in the world. He pointed out that they had to learn their magic from somewhere . . . and that *is* the border over which the Nameless Ones came."

She bit her lip. "That is another thing I would rather not think about. The Nameless Ones . . . what if we must face them again?" She rubbed her hands together nervously. "And another thing . . . we *thought* we knew why Aerie and Sanctuary were deserted. But what if we were wrong? What if it was magic that lured their people away—magic of the Nameless Ones—"

He grimaced; he didn't want to think about this either.

That is for wiser heads than mine—Ari and Nofret, Kaleth, and the Chosen of Seft. Not one simple wing-leader. "How are your Jousters?" he said instead, changing the subject, and grinned. "Have you found the need to set a watch on beds yet?"

She groaned. "I cannot do that, they are adults. Much though I wish I might. And when I move them to Aerie, it will be worse."

"Why move them at all?" he asked, invoking logic. "There is no real need, is there?"

"I—" she began, and was interrupted by the entrance of the Great Queen, who looked every inch the Great Queen indeed.

Nofret wore the tall ceremonial headdress, rather than the soft, draped cloth with the cobra headband. It was not as heavy as it looked, being made of starched blue cloth, adorned at top and bottom with a ribbon of gold. The head-dress, however, was the only thing other than her dress about her that was not heavy. She wore a collar of gold, coral, lapis lazuli, and turquoise beads, and a matching belt that encir-cled her hips and dangled two ends down to the floor. This, in turn, matched the beading on her sandals. She sported both upper and lower armbands of enameled gold as wide as Kiron's palm, and carried the same ceremonial crook and flail as Ari did; both of enameled gold, the stringers of the flail being composed of beads that matched the rest of her jewels.

Underneath all this, she wore a gown of closely pleated mist linen. Each such gown took one girl the better part of a day to wash and iron all the pleats back in. The jewels were so heavy that Nofret often changed gowns four and five times a day.

And the first thing she did when she entered the room was to hand over the crook and flail to the appropriate attendant, while her hairdresser came to lift the headdress from her head, revealing that she kept her hair cropped closely. It was the only sane solution. There were so many ceremonial hairstyles for a Great Queen, and all of them were so complicated, that the only way to deal with them was to wear wigs.

Another attendant came to lift the collar over her head with both hands, while a fourth removed the belt. Nofret herself kicked off her sandals and sank onto a couch with a sigh.

"Court would not be nearly so difficult if I didn't wear enough jewels to sink the royal barge," she complained, reaching for the fruit juice a fifth attendant brought her. The gown was now in crumpled ruins, rendered distinctly sorry looking by the heat and humidity and the press of the jewels. It hung limply from her shoulders, all the fine pleats vanishing. She sprawled onto the couch and allowed her attendants to fan her. "So, Ari told you the simple version, I trust?"

Aket-ten nodded her head.

"The complicated version is still simple at this point. There is too much we do not know, and the gods are not speaking to Kaleth. Tedious of them. Life would be so much simpler if they revealed everything to us like sensible beings." She handed the empty goblet to one of the attendants. "Kiron is here to transport whatever priest the Chosen of Seft designates to go back to the town. We want Kiron to do this because he is the *most* trustworthy of an already trustworthy lot and because of all of his experience. And because the Bedu trust him. That is no small thing."

"I feel very badly that I can do nothing," Aket-ten said plaintively. "It seems as if there should be something I can do. . . ."

"Train your couriers," Nofret replied instantly. "No, do more than train them. Your young women will be carrying messages of a sensitive nature, and it is imperative that they learn discretion. Make them see that they cannot conduct themselves like the little temple gossips they once were."

Aket-ten rolled her eyes. "Ask for a miracle," she muttered though Nofret probably couldn't hear it.

"Seriously, Aket-ten, if they become nexuses

of gossip, they will ruin the reputation of female Jousters for all time." Kiron put in. He had not wanted these women, but now that they existed, he had no intention of permitting them to fail. For all of their faults, he had seen them with their baby dragons, watched them grit their teeth and throw themselves into training. They *were* Jousters. "Just tell them that."

"Precisely." Nofret passed her hand through her cropped tresses. "They are not stupid, Aket-ten, or you would never have chosen them."

She nodded, chin firming.

"Enough of that," Nofret continued. "It is of little importance." She leaned forward and fixed them both with a steady gaze. "Kiron, the Chosen of Seft wants you here. So, Aket-ten, I am promoting both of you. Kiron, you are, as of this moment, confirmed as Lord of the Jousters. Aket-ten, you are his wing-second and speak with his authority. Ari agrees."

As the two of them started, and then stared at each other in shock, Nofret continued. "Above all else, Ari is a scholar and a scribe, and he has remembered most of the little that is known about the Nameless Ones. And if everything he thinks is true—" She paused.

"Then the Jousters may be the one thing that stands between us and their darkness."

# THIRTEEN

AKET-TEN gave Kiron a sharp look, but said nothing.

Then, crumpled dress and all, Nofret once again became the Great Queen. "And make it clear to the Queen's Wing that we are going to teach them combat," she said to Aket-ten, with a touch of challenge in her voice.

Kiron started. "Wh–what?" he stammered. He glanced at Aket-ten to see if she had instigated this, but she looked just as startled as he was.

"I am going to order you to either teach them combat yourself, or assign a senior Jouster to do so, Kiron," said Nofret, fixing him with a gaze that warned him she would accept no other an-

swer than "yes" right now. "When Aket-ten
began this project, I had no intention of ever letting these young women within a hundred
leagues of fighting. We may not have such luxury now. The Chosen of Seft has emerged from
his seclusion. The High Priest of Haras tells me
that this happens only when . . . there are drastic changes in the wind."

"More drastic than the destruction of Alta's
capital?" Kiron managed.

Nofret grimaced. "That," she pointed out del-
icately, "would not at the time have been the
concern of the Chosen of Seft, who is, after all, a
god of Tia."

"Hmm." Kiron had to agree with that.

"So we have not the luxury to plan for anything but the worst." Again Nofret hesitated.
"Ari is not happy. But we are one in this. We
may need every Jouster we can muster and if
some of those are women . . . so be it. If need be,
Ari and I will ride to battle."

"There is something you have not told us,"
Aket-ten said suddenly. "It is more than just the
Chosen of Seft coming out of seclusion."

Nofret bit her lip. "It is not just that Ari has
unease about the Nameless Ones. The gods are
not speaking to Kaleth because of a sudden
there is no clear future. Those with the ability to
see into the futures see nothing but mist and
shadows. *Something* has changed. Some new fac-

tor has entered onto the stage, and with that, everything has changed."

Aket-ten blinked. "How is that possible?"

Nofret shook her head. "Do not ask me these questions! I am no Winged One! I only know what Sanctuary has told us. If I had even a hint, it would help."

There was silence for a moment as even the discreet handmaidens paused and tendered each other worried glances. "Bah!" Aket-ten said finally. "We managed well enough when the Winged Ones were drained and could not Foresee. And what do peoples do who have no Winged Ones? We will find ways."

Nofret regarded her for a moment, then nodded. "So we shall. And now you know what I know." She paused a moment more. "Now that I have spoken to both of you, I would like you to do something, Aket-ten. I would like you to go to Aerie and speak with our friends, as their friend, and rather than having Kiron order someone to train them, find one *willing* to help to train the Queen's Wing. It may be that if *you* were to go and ask them yourself, there would be less . . . friction. I do not know, but it is worth trying."

"You can use my quarters, if it takes you more than a day," said Kiron, with a shrug, then felt moved to add, if she was feeling sensitive about it. "I will be here, so I will not need them. Or if I am not here, I will be ferrying the Chosen of Seft. In either case, I will not be *there*."

She had the grace to look uncomfortable. "I have not been the easiest of friends," she began awkwardly.

Nofret snorted, an unusual and un-queenly sound. "Take the reconciliation of lovers' quarrels elsewhere, if you please," she said dryly. "If your quarters are not sufficiently private, then tell my vizier you may have use of the royal barge."

Kiron couldn't help it; he burst out laughing. Aket-ten flushed, glared, then gave in with a wry shrug. "Very well, O my Queen," she said. "How else may we serve you?"

Peri could scarcely believe her good fortune. Lord Kiron was remaining for at least a day, perhaps more, and would be supervising their training in Aket-ten's absence. Now was her chance to impress him with her diligence. Not that she wasn't diligent all the time, but now he was here to see it.

She threw herself into the training with an enthusiasm that only grew whenever he complimented her. She listened with fierce concentration when he gave instructions or related some story pertinent to what they were learning. Today was only the second day that they were using the suspended barrel, and she stayed on it far longer than she would have thought possible.

When they'd all had their turn, he chuckled a bit, and motioned to the servants manning the ropes. "A *real* workout, if you please," he said, climbing into the saddle, and not fastening any but the main strap. "I would like the Queen's Wing to see what turbulence looks like."

The slave hauled the barrel aloft, and at his signal, began pulling at the ropes with twice and three times the strength they had been using with the girls. The barrel, with Lord Kiron firmly in the saddle, began to move.

Peri's eyes grew big as she watched the barrel being thrown about the air above the converted pen like a bit of debris in a windstorm. And he stuck to the barrel as if he was part of the saddle. She could scarcely believe her eyes. As for the others, when she glanced at them, she could see that they were also dumbfounded. There were at least two instances of the thing being sent up-side down.

Lord Kiron signaled to the servants, who ceased their tugging, and once the barrel had stopped moving, lowered it back down to the sand.

"This, Jousters, is why you need to practice before you take your dragons up for the first time," he said, as he unstrapped himself and stood up, breathing heavily. So it hadn't been as easy as it had looked from the ground. . . . "I am not saying that having your dragon in the midst of a thunderstorm is like that—it is different, and thus far we have managed no way to imitate that. For instance—there is the nausea-inducing plummeting spiral, that makes you certain you are going to die. But this, at least, begins to prepare you for the experience."

"But—" one of the other girls began. "We are only to be couriers—"

"And as couriers there is no telling when you *must* deliver an urgent message. But—" Lord Kiron looked them over measuringly, "circumstances are such that the Queen has ordered you to have combat training as well."

Shocked silence descended.

"If any of you do not feel that you can accept this, please say so now," Kiron continued. "We know that while baby dragons much prefer their surrogate mothers over anyone else, that affection can be transferred to a new surrogate if—"

He was interrupted immediately by all of the young women trying to talk at once. He folded his arms and put up with it for a little while, then cut them short with an abrupt gesture for silence.

"You will be carrying messages of great importance," he pointed out. "Urgent enough to require that a Jouster make all speed with them. Enemies both within and outside the Two Lands may often want to stop you. *How* our dragons are trained is no secret now, so it is entirely possible that some enemy could train a dragon and rider of his own to come after you. A single skilled archer could be sent to shoot you down. And if there is fighting, you may well find yourself carrying messages to those in command of our troops. The Queen is not minded to send you into danger without preparation, and neither am I. But if you do not feel equal to this task, there is no shame in stepping down, and there are a dozen male Jouster candidates waiting for every new dragon that I—"

This time he was interrupted, though most respectfully, by Kene-maat, who, when the former priestesses were all responding as a group, tended to be their spokesperson.

"We are equal to anything, Lord Kiron," she said, raising her chin as the others nodded. "Whoever thinks that women have no courage is a fool. But we had thought that there were objections enough to our mere existence, without encouraging further ire against us by giving us combat training."

"And who but you of the Queen's Wing and I and the Great King and Queen are to know it is combat training?" he countered, giving her a hard look. "Consider this a test of your discretion."

She blushed, and Peri knew why. Of all of them, bold Kene-maat had the loosest tongue.

"I am taking you seriously," Lord Kiron said at last. "You should take yourselves seriously. Certainly the enemies of the Two Lands will do so. They cannot afford to do otherwise."

It had been a strange day. It was about to get very much stranger.

Peri was helping Sutema exercise her wings, getting the little dragon to chase her and play "tag," wings flapping with excitement as she did so. Sutema's eyes flashed with delight; this was one of her favorite games, and she would play it until she had to flop down in the sand, panting with exertion. And eventually she did just that, then dozed off suddenly as all young creatures tended to do. Peri took the moment to go looking for something—a bench that could be weighted down with stones, perhaps—that Sutema could jump onto and hold while she flapped her wings, as Peri had seen young birds do on the edge of a nest.

But she had not gotten very far before she ran into a servant who was evidently looking for her.

"There is a person in the kitchens, Jouster, looking for you," the servant said, looking at her oddly. "She says that she knows you, and seemed surprised that you were not in the kitchen." The servant sniffed. "We thought at first she was looking for a place herself. Her name, she says, is Letis-ha—"

And at that moment, a harried and slightly overheated looking Letis came hurrying around the corner from the same direction as the servant had come. "Peri!" she exclaimed, catching sight of her younger friend. "I thought that as today was your free day, and mine, too, I would come spend it with you, but these people did not seem to know—and what are you doing out here—"

And at the exact same moment, rounding another corner, came Lord Kiron. "Jouster Peri!" he called. "I wanted to ask you—"

They both stopped short, staring, not at Peri, but at each other. Letis turned white, and put her knuckles to her mouth. "Kiron?" she whispered, eyes as large and wide as any gazelle's.

Meanwhile Kiron had put one hand on the wall beside him to steady himself. "Mother?" he gasped. "Mother—is that—"

Letis shook her head, hard, and rubbed her eyes. "Kiron?" she faltered. "S–son?"

And in the next moment, oblivious to anyone else, they ran to each other's arms. Both talking at once, laughing and crying, Peri could only catch snatches of what they were saying.

". . . look just like your father . . ."

". . . Ari's vizier searched, but couldn't find . . ."

". . . Iris is with me . . ."

". . . thought you must be . . ."

". . . knew you would be . . ."

Finally, Letis pulled a little away from Kiron and actually looked at him. "What are you doing here? This is where the Jousters are. Are you a dragon boy?"

Kiron flushed. "I'm a Jouster, Mother. Actually, I'm Lord of the Jousters. At least for—"

Letis frowned suddenly. "This is no time to be making up—"

"Lord Kiron!" Yet another servant came pounding up. "Lady Aket-ten wishes you to come to the Palace. You are urgently sought for by the Great Queen."

Kiron cursed. "Of all the times— Mother, this is Peri-en-westet—"

"I—" Peri just knew that Letis was going to say "I know who she is, I came looking for her," but Kiron didn't give her the chance.

"She's one of the Jousters from the new Queen's Wing. She can tell you all about what is going on. I will be back as soon as ever I can. *Don't leave* until I am back." With that, Kiron set off at a run, the servant that had come to get him trailing along behind.

Letis turned slowly to look at Peri, clearly still in something of a state of shock.

Finally she spoke, her eyes narrowing. "What did he mean, you are a Jouster?"

"You cannot be a Jouster."

It was about the sixth or seventh time Letis

had said this, and Peri was getting rather tired of it.

"Are you saying that Kiron, Lord of the Jousters of the Two Lands, friend to the Great King and Queen, *and your son,* is a liar?" she finally snapped.

Since she had rarely used even a harsh tone with her friend before this, the anger in her voice took Letis aback. She stepped back a pace, and regarded Peri with narrowed eyes and furrowed brow, an expression which made her crow's-feet wrinkles even more prominent.

And, in fact, which made her look rather like the evil old mother-in-law of storytellers' tales.

But she isn't, Peri reminded herself. *It is hardship and suffering that put those marks on her. Not an evil temper.*

"You never said you were a Jouster. You said you had work at the Dragon Courts," Letis finally said.

"And so I do. Being a Jouster-in-training. Would you have believed me if I had told you I was to be a Jouster of the Queen's Wing?" Peri countered, reining in her own temper.

"You cannot be a Jouster," Letis said flatly. "This is some foolish whim of the foreign Queen. Women cannot be Jousters, commoners cannot be Jousters, and no Tian will allow an Altan Jouster to exist for very long. Once the nobles of Tia get wind of this, you will find yourself on the street outside the Dragon Courts, and count yourself fortunate if you have not got stripes on your back to boot." She nodded decisively, convinced by her own arguments.

"Your own common-born Altan son is Lord of the Jousters of the Two Lands, the Queen's Wing is approved by the Great King as well as the Great Queen, and there are both Altan and Tian Jousters in Aerie at this moment," Peri countered, with growing irritation. "The wingleader of the Queen's Wing is Lady Aket-ten, *also* Altan, *also* a woman."

"But *not* a commoner!" Letis pounced on that like a bird on a beetle.

Peri sighed in exasperation. "Fully half the Jousters of the Two Lands are common-born now," she retorted. "High birth is no great recommendation for getting a dragon."

"You will never get a dragon," said Letis.

"I *have* a dragon, which I am going to now!" Peri snapped, and turned on her heel to stalk off in the direction of Sutema's pen. Letis remained where she was for a moment, then ran after her. Peri did not look back. She had never before seen this side of her friend—angry, bitter, and determined to be right even when she was completely wrong.

It made Peri wonder belatedly what sort of mother-in-law she *would* make.

No matter. Sutema's pen was not that far, and

Letis had kept her arguing for so long that the little dragon was awake and looking for her surrogate mother. With a yelp of joy, she lumbered across the sands to Peri as soon as Peri appeared in the door.

With a yelp of a different sort, Letis leaped backward into the corridor.

Peri paid her no mind, being far too busy reassuring Sutema that all was well, for the dragon was acutely sensitive to mood and had sensed Peri's irritation. When golden chin was scratched and emerald brow ridges were rubbed, and Sutema was soothed into happy playfulness again and busy with wrestling a bull's leg bone into submission, only then did Peri turn back to the doorway where Letis stood uncertainly.

"Rather substantial for something that doesn't exist, don't you think?" Peri said.

Letis eyed the dragon with apprehension. "They'd take it away from you," she said weakly.

"Sutema is a *she*, and they can't take her away. She is bonded to me. It is how the new Jousting dragons are raised, from the egg or nearly, tame and bonded to one rider." That was not exactly the truth, but Letis would hardly know that. "She cannot be taken from me."

Letis eyed the dragon with misgiving. "But women—"

"Make as good a Jouster as a man, if all one is doing is courier work," Peri said firmly. "This frees men to hunt bandits."

Letis looked as if she was digesting this. "I cannot like this," she said sourly. "This is too much rising above your place."

"Your son is Lord of the Jousters of the Two Lands," was all Peri said. "And now it is time for me to feed my dragon."

Letis beat a hasty retreat, and Peri did not see nor hear from her for the rest of the day, although the servants said she had gone to Kiron's quarters and was waiting there for him.

That was fine with Peri. This was not at all how she had planned for this to go. . . .

Kiron's head was swimming by the time he got to the Palace. He could hardly believe it. After all this time—

And it wasn't as if he hadn't been looking for her . . .

Well, admittedly, he hadn't personally been looking for her. One of the scribes in Ari's service was, trying to trace her through the various sales of their land. But hers was not an uncommon name, and the war had complicated matters, and so far the scribe had had no luck.

But to have her simply turn up like that—

He was happy—oh yes—but he was as much

shocked as he was happy. And she looked *old*, old and bitter.

Well . . . given all that she had suffered, it was no surprise that she looked bitter. Really, he should have been surprised if she had not.

Still, Jouster Peri-en-westet was Altan, and would take care of her until he got back. He ran on to the Palace, trying to regain a sense of calmness. This was duty, and duty came first. Duty always came first.

Where did she come from? Where has she been? And how did she come to the Dragon Courts? And as important as how, *why?*

She couldn't have been looking for him. She had been as shocked to see him as he was to see her.

By now, he was a familiar sight in the Palace. Servants parted crowds to let him through. He arrived at Nofret's rooms without any significant delay.

He half expected Rakaten-te to be there, but it was another, a junior priest of Seft, who waited diffidently for his arrival.

Nofret gazed at him somberly, as did—Ari! He had not expected the Great King to be here in the middle of the day, but one look at Ari's face told him why. The Priests of Seft had no good news for the Two Lands.

"This will be ill hearing," Nofret said, as he bowed to her and to Ari, then waited for the latter to wave him into a seat. "The Chosen of Seft had already sent word, so I decided to wait until we were all here to listen to it."

Kiron nodded and sank into a chair. The young priest cleared his throat with care.

"Our sort of hunting has found a place where the darkest of magics have been performed," the priest said. "And, as was warned, there are many deaths in that place. It is not far from where your trail from the city ends—

"So the deaths were probably the children and elderly." Kiron felt ill. The priest nodded.

"We all will want you to confirm that," Ari said into the awkward silence. "When you go back out there, we'll want you to find the place where the bodies are."

Kiron nodded; there didn't seem to be any sort of graceful response to that order. Then again, a graceful response really wasn't what was needed. "Has anyone been chosen to go from your temple yet?" he asked with great care and deference.

"The Chosen of Seft believes it will be himself, but the god himself will decide," the priest replied, with a look that warned he should ask no further. Kiron closed his mouth on all the other questions he wanted to ask. "And, as yet, we have been as unable to See past that barrier as the priests in Sanctuary."

Kiron shivered at that, for it implied that the

magic that had hidden the town was either very dark indeed—or very powerful. Or both.

"There is a flavor about it of the Magi," the priest was continuing. "But also a flavor of another sort. Something very . . . foreign. And that is all that I can tell you at this time about the magic. As for when you must be ready to leave, Lord Kiron, it will be at the end of three days. By then, the Chosen will have completed his preparations."

Kiron nodded, as did Nofret and Ari. "By then, Aket-ten will be back," Nofret observed, "and Kiron will be free to go. You had better begin making your own preparations, Kiron."

Taking that as a dismissal, Kiron bowed and backed out of the room.

Nofret and Ari scarcely noticed, so deep were they in plans with the young priest. This was fine; Kiron had no real head for strategy, and he knew it. The best thing he could do now was to go back to the Dragon Courts and begin writing out his requisitions.

And, of course . . . deal with his mother. Who was probably still waiting for him

He made himself hurry.

He had expected to find Letis with Peri. Instead he found her waiting in his rooms.

"By the gods, it *is* you," she said from out of the shadows of the little palms planted in their jars beside the pool. "Kiron—you look so like your father—"

And then she began to weep, and he caught her in his arms. He felt helpless and awkward then, and gradually it dawned on him why.

This might be his mother, but she was also a stranger to him.

The mother he had loved and cherished was gone into the past. He had no doubt that this *was* his mother. The trouble was, he had no idea who that person was anymore.

And he had even less of a notion how to let her know this thing.

# FOURTEEN

THE Chosen of Seft might be blind, but there was nothing wrong with the rest of his senses. He sat in a shaded corner of Avatre's pen, wearing the same tunic as Kiron himself, and because he was not used to riding, a pair of the leggings that Heklatis called "trews" such as the barbarians wore, to keep his legs from being chafed raw on the inside. "Curious," he said to Kiron, as the latter patiently tested every bit of harness and rigging on an increasingly impatient Avatre. "You seem both apprehensive and relieved at the prospect of this journey. I can understand the apprehension, but not the relief."

Kiron took his time in answering the implied question, and not just because he was trying to

avoid that particular subject. Even if Avatre was
getting impatient, Kiron had no intention of taking off without making sure of every piece of
equipment, every buckle, every strap. There
would only be three people out there this time;
himself, the Chosen, and—Aket-ten. If anything
went wrong, there were only two that really had
the skill to fix things. And if one or both of those
two were incapacitated, the result could be very
ugly. So Kiron was taking every step he could
think of to prevent anything from going wrong.

The Chosen said that the fewer living people
there were in the area, the easier it would be
for him to "read things." He did not specify
what "things" he would be reading, nor how,
and Kiron was not entirely sure he wanted to
know. The more he learned about magic, the
less he wanted anything to do with it himself.

The surprise had come when the Chosen in-
formed all of them that he wanted Aket-ten to
accompany them and assist him. Kiron gave the
priest a sideways glance as he tightened another
strap, then adjusted it minutely. And not for the
first time, he wondered; could they really trust
this man?

The reasons seemed good, sound, logical as he
enumerated them for the little conference. Aket-
ten was still technically a priestess, was definitely still a Winged One, had been trained to
assist at rituals. "She also has been used by the

Magi," the Chosen had said bluntly. "That left a mark on her that I can use for many purposes. It is one of the laws of magic, that things that have once been touched still retain the traces of that touching."

Oh, Kiron could certainly understand it. He didn't like it, but he understood it. And there was no real reason why she shouldn't go, no pressing duties with training her wing, because she had returned from Aerie with two victories. Huras, the patient, had agreed to be the trainer for her new Wing—and word from Haraket that he was, grudgingly, giving living room to the Queen's Wing in Aerie once they were trained and on duty. Aket-ten was thrilled, though she would have been less than thrilled had she heard what Huras had to say privately about it.

"Haraket's still predicting doom," the big man had said with a rueful smile, and an apologetic shrug. "He says that the girls will only serve to make the men act like idiots. But, he says, 'Better to have them acting like idiots under my nose, than having them finding excuses to fly off to Mefis every time I'm not looking.' He also thought it might discourage them, or even make them quit, if they left the luxurious life they have here and had to put up with what our life is like."

Haraket definitely had a vindictive streak in

him. And no, although Peri was used to hard living, none of the priestesses had ever done without very much. When they discovered the state of the food, the fact that they were unlikely to get twice-daily baths or relax in bathing pools, and that everything was in short supply, it would not make them happy. They would not like Aerie, or at least, they would not like it as it was now.

Well, none of that was going to happen until the little dragons were old enough to fly the enormous distance from Mefis to Aerie. And that would not be any time soon. They weren't even flying yet, much less flying with weight or for any distance at all. Who knew what would happen between then and now?

But having Huras in charge of training the Queen's Wing freed Aket-ten for this journey, which pleased the Chosen. Kiron was still not entirely certain how he felt about her coming with them. On the one hand, it would be very good to have Aket-ten to himself for a while. On the other hand, it meant that she was going into a potentially very dangerous situation. On the one hand, she was capable and competent. On the other hand, this was magic, and unknown magic to boot.

"So," the Chosen prompted, breaking into his thoughts. "What is it that makes you relieved right now? I would have thought, with all we are hazarding, you would have been entirely uneasy."

Kiron sighed, and gave a last tug to his saddle harness. "It is nothing, really."

The Chosen gave him a skeptical look.

He felt oddly like someone who has been caught in a lie. "Why do you want to know? It is only something personal . . . ."

"In magic, all things reflect one another and are reflected in one another," the Chosen said calmly. "I would not ask if I did not feel the need to know."

Kiron considered that. He really didn't want to discuss his feelings . . . but if this was going to affect the magic, he didn't have a choice. "It is truly nothing. Only that . . . my mother—"

"Ah. I heard something of that. Long lost to each other, discovered by accident in the Dragon Court. Like a market storyteller's tale." The Chosen's lips quirked a little. "I take it this was not the storyteller's ending."

Kiron sighed. "No . . . she wants me to . . ." He shook his head. The Chosen tilted his to the side.

"She wants you to be something you are not. She wishes to have again the small boy that was separated from her, who is always at her side, like a faithful hound, has no inconvenient duties that take him away from her, and who always obeys the least little wish his mother might have."

That was close enough. Too close for comfortable hearing, actually. He shut out the far-too-clear recollection of unceasing demands that he drop everything and get the family's farm back, that he give up being a Jouster and go back to his "real work" of being a farmer. Assertions that he would do this if he really loved his mother. Prim lectures on "knowing your place," and dark hints that all the people he called "friend" were merely using him and that once he had done what they wanted, he would find himself out of the Jousters and without a dragon. Three days of this, nonstop, every waking minute he had been with her. It had begun with subtle hints. It was far, far past subtle now. "Something like that . . ." He gave a last tug to the harness; good, it was as solid as the hand of man could make it. "It will be easier on you, sir, if we take off from the landing courtyard."

The Chosen got to his feet. "Very well. Lead the way. I shall follow."

Kiron gave a soft whistle, and Avatre got to her feet. He led the way into the corridor; usually, they took off straight from the pen, but he and Avatre had taken off from the landing courtyard often enough that she followed him with no sign of confusion.

He couldn't help but contrast this mentally with the "old days," of the dragon boys having to lead their charges with chains. Mostly they had been so drugged with *tala* that they didn't resist, but sometimes—sometimes it had taken two or even four strong handlers, with the danger that the dragon might stop resisting and start clawing or biting.

Aket-ten was waiting for him, already mounted on Re-eth-ke, when he arrived. In fact, there was quite a little audience to see them off, even though only he, Aket-ten, the Chosen, and Huras knew where they were going and why.

Letis was there, of course, and to his relief the presence of the Chosen of Seft was enough to keep her from asking questions he couldn't answer, or making any kind of a nuisance of herself. Huras had brought the Queen's Wing, under the guise of having them watch an expert flat take off. He and Kiron exchanged nods, while Aket-ten gave him detailed instructions that she had probably already given him twice over.

Kiron went straight to his mother and hugged her tightly, then kissed the top of her head. "I will see you soon, Mother, as soon as the Chosen releases me," he told her. She had begun hinting that he should allow her and Iris to move here— but Jousters had never had family here before, and at the moment he was reluctant to break that tradition. Instead, with the help of the Dragon Court overseer, he had settled her and his poor, damaged sister in their own little house, and arranged for them to get provisions and anything else they needed from the Dragon Court. There was that tradition, thank the gods; though Jousters seldom married, there was an arrangement for the care of dependent parents or siblings within reason; small houses in a little area near the court, mostly now as empty as the court itself. For now that would do, until he came up with another solution.

"When will that be?" she asked, her voice anxious.

"Only the Chosen knows, Mother," he was able to answer. She spared a nervous glance for the man who had already been helped into the second saddle behind Kiron's. Kiron gave her another kiss, then turned and trotted for Avatre, not even waiting for the dragon to extend her leg to scramble into the saddle ahead of the Chosen.

"Ready?" Aket-ten asked, and didn't wait for his answer, sending Re-eth-ke into the sky.

And Kiron was only too pleased to follow.

"Wings!" shouted Peri, raising her arms, and Sutema flapped her wings madly, raising a huge dust cloud that made her very glad she had decided to do this in the landing courtyard rather than the pen. The little green-and-gold dragon clung for her life to not one, but two perches, one for the hind feet and one for the front, made

of palm-tree trunks on legs that were weighed
down with bags of sand and gravel. It had taken
some persuasion to get her to climb up there,
and more to get her to understand what Peri
wanted, but now this was one of her favorite
games. It made Peri wonder if there was something about the strengthening wings that gave
the little dragons a strong urge to flap. The others, all younger than Sutema, were starting to do
the same thing, and Huras had ordered three
more sets of the perches after seeing Sutema exercising on them.

Despite the dust, Peri was enjoying herself.
The wind from Sutema's wings was a fine thing
on a hot day, and the way Sutema's eyes flashed
suggested that she was having a lovely time.

The other dragons were being exercised, each
by his or her own Jouster, as Peri had been exercising Sutema a few days ago, by running them
about in games of "chase." Huras had a very interesting way of dealing with the tendency of
the other girls to delegate such things to someone else—usually Peri. Aket-ten had confronted
them on it, which had simply made most of
them shrug and privately roll their eyes and
mostly ignore them. Huras had caught them at
it, telling Peri that they were going bathing and
"would she play with the babies" then starting
to walk off in a giggling, gossiping group without waiting for her answer.

But Huras had blocked the door with his considerable bulk and looked at them all reproachfully.

"If it was only once," he said, as they stilled, "I would have no issue with this if Peri does not. But the servants tell me that you do this every single day. Is this fair? Does Peri somehow *not* want to bathe in the heat of the day because she is not a priestess like all of you are? Is this how you want others to think of you, as the pampered priestesses who foist all of the work on Peri? Because they do."

It had been an interesting moment. Some had looked crestfallen, some shamefaced, some astonished, as if it had not even occurred to them that they were doing this. Peri had felt rather gratified, because on the whole, she *liked* all of them, and she wished that they were not doing this to her. They made her feel like—

"You are treating Peri as a servant, not as a fellow Jouster, nor a friend, which—if she is not—I am sure she would like to be," Huras continued, in an echo of her own thoughts. "She is senior to all of you in this wing, yet she does not demand that you defer to her."

Left unspoken, but certainly not unfelt, was the rest of that sentence. *Do not require or expect that she should defer to you.*

The entire encounter had been very gratifying for Peri. It remained to be seen whether the others would truly take it to heart, but she suspected that Huras would be continuing to keep an eye on them.

As for Sutema—

This was *much* more vigorous an exercise than being chased by Peri around a pen, or even the landing courtyard. It did not take long before Sutema was open-mouthed, panting, and exhausted. It was time to take her back to the pen, and there would be time afterward, once Sutema was napping, for Peri to have a swim herself.

And she wanted one; she was hot, sweaty and dusty, and the shaded pool in the center of the courtyard she shared with the others was appearing more inviting by the moment.

Only Sit-aken-te was there, and the lanky young woman waved languidly at Peri from where she was immersed up to her neck in cool water. Her body was invisible under the water-lily pads that covered the surface of the pool. For once, careless of the extra work for the servants, Peri stripped off her tunic and dropped it to the pavement, then sank into the cool water herself.

"A pity Lord Kiron is gone," Sit-aken-te said lazily.

"How so?" Peri asked, with a faint feeling of guilt. Had the others noticed all the time she had spent with Kiron? Did they guess at the game she was playing? It was a delicate balancing act.

Because Letis, along with the other demands she was making on her son, had wanted to present him with his wife-to-be as a *fait accompli*, and press him to wed her.

Peri was absolutely certain in her own mind that this would do her no good at all. She managed to persuade Letis to concentrate on what was, in Letis' mind, the more important issue anyway: getting the family home back.

It had been a long and tiring "discussion"—it was an argument, but that was not what Letis called it. Patiently, Peri had pointed out that Jousters seldom married, to which Letis replied that Kiron wouldn't *be* a Jouster once he had the farm back. That was when Peri had nodded and said, "So the important thing is for him to concentrate on that, then, and not get diverted."

She hated being so duplicitous, but she knew that having Letis present her *now* would only mean that Kiron would lump *her* in with all of the other pressures his mother was putting on him, and that would spell the end to any thoughts of love.

No young man really cares to have his mother pick out his wife, after all. Perhaps the noble-born and wealthy were used to that sort of thing, but they could afford concubines and mistresses and more than one wife. A young farmer needed to be sure that the wife he was getting was one *he* wanted. And though Kiron was no longer a farmer, and probably never would be one again, he *thought* like one of the young men in her village.

Meanwhile Peri had continued her quiet campaign. But if the other women had noticed . . .

"How so?" the other woman laughed. "He is easy on the eyes, that one. And much more amusing than our sober trainer or our quarrelsome wingleader."

So they hadn't noticed. She smiled with relief. "Now that is a true thing."

Her campaign was going well. Kiron sought out her company when he had time. He called her "restful." She spoke always of things he cared about—dragons, mostly, telling him of Sutema's antics, asking his advice. A man liked having a restful wife. Peace in the house; that was what they liked. A man liked to be deferred to.

It would be a strange sort of life. She could not imagine giving up Sutema, so they would be Jousters together, of course. What would that be like?

Hmm. Probably much like life now. Well, that was hardly a bad thing. Life now was very good, and she really could not see a way to improve on it.

"Hesh-ret is flapping his wings hard now," Sit-aken-te said into the hot silence. "I was glad when he tired, because he had long since worn me out. I think I will persuade him to use those perches tomorrow."

"You should use some other command than 'fly' when you want him to exercise his wings," Peri warned. "You'll want to use the word 'fly' later when he is really flying. I use 'wings.' But it really doesn't matter what word you use as long as the dragon understands what you mean."

Sit-aken-te laughed quietly. "Now that is a very true thing. Are you cool now? We could go study one of those scrolls Huras brought with him."

Peri flushed. "I cannot read," she said reluctantly.

Surely Sit-aken-te would stare at her in uncomprehending astonishment.

"I did not think you could, which is why I said we should study it together," the young woman replied. "You are sensible and practical, and we can, I think, do a commendable job of sifting grain from chaff together. Unless you had rather go to placate that friend of yours."

"Placate?" It hadn't occurred before to Peri that this was what she was doing with Letis. But it was, of course. That was exactly what she was doing.

The lily pads moved a little as Sit-aken-te shrugged. "One doesn't choose one's friends' friends. But I would not spend nearly the time with her that you do, if it were me. She does not approve of us, nor of your being one of us, and will not accept that you wish to be here. I would have reached the limit of my patience long ago. But then, she is not my friend. She may have many worthwhile qualities that I cannot see." The other woman chuckled a little. "And I must admit, her voice grates on me. I never could bear people whose words say one thing, while their spirit says another."

Peri blinked. "I must be missing something," she said carefully. "Whatever do you mean?" Was this a priestess attribute again?

"Hmm. It is a matter of paying a little less attention to what she *says* and more to the tone of her voice and the look in her eyes, the way she moves," Sit-aken-te explained. "She says that she is proud of her son, and yet I can tell that she is angry that he has risen to so high a place. She defers to us, and yet I can tell that she despises us because we are nobly born. Her words are soft and mild, yet her heart is full of bitterness and anger. I can understand why she would be so, of course, and in her place I should probably be just as bitter and angry. But this does not make her a comfortable person to be around. And if she would simply admit to you and to herself that this is how she feels, perhaps she could rid herself of some of it."

"She lost much," Peri replied, feeling as if she had to defend Letis now.

"So have others, on both sides," Sit-aken-te pointed out with justification. "But—there, you see, it is not my place to judge. I merely say I do not find her a pleasant person, and I would spend less time in her company than you do. If you would rather—"

The other woman rose from the water, and reached for a cloth to dry herself, though it was so hot that the faint breeze dried her before she even picked the oblong of linen up.

"No, no, if you will be so kind as to read the scroll to me, I had much rather do that while the little ones nap," Peri said hastily, also standing. "You do me a great favor."

"Well, and I do owe you for far too much time you spent watching over *my* dragon," the young woman replied, with a smile over her shoulder, as she shook back her hair and wrapped the linen around herself.

Peri did the same, feeling touched and a little surprised at the same time.

"Huras is right; we have been . . . hmm . . . taking advantage of your good nature," Sit-aken-te said. "It is time to change that."

Them-noh-thet, the Priest of Haras who had gone with Kiron the first time, had spent hours setting up elaborate ritual equipment to work his magic.

Rakaten-te, the Chosen of Seft, set up nothing but himself.

Kiron had more than expected the Chosen to ask him to find some other venue than the Temple of Haras and had resigned himself to moving all of the provisions that they had found to a new location.

Instead, Rakaten-te had dismounted—a bit stiffly, which was hardly a surprise, given his age—and followed Kiron into the temple by the simple expedient of keeping one hand on Kiron's shoulder. He had stood in the middle of the sanctuary floor for some time, with his head cocked a little to one side as if he was listening to something.

"Properly cleansed and purged," he had said at long last, with an approving nod. "I shall have to tender Them-noh-thet a compliment when we return."

Then he had sat down where he stood, without any preparations, elaborate or otherwise, and apparently went off into meditation.

That left Kiron and Aket-ten to set up the living space, fetch water, prepare food, and hunt, all in blistering heat. From time to time Aket-ten would glance at the Chosen with resentment.

"I don't know why he wanted me," she finally

said, crossly, as she kneaded dough. "All I'm doing is acting as a servant."

"So am I," Kiron reminded her, thinking as he did so that being made a wingleader, the one thing she had wanted above all others, had not improved her temper any.

"Yes, but I'm having to cook," she continued, looking down at the dough resentfully.

"So am I," Kiron reminded her, as he banked coals around the pot of lentils they would be having for dinner.

"Yes, but anyone could have done this," she responded. "Probably better than I could."

At this point, it was clear to Kiron that Aket-ten didn't want to hear anything logical, she only wanted to vent her frustrations. On the one hand, he could agree with her. After all, he was certain that, eventually, Rakaten-te would have magical need of Aket-ten's training and skills. All *he* had served as was a kind of cart driver on a very superior cart indeed. And now his only purpose here was to attend to whatever need the Chosen had.

Aket-ten fretted and fidgeted, wondered aloud what she was doing here, and became more irritated and irritating as the chores they were doing to make things livable clearly made her feel as if she was nothing more than a servant.

And how would she feel in Aerie? he wondered. Perhaps that was the real reason why she had not wanted to stay there with him. There was too much drudge work for her. Now he began to be irritated with her, and some of his mother's comments about the noble-born who had never known what it was to work hard began to ring truer . . . .

Perhaps he didn't fit so well with her. Perhaps this was the true Aket-ten, nobly born, she who had never had to do without servants, who had never known what it was to take care of herself. Life at Aerie, life as the new sort of Jouster, was going to be hard for a very long time. Perhaps the feelings they had for each other could not stand up under that hardship.

Despite the bright sun, a shadow seemed to fall over them both, and his spirits sank further and further. He had been deceived, or he had deceived himself. Why should someone like Aket-ten waste any time on someone like him? He was nothing more than a novelty to someone like her. Exciting for a while, certainly, but after that, after the novelty wore off . . .

And what had he seen in her anyway? Oh, she was pretty, and he supposed she must be a good lover, though he certainly didn't have anyone else to compare her to. But to listen to her whine about how terrible it was to have to make the bread that she was going to

eat, to have to sweep out the spot where she
was going to sleep—oh, it was maddening!
He'd have spanked her like a petulant child
if he hadn't felt so leaden. It was just too
much effort.

No, what he really wanted to do was just
leave. Leave this place, this whining girl, this
old blind cripple. Leave them to their own de-
vices and let them take care of themselves without him. He didn't have to be their servant. Why
should he be, after all? Who had appointed
them as his master? He wasn't a serf anymore,
to be loaded down with common labor.

He should go back to Alta. He *would* go back
to Alta. He would do that right now, this instant! In fact, there was nothing in this world
he wanted to do more than to go home, back to
the farm, where someone else would take care
of him.

He left the loaves he had been shaping, and
turned to march out of the kitchen-court of the
temple, into the east, heading home with a determination that nothing and no one would stop
him. It barely registered with him that Aket-ten
had done the same. And for a brief moment
there was uncertainty—a flutter of a thought—
Alta is not in the east, and the farm—but the
thought was gone in the next moment, and the
need to go east rose up and crested over him like
a flood wave—

He saw the old priest stepping into his path and thought only with annoyance that he was going to have to shove the old man aside—

And then the Chosen of Seft lashed out with his staff and shouted a guttural phrase, and lightning exploded in his skull.

"I am very sorry about that," Rakaten-te said, as Kiron sipped at a cup of some herbal stuff that was as thick as silt-laden flood-waters and tasted green. Whatever it was, Kiron hoped it would go to work soon, because his skull felt as if it was going to crack in half at any moment.

Aket-ten didn't look as if she felt any better. There were black rings around both her eyes, as if someone had punched her, and her face was pasty. She sipped at a clay cup of the same herbal muck.

"Couldn't you have shielded against that?" she asked the Chosen of Seft.

He shook his head. "Regrettably, I am finding that Them-noh-thet was correct. Something around here drains magic. Fortunately, mine is of the sort less susceptible to such things, but if I had set some sort of shields upon you, they would still have been reduced to nothing, and the result would have been the same."

"Shouldn't we go out there?" he asked. "Go to the spot where the townspeople were taken? We could catch whoever set this—"

Again, the priest shook his head. "We would catch only the slavemasters who had been told where to go," he corrected. "And perhaps—not even then. I do not think that anyone is aware that we are here. I think it was simply set up in the full knowledge that sooner or later, someone would come to investigate, and when they did, the trap would close and they would walk out into the desert and die."

Kiron shuddered, remembering his conviction that he *had* to go home, and that home lay in the east. He knew what would have happened had the Chosen not stopped them. He would have gone out and kept walking. . . .

"An insidious trap, too," Rakaten-te continued, in a musing sort of voice. "The magic caught you both in moments of doubt, amplified those doubts out of all proportion, then offered you a way out of the bitter unhappiness it had created in your minds. You actually supplied what would have been the instrument of your demise. If you had felt a simple compulsion to walk into the east, you likely would have fought it. But instead, you had *reasons* to walk into the east. Reasons that were vitally important to you at the time." His lips twisted wryly. "A masterwork of magic."

"Please tell me you broke it," said Aket-ten.

His mouth quirked in a sour smile. "Oh, yes. I broke it. Which is a pity, because now I cannot study it. I can only tell you that there was more than one hand involved in the making of it. And more than one kind of magician."

"The Magi?" Kiron asked, mouth going dry.

Rakaten-te sighed. "Now that—I do not know."

 # FIFTEEN

"**T**HE first thing is to find the source of whatever is consuming magic."

There had been silence for a long time as Kiron and Aket-ten finished the last of the green muck and waited for their respective headaches to fade. Though "headache" was far too mild a word for something that made him want to crack his own skull open to let the pain out. Neither he nor Aket-ten had wanted anything to eat, and the Chosen had seemed happy enough with bread and some cold meat. Well, that would just leave the pot of cooked lentil stew for the morning; it would certainly stay warm enough in the ashes, and if the bottom was burned to the pot, no matter; there were a hundred pots where that one had come from.

They sat in silence for a very long time, as the oblong of sun coming in through the ventilation slit crept up the wall.

When the silence was finally broken, it was with those words from Rakaten-te.

"That seems logical," Kiron said slowly, trying to be very careful not to set his head off again. He worked his tongue against the roof of his mouth, trying to get the taste off. "And there must be a way in which we can be useful in that hunt, or you never would have said anything about it right now. Correct?"

"Correct." The Chosen's face was unusually hard to read because of the bandage across his eyes, so Kiron had not a clue as to what he was actually thinking. "In a moment, you will begin to feel sleepy. You should go to rest as soon as you do. You will need all your senses alert in the morning."

Right on cue, Aket-ten yawned, and he found himself yawning in return. "Go," said the Chosen, then a very faint suggestion of a smile crossed his lips. "You feared I had selected you as little more than my servants. I assure you, I pondered all my choices with extreme care. I need the two of you, specifically. You will find yourselves using skills you did not even know you possessed."

Ah, Kiron thought. *Grand*. So now he was going to be mucking about with magic, which was perhaps the very last thing he wanted to do. He didn't much like it, he didn't much trust it, and truth to be told, if it weren't for the useful things it could do like heating the sands of the dragon pens and making the cold rooms, he could well do without it.

He got up carefully and offered Aket-ten a hand when she didn't move. She looked up at him, sighed, and took it. The only lamps were here, in the sanctuary, and they only lit the center of the room where the Chosen was, and where, since he had directed them to place his pallet there, he would presumably sleep. But there was enough of the fading twilight for them to find their way into the chamber they had taken to sleep in—not one of the inner chambers, but one that had probably once housed servants, at the back of the temple. It opened onto the kitchen-court, which suited Kiron fine. The wind off the desert that carried away the kitchen smells also served to cool their room.

Their room. Without thinking about it, they had placed their pallets together, in the same room. But after this afternoon . . . she had surely had similar thoughts to his, unflattering at best, downright hostile at worst. It seemed almost impossible to span the gulf the things he had been thinking had cut between him and her. She didn't know what he had been thinking, of course, but she could surely guess. And the worst part, perhaps, was that there was a grain of truth in all of it.

He dreaded what she was going to say.

But, in fact, she said nothing. She only shoved their pallets together with her foot and collapsed on one. And when he gingerly laid himself down on the other, she turned to him and put her arms around him, slowly, as if they were weighted with stones and she could hardly move them.

He found himself doing the same. Found himself unaccountably relaxing, and felt her going quiet and losing the tenseness in her muscles. And without a word, they fell into healing sleep.

Breakfast, over bowls of lentil stew, came in the still cool light of dawn. They woke fitted together like the stones of a wall. He didn't want to say anything, and he suspected Aket-ten didn't either.

They found the Chosen already awake. "You must be my ears and eyes, feet and hands," said Rakaten-te. "Here is what you need to know. Some creatures are sensitive to magic; the presence of it, the lack of it, and even to specific kinds. The scarabus beetle, for instance: one can hardly keep the creatures away from any place where there is Healing magic present. Flies swarm to the rituals of blood and death, and to the practitioners of those magics."

They both nodded, Aket-ten knowingly, Kiron only because he did understand to this point, but frankly expected to become confused very shortly.

"Whatever is consuming magic here must have a physical focus. There is probably more than one, in fact." Rakaten-te pursed his lips. "I think that someone must have come here and planted these things. A stranger would not have been out of place in a town like this."

Kiron nodded. That was certainly true. A border town saw all manner of wanderers coming through at irregular intervals. There was no state of war here, no reason to be alert, really, and the men who were garrisoned out here in this least desirable of all postings did not tend to be highly motivated at the best of times.

"Now as for the magic that caused you two to decide to take a sudden journey—I do not know if it had a physical focus and, alas, I may never know. Nor am I certain how it was able to work when all other magic was being drained." He shrugged. "Whoever did all of this is a magician of great skill and subtlety."

Greater than you? But Kiron knew that was an unfair question. Rakaten-te had the unenviable task of trying to unravel what another mage had done without knowing anything about the ma-

gician or his magic. He hid his eyes and his unfair thoughts by looking down at his breakfast.

"But before I can do anything, we must find
and destroy the objects that are absorbing
magic." The Chosen set aside his empty bowl.
"Now I do not know what creatures will react
to these things, but I do know that some will.
That is what you must look for. Some sort of
live thing either avoiding a place or swarming
to it."

Kiron felt very dubious, but decided it was
better not to say anything. What could he say,
after all? That this was a very thin clue, and not
much in the way of direction? The Chosen
surely was aware of that.

"Failing this hunt working to uncover the foci,
the only other expedient will be for me to walk
every thumb-length of this town, and for some
distance beyond," Rakaten-te said rather grimly.
"My god is not offering any sort of hint, which
means that Seft sees that I can solve this myself.
He is . . . a very challenging god to serve. But we
can hope that the creatures of the earth will
show us what we need to know."

"And if they do not, we will need to guide you
across the town, back and forth until you find
something" said Aket-ten. "But how is it you
think you can find these things, if you cannot
use magic to find them?"

"Ah, but I can, just in a more roundabout

way." The Chosen shrugged. "If I do the search in this way, I will have to cast small magics and try to determine where their power is being drawn to."

"That could take weeks!" Aket-ten exclaimed, her eyes widening in open dismay. Kiron couldn't blame her. The prospect of remaining here for more than a few days was not a pleasant one.

Rakaten-te nodded. "Yes, it could. But it is another possible solution. I had rather not use it, but if I must, I will. Seeing if the animals react will be faster. You two will either notice something, or not. If this does not work, we will approach it the hard way. And if that fails—I shall think of something else."

The determination in Rakaten-te's voice surprised Kiron. He was not used to hearing that sort of response from a priest. Like Kaleth, they tended to cultivate an aura of serenity. Kiron had the feeling that if this man had not been blind, he would have been a warrior. He had the "falcon look." As Ari called it.

"If we are going to look for things as small as flies," Aket-ten mused, glancing at the open door and the growing light outside, "We had better go on foot."

Kiron groaned, but silently, only within his own mind. Aket-ten was right. They could not spot swarms of flies from dragonback.

"Do we dare turn Avatre and Re-eth-ke loose to hunt for themselves?" he asked aloud instead. Aket-ten turned to smile a little at him.

"You read my thoughts, I think. Yes, not only do I think we dare, I think they will be fine. There are plenty of goats about here, and goats are scarcely a challenge for those two. I shall put it in their minds what we want, and we can then go out and hunt for—well, I suppose I must say, hunt for unnatural nature." She raked her hair with her fingers and stood up. At least this morning they were all fully and nicely fed. The lentil stew had improved with overnighting, rather than burning as he had feared it might.

Avatre gave him the most comical look of astonishment he had ever seen on the face of a dragon when Aket-ten persuaded her that she was to go hunting in the town alone, without her Jouster. She blinked at him for several long moments, then, with a hard headshake, she launched herself into the air—

Only to come down almost immediately, just on the other side of the wall around the temple. There was a bleat swiftly cut off with a crunch, and it was quite clear that Avatre was having an early success.

Re-eth-ke lofted into the air going in the opposite direction, showing none of the signs of surprise that Avatre had.

"You've done this before, haven't you?" he

said, suddenly realizing the implications. "Let her hunt on her own—"

"Not often, and only in the desert, but yes," she admitted. "I thought it might be good practice for times, well, like this one. Where we don't want to tie up time hunting with them."

He gave her a look. She flushed.

"All right," she said slowly, with a shrug. "I admit it. I was being lazy. But it is a good idea."

"And I'm jealous I didn't think of it first," he admitted. "You have a lot of good ideas, like getting all the babies to sleep in one pen, like they would in a nest, so that only one person has to look after them."

"That's open to abuse, though," she said, frowning, then shrugged. "You go in Avatre's direction, I'll follow Re-eth-ke. Let's hope we see something."

The goats were acting like goats, tame or wild. The cats—the few that he saw—were rapidly going feral, slinking away from him when they saw him. The dogs had all packed, holding several territories, and were also going feral. The fowl had long since been killed and eaten. The camels had created herds and wandered off into the desert. The donkeys had created a herd that was wandering through the streets, eating whatever green things they could find, and were keeping a wary eye on him.

None of them were acting in any way out of the ordinary that he could tell. The cats dozed in the sun or slunk away into the shadows, the dogs barked from a distance, and dozed in the shadows. The goats and donkeys wandered, looking for forage.

Maybe the birds, he thought, and turned his attention from the animals to the sparrows, pigeons, and the few desert birds that had decided to investigate the now-silent town.

But as the morning became afternoon, and he stopped long enough to eat the flatbread and dried meat he was carrying, he decided he was going to take a different tactic.

The Chosen said he thought that someone had carried objects into the town; a stranger, in fact. So where would a stranger actually be able to go without drawing notice? He certainly couldn't wander about the fortress and garrison, nor could he poke about in peoples' private houses nor their shops.

Taverns and inns, of course. The town square and market. Not the temples; if you were not from Tia, you wouldn't know the gods or the rituals, and you would stand out.

Taverns and inns, though, that would be perfect. If the object was something small, you could pick one that wasn't exactly clean, kick it into a corner, and it would probably stay there for a season. If it was something large, you could pick one that was honest, ask the tavernkeeper to hold it for you until you got back from a journey, and go off and leave it.

He turned on his heel and retraced his steps. There were at least three back the way he had come; a simple beer shop, a full tavern that served food, and an inn that took in travelers.

He checked the tavern first, going over it minutely, but couldn't really find anything. The beer shop was next, nearest the garrison, and a wretched little place it was, too. Even with the town being deserted for so long, it still stank faintly of beer and unwashed bodies and things best not named.

Roaming animals had pretty much cleaned up everything there was that was large; now it was up to scavenging insects to actually scour it.

Bearing in mind what the Chosen had said, Kiron paid very close attention to those insects . . . even going so far as to take a polished plate from another home and use it to reflect some light into the noisome and dark corners.

And that was when he found it.

It was the ants that told him.

At first, he thought there was nothing unusual there, just the work of a horde of ants, taking advantage of the situation to scour the very mud bricks bare of anything even remotely edible.

But then he saw it. Yes, the ants were scouring the corner, a steady stream of them coming in and leaving with their tiny burdens. But while they were actually *in* the corner, they moved in a circle. An anti-sunwise circle. There was, in fact, a swirl of ants on the floor in that corner, all moving in the same direction.

He went to get a metal signaling plate from the garrison. He was going to need more light.

By carefully reflecting a spot of sun into that dark corner, he was able to search it for anything that the ants were surrounding but leaving alone. And, eventually, he found it.

A bead.

A tiny, ordinary, dirt-colored faience bead. When he took it away, the ants stopped moving in a circle and went back to behaving like ants.

And when he took it out into the sunlight, he saw that what he had taken for irregularities in the glaze were, in fact, some sort of writing. At least, he assumed it was writing. The minute shapes were very regular and marched around the surface of the bead in a swirl, the way the ants had marched around it.

Now it could be that this was just an ordinary talisman; there was no way for *him* to tell that. It would have to go to the Chosen.

But he could not imagine how a talisman would have survived the magic-consuming spell enough to still have affected the ants, if it was not, itself, part of that spell.

So he ran as fast as he could back to the temple, excitement giving his feet an extra boost. Finally, *finally*, there was some change in this situation. It was only a toehold, but by the gods, a toehold he would take!

And in fact, his efforts were rewarded when, just as he crossed the threshold of the Temple, he heard Rakaten-te shout, *"Stop!"*

Obediently, he did just that. Rakaten-te got up slowly and walked with careful steps toward him. "You found one of the objects, and you brought it with you." The blind face showed some of the same excitement that Kiron felt. "I sensed the magic draining from the holy fire I had kindled on the altar just as I heard your footsteps. Describe the object to me."

"It is a faience bead, about the size of the last joint of my smallest finger," Kiron told him. "It is the same color as dirt, making it hard to see. There are black markings in a spiral around it, but I cannot read them. They look like the tracks of birds."

"Alas that I do not know either what writing looks like, nor what the tracks of birds look like," the Chosen said dryly, and Kiron flushed. "No matter. How did you find it?"

Kiron laughed nervously. "I thought like a stranger who wanted to leave these things in a town and a land that was not his own. I went to a filthy tavern and looked for anything strange.

Ants were swirling about this thing, and when I looked closer in the dirt, I saw it."

"Ants . . . so it may be an earth power. Hmm." The Chosen pursed his lips. "That does not sound like the Altan Magi. Their power was based in water."

"Whose power?" Kiron turned at the voice. Aket-ten stood wearily in the door. "Please tell me you have found something. I have been chasing a goat that I thought was acting oddly, that in fact had only gotten into something fermented, or perhaps had eaten an intoxicating drug. Do you know how high a drunken goat can leap? And what he will try to leap up to?"

"Yes, Kiron has found one of the keystones," Rakaten-te ignored her question about drunken goats, which was probably just as well. Quickly, at an impatient hand gesture from the Chosen, Kiron described what he had done and where he had found the thing. "I would like you to collect as many of them as you can find between now and sunset, and bring them here. Even if I cannot decipher the magic, with some of the keystones in hand I can destroy it."

"Think like a stranger," Kiron prompted her, as she turned to go. "A stranger in a hurry to place these things, perhaps. They are the color of dirt, so perhaps places where there is a bit of debris. But it will have to be a place that a stranger would not have to hunt for."

Aket-ten nodded. "I reminded the dragons that they are to hunt on their own. They don't much like it. Avatre was positively sulking. When we hunt with them, they never miss kills, and the goats and donkeys here are getting much more aware of a dragon in the sky."

He shook his head. Poor Avatre; well, he need never worry about her wanting to fly off and leave him then. Her belly would keep her right at his side, even if love and loyalty didn't.

Not that he had any doubts about the latter.

Consulting his mental map of the town, he headed off in the direction of the next seedy beer shop. This was a garrison town. There were many such. It might be a long afternoon, especially if there were no more helpful swarms of ants.

A half dozen of the dirt-colored beads lay in a pile in a flat bowl Aket-ten had fetched from the kitchen and placed in front of the Chosen. Kiron stared at them. They seemed very innocuous to have made such trouble.

"Is it fully night yet?" Rakaten-te asked, turning his sightless eyes toward the door. Kiron shook his head, then remembered that Rakaten-te could not see it, and said "No. The sun-disk is just now passing below the horizon." Rakaten-te did not have to explain why he wanted to perform his ritual after dark. Seft was the god of shadows, after all.

Rakaten-te pondered his course of action. Finally, he spoke aloud. "This magic is strange to me, yet all magic comes from the same roots. It either comes from the elements about us, or the gods themselves. I do not *think* this particular spell is of the gods. This means it is of the elements . . . ."

"You said something earlier about it being earth-magic, Chosen," Aket-ten reminded him.

He nodded. "And that in turn would make a great deal of sense. The earth can absorb a great deal, and that could account for so small a thing having so great an effect." He smiled a very little. "I muse aloud here, so that we all may learn. I find that those who come to a path with few or no preconceptions are often the ones to suggest new directions. Now . . . earth's opposite is air, and unfortunately, air is not very strong against it." He grimaced. "Nor, I fear, is the magic of Seft strong in the element of air. That would be for a Priest of Haras—I think I shall have to oppose earth with earth, and that is where you two come in."

To Kiron's surprise, Aket-ten began to blush. "I know that some magic requires that—" she stammered. "That—ah—certain—conditions—"

What is she on about? Kiron was baffled as to what the problem could possibly be. But not so the Chosen. He chuckled dryly.

"Not that of Seft," he said. "I told you, I had made a very careful choice in you two. Just because I cannot see, it does not follow that I am blind."

Aket-ten was quite scarlet by this point, and Kiron decided that this was one of those points on which he was probably better off remaining silent.

"I have no sense of whether our time is running short," Rakaten-te continued, "but it is better to err on the side of caution. So to counter this magic, I am going to use brute force. It is faster. The drawback is that it is . . . likely to draw attention."

Kiron frowned and rubbed the back of his neck. He had spent most of the afternoon hunched over looking for ants. He hadn't spent that much time hunched over since he had been a drudge of a serf.

"What does that mean?" he asked, and shook his head. "I confess all this magic business leaves me baffled."

"It means that if the magus or magi who set this spell happens to be—for lack of a better word—'watching' it for interference, then it will be as obvious as a club to the side of the head that I am destroying it, where I am, and possibly even who and what I am." The Chosen nodded, and so did Aket-ten. They apparently knew exactly what this entailed. Kiron could only guess.

But it wasn't difficult to imagine that if these unknown magicians could, they would probably attack Rakaten-te. The only real question was what form that attack would take.

Since the Chosen himself probably couldn't predict that, all Kiron could do was be ready and try to react quickly, whatever happened.

"If you can try and find me two large flat stones that have never been carved or altered in any way—" the Chosen began.

Aket-ten had revived from her earlier confusion, and now wore a look of triumph. "I already have, Chosen," she said. "A half dozen of them, in fact. I also have fuel for a fire that are sticks that were broken and not cut, and I have been harvesting such herbs as I can find in what is left of the gardens. I *think* I can collect water without using a container that was made by man—"

"That will not be needed. It is earth and fire that are the elements Seft's priests use. I knew I had chosen wisely," Rakaten-te said with satisfaction. "Well done, Aket-ten; please bring me two of those stones. Then the two of you do as you please until I summon you."

None of this made any sense at all to Kiron, but he was fairly content to leave it at that. Why the Chosen would need unaltered stones, or sticks for a fire that had been broken and not cut, he could not imagine. Since Aket-ten was practically glowing after Rakaten-te's praise, that was enough for him. And besides, he was starving.

"Is there any reason why we should not eat?" he asked hopefully. She shook her head. "It's probably a good idea, and also not a bad idea to bring some oil for the lamps to the sanctuary," she said. "If it's a long night, we might need to refill them several times over."

"Oh, *we* meaning me," he said, with a good-natured grumble. "Since the oil jars weigh as much as a donkey—"

"As a donkey?" She raised a skeptical eyebrow.

"A *small* donkey. A foal." He chuckled as she sighed with exasperation. "Nevertheless, I shall move one of them into the sanctuary, in obedience to your wishes."

"You make me sound like a small-minded overseer," she complained. "Isn't it better to have the jar there if we need it?"

It seemed to him that this was unnecessarily cluttering up the sanctuary, but he didn't say so. Instead he carefully wrestled and rolled the big jar to the room, leaving it just inside the door. Rakaten-te was chanting something and seemed deep in concentration. If he noticed Kiron, he said nothing and reacted not at all, which was exactly the way Kiron liked it. He was of two minds about the blind priest. On the one hand, Rakaten-te for himself was someone that Kiron was coming to like. He had a dry wit and sense of humor Kiron appreciated. He might not be telling them everything, but what priest ever did? There was a reason why the rites of the gods were called "Mysteries."

On the other hand . . . Chosen of Seft. Seft the Prince of Lies, Seft the Treacherous. And the Chosen of Seft might have a plausible-sounding explanation for the story of Seft's betrayal, but . . . that could be just as much a lie as anything else.

But Avatre liked him, and so did Re-eth-ke. Perhaps that was what he should go on. The dragons did not care about gods and their histories; they relied on their instincts. They had hated, loathed the Magi of Alta, one and all; every dragon in the compound would go mad whenever one was near. Avatre and Re-eth-ke not only tolerated Rakaten-te as a rider, but they would carefully, gently nudge him to solicit scratches.

He relaxed a little at that thought. If he could trust nothing else in the world, he knew he could trust Avatre as a guide.

Aket-ten came to stand beside him just as he came to that conclusion. She watched the Chosen chanting with a furrowed brow. "Not only do I not know what he is saying," she confessed in a low voice, "I don't even know what language it is in. It sounds like Tian, but . . . it isn't, exactly."

"Huh." He became aware of a sense of . . . unease? Portent? Both really. A feeling of pressure in a way. Despite the fact that the sanctuary still held the heat of the day, he felt a chill and shivered.

But then he felt more than a chill, as Rakatente's chanting increased in volume and intensity, and the Chosen of Seft raised the smaller of the two stones and smashed it down on the collection of beads.

Suddenly every hair on Kiron's body threatened to stand on end. A strange, dry silence dropped over them all. Kiron could hear his own heart pounding in his ears. But then, he heard something else entirely.

Something that sounded like—rain? Or a shower of sand on a roof?

Movement on the floor by the door caught his eye. It looked as if the shadows there were moving. And that was where the sound was coming from, too . . . a strange, sharp, musty odor suddenly assailed his nose, and as his heartbeat quickened, he peered at the moving shadow, trying to make out what it was.

Wait. That was no shadow. That was—

A living carpet of black scorpions, moving slowly toward them.

Aket-ten gasped the same moment he realized what they were. She stood there, paralyzed with fear, her eyes blank and black with sheer terror.

The deadly creatures paused at the edge of the light, as if making up their minds whether to go on or not. Their eyes glittered in the lamplight like a myriad of tiny black gems, and the sound of their claws on the sandstone floor was exactly like the sound of a rain of pebbles on a roof. They stared at him, and he stared back.

"Kiron!" Rakaten-te's voice cut across his paralysis. "Aket-ten! What do you see?"

"Scorpions," Kiron said, as Aket-ten whimpered the same word. "There must be hundreds of them—"

The carpet of insects surged forward at that moment. Reflexively, Kiron grabbed the object nearest to him and hurled it at them.

It was a lamp.

It broke just in front of the scorpions, spilling its fuel all over the stone floor. The oil caught fire before the wick spluttered out—

And with a scuttling of claws, the scorpions got out of the way of the flames.

Fire! Kiron ran for the jar of oil. Ruthlessly, he broke in the top and tilted it over. The oil spread toward the scorpions, forming a barrier between them and the venomous insects. Paying it no heed, the scorpions scuttled forward again, into the oil.

And Kiron threw another lamp into the middle of the pool of oil. Flames spread across the surface of the oil, catching some of the scorpions before they could escape.

Yes!

Shaking off her paralysis, Aket-ten ran out of the room and came back with unlit torches. He seized one from her, lit it, and began beating at the scorpions with it. The insects retreated, making an angry, dry clicking sound. Some of them tried to find a way around the burning barrier of oil; Aket-ten spotted them first and ran to intercept them with her torch. He gave her his and turned and sprinted for the overturned jar; there was still plenty of oil in it. He manhandled it into his arms, then staggered with it to Aket-ten's side, sloshing the oil clumsily out to finish the barrier that accident had started.

Wave after wave of the black creatures surged toward them over the burning floor. Each time they met the wave with torches and more oil. Even as they tried to build a bridge across the burning oil out of their own bodies by smothering it, he and Aket-ten threw more oil on them and then set fire to them.

Kiron's world narrowed to the oil jar, the torch in his hand, and the army of scorpions.

He fought them until his hands were burned and his body dripping sweat.

And then—suddenly—they were gone. The only trace of them was what was left of the ones that had burned.

Kiron let his knees go and sat down rather abruptly on the floor, with Aket-ten beside him.

"Well," said the Chosen of Seft. "That was unexpected."

 # SIXTEEN

AKET-TEN jerked her head around to stare at the priest, suddenly filled with fury. "You *knew* something like that was going to happen!" she snarled. "You knew it and you didn't warn us!" The heat of the dying flames was nothing to the heat of her anger. How dared he? Priest or no priest, how *dared* he?

"Aket-ten—" Kiron said, making a placating gesture. "I don't—"

"I knew? Child, my life was as much in danger as yours. More." The priest's tone was mild, with no hint that he was affronted by her accusations. He made a little gesture at his bandaged eyes, as if to emphasize his point. "I could not even detect what had been sent against us with my magic, which requires preparation and spells. Had you not defended me, I would have been swarmed within moments. You, at least, could have run away."

Shame overcame her. She bowed her head. *Of course. I'm being stupid. What was I thinking?* Rakaten-te could have been killed far more easily than she or Kiron.

"Now I will say that I guessed that breaking the spell so abruptly might draw unwanted attention," the priest continued, sounding a little shamefaced. "But I honestly thought it would come in the form of magic sent against magic, directed at me, and not at all of us. I anticipated retaliation that was magical in nature rather than material. It was a clever strategy. And one I did not anticipate." Now he sounded irritated. Aket-ten guessed that it was irritation at himself, and his next words confirmed that. "I am at fault there."

"Well, now what do we do?" Aket-ten demanded, bringing her head up. This was not the time to indulge in recriminations, self or otherwise. "Whoever 'they' are, 'they' know we've uncovered them—"

"You two remain on watch for things I cannot deal with," Rakaten-te said, firmly taking charge of the situation. Aket-ten bristled a little, then forced herself to back down. He *was* in charge. They were there as his hands and eyes, no more.

She was spoiled, really, having a leader who simply didn't act like one most of the time, and that even more so with her. Her nose twitched a little at the smell of hot stone and the odd scent of fried scorpion. She really needed to sweep those things out the door. The cats would probably love them.

She gritted her teeth and nodded acceptance. "Now that you can use magic, can't you do something about helping us keep watch?" she asked instead. Surely there was something he could do! Neither she nor Kiron were in any shape to stand on watch all night. Her hands were already starting to hurt in the places where hot oil or torch fire had scorched them.

He shrugged. "Not until I use that same magic to speak with my own priests, and if possible, with the priests of other gods in Sanctuary. After that, we will see. Magic is like anything else. You spend it, and it is gone, nor can you do more until you have more of it."

She sighed; she knew that of course, it was one of the fundamental tenets of magic. She had hoped he had reservoirs of power stored . . . but if he didn't or if he had used them, then so be it. There was no arguing with that. As he turned his attention back to his simple tools and preparations, she turned to Kiron.

He was frowning, black brows furrowed together. "If he's at this all night, we'll be hard-pressed to stay awake, much less on guard," he said quietly, echoing her thoughts exactly. "It's all very well to tell us to guard him, but I was tired before this started, and now . . ." He let his voice trail off. He looked about as bad as she felt; his eyes were puffy and red, with dark shadows beneath them, he had soot smudges all over him, and the red of burn marks on his hands and arms. He did not look as if he would do well in another fight.

She chewed on her lower lip. What they needed was some help, something that would at least make a fuss if there was something dangerous about. A couple of geese would have been ideal, but of course, there was little water here and she doubted this town had seen a goose outside of wall paintings. If only they had a dog! But the dogs around here had gone thoroughly feral, and were not approaching humans. Even if they could catch one in the dark and tied it in here with them, it would spend all its time fighting the rope, or whining and making a fuss, and it would be hard to tell whether noises it was making were because of danger or because it wanted to get loose.

The dragons would be too sleepy to be of any use, and besides, they would never notice anything as small as a scorpion, not even a legion of them. Things that would kill a human, the dragons could often merely ignore. More scorpions, snakes, poisonous spiders—those were the things most likely to be thrown against them, by Aket-ten's way of thinking.

She racked her brain for a way to guard against such things for as long as need be. What they needed were barriers across the two thresholds. The scorpions had come swarming in through the doorway that led to the open court in front of the temple. Closing the door wouldn't help; there was more than enough of a gap under the door for them to squeeze in. Short of bricking up that gap, nothing was going to stop them. Stuffing cloth or straw under it wouldn't hold them for long. The stones she had collected for Rakaten-te were too irregular to serve as a barrier. Was there any way they could use the oil to create a regular fire barrier?

Kiron was also frowning in thought. "Dishes of oil with wicks in them?" he said, sounding doubtful. "Set across each threshold? If we can find troughs, maybe . . . bread molds? Kneading troughs? I don't know, maybe we can stack enough dishes to cover gaps?"

It was as good a thought as any. Better than the half-formed notions she'd had so far. The flames would keep the oil hot, and enough wicks would even heat the dishes until they burned at the touch. "We don't really need to kill anything, just keep them back," she agreed. "At least . . . I hope."

They took a discarded torch, lit it, and went back to the stores together. They found a number of objects that looked as if they would work, and there were years worth of linen lamp wicks in bundles there. As she gathered them up, Kiron looked over an assortment of salves from the shelves, selecting some that appeared to be beneficial, as well as some flat-bread and honey, and took them into their haven. While she was at it, Aket-ten got a broom. Before they did anything else, she wanted the charred remains of those scorpions out of the sanctuary.

With the room swept clean and both thresholds guarded by these improvised barriers three dishes deep, food and water and whatever else they could think of in a corner, they settled down. At least there was plenty of light. The Chosen of Seft had settled into his silent attempts at communion with his fellows. The room smelled of hot oil; it was too warm, and sweat made her scalp itch and trickled down the back of her neck.

"I'll take first watch," Kiron said, opening one of the jars of salve. "When I can't keep my eyes open anymore, I'll wake you."

She was too tired to argue, and made herself as comfortable as she could on the floor of the sanctuary. She felt the stone start to pull the heat out of her body, and spread herself out to get as much of her flesh in contact with the stone as possible.

The next thing she knew, Kiron was shaking her shoulder, and she struggled up out of half-formed dreams of flames and glittering eyes.

"I can't even stay awake standing up," he said, swaying where he stood. She scrubbed at her eyes with one hand and nodded, getting up to take his place. At least she wasn't sweating. But she wanted a bath.

She kept an eye on the dishes of oil. Carefully topping them up when they got low, keeping the wicks alight. It was more work than she had thought it would be, and hard to do without getting burned. Or rather, burned more. Her hands were laced with burns that she was awake enough to start feeling, and she began trying every unguent she could find in the things that Kiron had taken from the temple stores in hopes that something would work.

Finally, something did. It was green, and had an odd, pungent aroma that reminded her of something she couldn't quite put a finger on. Whatever it was, it seemed to cool the burns and numb the pain significantly, for which she breathed a sigh of relief. It might have been what Kiron had used; there was a completely empty jar there that might have held something similar.

So she paced, salved her hands and arms,

tended the lamps and paced, until she, in her turn, found herself swaying on her feet and awoke Kiron, who had been sleeping so soundly he might have been a stone image. Like her, he had spread himself out on the cool stone floor, and that looked as comfortable as any bed to her right now.

And she was asleep again without a clear memory of lying down.

"The priests at Sanctuary and I are of the same mind," Rakaten-te said rather grimly as the two groggy Jousters joined him at breakfast. "If it is possible, we must secure whatever amulet or focus has been used for the spell that sent our people into the east. But we must not delay too long. A day, no more. If I cannot find it by then, we must leave in the morning anyway. There is too much at stake, and there is only a limited amount of information that I can send by means of my magic. I need to be back among other priests, so that we can compare what we know, and among scholars, so that we can look in the oldest scrolls for more wisdom. The Great King and Queen are debating how best to alert the Two Kingdoms."

Aket-ten blinked him. What was this? They already had a good idea how the first stage of this tragedy had been put into place! All they had to do was to intercept the first bearers of those insidious amulets! "How best?" she said. "But surely we must send urgent messengers, couriers, to every village and estate! We must send soldiers to every trade road, to every inn and tavern and beer shop, to stop strangers, search—"

"That," the Chosen said crisply, "is precisely what we must *not* do."

She stared at him openmouthed. Had he gone mad?

His mouth firmed, and his tone took on an edge of exasperation and sarcasm. "What? Blanket the Two Kingdoms with soldiers? Oh, surely *that* will make relations with Alta *so* much better! And are we to begin intercepting each and every traveler? Stop and search each and every person who is a stranger to a village? And how are soldiers to know who is a stranger and who is not? Do you think, with all these soldiers, who are strangers themselves to a town, that the townsfolk will warm to their presence and come running to them to identify every new person on the road?"

"But—" Aket-ten protested, "surely they—"

But Kiron, who had lived in a small village, was shaking his head. "No, Aket-ten, they will not. The soldiers will be regarded with suspicion, scorn, and anger for interfering in village matters. Worse, every man that has a quarrel with a neighbor will come to the soldiers to report his neighbor as suspicious. The soldiers themselves will do what they were trained to do for the war—harass and intimidate all civilians to bully information from them. It will be bad if only Altan soldiers are in Alta and Tians in Tia, but worse, much worse, if the borders are crossed."

The Chosen nodded forcefully. "A fool's course, and a waster of time while the real villains find some other means to cast their spells, or even begin a different sort of campaign altogether. Meanwhile our soldiers are scattered from one end of the Two Lands to the other, accomplishing nothing save to raise the level of fear and distrust. No, and no again. This is trying to catch the wind in a sieve."

"A wall—" Kiron began, then shook his head. "No, that is just as foolish. How can we wall a whole border? A wall will not keep out magic, and any man can find a place to go under, over, or around it."

"And we do not have the time to build a wall even if we could," Rakaten-te said bluntly. "Which we cannot. The cost would bankrupt both nations. Whatever the solution that the Great King and Queen arrive at, it will not be any of those. Meanwhile, we must try and accomplish the task that was set for us. We must find one of the amulets that sent our people out into the wilderness, sure that this was the thing they wanted to do the most."

Once again, Aket-ten and Kiron found themselves standing by while the Chosen performed a series of arcane rituals, things which appeared absurdly simple. Some chanting to a shaken sistrum, the burning of pungent incense, a few gestures with hand or staff, and a great deal of sitting or standing in silence. Aket-ten had the distinct feeling, however, that this impression was deceptive, and as the morning wore on, she found herself thinking that if one of the powerful Magi of Alta had gone head-to-head against Rakaten-te, the Magus would have come off distinctly second-best.

But the old man was definitely flagging. And when, in midmorning, he exploded in a fit of temper and threw his staff to the ground, she was not entirely surprised.

"Curse it!" he swore. "How can an amulet *move?* And more, how can it waft through the air? I find them, I have found three of them, and yet they are traveling all over this town! Twice now I have sensed one over my head for a moment, before it moved off! I cannot pin these things to a place! This is impossible!"

Waft through the air . . . How could an amulet fly? Perhaps part of the magic was to make it fly? Like the enchanted rug in the tale? Aket-ten thought for a moment, then went outside. She looked about in the kitchen-court, where a flock of pigeons was pecking at the remains of the

stale flatbread she had torn up and thrown to
them—as she did every day. Her presence startled them into flight, and as they circled above
the roof of the Temple, she heard Rakaten-te
howl, *"And there it is again!"*

Waft—

It struck her like a blow to the head, and she
ran inside. "An amulet can fly, when it is bound
to the leg of a pigeon," she shouted, as soon as
she was in the sanctuary.

Both Kiron, who was picking up the much-
abused staff, and the Chosen, who had both
hands cupped to his head, shaking it in frustration, stopped dead. For one long moment, both
stood frozen, without saying a word. The Chosen was the first to speak.

"A pigeon?" he exclaimed, for the first time in
Aket-ten's knowledge looking honestly bewildered. "But—how would—" He shook his head.
"These things came in from outside, as the
amulets that ate magic did. How—"

"By putting out bread and netting one," Aket-
ten said excitedly. "Or grain. Or making a
sticky-trap. Whoever did this would have to
take care that no one saw him, because I am sure
all the pigeons in this town belong to someone,
but it is not hard to take a pigeon." Pigeons were
a good source of meat for anyone who could afford the bit of grain it took to bring them home
to roost at night. During the day, they could

scavenge whatever food they could peck up. And of course, there were dove sellers who raised doves and pigeons to offer as sacrifices for those who could afford a slightly better gift to the gods than a loaf of bread, a bunch of *latas* flowers, or a jar of beer.

"And pigeons always come home to roost," said Kiron, straightening, and handing the Chosen his staff. "That was one of my jobs as a serf, tending to the pigeon cote. They always come home to roost. If you sell one and the buyer is foolish enough to turn it loose, it will come back to you. Khefti-the-Fat, my old master, gulled many a fool in that way."

"In Alta, traders sometimes carry pigeons with them to send messages home," Aket-ten explained with growing, if weary, satisfaction. "It is a one-way journey, of course, which is why a dragon courier is so much better. But—if I wanted to slip amulets bearing spells into a city, I would buy some pigeons from a cheat, and I would tie the amulets to their legs, and then turn them loose. Or I would buy doves from a dove seller in the temple court, and instead of taking it inside to sacrifice, tie the amulet to its leg and turn it loose."

"By all the gods . . ." The Chosen stood stark still, but then his face darkened. "And how are we to get our hands on one of these birds? *You* cannot sense which one it is, *I* cannot see to aim a sling or a bow! We cannot net every bird in the town!"

Aket-ten laughed, and both Kiron and the Chosen stared at her as if they thought she had gone mad. "You cried out 'there it is again' as I startled the flock that was feeding in the kitchen court. They will already have settled again and are surely the ones that eat here every day. We have more bread, do we not?" she countered, with memories of birds lurching around her mother's courtyard after feasting on fermented berries flashing through her mind. "And we have palm wine? Trust me. We will have one of those birds before the sun sets."

Every scrap of their bread was soon soaking up the wine as Rakaten-te made certain that the flock that held his amulet did not venture off somewhere else, by the simple expedient of sitting in the courtyard and distributing a miserly few grains of barley at intervals. The continued promise of food held the flock on the roof until the bread was ready. Then Kiron and Aket-ten carried it out in platters, and the three of them retired to the shade of the kitchen to wait.

It did not take long. The pigeons quickly swarmed the pans of bread, gobbling it as fast as they could, and before very long, the entire flock was lurching around the courtyard completely unable to fly. It would have been funny at any time, but in their exhausted state, Kiron and

Aket-ten found it hilarious. Aket-ten laughed herself weak in the knees, watching the poor birds stagger, flap, and fall over. Rakaten-te was in the sanctuary, which was just as well in a way, since he would never be able to appreciate the sight.

Even funnier, in a macabre way, was what they did next.

Kiron had gotten a pair of bird nets used for taking up pigeons from the cote, and he and Aket-ten slowly made their way around the courtyard, scooping up birds, examining them for anything fastened to them, then tossing them over the wall to avoid netting them up a second time. After a while, Aket-ten began hearing snarling and spitting, then barking. Curious, she tossed the bird she had rejected over the wall, and found a box to stand on so she could see what was going on.

She was just in time to see an uneasy standoff between one of the dog packs, and a loose conglomeration of cats end in a swirl of angry barking and flashing claws, as one of the cats darted in, snatched the poor bird, then whisked itself over the rooftops with the pigeon in its mouth as about a third of the cats arrowed off in hot pursuit. There was some more snarling and spitting, then the fight resolved itself, and about two dozen pairs of hopeful eyes turned back to the top of the wall where Aket-ten was looking over.

She began laughing helplessly, and Kiron climbed up beside her to see what was going on.

"Oh, dear—" Kiron shoved his hand up to his mouth to smother his own reaction. "I should be appalled—"

Aket-ten giggled. "I know. But it's funny—"

"It's hardly fair," Kiron pointed out. "I know the dogs and cats are hungry, but it still seems unfair—"

"So maybe we should stop tossing them over the wall—"

Kiron looked around, and shrugged helplessly. "Where do we toss them, then? If we throw them on the roof—"

"Maybe the cats will get them, but at least the dogs won't," she said, still giggling, and then broke up into gales of laughter, until her sides ached and tears came, as something else occurred to her. "Bounty from the temple court! They must think that the god Anbas and the goddess Pashet have come here to reward their creatures!"

But as it happened, the poor pigeons got a reprieve, and were permitted to recover from their inebriation without further decimation of their numbers, since the very next bird that Kiron took up proved to have a tiny scroll of leather so thin it was translucent bound to its left leg. Kiron tried not to touch the thing. It was magic, and it was not something he wanted to take a chance on. For all *he* knew, this was the same amulet that had sent him and Aket-ten off to wander. Would the spell work now that they knew about it? There was no telling, but he wasn't going to risk it.

Bearing the bird, scroll and all, they hurried into the Sanctuary.

The Chosen "examined" the bird without touching it. "Kill the bird," he said shortly. "Get the scroll off the bird without cutting the binding or letting it unroll. Then put the scroll in one of those empty unguent jars we found and seal the jar."

Kiron and Aket-ten exchanged a glance, and Kiron took the bird from her while she hurried off after a jar. When she returned, the bird was gone, and Kiron was just cutting the foot off the birdless leg, carefully not touching the scroll, leaving only the bit of skin and bone with the amulet attached. Wordlessly, she held out the jar; he dropped it in, and she gave the jar to the Chosen.

With heavy weariness, Rakaten-te made some gestures and muttered something and a bit of that odd darkness billowed up out of the ground at his feet and wrapped itself around the jar, vanishing as it did so.

"Have we enough provisions for the journey?" he asked, raising his head slowly as if it ached. "Now, I mean. This very moment."

Kiron shrugged, then seemed to remember that the Chosen couldn't see the gesture, and coughed. "We've got no bread, but other than that—"

"Then call your dragons, gather no more than what we need, and let us be gone from here," Rakaten-te said grimly. "I do not believe this city will be safe for us to be in for much longer."

Rather than flying back to Mefis, the Chosen of Seft insisted that they go to Sanctuary. Kiron could not have been happier; though Aket-ten fretted about leaving her wing for so long. Sanctuary was closer by far, and after the ordeal of the scorpions, Kiron wanted nothing more than to be able to get a sound night's sleep in a place that had so many priests and priest-mages in it that surely not even the strongest magician could slip an attack inside. Or even if they could, there were hordes of acolytes and servants to deal with it.

They pushed the dragons to the limit, taking straight off as soon as there was light, pausing to hunt the moment they saw something large enough to be prey rather than hunting first before going on, and stopping to make camp and hunt again well before sunset. Each night the Chosen settled for wordless communion with other priests long into the night. He slept little, ate little, and spoke no more than a few words at a time.

They reached Sanctuary as the last of the light left the sky on the third day. The dragons were ravenous, and it was with profound relief that Kiron saw the servants waiting below as he and Aket-ten spiraled down to the pens. Rakaten-te slid off the saddle as soon as he could unbuckle the strap holding him; two acolytes led him away without a word, with his hand on the shoulder of one of them.

Kiron did not give the Chosen another thought, for more servants arrived with meat for the dragons, who fell on it avidly, snatching the chunks out of the barrows and wolfing them down so fast that one chunk was still visible traveling down as a lump in their necks while they were gulping down a second. For the first time in Kiron's memory, there was some jostling and snapping between Re-eth-ke and Avatre over the food. It took Aket-ten to get them to settle again, but Kiron took this as a warning of trouble if dragons were ever allowed to go hungry. Even tame dragons had their limits.

And so did even the strongest of Jousters. As he pulled the harness from Avatre's back, he felt himself flagging. Food was not his need, of course, but oh, sleep, sleep—

He grabbed the arm of one of the servants as the man passed. "Are we needed, Aket-ten and I?" he asked, more harshly and abruptly than he intended.

The man shook his head. "I have no orders—" he ventured.

Avatre finished the last of her meat, and with an enormous sigh, settled into her hot sand, wiggled a little to work herself into it, and was instantly asleep. That was all Kiron needed.

"Good. Then until someone comes to fetch us, I will be here," he replied, and without even pausing to fetch bedding or ask the servant for some, he settled in next to Avatre's warm bulk, as he had when she was just an unfledged baby, and grabbed for sleep with both hands.

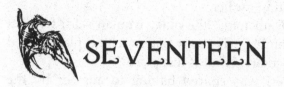 SEVENTEEN

THE baby dragons were not such babies anymore.

All of the things that Ari, Kiron, and the
Altan wing had learned when raising their babies were showing impressive results with the
babies of the Queen's Wing. They were growing faster and stronger than any wild dragon
could. Sutema was already flying short dis-
tances with a weighted saddle, although she
was not yet up to Peri's full weight. The others
were at the same flapping stage that Sutema
had reached a few days ago. They would all be
flying soon.

That was what was really on her mind, when
she came back to her courtyard to have a bath

before dinner. She had not expected to find Letis waiting for her.

"I am told," the older woman said, without preamble, "That my son is in the place called Sanctuary. What is this place?"

Peri was spared having to answer by the timely appearance of Helet-ani, which was just as well, since she didn't actually know the answer.

"Sanctuary is the desert city of priests," the former priestess said. "Priests of both Tian and Altan gods gather there. It was the refuge for the Altan priests against the depredations of the Altan Magi, and when those Magi tempted the Great King of Tia and became *his* advisers and the same troubles began here, as many as could escaped to its shelter.

"Ah," Letis said enigmatically. Helet-ani gave her a curious look, but when nothing else was forthcoming, shrugged and went on her way.

Peri, who wanted a bath far more than she wanted to be polite and deferential, went on her way to her quarters. The sun was very hot, and she had just spent far too long in it, exercising Sutema. Letis followed her, the mulish look on her face telling Peri that her putative mother-in-law had something to say and was not going to leave until she had delivered her lecture.

Peri pulled her tunic over her head as soon as she entered the door of her own rooms and

dropped it on the floor. Once, it would have
been she who would have scuttled in afterward
to retrieve the soiled garment and take it off to
be cleaned. Now that was someone else's duty.
She reflected, as Letis' lips tightened, that she
was getting used to being waited on instead of
doing the servants' work herself. Not that long
ago she had tried to tidy her own quarters and
make as little work for the servants as possible.
That was, until the Overseer for the Dragons'
Court took her aside and explained to her, in the
kindliest possible manner, that she was making
the servant assigned to her unhappy by doing
that servant's job.

"If you do not let her tend to you, not only
does she lose pride in thinking that you feel she
will not do her work properly, she then, because
there are no idle hands here, has to do work she
would really rather not do. Much harder and
less pleasant work."

So now she made as much light work as possible for the nearly invisible girl to do.

But Letis, of course, frowned, then with an ex-
aggerated sigh, picked up the tunic, folded it
neatly, and put it on the bed before following
Peri into the bathing room. This place was a true
wonder to Peri, what with cool water appearing
like magic in the bath jars every day. It wasn't
magic, of course; it was the servants, but it
might as well have been magic.

Peri dipped out water and cleaned herself, sighing with relief to feel the sweat and grime sluice away. This was usually a peaceful part of the day for her, but Letis clearly had something on her mind, so Peri thought it best to get it over with.

"So Lord Kiron is in Sanctuary?" she said quietly.

"And I would like to know why he is not here, with his mother!" Letis said angrily.

"I presume because his duty took him there. He was escorting a priest, after all. Is there something that you need?" Peri asked. "I can certainly see that you get it—"

Letis gave her a withering look. "Only my son. And what of you? Are you not anxious for him to return?"

Peri flushed a little. Letis took that for maidenly blushes, and finally smiled and nodded knowingly. But the truth was that Peri had been so busy with Sutema that she hadn't actually thought much about Kiron.

"It would be good to have him here, but his duties truly rest in Aerie," she pointed out. "And that is likely where he will return."

That made Letis frown again, and she was off on a scolding plaint about filial duty, the lost farm, and all the worn old complaints, until Peri was close to telling her to hold her tongue.

And long before the screed was over, Peri
wished she had.

"Kiron . . ." Aket-ten was shaking his shoulder, as
Kiron swam up out of dreamless sleep. He
vaguely recalled someone rousing him earlier,
about dawn, and steering him into the darkened
comfort of the little room attached to the pen and
the bed therein. Just as well; he'd have been
turned to a strip of dried leather if he had slept
out in the sun.

He yawned, stretched, and in a burst of mischief, started to reach for Aket-ten to pull her
down beside him.

But the seriousness of her expression made
him halt that impulsive gesture before it began.
"You look as if we're needed," he said instead.

She nodded. "We are. There are three other
Jousters here, and Kaleth has a task for us."

Kiron made a face. "More courier duty—"

She shook her head. "I don't think so. At least,
it didn't seem that way to me. But he wanted me
to get you, so he can explain it to all of us at the
same time."

He became uncomfortably aware of how
grimy he was, especially after noting that Aket-
ten had apparently had a bath and a change of
clothing already. "Before I see anyone, I want to
be cleaner."

She nodded. "I'll tell him you're coming. Get

something to eat, too. It might be a long meeting, I don't know."

Well, that was not exactly what he wanted to hear.

Bathed, in truly clean clothing for the first time in days, and fed, he checked on Avatre and Re-eth-ke again. A servant was just taking away the last of the empty barrows, and Avatre had flopped down in the sand again to sleep. Re-eth-ke was already dozing. The fast flight here had taken a great deal out of both of them.

He knew exactly how they felt, too. It seemed to him that he could easily sleep for a week. Unfortunately, he did not have that luxury.

One might have thought that the Mouth of the Gods and his mate would have the use of the largest temple building in all of Sanctuary. In fact, their choice was to have the smallest. Because there were priests of both Alta and Tia here now, and because even the least and littlest cult had sent representatives here, the largest was dubbed the "Temple of All Gods," and there was a shrine to every deity with a representative here in the city. The next largest was given over to Haras, in no small part because ornamentation and carvings indicated it had once been the home to priests of the hawk-headed god before the city vanished under the sand.

After that, Kaleth had somehow apportioned out buildings to various sects without anyone having apoplexy. How he had done that, Kiron could not imagine. Perhaps the gods themselves had gotten involved.

However it had happened, the end result was that Kaleth and Marit, the Mouth of the Gods and his beloved, ruled over a building of only two rooms. There was the sanctuary, and behind it an all-purpose living space. There was no kitchen, but a kitchen wasn't really needed, as food was brought over from other temples.

And, in fact, as Kiron entered the door to the sanctuary, he sidestepped a couple of young women in the robes of those who served the goddess Mhat, who were just leaving with large, empty platters. The sanctuary was empty, but voices coming from beyond the door curtain told him where everyone was. Like all buildings in Sanctuary, here in the heart of the desert, the walls were as thick as his arm was long, and had very few openings. Even the customary ventilation slits near the ceilings of Tian buildings were missing here. Small wonder. The sand crept in through every aperture under normal circumstances, and when a midnight *kamiseen* blew, you could have found yourself buried alive in your own home as the sand flooded in.

So the interiors of buildings were dark, except where there were lamps. But lamps made heat, so for the most part people preferred the dark.

He took a moment to let his eyes adjust to the darkness before walking across the cool stone floor of the sanctuary to the curtained doorway at the rear.

Pushing aside the curtain, he found Aket-ten, Rakaten-te, Kaleth, Marit, and two priests he did not know sharing a somber meal. Rakaten-te turned his bandaged eyes toward the doorway, detecting Kiron's presence before anyone else did.

"Ah," he said. "The last of our group."

Kaleth looked up and nodded at him somberly. "Kiron, come eat, and you will hear what we have been doing here in your absence. It bears directly on what we will be asking you to do."

With a certain amount of trepidation, Kiron folded his legs beneath him and helped himself to food. One thing was certain, they were eating better in Sanctuary than they were in Aerie.

I am very tired of desert, he thought suddenly. He thought with sudden longing about Alta, the estate of Aket-ten's aunt. Streams and ponds, and the river running alongside it. Not like Sanctuary, where the air was so dry it sucked water out of you.

He pulled his wandering attention back to the conversation, which had started up without him.

". . . Heyksin," one of the two stranger priests was saying somberly.

That got his attention.

"How sure of this are you?" Kaleth asked sharply. His head was up and he frowned, and well he might. This was not good hearing.

The priest shrugged. "We have but a few words from the written tongue of the Nameless Ones, copied down centuries ago, recopied over and over without the scribe that made the copies knowing what the words were supposed to mean. And we have the words on this amulet. Some of the characters are identical. Some are a mismatch. Does that mean that these Magi are of the Nameless Ones? We think so. Our written tongue looks nothing like this, the Bedu have no written language, and Heklatis tells us it looks like no language he knows."

All fell silent at that point. Kiron felt chilled as a stone in winter. If there was one thing that the people of Tia and Alta feared equally, it was the Nameless Ones. And if *they* were the ones responsible for the disappearance of a town full of people . . .

"Then I must tell you still another unpleasant thing," Rakaten-te said slowly, fingering the carvings on his staff. "You know that we of Seft are accustomed to keeping our own counsel and hold many secrets."

Everyone nodded at that, but none more emphatically than Kaleth. The Mouth of the Gods raised an eyebrow but held his peace.

The Chosen of Seft coughed lightly. "Some seasons back, one of our . . . agents . . . got his hands on a book of spells of the Magi of Alta."

He could not have secured their attention more fully if he had stood up, smashed Kaleth over the head with his staff, and proclaimed *himself* the Mouth of the Gods. Every eye in the room was riveted on him, as he sat there with the hint of a sardonic smile playing about his lips.

For that matter, Kiron felt rather as he had right after the Chosen *had* smashed him in the head with his staff.

It was Kaleth who finally spoke first. "But—how—"

"It was when those so-called advisers to the Great King first turned up, and we of Seft got whiffs of darkest magic about them," Rakaten-te said and shrugged. "Caution bid us work in silence and in secret, as we are wont to do anyway. These men were respected, and not all dark magic is turned to evil ends. It was early days, the would-be adviser was living in a house he had rented, and our agent caught the fellow at something unsavory. Trust me, you would rather not know the details. There are some things that even one who lives in the shadows will not tolerate, and the Magus met with an—accident."

"And the crocodiles with an offering?" asked one of the strangers.

The Chosen of Seft tilted his head to one side. "It is true that we of Seft have an understanding with the spawn of Sobekesh. And from time to time we offer them tribute. It might have been that the Magus fell into a pool where they were accustomed to be fed. Of course, we did not know he was one of the Magi then, nor did we have any clue of this until very recently. To avoid difficulties, our agent took all of the man's personal belongings, making it look as if the fellow had run off on his own. He brought the belongings to his master, the master brought them to the temple, and an underpriest, not knowing what to do with them, took them to the Chief Scribe of Seft who ordered them put away in a chest. Recently a number of such storage chests were being gone through, and that was when we uncovered the book." One corner of his mouth quirked up. "Our scribes are very thorough. The antecedents of the contents of that chest were tallied in a scroll on top of everything in it. Knowing *now* that this adviser must have been an Altan Magus, the contents were searched and the book found. It was no bigger than my hand, and I am told, written in such small characters that a man was like to have his eyes cross trying to read it."

Kiron was waiting for the other sandal to fall. Rakaten-te had certainly been dangling it in one finger long enough. He took pity on them then and let it go. "When we realized it was written neither in Tian nor in the Altan variant script, we began trying to find someone who could read it. When that was fruitless, we began a search of the library for scrolls in obscure tongues. To shorten this tale, it appears that the book of magic is written in the tongue of the Heyksin."

The silence was like a shout.

"The Magi of Alta were really Nameless Ones?" It was Marit who asked this, in an oddly calm voice. But Kaleth's beloved moved to take his hand, and he to hold hers. Her slightly slanted eyes were wide with alarm that she otherwise did not show.

"Let us say that we think that the Magi of Alta were—perhaps I should say 'are'—*descended* from the Nameless Ones." Rakaten-te shrugged. "It is difficult to say whether they still had any connection with their former peoples."

Kiron was still trying to get his mind to work. He thought it might be some time before he got his mouth to do so.

It was one thing to have his worst and yet most nebulous fear confirmed, that the shadowy attackers were in fact the Heyksin. At least he had anticipated that much.

But that the Magi were Heyksin—this smacked of a plan, a conspiracy, that must have been going on ever since the Nameless Ones were expelled from the Two Kingdoms.

"This . . . explains something," Kaleth said slowly. "I may be the Mouth of the Gods of Alta and Tia but . . . there are other gods. . . ."

The stranger priests now turned to stare at him as if he was speaking nonsense. But Rakaten-te nodded, his lips compressed into a thin, hard line. "There are other gods. And mine is the god of difficult choices. When gods war, it is often we mortals who serve as the armies."

The two stranger priests blanched.

Rakaten-te ignored them. "Go and commune, Mouth of the Gods of Tia and Alta. Ask them if it is war in heaven we face. And I hope you will return to me with an answer."

The quietest and coolest place in all of Sanctuary was the cavern beneath the city where a tributary of the Great Mother River ran hidden beneath the sand and rock of the desert. At the downstream end, past where people were pulling out their water for drinking and cooking, the current inhabitants had made a kind of area for swimming and bathing. Lit by a few lanterns whose light was reflected in the placid, deep waters, when there was no one else present, it was a place of deep peace and very, very quiet. This was where Kiron took his dazed and aching head, to immerse himself in the slowly-moving water and try not to think.

This was just too big. It had all gotten completely out of hand—

Except that wasn't it already out of hand? If what Rakaten-te had said was true? If this was all about the Gods of Tia and Alta at war with the Gods of the Nameless Ones . . . and had been all along . . . then the only difference was that now the poor mortals caught up in this conflict knew about it.

It made him feel as if he was in the middle of an earthshake.

I don't want to be in the middle of this.

But he was in the middle of it whether he liked it or not.

I'm not like Ari and Kaleth. I'm not royal, I'm not a priest, I'm just the son of a farmer. . . .

He lay there with his eyes closed, listening to the slow lapping of the water against the stone and sand of the verge, with the cool water covering all of him but his chin and face. This was insane. How could he be caught up in something this big?

Someone padded softly, with bare feet, down to the waterline and dove in, being careful to do so far enough from him so as to not splash him unduly. He opened his eyes and was not surprised to see Aket-ten's head surfacing nearby.

She looked at him out of the shadows as if she knew his thoughts. "This changes nothing, you know," she said calmly. "We'd still defend our land and our people. The Nameless Ones would still try and conquer us again. It's just as valid to say that *we* are causing this 'war in heaven' as it is to say the other way around."

He blinked. "It is?"

She smirked a little and pulled damp hair out of her eyes. "The Seft cult isn't the only one to have its little secrets. As a Fledgling, I was taught that 'as above, so below' also works the other way. As we, the worshippers, tend, so tend the gods. That's one reason why Kaleth is working so hard at reconciling the cults of Alta and Tia. Eventually in every Altan/Tian pairing, if the worshippers and the priests become reconciled . . . the two Gods *will* become one."

He had a funny mental image of two gods melting together like two unbaked *abshati* figures left out in the rain, and started to laugh. But then he sobered. "So we affect the gods?"

She nodded. "This 'war in heaven' may only be a reflection of the war the Nameless Ones brought to us so long ago. There is no telling for certain."

She swam over to him as he moved into the deeper water. "I just—don't like the whole idea of the gods swooping in and using us as pieces in a game," he replied, his stomach clenching.

She said nothing, for a very long time. "It's not a game," she said very quietly. "Not for us, certainly, but not for Them either. It's more complicated than that. I've been told that if they lose their followers, Gods can even die."

"Well, maybe the Gods ought to think twice about sticking people in wars where *they* can die, then," he said, irritated. It still made him queasy to think about it. Life was complicated enough without the Gods mucking about with it. "How long do you think they'll want us to stay here?" he asked, changing the subject. "The Chosen and Kaleth, I mean."

"I don't know." She swam over to the side and climbed out on the rocks to dry herself off. "I'm anxious to get back."

He felt a pang. So she would rather be with her new wing of dragons than with him for another day. . . .

The moment he had that thought, he knew it was unfair, but he couldn't help it. She had her duty. And these young women—they were shaping up well. Of course she needed to be with them.

He just wished she needed to be with him as much.

And he suddenly realized, with a very sour feeling in his gut, that he did not *want* to go back to Mefis. Not at all.

"Do you think you and Re-eth-ke could manage Rakaten-te alone?" he asked. She pulled a clean tunic over her head and tugged it down in place before turning to look at him, a hurt expression in her eyes. "It's not you!" he exclaimed quickly. "It's . . . my mother."

He clambered out beside her as she eyed him with a peculiar expression. He pulled his own clothing on without bothering to dry himself off. "She's driving me mad," he said pathetically. "She's my own mother, and she's driving me mad."

"She might be your mother, but you have seen nothing of her since you were very small." Aketten sat down on a rock, chin on her fist. "How can she possibly drive you mad? Now *my* mother—she knows exactly how to get me to do what she wants. She can make me feel guilty without saying a word, just using a look! She knows me too well. Your mother knows you not at all."

He ducked his head a little, feeling guilty already. "I should be happy to see her. I should want to spend as much time as I can with her and my sister. But my sister sits in the corner and plays with toys like a child because of how badly hurt she was. And my mother . . . all she talks about, all she wants to talk about, is getting the farm back."

He couldn't bring himself to call it "our" farm. He didn't belong there. He hardly remembered anything about living there, and he certainly didn't want to go back.

Ever.

Aket-ten blinked. "What would she do with it if she had it?" she asked logically. "One woman and a feeble-minded girl could not possibly keep up with the work. Does she have a man interested in her? Could she marry again if she had the land?"

Kiron groaned. "No, she does not, and would that she did! I know what she wants me to do. She wants me to find some girl in our old village, marry her, and become a farmer myself."

Somewhat to his indignation, Aket-ten burst into laughter.

"She does! And it is not funny! Even if I did not . . . love you . . ."

There, it was out. Words that hadn't been said between them for too long.

Words that broke the unspoken tension that had been between them. She looked up at him, eyes wide. He reached for her.

And for a long while there were no words between them, nor any need for them.

Dawn brought another summons to Kaleth's tiny temple. This time there were only the five of them there to confer; Kaleth and Marit, Kiron and Aket-ten, and the Chosen of Seft. Kaleth looked worn; Marit, worried.

And the word was not what Kiron had expected. "We're going back to Aerie? All of us?"

Kiron repeated what Kaleth had just told them with some incredulity. "But I thought—"

"The gods have not said much, Lord Kiron," Rakaten-te said somewhat sardonically, "But they have said that Aerie is the place where we must all be."

"The place where it began and where it all shall end to be precise," Kaleth added, equally sardonic. "Though they were exceedingly vague on what *it* was supposed to be." He sighed. "Sometimes even *I* grow weary of cryptic pronouncements.

"An end to bad poetry, perhaps?" Aket-ten suggested lightly. "Or the end to watered beer? Since no one has Foreseen the end of the world, I prefer to assume that the world will go on." She helped herself to a honeyed cake and nibbled it.

"Well," Kaleth said reluctantly, "we were given certain . . . directions. *Seek at the source of the life giver, once gracious and free, choked by enmity, now free again but crippled.* If that makes any sense to all of you—"

"Only that, as ever, the Gods are fond of bad poetry and—" began Aket-ten, shaking her head.

"—not as cryptic as you think," Kiron said slowly, interrupting her.

They all turned to face him as he spoke, the picture of the debris-choked cavern of the main spring of Aerie vivid in his mind. "The spring that once supplied water for most of Aerie in its prime was blocked up by an earthshake in the distant past, the same one that did most of the damage to the buildings there. We think that is why the city was abandoned; without that water, they could never have supported all the people that once lived there. The water's been working a way out toward the surface for—centuries at least. Before we found the city, the spring created another outlet, but we'd been planning to dig the entire area out when we had time—"

"It sounds to me as if that time has more than come." Rakaten-te sat up alertly. "The rest of your pronouncement was blessedly clear if wretchedly inconvenient for me. Fortunately, there are two messengers here already, so at least there are dragons enough to haul us like so many sacks of provender off to the middle of the howling wilderness. I am too old to endure a jaunt on a racing camel in the ungentle care of one of the Blue People." One corner of his mouth turned up a little. "Here I am, who wished for adventure in his youth and got none, now beset by adventure uncomfortable and hazardous in my declining years. Truly it is said, 'Take care what you wish for, the Gods will deliver it at the worst possible time.'"

But he did not sound unhappy about it. Not in the least, in fact. Kiron had the distinct impression that Rakaten-te was enjoying every minute of this, even (or perhaps especially) the danger.

"It's not the middle of the howling wilderness," Kiron protested mildly. "I will admit that you can *see* the middle of the howling wilderness from there, but—"

"—there is no point sitting about and nattering about it," Aket-ten said briskly, standing up. "The sooner we get there, the sooner we will discover what it is the Gods want us to find."

"And that is truth. Let us gather our things and go. Marit and I can be ready by the time the dragons are finished eating." Kaleth stood up, and Marit with him.

"I never unpacked," sighed Rakaten-te.

"Anything Aket-ten and I need is already there," Kiron put in, with a glance at Aket-ten. She returned his look warmly.

They had agreed on a few things, down there beside the slow-moving, hidden river. She wouldn't be going back to Mefis. Certainly not until this crisis was over, and after that—

She told Kiron that she had more than half made up her mind that Huras was a better teacher than she, certainly more patient and definitely better able to get things out of people. It might be, now that the group of female Jousters had been more-or-less (if grudgingly) accepted, that it would be good for them to get their training from someone who was actually suited to teaching. And one thing was certain. The Queen's Wing would be led, for the nonce, by the son of Altan bakers.

But first, before any plans for the future could be made, it was time to defend the Two Kingdoms.

"Then we will gather at the pens when you are ready," Kiron said. "I will alert the other two Jousters. Let us be gone and quickly."

"Aye," Rakaten-te said, all of his humor vanishing. "All we know about our enemy is that he has been a step ahead of us until now. We must hope he is not still, but act as if he was."

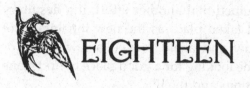 **EIGHTEEN**

WHEN *the Gods speak . . . things get done.*

Kiron wiped the back of his neck and his forehead with the rag he'd had tied around it, and took a much-needed break from what at any other time he would have balked at doing. Virtually every able-bodied person in Aerie that was *not* out patrolling or supporting the day-to-day activities of the place had put in some time on clearing the rocks from the cave-in.

It helped that one of the priests had some sort of magic that told him what places were unsteady and needed careful work. It also helped that the initial effort at clearing the tunnel must have taken place immediately after the earth-shake until the presumably desperate inhabitants had given up and packed themselves out. It also helped that another effort, if a desultory one, had taken place as the new inhabitants of Aerie now and again moved a few rocks, or even came looking for a good place to find stone for partitions and the like.

But now . . . now the real effort was underway, and even Lord Kiron, Captain of the Jousters, was stripped down to a loinwrap and was part of a human chain moving rocks out to be piled beside the ever-more-freely-running spring. And Aket-ten, Wingleader of the Queen's Wing, was carrying water like any serf girl.

It was brutally hot, even deep in the tunnel, and the air was thick with sweat and dust. Although most of the labor was of the unskilled, brute-strength variety—barrow-loads of smaller stones being carted out and dumped, those rocks that could be lifted being passed from hand to hand, and the truly enormous boulders being levered from where they were wedged and pulled by teams of the strongest hitched to ropes—Kiron was seeing more real magic in this place than he had since the use of the Eye in Alta. And now he knew why priests and Magi so seldom did purely ordinary things by means of magic.

There was the priest who could somehow "read" instability, of course. That was not what Kiron would have called "impressive" except in that there had been no rockfalls and no cave-ins. But three times now, they had come upon a huge boulder that was far, far too big to lever out, and even if it could have been freed, it was too heavy to move. Three times, a different priest had come forward with a different solution.

The first had sent everyone out of the cave. What happened next, was known only to the priest and presumably others of his rank, but there was a thunderclap from within the cave, followed by a violent blast of dust-carrying wind rushing out of the mouth of it. They all scrambled back in, to find the boulder shattered and the priest unconscious on the ground.

Kiron was in a panic at the sight of the unconscious man, but his fellows seemed perfectly at ease, and merely picked him up and carried him out without any fuss.

The second time, the rectangular rock was not wedged in like a cork in the mouth of a bottle, it simply filled most, not all, of a rather narrow space. This time another priest came forward and directed them to clear all debris out of the way and from around the sides of the boulder. Then, chanting and gesturing, he "went to work" with all of them watching.

With a grating sound, the rock began to move.

It moved forward at an agonizingly slow pace, hardly more than the width of a nail paring for every breath. The priest was soon white-faced and sweating as hard as any of them; it looked for all the world as if he was moving the wretched thing himself, by main strength.

Maybe he was.

Finally, just as he got it far enough out of the bottleneck that it would be possible to get ropes around it to haul it out over rollers, *he* collapsed and was in his turn carried out.

And now the third. Another fall of rock, again bottlenecked in with the spring creeping under some hair-thin gap beneath it, and another priest.

"This is the last," said the one who could sense when falls were about to take place. Eyes closed and sweating as hard as any of them, it was clear that what he was doing was no light task either. "When this is gone, the way will be clear."

"But there is much water built up behind this stone." The new priest placed both hands on the rock and leaned his forehead on it. "Hmm. This will be tricky—"

"Not to mention dangerous," the stone reader replied. "If it is released all at once—"

"I do not speak to you of the ways of stone, Tam-kalet; do not preach to me of the paths of water!" the priest snapped, then immediately apologized. "Forgive me. Great Mother River is no easy mistress. And she wants her child released."

The reader of rocks chuckled, opened his eyes, and mopped his brow. "They all move in us this day, and it seems we deal in more tasks for them than just one. Need you my services?"

The newcomer looked around the cavern. "Indeed, I need none save perhaps Lord Kiron. . . ."

"Why me?" he asked, astonished. "The other priest—"

"The other priest was not me." That was all the explanation Kiron was going to get, it seemed, for as everyone else took the hint and began an ordered but hurried evacuation of the tunnel, the priest turned his attention back to the rock. "Have I your consent to draw upon your strength?" the man asked brusquely, eyes closed and one hand on the rock.

As if I have a choice? This was the final barrier. It needed to come down. Whatever lay on the other side of it, they *needed* and needed swiftly. "Yes," Kiron replied, just as brusquely.

The priest grunted, then said, "Sit somewhere near me. And be silent. This is not a magic of brute force, but of planning and concentration."

Kiron obeyed, throttling down his own impatience. From Aket-ten's explanations, he had a good idea what the priest was asking for. The strength for a spell had to come from somewhere. Either it came from inside the magic worker himself—which was why those other priests had collapsed—or it came from some source outside. The Altan Magi had stolen their power, stripping it from the god-touched priests and acolytes of Alta, and from the premature deaths of the war. The Tian priests—the ones he'd seen so far, at any rate—were more ethical.

This one wanted to use Kiron as his source of strength.

Well, if it would get the job done . . . from Kiron's perspective, this was certainly preferable to hauling stone.

So he sat where the priest directed and put his back against the wall. He had the feeling he was going to need the support before it was all over. Now there was nothing but silence, and the very occasional plashing of the spring running under that final blockage.

He knew when the priest was taking—whatever it was—too. It felt as if he was running, except that he wasn't. It was just a steady drain of strength and energy. Not a lot, nor all at once, and not debilitating to the point where *he* was passing out, but there was no doubt that something was going on, that in some way, life energy was sapping from him and going somewhere else.

Even though all he could see from where he sat was the priest with his hands and forehead pressed up against the rock.

But then a new sound in the tunnel made him look more closely.

It was the sound of dripping water.

The departing workers had left all their lamps and torches stuck wherever they could be wedged or balanced, so there was plenty of light, and in addition, sheets of reflective, polished metal outside were sending bright patches of sunlight down here. And now, in that light, Kiron first noticed that the volume of water running through the channel at his feet had easily doubled.

The next thing that he noticed was that all around the edges of the bottom half of the stone jamming the bottleneck, there were little trickles, tiny streamlets that had not been there before. And even as he watched a spot that had been previously dry, he saw first a single drop of water well to the surface of the hairline crack, then a second and a third, then the drops became a trickle, then the trickle a thin stream down the face of the rock,

And he realized a moment later that somehow that crack, almost invisible to the eye, was widening.

He had to pull his feet up now, the water was getting so deep.

Then there was a wet *pop,* and the rock itself cracked across the middle from right to left, and water began to trickle from the crack.

That was the beginning of the end. The rock cracked, and cracked, and cracked again, but only the bottom half. Soon the bottom half of the rock shimmered with water, and even with his feet pulled up, Kiron was ankle-deep in the stream.

Then the priest pulled away from the stone, and the steady drain on Kiron ended.

"I think we need to leave here and let Tam-kalet do his work," the priest—whose name Kiron still didn't know—said hoarsely. "The water has undermined the entire bottom half of that blockage; that is why it was cracking. I do not know when it will succumb to the stress."

Kiron didn't need a second invitation. He shoved himself up off the rock and realized, as he staggered away, that he was as completely spent as he had ever been in his life.

And cold, cold. As he stumbled into the harsh sunlight, the warmth felt good on his numb skin. He sat down abruptly on the first place that looked comfortable, as the priest's fellows came and assisted him away. Tam-kalet and two others went back inside the tunnel, after warning everyone else to stay back.

Just as Kiron was actually starting to feel warm again, they came running out, a grinding sound echoing from the tunnel behind them.

Tam-kalet jumped up onto the rocks stacked up to the right of the tunnel entrance. The other two scrambled over the ones to the left. And just in time, for a muddy wave of water and rocks tumbled together surged out hard on their heels with a roar.

When everything had settled again, the spring was back in its old bed. As near as Kiron could tell, the stream it fed was back at the highest level it had been in when Aerie was in its prime.

The priests that remained stared at the stream in satisfaction, but it was Rakaten-te who spoke, standing off to one side and leaning on his staff.

"Kaleth, Marit. It is our turn now."

Kaleth gestured to two of the younger priests. One stepped forward to act as Rakaten-te's guide, the other followed the trio. Kiron was curious, but his exhaustion overcame his curiosity. He knew he would find out what, if anything, was in there eventually, and for the moment, recovering his strength seemed more important than anything else.

It was not very much later that all five of them came out again. This time it was Kaleth who led the elder priest, while the two junior priests carried a small chest between them. It seemed very heavy for its size; after a moment, it occurred to him that it must be made of stone, and he wondered what could be so important that it required a stone chest to hold it.

Well, whatever it was, it seemed to be what Kaleth and Rakaten-te were looking for. They paused, as the two young priests went on with the chest, presumably to the Temple of Haras.

"We have found what we were sent to find," Kaleth said into the waiting stillness. "The Great King and Queen have been sent for, because the enemy comes apace, and the time has come to end what was here begun."

His words did not have the otherworldly ring about them that they had when he was speaking directly for the gods, but Kiron had no doubt that his words came from them anyway. As the rest of those waiting, Jousters, workers, priests and all, looked at one another in befuddlement and began to murmur, Rakaten-te rapped his staff three times on the stone to silence them.

"Prepare yourselves, people of Aerie, of the Two Kingdoms. The Heyksin come. And this time their Magi, and perhaps their gods, come with them."

Outside the temple, even through stone walls as thick as his arm was long, Kiron could hear the murmur of voices. Not surprising since just about every living soul in Aerie was out there right now.

With that single word, "Heyksin," every difference that had ever existed between the people, and the Jousters, of Tia and Alta had disappeared. It was what Ari and Nofret had wanted so badly—

Be careful what you wish for . . .

Kiron could not help thinking about those

words, now so grimly prophetic. And yet, that wish had nothing to do with a plan that must have been a-building for tens of tens of years. Even if the Magi of Alta were *not* in league with their Heyksin cousins, it still must have been a-building for that long. It was just too well-plotted, too well-executed. Had not that one single man escaped . . . had he not gotten far enough and at the right time for his body to have been spotted by patrolling Jousters . . . then all of the border towns could have been removed and the way would have been clear for a Heyksin army led by Magi to strike straight at the heart of Tia. Alta was already weak and shaking. Tia's troops were decimated even if the land itself and the majority of the people were still secure. It would have been the ideal time to strike. Heyksin forces could have taken Mefis with scarcely a battle. And even if Ari and Nofret had escaped by dragon, where could they have gone?

They were here now, and along with the strongest priests of Sanctuary, and Aket-ten and Kiron, they waited to see what it was that the gods had wanted Kaleth to find.

Kiron had suspected a weapon of some type, perhaps something like the great Eye of Alta—though hopefully, one that could be powered without the dreadful cost of lives—but the box was far too small for that. Kiron had thought it was stone; it wasn't. It was made of some metal he could not identify, black either by design or blackened with age. And utterly plain, without any of the bas-reliefs or carved letters beloved of the craftsmen of the present day. In fact, in its simplicity, it seemed of a piece with this very city, a place where even the statues of the gods were curiously simplified and refined down to a few basic lines.

No one, not even Kaleth knew what was in there. He had been waiting for Ari and Nofret to arrive. And now was the moment of truth. . . .

With great care, Kaleth reverently put his hand on the lid. Kiron held his breath—and truth to tell, he more than halfway expected that the box would be sealed, either by some invisible lock or by age. Or maybe by magic.

But the lid came up easily in Kaleth's hand, swinging on hinges that *were* invisible. Kaleth reached inside—and pulled out an oval, flat package, wrapped in age-yellowed linen that literally fell to pieces in his hands, revealing the gleam of gold.

It was a circlet, a crown, of the sort that could be worn alone, or over the Greater Crowns. This one, though—the hawk head meant to be worn on the brow was of nearly identical design to that of the statues outside, and standing in the sanctuary of this very temple. Very simple. Very stylized. The hawk head was all smooth curves, suggesting beak, eyes, the hunch of wings, rather than actually depicting them. Kiron stared at it, fascinated by the gleaming metal. He wanted to touch that little casting, feel the metal smooth beneath his fingertips. . . .

But there were more. Five more times, Kaleth reached into that box and came out again with a crown, until he had placed the sixth and last on the floor, in a circle.

There was a stylized cobra and a scorpion. The hawk and the arching horns of a cow. The curled horns of the ram and the long-necked head of the vulture. Six crowns.

The representations of six gods and goddesses.

"The crowns of the gods?" Kaleth asked out loud.

"Ah, I wondered what you had uncovered." The Chosen of Seft nodded. "Such things were said to have been made. By the gods themselves, in fact. One wonders now if the blocking up of that spring was deliberate, not to stop the water, but to prevent the priests of this city from getting their hands on these relics."

For Siris, chief of the gods and lord of the dead, there was the ram. For his wife Iris, the cobra, wise and cunning. For Haras, the hawk of course, and for his wife Hattar, the curved cow horns surrounding a fertile full moon.

And for Seft . . . the scorpion crown. And for his wife Nebt, the vulture.

For a long time, everyone stared at the six crowns and no one moved. Finally, though he could not have said why he did this, Kiron reached avidly for the hawk crown.

Just as his fingers caressed the smooth surface of the gold, the crown suddenly flared to life. To his credit, Kiron did not even flinch. White-gold light blazed from the circlet for a moment, making them all squint, then faded to a soft, warm glow.

"Do—can I hold that?" Aket-ten said, hesitantly. Without a qualm, Kiron handed it to her.

The light was quenched as suddenly as if a lamp flame had been blown out. Aket-ten bit back an exclamation of disappointment and handed the crown back to Kiron.

The moment his fingers touched it, the light returned.

"I sense the magic," said Rakaten-te mildly. "If I were you, I would not put that on just yet."

Kiron blinked. He had, in fact, been thinking of doing just that. But the Chosen of Seft's words made him think twice about that idea. "Ah . . . you may be right," he said. But he didn't put the crown down.

He couldn't. Not even when another thought occurred to him. He hadn't been at all happy about the notion of the Gods pulling them about . . . and now, here he was . . .

"So. Kiron has—what?" Rakaten-te asked.

"The diadem of Haras," replied Kaleth. "So this, Chosen, is surely meant for you—"

Kaleth gingerly picked up the diadem of Seft and began to put it in Rakaten-te's hands. But as soon as the metal circlet got even close to the Chosen, a darker, redder light blazed from the gold, and Rakaten-te gave a swift intake of breath.

He reached out his hands, and Kaleth quickly dropped the circlet in them. He let out a long sigh, as the light dimmed to a ruddy glow. Meanwhile, with some hesitation, Aketten was reaching for the diadem of Hattar. As her fingers neared it, silver-gold light blossomed as if to welcome her, and she picked up the circlet with wide eyes, lips parted a little in wonder.

"I—feel the power, too!" she said. "I have never done that before—"

"You have never held something that the gods themselves have made," Rakaten-te said with a slight smile. "And I think there is a reason why the Great King and Queen were called for—"

But Ari hesitated, looking dubiously at the remaining three crowns. "I didn't want, didn't choose to be King," he said slowly. "This—this is so far beyond being merely *King*—"

The Chosen of Seft raised his chin, frowning. "And this may well be the only way you can save your peoples, Great King. You did not choose this task, it chose you. Nevertheless—"

"Nevertheless . . . it is a task I accepted. And this is a piece of that task." Ari took a deep breath and reached for the diadem of Siris, as Nofret reached confidently for that of Iris. Blue-white light, a little darker for the crown of Siris, answered their touch.

I am holding the crown of Haras. I am about to become a hound on the game board of the gods. He felt a chill, a sinking feeling in his gut, and yet . . . now that it had come this far, he could not put down that diadem. He could not back away from the game. More lives than just his depended on this.

And the game had been put in motion long, long before he was born. If Aket-ten was to be believed . . . maybe it had been started, not by the gods, but by men. As below, so above, she said. He clutched the crown and willed himself to be steady. He was on the path now. There was no turning back.

That left only one crown, that of the wife of Seft, Nebt, the Lady of the desert, the Voice of Prophecy, the Dweller Between, unclaimed. Kaleth stared at it for a long time. Finally, he picked it up. It remained lifeless gold in his hands.

He placed it reverently back in the metal box. "Not today, I think," he said, and put down the lid, which closed with a muffled click. Then he turned back to the Chosen of Seft. "I assume you know something of these objects?"

Rakaten-te shook his head, but he was smiling. "Only that they once existed and were lost. But the gods do not leave anything to chance when the situation is as grave as this one, and they will guide us as to what we must do next. I suggest all of you *listen* to your crowns. *They* will tell you what you need to know."

Kiron shook his head, even as his fingers caressed the cool gold. Listen to the crown? That was ridiculous . . .

. . . wasn't it?

But he closed his eyes for a moment, and felt the weight of the thing that he held in both hands, felt its solidity, its power, and . . .

Blinked, as his head jerked up, as if he had been nodding off, and he knew in that moment exactly what it was he needed to do, and when. He didn't know what would happen after that, but he did know that much. The crown was a conduit for Haras, somehow, and made it possible for the god to manifest when it was worn by a living human.

Provided, of course, that *Kaleth* knew what *he* needed to—these things required a ritual, it seemed—

"The crown has given me the ritual that we will need, Mouth of the Gods," Rakaten-te said, with great formality. "I shall teach it to you as soon as may be."

Kaleth looked around the circle of faces, lit from beneath by the softly glowing diadems on their laps. "You all know what you have to do?"

As he met the eyes of each of them in turn, they nodded.

He let out his breath in a sigh.

"Then teach me, Chosen of Seft, and let it be now," he replied. "The gods have spoken. Tamat the Render is coming, the ravaging goddess of the Heyksin, and there is very little time to waste."

The Chosen of Seft could not look at him, but Kiron sensed all of Rakaten-te's concentration was focused on Kaleth, with a fierce heat like that of the sun on the Anvil of the Sun.

"There is *no* time to waste, Mouth of the Gods," the Chosen said, in a very controlled voice. "No time at all."

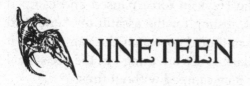

NINETEEN

THE tallest flat spot in Aerie—on the top of the cliffs overlooking the main chasm—was their rallying point. Whatever Tamat the Render was, she was not coming alone. The Heyksin were bringing an army, the like of which only the Heyksin could field. For the Heyksin had in abundance something that was rare in Tia and unheard of, practically, in Alta.

The Heyksin had horses.

Now, the Tian army did have chariots, about as many as they had dragons. Which was to say, formidable against foes afoot but nothing like what the Heyksin were bringing.

Orest's wing was running scouting forays, and caught them just leaving the Anvil of the

Sun, at the farthest point of practical scouting range. The Heyksin force paused and camped overnight, resting for the assault on Aerie, and Jousters continued to watch the camp until it was too dark to see anything but the occasional torch, for they camped without fires.

That morning, a final set of scouts had gone out to take actual numbers, if they could. Orest himself returned, white-faced and shaking, to give the report.

"I've never seen anything like it," he stammered, balancing in his saddle as his blue dragon Wastet perched gracefully on an outcrop that really looked too small to support so much weight. "They cover the land from edge to edge. You can probably see their dust cloud from here. Thousands of them. And not like our chariots, no, these things have slicing blades on the wheels, and armor. They'll mow down foot soldiers like so many farmers cutting barley." He wiped his forehead with his hand. "Those blades and things weren't on the chariots before. They must have had them all stored and put them on last night."

The Chosen of Seft nodded gravely. "This was how they conquered before. But we will have no foot soldiers on the ground today. We will have archers, spearmen, and sling wielders on the cliffs of Aerie. And we will have the Jousters in the air—"

"Every Jouster that can drop a pot," Kiron said grimly, shading his eyes with one hand as he peered toward the horizon, looking for the haze of a dust cloud. "We have had every pair of hands that can busy brewing Akkadian Fire and sealing it in beer jars. The Jousters, too, are trained with javelin and sling. And I hope that the Heyksin horses are not accustomed to dragons."

"Do not count too much on that," Ari cautioned. "They have had a very long time to learn about our dragons. They might not have any themselves, but they surely have some weapons to counter them." He looked to Kiron. "Only our newest techniques are likely to work."

Kiron nodded, and turned to Gan. "Tell the Jousters that they must stay out of reach of the ground. Ari is right; the Nameless Ones *must* be expecting dragons and plan on us using the old tactics. I don't want anyone flying down to seize an officer. Stick to attacking from above, and choose your targets with care."

Gan nodded, and strode off to the edge of the cliff. He whistled shrilly, and with a flash of green, his Khaleph rose up from a ledge below to land beside him. He swung himself up into the saddle and Khaleph pushed off, carrying them both to pass the word on to the Jousters.

And perhaps the diadems they all held in uncertain hands would not be needed. He could hope for that. Perhaps whatever it was that the Heyksin had in mind to conjure up this "Tamat"—whatever it was—wouldn't work. Perhaps the real battle would be won by mortal hands, hands that the Heyksin had outnumbered by as much as a hundred to one.

And perhaps you will do as your mother wishes, take back the farm and house, marry whatever girl still living in your village happens to consent, and settle down to raise barley. One was as likely as the other.

The dust cloud that stretched across the eastern horizon grew nearer. And now Kiron heard it, felt it, a rumble like distant thunder, except the thunder didn't end, and it grew louder, nearer. He felt the faint vibration of the stone beneath his feet. And the Heyksin army still was not in sight, only the dust they raised.

The dragons shifted, stirred, complained. Below him, in the valley and on the cliffs, they turned their heads to look at their riders. Those few that had been in battle *knew* what this meant, and they wanted to be off. The rest took their cue from those few.

But Ari's—and Kiron's—orders were explicit. *Let the Nameless Ones wear themselves out to come to us. Let the sun and the heat be our weapons.* For there was a small, an infinitesimal bit of luck on their side. The season of the rains was not yet come. The sun still burned his way across the sky in the fury of full summer. The Heyksin were driving chariots, not riding camels.

Down below, the last of the feverish preparations ended, and people retreated behind their barricades of stone. The way had been made as cruel for horses as possible with every handspan of open ground strewn with sharp-edged shards of rock. The ways into the city were barricaded with piles of thorns. There was not a drop of water to be had; what water was freely available came from within the city, and those water-courses had been rerouted.

And *now* it became clear why every dwelling in the city had those sunken ground floors that seemed so perfect for dragon pens.

They were for water, probably in the event of just such a siege as they were facing. With a minimum of effort, each could be filled in turn from the now freely flowing spring. It would take days, weeks to fill them all, during which time the water was *not* going out to where the Heyksin army would be. Of course, those that had been made into dragon pens couldn't be filled with water, but those were few compared to the number of empty dwellings, or those that held folk who were not Jousters.

The Heyksin army might be huge, but they were facing a more implacable enemy than the united force of Alta and Tia.

Time.

They were living on only what they had brought, food and water both. They were under the punishing sun. Their supply line was impossibly long, unless they could somehow send supplies across the Anvil of the Sun in the blink of an eye. They *could not* wait out a long siege. For once, the advantage was to the besieged, not the besiegers.

But they had to know that. Either they were mad and did not care, or . . .

Or what they bring with them is worse than anything we could possibly imagine.

Kiron clutched the diadem so hard his hands ached. It still had not lost that soft glow, nor had any of the others.

But as the thunder of the approaching chariots neared, as a dark line beneath the dun-colored dust cloud resolved into a mass of tiny, moving figures, he had a final fear that he could not still. Off to one side stood the Chosen of Seft, his own diadem held lightly in his hands, his bandaged eyes betraying nothing.

Seft the Liar. Seft the Betrayer.

Could they trust the god, or his Chosen?

Kiron didn't know, and that terrified him as much as that army of chariots.

But it was too late now. Their feet were on the path, and there was no way to turn back, as the chariots finally came within easy range of the first dragon attack.

Kiron watched with sick longing as the wing in his colors of scarlet and black led the attack, and tiny jars rained down on the line of charioteers from above. They must have laughed—

Until those jars shattered, and their evil contents splattered over drivers, warriors, and horses alike, bursting into flame.

Obviously not all, nor even most, of the jars hit their marks. Nor did the contents find useful targets. But enough did that suddenly the front line erupted into chaos. Men screeched and horses screamed in pain. Flames blossomed out of the cups of the war chariots, eating everything they touched. Horses reared and bolted, trying to escape the fires burning on their backs, their rumps, making brief, fiery banners of manes and tails. Kiron cheered with the rest, although there was a part of him that felt sick at watching the horrible sight—a flaming chariot careering wildly across the space between the army and Aerie, with neither driver nor fighter aboard, with the horses crying their fear and pain until they encountered one of the many traps set for them and went down in a tangle of metal and broken legs, slashing wheels and blood. Or two chariots locked together, scything their way through the Heyksin's own ranks until a quick-witted archer on their own side brought the horses down. Men lying on the ground aflame, howling out their agony until the fires, or one of their fellows ended their pain.

A second wave of Jousters, this time in Menet-ka's green and white, bore down on the line with another round of their deadly cargo.

But this time they were met by a storm of arrows, rising from the ground so thick they formed a black cloud. Kiron began waving his diadem in the air and shouting wildly, even though there was no chance that Menet-ka could hear him. His heart plummeted. No dragon could fly into that—

But Menet-ka made the right decision; a signal from the indigo-blue's rider told the whole wing to veer off. There was a groan of disappointment from the defenders of Aerie, but Kiron breathed a sigh of relief.

They came at the line again, but this time from high above the point where the arrows were falling off and arcing back to earth. Unfortunately, from that height most of the jars missed their marks and splattered their contents on the ground, flames boiling up from the ground uselessly.

Trumpets sounded in the enemy ranks and the chariots reorganized, protected by the archers, as foot soldiers ran out to collect the spent arrows. They were still out of reach of weapons from the cliffs of Aerie.

"They can't charge," Ari murmured. Kiron turned his head.

"What? Why?"

"They can't charge, because if they do, their archers can't protect them. But if they advance slowly, they lose all the advantage those chariots give them. They weren't expecting the Akkadian Fire . . ."

He was interrupted by Aket-ten's gasp, which, as she pointed to the northern end of the enemy lines, was echoed all over Aerie.

A pillar of black cloud and purple lightning was forming where she pointed, a slowly rotating pillar growing taller and broader with every passing moment.

As a chill fell over Kiron, he vaguely heard Kaleth beginning to chant behind him. The diadem in his hands grew warm as he stared at the apparition that grew and grew until it towered overhead and blotted out half the sky. A cold, harsh wind sprang up, spiraling toward the pillar, whipping up sand and dust, lashing them all with punishing gusts and carrying with it a stench of stagnant water and decay.

Thunder growled from it—real thunder—and the lightnings that laced the thing grew hotter and brighter until—

A bolt sizzled out of the pillar and lashed at the outermost cliff face. With a roar, stone exploded in every direction, and dragons reacted by launching themselves into the sky, in every direction, propelled by fear.

They weren't the only ones jolted into terror by the lightnings that now arced toward Aerie's cliffs. Everywhere, the defenders were screaming and trying to scramble down off the heights. But the lightning wasn't what riveted Kiron's attention. His eyes were fixed on the vague shape forming near the top of the pillar, and the six baleful green eyes glaring down from within.

Then the great wings unfolded with a booming sound that rivaled the thunder, Tamat raised her three heads to the sky and sang her song of death.

She was not a dragon, although she sported wings. These were huge, tattered things of bone and black feathers, like the wings of the carcass of a bird that the insects have almost finished with. The rest of her body was an unhealthy shade of pale, corpse-blue, a naked woman's body, skin a glowing pallor with a faint, slick sheen of scales. She had legs like a bird, too, a great vulture perhaps, but a lizardlike tail, and her three heads were like nothing that Kiron had ever seen before. Scaled, enormous jaws, bulging fish-eyes glowing green, the curving horns of a ram, all of it the same sickly blue as her body.

And she must have been the size of the largest building in Aerie. Maybe larger.

That corpse stench came from her. With every

beat of her wings it drove down at them as she
looked down at them and sang.

Give up, said the song. *Give up, despair, and die.
Death is inevitable. I will have you, and you will go
down into the darkness and be forgotten. I am the
End of All Things, and you cannot escape me.*

Kiron felt his will being sapped, his knees
weakening, and black depression surrounding
him, smothering him, drowning him.

*Surrender to me. I am Inevitable. Hope is an illu-
sion.*

This was where that insidious, corrupting
voice had come from, the voice that had whispered in his mind and told him how foolish it
was to believe that Aket-ten cared for him—

That moment of recognition flashed across his
spirit and jolted him awake, out of the mire of
despair, giving him one tiny moment of freedom
in which to act.

He put on the diadem.

Around him, he sensed the others doing the
same, as some strength in each of them lashed
back at Tamat's Song.

Then his mind was clear, clearer than it had
ever been in his life.

Of course, his mind was no longer in control
of his body. Something—Someone—else, was.

That Presence filled him; he felt his mortality
straining to contain it, like too much grain being
poured into a sack until the fabric was tight

enough to drum upon. It was Light. *He* was Light. He was Haras, offspring of Siris and Iris, the Hawk of the Sun. But . . . what that was . . . was so much more than anyone had ever written.

Beside him, his other self, his complement, She who completed him.

In fact, Kiron sensed all of this only dimly. This Being that had taken him over, and was using him as an anchor to the mortal world, was too enormous to grasp, and as for comprehending it—he might just as well as a beetle could comprehend the thoughts of a man.

And yet to act in the mortal world, these immortal beings required a mortal anchor, one person who would give them that right-of-usage. He had given that consent, and Haras had taken it.

And Kiron was now only baggage.

Peri stood on the edge of the path leading up to the top of the cliff where Kiron and the others had been overseeing the battle. She had brought them water—no, truth, she had brought *Kiron* water, and the others would be welcome to have some, but she had brought it for Kiron—

But now she clutched the water jar to her chest, unthinking, as she stared up at the monstrous shape of the column of darkness looming over them all. A cold storm wind whipped her clothing against her body, and the lightning that lashed out of the column to strike nearby made her jump and scream, dropping the jar, which shattered at her feet.

What have I done? she thought, as terror froze her.

When Huras had told them all he was returning to Aerie, that he was needed there, and that there was going to be a battle, she had begged him to take her with him. Sutema wasn't strong enough to make such a long, grueling trip with a rider, but she could and would follow, if Peri was carried behind another Jouster. In fact, that had been one of Peri's own ideas, to train fledglings too young to carry much weight how to fly. Sutema had been flying strongly for a sennight or more now.

Huras hadn't hesitated, not for a moment. "We'll need every hand," he had said, somewhat grimly, and gave her only as long as it took for Sutema and Tathulan to eat their fill to gather what she needed. She realized just how urgent it was when he did not stop for the dragons to hunt midway through their journey. Sutema had been tired beyond measure when they had arrived, and Peri hadn't been in much better shape. They both ate and drank enormously and curled up to sleep together in a strange sort of cavelike house that had a dragon pen in the bottom of it, alongside Huras' Tathulan. Peri had not even had the strength to go up the stairs to try and find a proper bed.

And when she woke, an army was already almost to Aerie itself.

She knew better than to pester Kiron; instead she made herself as useful as she could. She had fetched and carried all manner of things, helped to build barricades, helped to channel water into a reservoir, even cooked and baked so that food would be ready and on hand when fighters needed it. Finally, she got a moment of respite and decided that there would be nothing wrong with taking water up to the commanders of this battle.

She had only really been aware of a harsh wind whipping up; the switchback path she had taken to the top of the cliff where they were faced away from where the army was assembled. So until she got to the rim, she'd had no idea of the horror hanging in the sky, a pillar of lightning and darkness that was taller than the cliff—and had eyes.

This was not what she had expected to see. There was nothing in this world that she could compare this to, and horror dried her mouth, knotted her gut, and froze her feet in place.

And *then* the—Thing—came out of the top of the pillar and began to sing, and she could not even scream. Her mouth opened, but all that

came out was a strangled squeal. Tears of fear
and despair poured down her cheeks, and she
wanted to throw herself off the top of this cliff,
because breaking her neck on the rocks below
would be a blessing compared to what that—
Thing—was going to do to them. To her. It *told*
her somehow, deep in her mind, in a whirlwind
of horror and panic, it *showed* her what her fate
was to be.

We're going to die. We are all going to die.

The Being that inhabited Kiron bowed with deep
respect to the One looking from Ari's eyes. The
five who wore the diadems now wore power and
glory like so many shining mantles. Their eyes
glowed with it; their faces were radiant, and
auras of light coruscated around them. *"Father,"*
he said, his voice sounding strange and echoing
in his own ears. The Being cast a glance at the
Chosen, who had discarded his staff and moved
to join them striding as surely as if he could see
despite his bandaged eyes. *"Uncle. I greet you."*

Tamat screamed, and all five of them looked
up at her. She hovered in place, wingbeats
spreading her noisome stench, all three heads
glaring down at them.

"She is not yet a god," observed Seft, through
his vessel's lips.

"Not yet," said Iris, as Tamat shrieked in outrage at the sight of the five of them. *"But enough*

blood has been spilled to unbind her. She is loose now in the world and if we do not bind her again, enough blood will likely be spilled to make her a god. And that would be an evil day indeed."

"She is stronger than we," replied Siris doubtfully. "We have never faced her thus. Always before, we have been on equal footing with her. We are constrained by the limits of our mortal hosts. She has made a body to suit herself."

"Then we must be wiser, faster, and more skilled!" said Haras, with all the fierce determination of a desert falcon. His words rang out against the screams from Tamat above them, and the whine of the wind in the rocks.

Seft's dark powers pulsed with the beat of his heart, and against the brilliant gold and incandescent white of Haras and Siris, he looked like a shadow. His words echoed ominously. *"Blood called her. It may require blood to bind her again."* Despite the bandages shrouding his eyes, there was no doubt that he was looking directly at Siris. *"As it was in the past, so it may be again. It may be that one must fall. It may be that only then will the power be sufficient to bind her."*

"No!" Iris moved forward in protest, but Siris waved her back.

"She cannot be left to rage across this mortal soil. So be it." The words had all the weight and finality that only a god could give them. *"But that moment is not yet. Let us see what mortal hands and*

immortal powers can do." He turned toward the waiting dragons, that had not moved in all this time. He spread his hands wide, and Power filled the cliff top.

The top of the cliff blossomed with light, as if the sun-disk itself had alighted there. At last the terror let her go, and Peri dropped to her knees, whimpering. She turned her face away from the shining creatures that had once been people she knew, or at least recognized. They were nothing she recognized anymore. They seemed twice the height of perfectly ordinary people; they radiated light and force, she didn't even dare look at their faces, and merely being in their presence made her gasp as if she had been running for half a day.

Gods. These were gods. How they had come to take the place of the people she knew, that was a mystery. But the gods were mysteries, not just mysterious, they were *Mysteries* and they did things she could not even begin to understand.

Blinding light filled the top of the cliff, making her cover her eyes, and when she could look again, four of the gods were in the sky, flying toward the hideous *Thing* in the midst of its darkness, mounted on—

Well, what they were riding bore as much resemblance to dragons as these Beings bore to humans. If someone had taken pure light and shaped it into the form of a dragon—well, that was the closest she could come to what was winging toward the demonic nightmare in the sky. A blue more intense than the sky itself, a scarlet that flames could only envy, a purple-shaded scarlet that would make the most glorious sunset look washed out, and a blue-black that vibrated with intensity; these were the colors of the celestial creatures that the gods rode. There was nothing in her experience to compare these colors, these creatures, to. The colors of jewels perhaps, but nothing less.

The monstrous vision screeched, a sound that made Peri cover her ears and duck her head, overcome by panic. When she could look up again, it was to a sky gone mad.

The Thing lashed out against the four attackers with bolts of lightning. Somehow they evaded these, and returned the favor with balls of light, great gouts of flame, and some lightning of their own. For Peri, it was impossible to sort out who was doing what, the sky was too full of light, the air too full of thunder.

The ground shook with the force of their exchange.

She felt a hand seize her shoulder and shake it, and turned to find Huras kneeling beside her. It gave her some small measure of comfort to see that he looked as terrified as she felt. "Peri!"

shouted Huras over the sound of the unearthly battle. "Peri, what's going on? Where are Kiron and the others?"

Hands glowing with dark power seized both their shoulders and pulled them to their feet. "What do you think is going on, Children of Alta?" shouted the one who held them.

He, too, must have once been a man; his eyes were bandaged, and he wore the robes of a priest and a coronet with the image of Seft's Scorpion. But he moved as surely as a sighted man, and his face was full of that same terrible glory as the others. It burned in his regard, it invested every word, and every tiniest gesture.

He did not wait for them to answer.

"The gods war to put back what should never have been released," he continued, shouting over the howl of the wind and the crashing and booming of strike and counterstrike.

Huras seized their captor's hand. "Is that *Thing* a goddess?" he shouted.

"Not yet, you mortal children of the Two Kingdoms. Not yet," the being shouted back, with a bitter laugh. "Foolish, foolish mortals— the Heyksin being fools, and not you—as below so above, the wretched Heyksin wanted a God of Vengeance, and so they strove to create one in their own image. Look at it!" he continued, flinging out an arm, and the power behind his words forced Peri to look back up at the raging battle, and at the dreadful Thing that was the center of it. "Look at it! Do you think for one moment that something like *that* is going to go quietly away when this battle is over?"

Numbly, Peri shook her head, sheltering her eyes with one hand from the wind.

"Wiser than they, you are. Of course it won't. If we lose here, it will not be content with that! It will remain manifest and demand blood and blood and still more blood, and it won't be the blood of bulls it calls for." The Being let them go. "The blood of men made it, and the blood of men is what it feeds upon. And one must fall to bind it again."

But he gave Huras a push. "You! There is another battle being fought, and it is mortal against mortal. Gather your Jousters, Huras of Alta! Strike now, while the enemy is as befuddled as you! It will serve you ill if the Gods win their battle, only for the mortals they serve to lose theirs!"

Huras did not hesitate for a moment. He turned and ran for the edge of the cliff, leaving Peri standing before—

—before a god.

Kaleth and Marit were chanting, lost deep inside ritual and magic. Essentially, Peri was alone with this god. Seft. Seft the Dark, Seft the Liar, Seft the Betrayer.

She turned her eyes back toward the four who

hung in the midst of Light and Darkness. "Kiron—" she whispered, without thinking. What were her dreams in the face of something like this?

What had her dreams ever been—when he could become—a god?

"He does not love you," the Being said flatly, without emotion. "Here and now, in this place and time where will can become manifest, there must be Truth. And he does not love you. He was being kind to you, nothing more."

She felt tears spring up in her eyes, and turned to the Being angrily. "You cannot know that!"

"Oh, I can, and I do. If he had loved you, it would be *you* up there beside him, wearing the diadem of Hattar, and not Aket-ten."

Her eyes stung, and her cheeks burned. But she could not deny what she saw. With a little mew of despair, she turned away. The Being seized her shoulders and shook her.

"Fool!" he snapped. "Look higher than the mud at your feet! Look at the Truth in you! *You do not love him either.* You love a dream of what you thought he was! The lies you hold give That thing power! You blundered into the place of power, and you can overset Us or aid Us by what you are! Now give over the pretty lie, and give Us your strength! *Be* strong, as strong as the one who survived the loss of all! Be strong as you do not yet realize you are! That thing came to life on the will of her worshippers—she is everything that they are writ large across the sky—now you are in this place of power—serve the same purpose for us!"

Shocked into silence, she looked, since she could not look into his eyes, at his mouth.

Why me? was her first thought. But he had answered that. She had stumbled inside a place of magic. He had said that "will became manifest" here. If she persisted in her illusions—

—would that weaken the bond between the Haras and Hattar that battled above her head?

She knew the answer before the question finished forming. *Yes.*

And if that happened—

"Any weakness, that *Thing* can exploit!" the Being said ruthlessly, giving her another shake. "Any doubt feeds her, any despair aids her. Face the Truth! Give Us your strength! Be strong, and become their channel to help us!"

He does not love you. That was hard, hard to face. But . . . *you do not love him*—that was . . . *Truth.*

She felt something turn inside her, as she faced her innermost self and saw—the Truth. She . . . she had wanted, not love but . . . protection. She had wanted to be dependent on someone else. For all that she had joined the Queen's Wing, for all that she had taken on responsibilities there—she had wanted, in her heart of hearts, to be told what to do. To be taken care of. Had wanted her story to end in some vision of unrealistic harmony, where nothing ever went wrong, where she and—this vague man-shaped image—never quarreled, never differed, never experienced the least little bump in their unending contentment. A story-teller's ending . . . *and they lived happily until the end of their days.*

And in that storyteller's tale of a life, she would tend to this image's every want, serving as a faithful priestess, and in turn, being protected and told exactly what to be, what to do, what to think, in return for this fat, stupid, sheeplike contentment.

That was what she had been in love with. Not a man. Not even a dream of a man. And not a woman's dream, but the dream of a child, lost and bereft, wanting only someone who would make her safe.

False and hollow, all of it. She was no longer that child, and safety was always an illusion.

She felt the fragments of falsehood falling away from her, like bits of a dragon's shed skin as she slowly straightened her back.

There was no safety in the world. This *Thing* howling and fighting above her head should tell her that. Contentment was for cattle and sheep—who were used, herded, and then slaughtered, never knowing the reason why.

Freedom was not safe. Love, if and when it did come, was not safe. Life was not safe, it was full of brawling and strife and terror and pain—and love and joy and bravery and passion.

She could choose to be a sheep, or a dragon. A child, or a responsible adult.

Without even being aware of starting to move, she found herself joining the priest Kaleth and his consort.

If the gods needed her will, her strength, then by all that was holy, they would have it. And it was more than time to grow up.

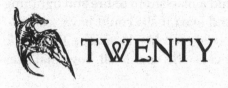 TWENTY

THE Jousters of Alta and Tia rained down jars of Akkadian Fire on the heads of the Heyksin.

That was a kind of strength that poured into those who wore the mortal shells of Jousters themselves. The Jousters believed that their Gods would overcome this abomination that the Heyksin had created and that bolstered the battle going on above their heads. *As below, so above.* Belief.

That, at least, was what Marit told Peri, as she paused for a precious drop of water to moisten a throat gone hoarse with chanting.

Peri could not watch the battle above; not because she was afraid—though she was—but because she couldn't see anything of what was going on, amid a maelstrom of fire and lightning and glare. And even if she could have seen it— it was all too *big* for her to grasp. The battle below, however—she could tell how that was going.

And at the moment, it was stalemate. The Jousters were able to keep the front lines of the enemy in a state of chaos, as flames blossomed among them, and men and horses screamed and tried without success to extinguish the Akkadian fire. As she watched, little eddies in the chaos emerged. Three chariots tangled together, dragging their drivers. The sickening stench of burning flesh, the sharp smell of Akkadian fire, the stink of flamed hair. The sting of sand whipped into her face and bare skin by the wind. The chill of the wind and the chill in her gut.

More bits emerged from the smoke below. Jewel-bright dragons swooping, kiting, diving and arcing back up again, clawing desperately for height to get out of the way of arrows. A red blossom of fire below.

A knot of archers taking a brave stand and sending volley after volley into the dragons, until someone, by plan or chance, dropped a jar onto the rim of a chariot, splashing driver and horses with liquid fire—and the horses bolted, screaming, straight into the archers, while the driver lurched out of the back, arms flailing, head a ball of flame.

But there, a long line of archers, keeping the dragons off the chariots they protected. A dragon suddenly stiffening, then lurching sideways, and floundering its way back to the safety of the cliffs, one wing web torn and shedding drops of blood.

A lucky arrow hitting a Jouster in Oset-re's colors . . .

And the battle in the sky was having its effect on those fighting below as well. Some were staring, doing nothing, paralyzed.

But it seemed plenty of them were encouraged by the appearance of their goddess. And there were still far more of them than there were of the people of the Two Kingdoms.

As below, so above. This was belief. And it was power.

The Avatars of Haras and Hattar, Siris and Iris, supported by Seft, flung their weapons of fire and fury at the unchained creature Tamat. Haras sent javelins of sunfire at the hideous creature's heads, while his father called down lightning from the stars themselves. Hattar shot silver arrow after arrow from the curved moon bow that was her own special weapon, while Iris rained down the Blood of the Earth upon it, white-hot molten stone that sizzled when it struck flesh. The transformed dragons they rode, though not god-ridden, were still possessed of their own vast courage and even greater loyalty. They dared as close as their riders would let them go, darting in and out, dodging Tamat's lightnings and the dreadful black sky-metal death swords in her hands, and trying to score her with teeth and talon.

From below, Seft's dark powers lashed out, and connected. They wrapped about the eyes of her three heads, blinding her as much as possible; his magic put fetters and weights on her arms, binding her for moments, making her clumsy, causing her to miss them when she could strike at them. She shook them off, but he sent them again and again and again, and while they lasted, they hampered her.

So far, none of them had taken any serious injury that a moment's attention from Iris could not heal.

As above, so below. This battle, too, was at a stalemate. Their weapons were marking her. But not fast enough.

They were able to distract her from the mortals below, and keep her from supporting her army, but Tamat's blood-fueled magic was healing her as fast as they wounded her.

And Tamat remained as strong as ever, and they, bound by mortality and their mortal vessels, were tiring. Their Light hammered her Darkness, but her Darkness could swallow it up.

From mind to mind, the thoughts flashed.

Her priests are feeding her. Iris lashed the unholy creature with the flail of earth-focused power she held in Her hand, as her dragon dove in beneath Tamat's blade to get the goddess in near enough to strike. The corn-gold chains of the flail struck home across the dark-blinded eyes of the third head, and the dragon writhed out of the way of a lashing claw to fling herself and her rider out of harm's way.

There is pain and death in abundance below Us. That feeds her . . . Siris fended off a volley of lightning with a shield made out of His own Being, and sent His dragon kiting sideways as the shield failed. *If we can stop her from being fed—if we can remove that source of her strength—*

No. It was the Avatar of Seft.

. . . no? One thought from four minds jolted by the response.

It is not that she is being fed. It is that she is not bound by flesh, except the flesh of her own creation. We are tiring. She is not. We are anchored by mortality. She is not. There was conviction in that. But more than that. There was Truth.

But surely one of Us can— The thought went unfinished. Yes, any one of them could, indeed, manifest enough power to equal, even to rival, Tamat.

And to do that, their mortal vessel would have to die, both because no mortal could encompass that much power and live, and because it would be the manifestation itself that destroyed Tamat.

One must fall. The answer was flat, implacable, inescapable.

No! Protest from three of the four.

Yes. Resignation from Siris, as he reached within himself, found the consent of his mortal vessel and prepared to make of himself a sacrifice—spurred by her own anguish and that of her vessel, Iris reached for him—

No! she cried, all the heartbreak of goddess and mortal together bound in that word. And as Haras hung his head in anguish, Kiron tried to think frantically if there was some other way—

Yes. Siris and Ari together shut them out.

Kashet hung in the sky, hovered, blinding blue against the churning dark. The dragon understood, too—and Kiron felt it, felt the dragon's assent. He and his beloved Jouster would take this together if that was what it would take to save all.

Together, they faced Tamat, and—

Not this time, my brother.

A blast of dark energies struck Siris in the back, knocking him from his dragon. With a cry of anger and despair, Haras dove Avatre down in the maneuver that Kiron had practiced so often. *Traitor! Betrayer! You show your true self at—*

A laugh. *Not this time, my nephew. I am the god of difficult choices. Remember that in the future.*

Just as Avatre got under the plummeting body, arced herself with grace and power, and caught him across the saddlebow, something dark bloomed on the cliff below them.

Across the face of Aerie, across the battlefield, a voice louder than the thunder and sharp as the kiss of a blade rang out.

"Tamat! Corruptor! Destroyer! I dare you to face Me! I am Seft, Lord of the Darkness and Despair, and I am your Master!"

A second pillar of darkness rose from the top of the cliff in the heart of Aerie. A second Being spread shadow wings against the sunlight, blotting it out. Unable to resist the challenge, Tamat roared her answer, and the two surged together—

—and in that moment of meeting, Seft snapped the bonds of His vessel's mortality, sending a wave of force across the battlefield that flattened everything in its path.

Kiron picked himself up off the ground. Beside him, Ari stirred and moaned a little. Both had been flung from Avatre's back when Seft and Tamat had met and—

Avatre! He turned at the sound of a whine, to

see the red-and-gold dragon, rather the worse for wear, climbing up over the edge of the cliff, with Kashet right behind her. They both flopped down next to their respective Jousters, stretched out their long necks and sighed with exhaustion.

The air stank. Burned flesh, burned hair, burned stone. A lingering taint of decay.

And the silence.

Gingerly, he removed the diadem of Haras from his head, and looked it over. It was in better shape than he was, for all its apparent fragility. But it no longer glowed with magic, and he was just as glad. Haras was gone, to wherever it was that the gods dwelled, and Kiron could quite do without the "honor" of serving as His vessel again. With careful deliberation, he removed Ari's diadem, too.

"Ari!" The-on flapped heavily down onto the cliff top, and Nofret tumbled from her back to cradle Ari in her arms. Her hair was half-scorched on the left side of her face, and there were burns on her hands. Ari, of course, was going to be black and blue from head to toe. He groaned once, then opened his eyes and smiled, and she burst into tears.

"If—if you ever—do that again—" Whatever she was going to say vanished in incoherent sobs and kisses. A little embarrassed, Kiron looked away—

And saw, with a shock of recognition, the crumpled body of Rakaten-te, Chosen of Seft.

And a shadow-enshrouded form that held that body in His arms.

Kiron, who had been struggling to his feet, instinctively bent the knee.

The shadow gently laid Rakaten-te down, and passed a hand over his face. The bandages that had always covered his eyes melted away and Lord Seft flowed to his—feet? It wasn't possible to tell, but Kiron got the impression of someone standing, someone with furled wings, or a cloak like wings, brooding down on him.

I am the god of difficult choices, said a voice that came from everywhere and nowhere. *Never forget that. He knew that, my Chosen did, and he knew that we must share that choice. And now—*

He turned toward the place where Tamat's army had been. Kiron stood, slowly and looked in that direction.

The army was fleeing, in disorder, in panic. No one pursued them; most of the defenders on the cliffs had been flattened when Seft and Tamat collided. As for the Jousters—like Kiron, Nofret, and Ari, they and their dragons were picking themselves up from whatever place they had been flung.

It matters not. They cannot cross the Anvil of the Sun twice unprovisioned and live. Oh, a handful will survive. And they will carry back the tale—the tale of how their goddess was immolated, how Tia and Alta are one now . . . and how that land is defended.

A kind of fierce, dark exaltation infused those last words. And Kiron shivered to hear them.

My remaining time is short. Kiron saw, as the shadowed god turned, that He had His diadem in his hands. *My Chosen has crossed the Bridge of Stars, and I am in need of a new avatar.*

For one moment of unbearable horror, Kiron feared that Seft was going to—

No! No! Never again! Never—

But the god turned away from him, and toward the trio that stood a little ways away, the first to have gotten to their feet.

I am in need of a Chosen One, Kaleth, Mouth of the Gods. I am the god of difficult choices. Will you make the choice to serve Me?

"You are a difficult master," Kaleth replied, regarding the form of shadow gravely.

And yet you have served Me already, as you have served all the gods. Will you serve Me alone? A pause. The choice that Rakaten-te assented to is not one that is asked often of My Chosen. But it is one that they must be ready to make. Could you make it?

Kaleth took a slow, deep breath and looked the God fearlessly in the face. "Aye," he said, as, to Kiron's wide-eyed astonishment, Marit nodded gravely in agreement. "For the sake of the Two Kingdoms, aye. And for their sake, I will be your Chosen," said Kaleth, the Mouth of the Gods.

Then this is yours. The diadem of Seft floated across the space between them, and down into Kaleth's waiting hands. *Keep it safe, against need, my Chosen.*

But then the shadow turned toward Marit. *The gods will need another Speaker, faithful one. And Prophecy, and standing between Life and Death, Light and Shadow, has ever been the providence of Nebt. Will you take your mate's place as the Mouth of the Gods?*

Marit nodded, and the diadem of Nebt rose from the box where it had been left. As it neared her outstretched hands, for a moment, it took on a soft, metallic glow.

All unnoticed, Aket-ten had landed Re-eth-ke and come to stand beside Kiron. The god merely glanced in their direction but said nothing.

Nofret had helped Ari to his feet again, and the god turned back to them. *Make the Two Kingdoms into One. Guard your borders, yet do not expel the stranger. Be vigilant, but not despotic. Remember that the difficult choice is almost always the right one. And now I go.*

With those words, the god vanished, leaving no trace of Himself behind.

The last trace of the Nameless Ones was gone from the desert outside the cliff walls of Aerie.

From where Kiron and Aket-ten had stood on the cliffs in the early morning light, you could not tell there had even been a battle.

Since the casualties had been relatively few on the Altian side—"Altia" being the name that Nofret and Ari had jointly decreed was to be the new name of their combined Kingdoms—in some ways the war had created a windfall for the desert city. Those horses that had died became dragon food. Those that lived had already been taken off to be traded for more useful asses, donkeys, and camels. The chariots and some of the weapons were already being converted into furniture and hardware, tools and other useful objects. So useful was the detritus of war, in fact, that scavengers from Aerie tracked the fleeing army well into the Anvil of the Sun to loot the fallen.

And there were a great many fallen.

And that was where the last mystery had occurred, in regard to all those fallen.

That first night, one of the things that the weary council that Ari convened tried to consider was what to do with the hundreds, thousands of corpses right on their doorstep. They were dangerous there; besides the stench that would start to arise when they began to decay, there was the disease, the flies, and all that to consider.

"We can't burn them," Ari had said helplessly. "There is not enough wood in all of Aerie to burn a tenth of them. We can't bury them, we haven't enough hands . . . ."

And just as he said that, there came the unearthly howl of a jackal cutting across the quiet night air. "Unearthly," because it hadn't come from the desert.

It had come from everywhere. And nowhere.

They all froze, then had looked at one another cautiously. Anbenis, the god of the dead, had the head of a jackal. . . .

The howl came again, filling Kiron's upper room where they all sat on mats, like so many scribes, because Kiron didn't have chairs.

"Perhaps we should sleep on a decision," Ari said after a moment.

And in the morning, the bodies were simply gone. Not as in "dragged off by jackals" gone either. As in "vanished, leaving even their clothing and armor behind" gone.

That, thankfully, was the last manifestation of the hands of the gods.

Kiron had felt very uneasy about stooping to the level of looting the dead so as to make use of that discarded clothing, but others were not so squeamish. After a thorough washing, there were plenty of folk walking about on this day sporting Heyksin tunics. Aside from the garish colors, which would soon fade, they were not so unlike Altian tunics.

So he and Aket-ten sat on the carved window

ledge of his uppermost room, and watched the unaccustomed splotches of bright crimson, eye-searing blue, and acidic yellow moving purposefully beneath them. There were too many weighty matters to be discussed, and they wanted to discuss none of them.

So, instead, they talked about furniture, of which there was very little here. It was a relief, a relief to speak of commonplaces, to debate the type of table, the style of lamp. It meant they did not yet need to think about what all this meant . . . or could mean.

Or what it had been like to play host to a god.

"I should like a proper bed," Aket-ten said at last, speaking aloud. "Raised off the floor, with a real mattress. There are enough rags now to stuff mattresses for every person in Aerie twice over."

Kiron decided to say nothing of his misgivings about sleeping on dead men's clothing; instead, he suggested, "Don't you think grass would be more comfortable?"

"Well, so would goose-down," she said, giving him a dubious look, but I don't see any parades of geese in Aerie—nor fields of grass either—"

"Perhaps the Lord of the Jousters can ask for a mattress to be brought," suggested Marit from the stair. "Ari and Nofret are off safely, which is just as well, considering that it would not be wise for her to be flying soon."

"Ah, goo—" The implications of that last sentence brought Kiron's thoughts to a crashing halt. "What?"

Kaleth followed his mate up into the dwelling room. "Oh, do give over. You are not so dense as that, Kiron," the Chosen said with a smirk. He now wore the same sort of robes that Rakaten-te had worn, and carried the very staff the former Chosen had used, but to Kiron's relief, he had *not* been blinded. Kaleth did not explain this, nor did Kiron ask.

"Why do you think that Seft made the choice he did?" Marit asked, and then at a look from Kaleth, amended, "All right, it was *one* of the reasons. There will soon be a Haras-in-the-nest."

"And you will have to give up the honor of being the wearer of the diadem of Haras if there is need," added Kaleth, and snorted at Kiron's expression of relief.

Kiron did not say what he was thinking, which was *I prefer my gods in Their Temples, and not in my head,* opting instead for "Why are you strolling about like any baker's son? I thought the Chosen of Seft was supposed to remain secluded."

Kaleth shrugged. "The god has not told me to scuttle into hiding. I assume that it does not matter here, nor in Sanctuary, which are both cities of the gods. We have tended to live somewhat withdrawn anyway, Marit and I, so I anticipate no great change."

Kiron was about to ask something else, when a commotion below made all of them turn and stare at the stairs.

"—I don't care if he is bathing or eating or speaking with the Mouth of the Gods!" said an all-too-familiar, scolding voice. "—I will see my son!"

Letis stormed up the last few steps and turned to look for Kiron. Since he was hard to miss, she made a little grunt of mingled exasperation and satisfaction, and strode up to him to stand in front of him with her arms crossed over her chest. "I have made enough allowances for you, and I have heard more than enough nonsensical reasons why you did not return. You are my son! It is time you obeyed me. You must return to Mefis now, and get back our farm. Then you can marry Peri, settle down to a proper life with a proper wife, breed me proper grandchildren who will honor their grandmother, and forget all this dragon foolishness." She scowled, and muttered, under her breath. "Wars with the Nameless Ones, indeed!"

Kiron simply stared at her. First of all, he could not imagine how she had gotten here. Secondly, he could not imagine how to answer her.

She stood there, utterly recalcitrant, completely unembarrassed. Peri, however, who had followed her up here, was embarrassed enough for three.

When he did not answer, Letis cast about the room for someone to support her. "You! Priest!" she said, arrogantly. "Tell him! Tell him it is his filial duty before the gods to obey his mother!"

Kaleth scratched his head. "As I am the Chosen of Seft . . ." he began. "My advice would be to make the difficult choice to tell you that his duties lie to a higher authority than his mother."

As Letis' eyes widened, Kiron seized the moment. "I am very sorry for you, Mother, but I have already provided for you every thing that a filial son should. You are well cared for. You have a house, a comfortable life, even servants, which is more than you had when Father was alive. The Chosen is right; my duty to my King and Queen, my land, and my Jousters supersedes any duties to obey you, when you demand things that are not only not possible, but possibly foolish." He crossed his arms over his chest and looked down at her. "In a word, Mother, no. No, I will not give up my duty. No, I will not get back the farm. And no, I certainly will not marry Peri." He looked apologetically at poor Peri, caught in the middle and red as a sunset. "Peri is a very pleasant young woman, but I will marry Lady Aket-ten, and we will train the next generations of Jousters, male *and* female, and we will make Aerie our home."

Letis spluttered for a moment, then turned to Peri. "Don't just stand there! *Tell* him!"

For a very long moment there was only silence. And Kiron was struck by the uncomfortable possibility that poor Peri—

She had spent a great deal of time with him. Gone out of her way to keep him company. He had put it all down to just being two people with a very similar background cheering each other up, but what if—his mother hadn't gotten his notion that he would be marrying her out of nothing. What if this was something that his mother had been cooking up all along? And what if that was what Peri wanted and expected?

"Then I must make a difficult choice, too," Peri said slowly. "Because it is more than time that I did so." She turned to Kiron's mother. "Letis," she said forcefully. "Shut up."

Letis could not possibly have looked more astonished if those words had come from the mouth of Kiron's cat.

"Kiron does not care for me except as another Jouster," Peri went on. "Nor do I care for him except as he is a kind and generous man. And I will not give up Sutema, nor my position here, nor all the responsibility nor all the pleasures that taking that responsibility brings. Especially not for the life of a farmer's wife, which is better than being a serf only in that I would be free." She snorted, clearly both amused and angry. "Free, that is until the first babies come, when I would be bound more closely than if I had been clapped on a slave coffle. So Letis, I love you as my friend, but no. I will not marry your son. Let him wed his love, and let them live as happily as they can."

Letis gaped at her, then managed to splutter, "Then you will die a childless old maid!"

"I think not," Marit said thoughtfully, looking at both Peri and Letis. "But even if so . . . there are worse fates."

"Aye, being a farmer's wife," said Peri.

"It is safe!" Letis cried out, her face reflecting her bewilderment. "It is safe, and certain! Great Mother River rises and falls, the seasons turn and every one is like the one the year before! You know where you are, you know your place, and Great Kings can come and go and it matters nothing at all!"

Peri went to the window, gesturing out at the dragons, perched and flying, everywhere. "Safe, true, but how boring! How confining! How sad! How could that compare with *this*? And what is safe? You were not safe on your little farm. War came to you and took all your safety away! If I am to be in this world, I want more than to be a hound upon the game board, tucked away in a corner until the jackals come and sweep all away!"

Letis looked from one to another of them. "You are all, all of you mad," she said at last.

Then mustering the shreds of her dignity, she raised her chin. "I am returning to Mefis and the daughter who appreciates me."

She stalked off. The three Jousters looked at one another, and then at Kaleth and Marit . . .

. . . hounds upon the game board . . . swept up by the Gods and now . . .

And given what Kiron had just been through . . .

"She may be right," he said finally. "We may all be mad."

Kaleth shrugged. "Then I choose to be mad, rather than blind," he retorted, and smiled. "Besides, if it is madness, it is glorious madness, a madness that builds rather than merely endures. I choose to be the hawk, not the calf. And there is a great deal to be said for that."

The hawk and not the calf . . . He thought about that, and about something else. *As below, so above.* If the Gods had moved him on the board . . . still, the people moved *Them*. The manipulation, it seemed, went both ways.

"A difficult choice," he agreed. "But yes. I choose the hawk."